Praise for *The Hunting Dogs*

'Yet again the novelist convinces with a satisfying, credible police procedural. This time, William Wisting faces a major life crisis: he is himself investigated, and forced to examine his police career in a new light. His journalist daughter Line plays an important role in the book, turning the novel into both a depiction of the father-daughter relationship and a portrayal of the relationship between the police and the media.'

The judges of the Riverton Prize Golden Revolver, won by Jorn Lier Horst for *The Hunting Dogs*

'An immaculately plotted, beautifully structured novel, complex and full of tension, both in terms of the action and the personal complications.'

Bob Cornwell in *Crimetime*

'There's a gritty atmosphere and a good sense of pace, while Wisting and his daughter make for excellent and companionable protagonists.'

Russell MacLean in *The Herald*

Praise for *Closed for Winter*

'Painstaking and swift, *Closed for Winter* is a piece of quality craftsmanship, with Horst meticulously bringing together an unexpectedly windy plot, highly intelligent characterizations and a delectably subtle 'noir' mood to create a very engrossing crime novel.'

Edinburgh Book Review

'On the evidence of *Closed for Winter*, which is the seventh book in the series but only the second to be translated into English, it would appear that we are about to be treated to another classic series.'

Bay Magazine

Praise for *Dregs*

'Jorn Lier Horst has, right from his debut in 2004, set a sensationally good pace in his crime novels, and has today gained entry into the circle of our very best writers in that genre.'
Terje Stemland, AftenPosten, Norway

'Just as good are the descriptions of the characters in Jorn Lier Horst's book. They are nuanced and interesting, absolutely human. Many have known it for a long time, but now it ought to be acknowledged as a truth for all readers of crime fiction: William Wisting is one of the great investigators in Norwegian crime novels.'
Norwegian Book Club (Book of the Month,
Crime and Thrillers)

Jorn Lier Horst was born in 1970, in Bamble, Telemark, Norway. Between 1995 and 2013, when he turned to full time writing, he worked as a policeman in Larvik, eventually becoming head of investigations there. His William Wisting series of crime novels has sold more than 500,000 copies in Scandinavia, UK, Germany, Netherlands and Thailand. *Dregs*, sixth in the series, was published in English by Sandstone Press in 2011, and *Closed for Winter*, winner of Norway's Booksellers' Prize, in 2012. *Closed for Winter* was also shortlisted for the prestigious Riverton Prize or *Golden Revolver*, for best Norwegian crime novel of the year. *The Hunting Dogs* won both the *Golden Revolver* and *Glass Key*, which widened the scope to best crime fiction in all the Nordic countries, in 2013, and the Martin Beck Award – from the Swedish Crime Writers' Aademy – in 2014. *Closed for Winter* (2013), *The Hunting Dogs* (2014) and *The Caveman* (2015) were all shortlisted for the illustrious Petrona Award in the UK.

Anne Bruce, who lives on the Isle of Arran in Scotland, formerly worked in education and has a longstanding love of Scandinavia and Norway in particular. Having studied Norwegian and English at Glasgow University, she is the translator of Jorn Lier Horst's *Dregs*, *Closed for Winter*, *The Hunting Dogs* and *The Caveman,* and also Anne Holt's *Blessed are Those who Thirst* (2012), *Death of the Demon* (2013), *The Lion's Mouth* (2014) and *Dead Joker* (2015), in addition to Merethe Lindstrøm's Nordic Prize winning *Days in the History of Silence* (2013).

Also published by Sandstone Press

Dregs
Closed for Winter
The Hunting Dogs
The Caveman

ORDEAL

Jorn Lier Horst

Translated by

Anne Bruce

SANDSTONEPRESS
HIGHLAND | SCOTLAND

First published in Great Britain
and the United States of America
Sandstone Press Ltd
Dochcarty Road
Dingwall
Ross-shire
IV15 9UG
Scotland.

www.sandstonepress.com

Published in English in 2016 by Sandstone Press Ltd.

English language editor: Robert Davidson

The moral right of Jørn Lier Horst to be recognised as the
author has been asserted in accordance with the
Copyright, Design and Patent Act, 1988.

This translation has been published with the financial support of NORLA.

Creative Scotland towards publication of this volume.

ISBN: 978-1-910124-74-1
ISBNe: 978-1-910124-75-8

Cover by Freight Design, Glasgow
Typesetting by Iolaire Typesetting, Newtonmore
Printed and bound by CPI Group (UK) Ltd, Croydon CR0 4YY

WILLIAM WISTING

William Wisting is a career policeman who has risen through the ranks to become Chief Inspector in the Criminal Investigation Department of Larvik Police, just like his creator, author Jorn Lier Horst. *Ordeal* is the tenth title in the series, the fifth to be published in English, and finds him aged fifty-five, the widowed father of grown up twins, Thomas and Line. Wisting's wife, Ingrid, went to Africa to work on a NORAD project but was killed there at the end of *The Only One*, the fourth title in the series.

Thomas as a helicopter pilot in the military at the time of *Ordeal*. Daughter Line is an investigative journalist whose career has frequently intersected with that of her father. Wisting, initially apprehensive, has come to value how she is able to operate in ways that he cannot, often turning up unexpected clues and insights. In *Ordeal*, she has given up her job in Oslo and returned to live in her home town, and this time she is embroiled in the enquiry in a different way, through her friendship with an old school friend, Sofie Lund.

After Ingrid's death, Wisting became involved with another woman, Suzanne Bjerke, but their relationship foundered in the course of *The Hunting Dogs* and Wisting is now unattached and living alone. Suzanne features again in *Ordeal* in her role as proprietor of the local café/bar, *The Golden Peace*.

Crucial to the series are Wisting's colleagues in the police. One of the themes of the novels is the tension between police personnel facing the pressures of investigating crime, and management whose priorities are balancing budgets and meeting targets. This comes to the fore again in *Ordeal*, when the new Chief of Police, Ivan Sundt, crosses swords with Wisting.

Wisting has more positive relationships with certain trusted colleagues: old school Nils Hammer, whose background in the Drugs Squad has made him cynical, the younger Torunn

Borg whom Wisting has come to rely on thanks to her wholly professional approach and outlook, and Espen Mortensen, the crime scene examiner who is usually first on the scene. Christine Thiis, more recently appointed as Assistant Chief of Police and police prosecutor, has established herself and consolidated her position as a trusted colleague.

The setting is Vestfold county on the south-west coast of Norway, an area popular with holidaymakers, where rolling landscapes and attractive beaches make an unlikely setting for crime. The principal town, Larvik, where Wisting is based, is located 105 km (65 miles) southwest of Oslo. The wider Larvik district has 41,000 inhabitants, 23,000 of whom live in the town itself, and covers 530 square km. Larvik is noted for its natural springs, but its modern economy relies heavily on agriculture, commerce and services, light industry and transportation, as well as tourism. There is a ferry service from Larvik to Hirsthals in Denmark.

At the beginning of *Ordeal*, Wisting is struggling to come to terms with Line's new situation and proximity, as well as confronting public and press criticism of his lack of progress with a missing person case that has remained unsolved for more than six months. Just as the enquiry is to be shelved, a lead turns up that uncovers links with organised crime. The ensuing twists and turns overlap with a murder case in a neighbouring jurisdiction and Wisting is forced to challenge not only his superiors but also his colleagues in Kristiansand.

Jorn Lier Horst's own deep experience of police procedures and processes brings a strong sense of the novels in the William Wisting series being firmly grounded in reality.

Jorn Lier Horst worked as a policeman in Larvik between 1995 and 2013 when he turned to full time writing.

Further information on Jorn Lier Horst and the earlier books is available in English at http://eng.gyldendal.no/Gyldendal/Authors/Horst-Joern-Lier

1

Twice she drove past the imposing white house and, on the third lap, stopped in the street outside.

The stately villa with its half-hip roof was located behind a white picket fence and a privet hedge fringed by ancient trees with sprawling branches. Lattice windows revealed nothing but interior darkness. Larger than she remembered, it was really far too big for her. Nineteen years had passed since she promised herself never to return. Now she was about to move in.

She lifted an envelope from the passenger seat and shook out the key, tagged with a small plastic fob on which the lawyer had written her grandfather's name on one side and the address on the other: *Frank Mandt. Johan Ohlsens gate, Stavern.*

He had held this same key, walked about with it in his pocket, fiddled with it, clenched his fist round it. She did not like to think of him as *grandfather*, and didn't use that word. Instead, she thought of him as the *Old Man*, which was how she remembered him, although he couldn't have been more than fifty back then: strong and well built with dark deep-set eyes, thick grey hair and a small white moustache.

One of the last times she had seen him was during a seventeenth of May celebration, Norway's National Day. She had passed the house in the children's procession, and the Old Man had stood on the glass verandah with his hands on his back, scowling through tight lips. She waved, but he had turned his back and gone inside.

Letting the key fall, she peered over at the house again, radiating coldness even on a hot July day like this. Snuffling noises from the child seat made her swivel round. "Are you awake, little Maja?" she said, smiling. "We're here now."

1

The girl gurgled and smiled, blinking all the while. Fortunately, she didn't resemble her father. She had her own dark eyes and hair. "And my dimples," she said, tickling her daughter's chin. They would manage. In the past, it had been her and her mother. Now it would be her and her daughter.

She put the car in gear and drove to the rear of the house. Stopping in front of the garage she picked up the key again, clambered out of the car and took Maja from the back seat.

The entrance had a distinguished appearance, with pillars and ornamentation in the style of a century ago. The key turned easily in the lock. Inside, everything smelled clean and fresh and not stuffy as she had feared.

The lawyer had done as she had asked. All the furniture, household effects and personal belongings had been removed; everything that might remind her of the past. She entered the kitchen and moved on to the living room, where sunlight spilled across the floor and her footsteps reverberated off the bare walls. We could be comfortable here, she thought, gazing at the little park across the street. This enormous house could offer an excellent new start.

The wide staircase to the first floor creaked. She eased Maja to her other hip and entered what had been her mother's room, lingering without really feeling any emotion before glancing at her watch. Quarter to ten. The removal van would arrive soon. She hurriedly checked the other rooms and dashed downstairs to inspect the rest of the house.

Hesitating for a moment she opened the basement door, switched on the light and took a few steps down the well-worn treads. It was down here that they had found him one day in January. He must have fallen from about where she was now standing. On the grey cement floor below she could sense rather than see a darker stain on the pale surface. They reckoned he had lain for three days before one of his friends had discovered him.

She was the only surviving relative, but had not attended the funeral or helped with preparations. At that time she had not realised she was the only heir to a million-kroner villa and

2

the money deposited in his bank account. When she learned, her first thought was that she did not want any of it, it was so dirty. She would prefer to have nothing to do with it, but then it struck her: Why not? It would be crazy to turn it down.

She carried Maja further down into the basement, aware that the air down here was more oppressive than elsewhere in the house: a stale smell, like old fruit or flowers kept too long in a vase. One of the below-stairs rooms was fitted out as a bathroom and sauna, another kitted out as a home gymnasium. One side was lined with wall bars.

In the innermost room she found the safe. The lawyer had informed her that it had been left behind because it was not only large and heavy, but apparently also bolted to the floor. The cleaners had hoped to find the key, but it was missing. She had full confidence in them, since they had handed over almost thirty thousand kroner they had found tucked inside an envelope in a kitchen cupboard. Perhaps they had found more money lying about, but she felt sure they had not found and used the safe key.

The safe stood alone in the middle of the room, taking up a great deal of space and making it difficult to furnish if that proved necessary at some point. She shivered as she ran her fingers over the cold steel. Irritated that the key was missing, she hunkered down and pushed aside the small metal plate suspended over the keyhole, trying to peep inside.

A horn tooted outside and she looked at her watch again: ten o'clock. The removal firm was bang on time. Outside, she opened the boot of her car, lifted out a box containing the doorplate she had ordered at home in Oslo, and hung it on a nail beside the front door.

Sofie and Maja Lund.

As the removal men reversed into position, a woman in the house next door peered out from behind checked kitchen curtains. Sofie waved to her but she did not wave back.

2

William Wisting stood in his bedroom doorway watching the woman who lay in his bed. Narrow bands of light flooded through the venetian blinds and across her face, but did not disturb her deep sleep.

He had worked with Christine Thiis for less than two years. She was fifteen years younger than him and had two teenage children. Following a divorce, she had left a well-paid job as a defence lawyer in Oslo and moved to Larvik with her offspring. Easy to work with, she was results-orientated, energetic and resourceful, and had a talent for making the right decisions at the right time.

When they spoke it was always about work, and she was less than expansive when it came to her personal life. When they attended conferences together, she always went home or straight to her room once the professional side was over. She never showed up after work if someone suggested a beer, and had never been present at a Christmas dinner. So, Wisting had been taken aback when she had accepted an invitation to a summer party at his house.

Her expression suggested she sensed his presence in the room. Wisting quietly re-closed the door and went downstairs to the living room. She needed to sleep it off. Nils Hammer had carried her up to bed, well into her second bottle of wine. The others had stayed until first light and the earliest birds began to sing.

He folded the blanket he had used overnight and tidied the cushions, collected the glasses and took them to the kitchen, filled the dishwasher and stood at the window looking at the bend in the road and the brown-stained house where Line lived.

Although not entirely comfortable with the reason for her moving back to Stavern from Oslo, and not best pleased that she had bought *that* particular house, he was glad to have her in the neighbourhood. The previous owner had been called Viggo Hansen and, eight months previously, he had been found dead in a chair in the living room. He had sat for almost four months without anyone in the vicinity registering the fact. Wisting felt that death pervaded its very walls.

The thought of the dead man did not worry Line, which was actually typical of her. Fearless, she had a pragmatic disposition. Besides, it was a good buy. Circumstances meant that it sold for considerably less than its valuation, and when he visited yesterday he had seen few reminders of its past. Everything unnecessary had been torn down and thrown out. The kitchen, bathroom and one of the bedrooms had already been renovated. Now it was the living room's turn.

His mobile phone rang somewhere. He found it on the coffee table, too late to answer. It was Suzanne though, her number still stored. Even after several months, seeing her name affected him. For a while they had lived together, but she decided to move on. Losing her weighed heavily on him, though not as much as losing Ingrid, mother of Line and her twin brother Thomas. Ingrid was dead and gone forever. Suzanne, on the other hand, was not far off, running a gallery and coffee bar in Stavern and living in the flat above.

He jumped when she rang again. 'Hello,' he answered, his mouth suddenly dry.

'It's Suzanne.'

'How are you?'

'Are you at home?'

Wisting surveyed the room. Someone had knocked over a dish of peanuts. Espen Mortensen had placed several layers of toilet paper on the carpet in an effort to soak up beer spilled from an overturned bottle. Christine Thiis' handbag was underneath a chair, its contents strewn across the floor. 'Why do you ask?'

'There's something I need to talk to you about, and I don't

5

want to discuss it on the phone. It's to do with the Hummel case.'

'The Hummel case?' Wisting repeated, though he knew exactly what she meant. Jens Hummel was a taxi driver. Both he and his vehicle had disappeared on the night before Friday 6 January, more than six months ago. The last person to see him had been a passenger dropped off outside the Grand Hotel in Larvik's Storgata at 01.23. The case remained a mystery.

'I can call in later this morning, before there are too many customers in the café.'

Wisting heard footsteps on the floor above. Christine Thiis must have wakened. 'I'm on my way out,' he said. 'I can drop in on you.'

'Before one o'clock?'

He glanced at the time, calculating how long it had been since he stopped drinking. 'I can be there in an hour,' he answered, and knew from the way she thanked him that there was a smile on her face.

He heard the sound of running water in the upstairs bathroom, crossed to the kitchen and took two cups from the cupboard. The coffee machine was humming faintly when Christine Thiis entered.

'Hi,' she said in a hoarse voice. Her chestnut brown hair was still dishevelled, but he could see that she had tried to tidy it. 'Sorry, it . . .'

'Coffee?'

'That would be nice.' They sat on either side of the kitchen table. 'Sorry,' she said again. 'That's never happened before . . . I usually make my own way home.' She drank from the cup and cleared her throat. 'That is to say, I don't usually go out. I'm not used to drinking alcohol.'

'Then you needed it,' Wisting said. He could see how uncomfortable she felt, sitting in the same clothes that she had worn when she went to bed. 'You probably really needed to let your hair down. Totally relax and not think for a single minute about the children or work.'

6

'But I should have made my way home.'

'There was nothing waiting for you there anyway,' Wisting said with a smile. He curled his hand round the coffee cup and appreciated again how good it is to sit with someone at the kitchen table. 'I can drive you home later.'

She shook her head. 'I can take a taxi.'

'I need to go out in any case,' he said. 'Something's cropped up in the Hummel case.'

Her eyes changed, shifting from slight embarrassment to total alertness. 'Jens Hummel? We went over the whole case last week and agreed to shelve it. Is there something new?'

'I don't know yet. I'm going to meet someone who wants to talk.'

Christine Thiis leaned across the table. 'What they said in the newspaper was all wrong,' she said. 'We really have done everything we could in that enquiry.'

She was referring to a newspaper article of the previous week. The disappearance had generated headlines in January as well, but not such enormous public interest. Jens Hummel had no close family to push the police and the press. Only a grandmother left alone with her loss.

When the media grew interested again, Wisting had hoped that the publicity would lead to fresh information. The time factor did not necessarily reduce the likelihood of a successful enquiry. In fact, it could allow rumour and gossip to spread in ever-increasing circles until it reached someone willing to talk. Fresh reporting could act as a trigger.

However, it had been angled extremely negatively against the police in general, and Wisting in particular as leader of the investigation. Nothing emerged about what specifically the police could have done differently, but the article gave a picture of low interest and substandard work. The lack of results spoke for itself. They had not even managed to locate Hummel's car, and recently published statistics on increased traffic control operations were used to support assertions of poor judgment and wrong priorities. Their sympathies in the case did not lie with the police who were faced with such a difficult task, but with the grandmother who had lost her only grandchild.

Wisting was used to criticism and normally it bounced off, but this time he felt differently. It was a reminder of their failure, and how the Hummel case had originally made him feel anxious, creating a nagging sense of inadequacy.

'*Disappeared without trace* has rarely been a more appropriate expression,' Christine Thiis said. 'You'd think with all our telecommunications networks, toll stations, taximeters and on board computers that we would be able to find something to tell us what became of him and his vehicle.'

Wisting agreed. He thought of the time spent investigating the Hummel case as days with no content. They had assembled a packed timeline for the twenty-four hours before the man vanished, but nothing pointed to his present whereabouts. In parallel, they had tried to form an impression of Jens Hummel as a person; it was a complex picture. He was thirty-four years of age and lived alone. He had worked in a variety of casual jobs until the age of twenty-five when he had started to drive a taxi. Five years ago, he had obtained his own licence and vehicle. Spending almost ten years behind the wheel had given him a wide network of contacts with very different people, most of whom they had interviewed.

Disappearance cases were always difficult, not only because there was no crime scene to examine, but also because it was difficult to unify a sprawling investigation.

They lingered over their coffee, discussing some of the most interesting theories. One posited a confrontation over narcotics. It was rumoured that Hummel had acted as a local courier and used his taxi to transport drugs. It was also suggested that he had picked up and delivered prostitutes, which had more or less been confirmed but had not led them any further.

Wisting looked at his watch. It was time to leave. In the car, their conversation turned to other topics, about the summer and their holiday plans.

'I'm not going anywhere,' Christine Thiis said. 'What about you?'

'I've promised to help Line with her renovations. She thinks I'm good at wallpapering.'

Christine Thiis looked pensive. 'My children are going to spend four weeks with their father; it'll be strange to be on my own for such a long time.' Wisting turned the car into the kerb outside her house. 'Thanks for the lift,' she said, 'and apologies again for not making my own way home last night.'

'No problem.'

'You must phone me,' she said, placing her hand on his arm.

He met her gaze. She blinked both eyes before withdrawing her hand. 'If anything comes of it, I mean. If you get an answer to what happened to Jens Hummel.'

3

The day was hot and oppressive with no breath of wind. Wisting found a vacant parking space beside the steamboat quay and stepped from the car. Two little boys stood at the quayside, each with a fishing rod. Seagulls flew above them in lethargic circles.

The streets were unusually crowded. Wisting nodded occasionally to familiar faces as they passed by.

Most of the small tables outside *The Golden Peace* were already occupied. Wisting hesitated at the door until his eyes adjusted to the dim light and he saw Suzanne seated at the far end of the premises, waving him across. She was wearing a white summer dress, her black hair drawn back in a ponytail. She stood up and gave him a hug. The skin round her eyes wrinkled when she smiled. 'Would you like anything?' she asked. 'Coffee?'

Wisting's head felt heavy. 'I'd like a *Farris*,' he said, clearing his throat.

She disappeared behind the counter and returned with a bottle of mineral water and a glass filled with ice cubes. 'I didn't know who else to talk to,' she said.

Wisting poured water into his glass. 'You said it was to do with Jens Hummel.'

'I don't really know if there's anything in it,' she said, 'but there's been a man in here on a few evenings recently. He sits at the bar, reads the newspapers and doesn't say much, but I've picked up that he's been living abroad for a while.'

Suzanne moved an unaddressed envelope that lay between them on the table before continuing: 'Last week, you said in the newspaper that you were going to shelve the Hummel case.'

10

'Hold in abeyance,' Wisting corrected.

'Is that different?'

He shrugged.

'Anyway,' she continued, 'in connection with their outline of the case, among other things they printed a photograph of Jens Hummel's taxi.'

Yet again Wisting was reminded of their unsuccessful media strategy.

'It was quiet here that evening. I noticed that the man's reaction was really strange when he read it.'

'How was that?'

Suzanne lowered her voice, even though there was nobody nearby to eavesdrop: 'He grew restless. He glanced up from the newspaper and looked over his shoulder before he went on reading. Afterwards, he stood up, went outside and waited for a while before coming back to read the article again. I went over to collect empty glasses and he said something odd.'

'What was that?'

'First of all I made a comment about the article, something about it being a peculiar case. Then he looked at me and said *it's sitting in the barn.*'

'It's sitting in the barn?' Wisting repeated.

'I didn't get to ask him more. "*It was just sitting there one day,*" he said, pointing at the picture of the taxi in the newspaper. Then he folded the paper, took it with him and left.'

'What barn was he talking about?'

'I don't know any more than what I've told you, but I've thought a lot about it and felt it important enough to phone you. That man knows something.'

'Has he been here since?'

She shook her head.

'Was he with anyone when he was here?'

'No, I've spoken to the staff. Nobody knows who he is.'

Wisting reeled off a list of questions about what the man looked like, what he had been wearing, what dialect he spoke, and whether he had any other distinguishing features.

Suzanne fiddled with the envelope in front of her. 'He paid

by bank card,' she said. 'I checked the till roll and worked out approximately when he must have paid. Presumably you can use the transaction number to find out who he is.'

Wisting smiled and took the envelope. This could be a breakthrough in the Hummel case. Among the detectives, various theories had circulated about what had become of the car. Some thought that Jens Hummel had driven out of town of his own free will, others believed that it was lying somewhere at the foot of a precipice after an accident or at least off road having been dumped. Wisting was among those who felt that it must have been stashed in a garage or somewhere similar after Jens Hummel had fallen victim to a crime.

Police patrols had explored all the side roads in the area. A helicopter had searched over increasingly extensive territory. Divers had scoured along the edges of piers and jetties. Multistorey car parks had been inspected. It had all been futile, so it was not unlikely that the car had been deposited in a barn.

Suzanne got to her feet. 'I need to start work,' she said. 'How's Line getting on?'

'Fine,' Wisting said. 'I think she's doing very well.'

It looked as if Suzanne wanted to say something further, but she let it drop. Wisting was grateful. What had happened to Line was difficult to talk about.

Suzanne took a few steps over to the counter. 'Good luck,' she said. 'With everything. Say hello to her from me.'

'Call me if he turns up here again,' Wisting asked, remaining seated. He opened the envelope and took out the slip of paper. The numbers on the printout from the point of sale terminal told him nothing. They would have to ask the card company for the name of the person behind that combination of digits. He had waited a long time for some sort of breakthrough in the Hummel enquiry. Now he was going to have to wait a bit longer: until Monday.

4

Wisting let himself into the police station as early as quarter to seven on Monday morning, flecks of white paint still on his hands after helping Line to paint skirting boards. On his way up to the criminal investigation department he nodded to the tired officers slumped over their computers, writing the final night-shift reports.

He spent the time until the other investigators showed up on trawling through the Hummel case once more, scraping the white paint off his hands with his nails as he read. A new piece of information could make him view the case from a different angle, and what had previously seemed insignificant could become extremely important in the light of a new hypothesis. He leafed through the case documents searching for something that had been left unexplained, chance events that might turn out to conceal significant connections.

One distinctive aspect of the case had been Jens Hummel's long distance drives. At least once a week he had gone on trips lasting hours to Kristiansand or Oslo. It *could* be sheer chance and, as a matter of fact, these were nothing more than statistics. What made Hummel's trips special were that they were paid for in cash, and were not booked through the taxi headquarters. Hummel had joked to his colleagues that he drove a rich old lady who was visiting relatives on the south coast, but no one had ever seen her and the police had not succeeded in tracking her down.

He found nothing new in the files. An electronic search through the list of tip-offs for the word *barn* did not yield anything specific either. His office door was open and he listened every time someone entered the department. At ten to eight he

13

heard Nils Hammer's footsteps as he shuffled to his office at the end of the corridor.

Hammer had become proficient at finding and following electronic traces, mostly due to his excellent ability to adapt. Investigation methods and possibilities that had not existed when they started their careers had now become crucial.

Wisting got up from his desk and went to see him. The burly police officer had brought a plastic beaker of coffee from the duty desk and sipped from it as he logged into the data system. Wisting placed the printout from the POS terminal on the table. 'How fast can you find out who paid with this card?' he asked.

Hammer put aside his coffee cup, picked up the slip of paper and gave it a quick once over. 'How urgent is it?'

'The person who used this card may know where Jens Hummel is.'

Nils Hammer sat up straight. 'Give me a couple of hours,' he said, draining his cup in one swallow.

Wisting turned to go back to his office.

'How did it go with her, by the way?' Hammer asked his retreating back.

'Who?' Wisting asked, wondering if he meant Line.

'Our Assistant Chief of Police,' Hammer said, grinning. 'She flaked out completely.'

'She was fine. She probably needed to wet her whistle.' He headed for his own office, smiling at the memory of morning coffee shared with Christine Thiis.

Routine tasks were next in line. He worked his way through the bundle of reports and notifications from the weekend. It looked as if the summer hiatus also affected the crime statistics. With the exception of some disturbances in restaurants, a few drunk drivers and a fire on a boat, there was little of note.

Christine Thiis appeared when he was nearing the bottom of the pile. 'Thanks again,' she said, smiling with a hint of shyness in her eyes. 'For driving me home.'

Wisting brushed it off.

14

'Did you find out anything about the Hummel case?' she asked, taking a seat.

'That remains to be seen.' He explained about the bank terminal and the unknown card owner's reaction to what had been printed in the newspaper, without mentioning Suzanne's name. She had not asked to be kept out of it, but he had not told Christine who he was going to meet and saw no reason to do so now.

Christine Thiis stood up. 'You've got a white spot here,' she said, pointing at the side of her cheek.

Wisting touched his face. 'Painting,' he explained, showing off his hands. 'I'm probably going to look like this for a few more weeks.'

She smiled again and closed the office door behind her when she left.

He returned to his notes. The door did not open again for nearly two hours when Hammer entered carrying printouts. He sat in the vacant chair.

'The bank card belongs to an Aron Heisel,' he said, putting one on the desk.

Wisting drew the sheet of paper towards him. In addition to the account number, the date of birth was printed, but no address. Wisting calculated that Aron Heisel must be forty-eight years old. 'Who is this Aron Heisel?'

Hammer showed him a photo from police records, taken from front and side, a younger version of the man Suzanne had described, with narrow shoulders, flat nose, a suggestion of dark rings under his grey eyes and a gap between his front teeth. Wisting asked how the man in the picture had come to be registered with the police.

'He was found guilty of being the linchpin when the police uncovered a big spirits factory outside Drammen in 1997. In 2002 he was arrested again and sentenced for smuggling alcohol and he was a suspect in another case in Østfold three years ago, but not convicted.'

'Where does he stay now?'

'His last place of residence is near Marbella in Spain.'

Wisting was familiar with the city, having once been there on police business with Torunn Borg.

'He's in Norway now,' Hammer continued, and set down a closely written list of transactions. 'The card's been used in different places in Spain,' he said, running his index finger down the list. 'The last time was at the airport in Malaga on 12 July. Then, as you can see, he's in Norway.'

Wisting squinted at the printout. The card had been used the previous day, at the *REMA 1000* supermarket in Holmejordet. The shop was located beside the main road into Stavern. Wisting himself stopped there now and again to buy groceries on his way home from work.

He searched for his glasses, but could not find them. Instead he continued to study the list with his eyes screwed up. The card had been used for purchases at builders' merchants, to pay for a meal at one of the restaurants at the inner harbour, and a larger sum had been paid out at the *Elkjøp* electronics retailer. He found several visits to Suzanne's café, *The Golden Peace*. With the exception of the last visit, he always paid his bill just after midnight. The subsequent transaction was always charged to the Vestfold Taxi Company.

'We can track him down,' he said, pointing at the line noting one of the taxi trips. 'Someone drove him home.'

5

It took Hammer three hours to find a taxi driver who remembered driving Aron Heisel. The first two he had spoken to did not recollect either passenger or trip, but the third recognised him from the photograph and told Hammer that he had driven him two nights in a row. Both times the passenger had been dropped off at Huken.

The journey from the police station took ten minutes. For Wisting, Huken had never been more than a place name on the inland main road that meandered out to Helgeroa.

Hammer reduced his speed as they approached, and Wisting leaned forward in his seat, studying his surroundings. Potato plants grew tall on either side of the road. They arrived first at a modern house that looked as if it had been built on former farmland. Children were jumping on a trampoline in the garden, and two older boys stood repairing a moped. Beside the road was an old workshop or garage for heavy goods vehicles, and behind that a number of red-painted outbuildings. No barn.

'Drive on,' he said.

They passed a paddock where horses were grazing. A man stood on a ladder painting the stable wall. In an open space, a tractor with a log splitter attached was parked beside a pile of wood. In the distance the sun reflected off the remaining panes of glass in an old market garden. They spotted a milk churn shelter in a layby and a blue sign indicating it was a bus stop.

'Here,' Hammer said, pointing. 'He dropped him off here.' Behind a dry-stone wall a narrow almost overgrown track led into the woods.

Hammer turned in. A flock of birds took off from a leafy tree, like a swarm of insects. The car bumped slowly over potholes and clumps of grass. A wide ditch filled with stagnant water, covered in unsavoury green slime, ran the length of the left side of the track. Only intermittently could Wisting see patches of black water.

The woods grew denser around them before the landscape opened out again, and the track ended at an abandoned small-holding, with a tumbledown barn situated at the edge of the woods. Half the roof tiles were missing, so it looked like a skeleton picked clean by vultures.

Hammer stopped the car in front of the farmhouse. Two outbuildings with corrugated roofs were located between the house and barn. Wild roses and clusters of purple foxgloves surrounded them.

Wisting stepped out, slamming the car door. Hammer left the driver's door open. A summery buzz of insects gyrating above the tall grass was the only sound. Once, the farmhouse had been painted white. Now it was grey and neglected. The downpipes hung broken at the corners, there were no curtains at the windows, and a wooden board replaced a broken pane.

Wisting approached the door and knocked. Without waiting for a response, he put his hands to the glass of the nearest window and peered inside: a blue-painted kitchen with plates, cup and glasses piled up in the sink, plastic bags, empty bottles and empty pizza cartons on the worktop. An ant trail led from one to the wall trim. On the kitchen table, a newspaper was spread out beside a coffee mug.

'No one home?' Hammer asked.

'No, but someone's living here,' Wisting replied. He rapped the glass with his knuckles and shouted before retracing his steps to the door and rattling the handle. 'Locked,' he said, and turned to face the barn. 'We'll see if we can get in there instead.'

They strode through the long grass to the double doors in the middle of the barn wall and a plank of wood that was tilted against them to hold them shut. Hammer kicked it away. The doors slid open a few centimetres, but they were still held closed by a bolt on the inside.

A door further along the wall was also locked. There were latticed windows on either side. Most of the glazing putty had crumbled away, but the panes were held in place by little staples bent towards the glass. 'We can't leave here without checking,' Hammer said, poking at the frame with his fingers.

Wisting nodded and stood in silence as Hammer went back to the car to fetch an ice scraper. He pushed it down behind the staples, forced them out and soon was able to lift out one of the panes. He thrust his hand inside and unhooked the catches.

Wisting held the window open while Hammer crawled inside. From the outside he could hear Hammer swearing and something scraping along the wall before falling to the floor. The bolt was drawn back and the double barn doors slid open. Throwing them wide, Wisting looked inside the barn's enormous interior. The smell of dry straw billowed towards them. Strips of light forced their way through cracks in the timber.

After a short delay, their eyes grew accustomed to the darkness, and the room took shape: two doors on one of the gable walls, a cargo trailer with two axles and four wheels, behind that a stack of hay bales and a pallet of white plastic containers, and along the walls hung hayforks, spades, rakes, a scythe and other tools. Various tractor attachments were scattered in a corner along with old milk churns.

There was a vehicle in the centre of the barn, covered in a grey tarpaulin that did not quite reach the floor. Wisting marched over, his feet stirring up fine dust that made his nose itch.

Hammer took hold of the tarpaulin and yanked it off, revealing a black Volvo V60 with a taxi sign on the roof. Taxi number Z-1086. Jens Hummel's car.

Wisting leaned over the windscreen and peered inside without touching anything. It was empty. The key was in the ignition. A half-empty bottle of cola sat in the centre console. On the passenger seat were a pair of leather gloves and a shrivelled, half-eaten mouldy baguette wrapped in plastic.

Removing the tarpaulin, Hammer went behind the car to open the boot lid. 'Empty. Totally empty.'

19

Wisting felt a tingling sensation; the Hummel case was opening up again. He took out his mobile phone to call Mortensen and arrange for a technical examination of the car and the barn. Then they would have to organise a search. Since Jens Hummel was not inside the taxi, it was fairly unlikely that he would be found anywhere else in the barn, but the smallholding would be the starting point for a search. They would have to dredge the streams and riverbeds, probe crevices, gravel pits and drained wells, everywhere that a body might possibly be hidden.

Before he managed to tap in the number, the phone rang: Suzanne. He answered by giving his name, and heard himself how curt and dismissive he sounded.

'He's here now,' she whispered into the receiver. 'The man who said that Jens Hummel's taxi was in the barn. He's in the café now.'

6

Taking two steps back, Line used her hand to sweep her fringe from her forehead and surveyed the living room ceiling. The newly painted surface was gleaming, and the room looked more spacious now that it was white. She glanced at the yellowish-brown pine panelling in the hallway. That could wait until tomorrow; she had earned a break.

Cleaning the brushes, she packed away the painting equipment and pulled off her white overalls. Her father had promised to paint the ceiling that afternoon and would be annoyed that she had already done it. Not really angry, but he wouldn't be pleased, given her condition. But she was looking forward to being finished and, besides, the paint did not contain any harmful solvents or gases.

Her hand automatically moved down to her large stomach; soon it would be eight months. Even before the baby was born, it had already changed her life. She had lost her taste for big city life and moved home to familiar and safe surroundings. Left an exciting job as a journalist where the pace was too fast and expectations too high to combine with life as the mother of a young child. Maybe it would have been different if she had someone to share the responsibility, but it wasn't like that.

She headed for the fridge, took out a bottle of tap water and, as she drank, stood in the living room doorway. She ought to give the window frames another coat now that she was started, but it would have to wait.

There was very little left of the living room she had taken over with the house, though she would probably never manage to free herself entirely of the man found dead in his chair, or the man who had hanged himself in the basement in the late

21

sixties, just after the house had been built. She shuddered at the idea and placed her hand protectively over her bump. It still felt quite strange that it was so huge, but she had been lucky. She had not put on much weight and was fighting fit. At present she was mostly aware of it in her back, mainly because of the painting. Apart from that, she had more energy now than she'd had in ages.

She returned the water to the fridge and went to the bathroom. She had no regrets about spending money on renovations before she moved in. The house was a good purchase, and with the sale of her flat in Oslo she actually had a generous budget.

She stripped off and scrutinised her belly from various angles. It had never been as tight as now, so tight she could feel the baby's movements when it changed position. She held her hand over a minuscule hard bulge that pushed the skin out on her stomach. Was it a hand or a foot?

She did not like to think about the actual birth, which was only four weeks away, and she dreaded it. She had done some reading, but did not know whether that was helpful. She would just have to take it as it came, she mused, shifting her attention to her face in the mirror. There were two white spots on her right cheek and another on her throat. She rubbed them off, washing her hands clean of paint, before stepping into the shower.

Half an hour later she was sitting in her car en route to the town centre. It was not easy finding clothes to fit her steadily increasing bulk. As a rule she wore tracksuit trousers or a tunic, but for now she had put on a light and comfortable dress with a high drawstring waist and a loose skirt.

The traffic moved slowly towards the centre where most of the narrow streets were closed, transformed into a pedestrian precinct for the summer. Usually she could find a parking space in one of the less congested side streets, but today she ended up parking in the fee-paying area set up in the old tennis courts.

She was hoping to find a spare table outside *The Golden Peace* or one of the other cafés now serving on the pavement, but first she wanted to go into the little interior décor shop with such a pleasant atmosphere on the corner of Skippergata and Verftsgata. Every time she went inside she gleaned fresh ideas about how to decorate her home. In addition to a great deal of elegant interior decorations, they also stocked jewellery and clothes.

The streets were swarming with people as usual. At one of the market stalls, she stopped to look at some handcrafted jewellery, but walked on before the stallholder engaged her in conversation.

She took off her sunglasses when she stepped inside the interiors shop. Here too there were lots of people, but the air was cooler, and every metre of shelving was filled with marvellous things: scented candles, mirrors, frames, clocks, decorative boxes, jars, pictures, cushions, rugs, cups, dishes, lamps, blackboards, hooks, signs, candlesticks, wooden boxes, pots, buckets and small items of furniture.

Tired of the trend for nostalgia in which every piece of furniture was required to look old and shabby she aimed for a cleaner and more modern style, but it was also important to put her own personal stamp on the final look. She would hang her own pictures on the walls. She was skilled with a camera, just as much a photographer as a journalist. What she looked forward to most was kitting out a workroom in the basement. She envisaged a rough unpolished design with rustic lamps, well-worn filing cabinets and the front-page stories on which she had worked framed and displayed on grey brick walls.

She stopped at a trendy wall clock with Roman numerals. As she lifted the price ticket, someone bumped into her.

'Sorry!'

A woman of her own age with a child on her arm and sunglasses on her head put her hand tentatively on Line's bump. 'Are you okay?'

Line smiled, nodding. She stretched out her hand to the clock again, but her eyes returned to the woman with the child. There was something familiar about her face.

'You're Line, aren't you?' the other woman asked. 'Line Wisting?'

23

Line smiled in confirmation before she cocked her head and frowned in an effort to recall who the other woman was.

'I'm Sofie. We went to primary school together. It's not so odd that you don't remember me, but of course I've read about you in the newspapers. Or at least, I've read a lot of what you've written.'

The name and face fell into place. 'Sofie Mandt,' Line said. 'You moved when we were in year seven, or something like that.'

'Year five. My name is Lund now. And this is Maja.' She tickled her daughter under the chin, producing a gurgling burst of laughter and two deep dimples.

'You're married?' Line asked, caressing the child's head.

'No, Lund is my grandmother's maiden name,' Sofie explained. 'It's just Maja and me.'

Line wanted to tell her that she was alone too, but left it unsaid. 'Are you here on holiday?' she asked.

Sofie Lund shook her head. 'I've just moved back.'

'Me too! I've lived in Oslo for five years, but that's enough now.' Line laid her hand on her stomach. 'I've bought a house in Varden in the street where I grew up. I'm doing it up now.'

'When are you due?'

'At the end of August.' Line concentrated on the child on Sofie's arm. 'How old is she?'

'She was one in May.' Sofie put the child down on the floor, where she took several unsteady steps before grabbing her mother's leg and holding on tight.

'Where do you live?'

'In the centre,' Sofie nodded in the direction of their house.

Line crouched down and chatted to Maja. After moving to Oslo she had gradually lost contact with her old friends, but gained new ones among her work colleagues. She was prepared to take time to build a new circle, and this could well be a start. 'Would you like to go for coffee?' she asked.

Sofie Lund did not answer immediately. She was studying a little sign stating that life was like riding a bicycle. To keep your balance you must keep moving. 'Yes, please,' she eventually replied and put the sign back on the shelf.

24

Line smiled and checked the price of the wall clock: nearly twelve hundred kroner. If they still had it at the end of the summer, she could probably buy it for half that price.

A young couple got up from one of the tables outside *The Golden Peace*, freeing a place for them, and a man with a skip cap at an adjacent table moved aside to make space for Maja's pushchair. Line went inside and bought the coffees. Suzanne was behind the counter, but one of the young girls took her order. When she came out again, she had bought two slices of cake as well as two lattés.

They made small talk about the weather and the heat, about the crowds of people, the tourists and old classmates. 'Why did you move back?' Line asked.

'I inherited a house,' Sofie answered, 'from my grandfather. It suited me to move. Begin over again, so to speak.'

'Who was your grandfather?' Line asked, noticing that Sofie did not like the question.

'Frank Mandt. I haven't had much contact with him. He died last winter.'

Line knew who Sofie's grandfather was. Most people in Stavern did.

'What about you?' Sofie asked. 'Why did you move?'

'Because I fell pregnant,' Line answered. 'The life I was living in Oslo was linked to my job with *VG* and my colleagues there. Without my job I had no connection to the place, and I'd prefer for her to grow up here.'

Sofie glanced at her stomach. 'It's a girl, then?'

As Line nodded, her thoughts turned to the little body she was carrying inside. If what she had read was true, she was more than forty centimetres long by now and weighed two point five kilos.

'What about the father?' Sofie asked.

'That's a long story,' Line said, smiling. 'He was out of the picture before I knew I was pregnant.'

'Just as well,' Sofie commented. 'Mine stayed, but found other women on the side. I'm better off without him.'

'It wasn't quite like that for me,' Line said. 'I met him

25

through my work. He was an American police officer working on a case here before Christmas.'

Sofie burst out laughing and pointed at her stomach: 'So that's the result of a one-night stand?'

Line joined in and felt how good it was to laugh. 'It wasn't just one night,' she pointed out. 'He was here for a couple of weeks.'

'But you kept it?'

'I'm twenty-nine,' Line said. 'And she's not unwanted.'

'Are you in touch with him, the American? Does he know about it?'

'Oh yes, we talk to each other online. He offered to move here to be close to us, but it wouldn't have been right. He has an important job where he is.'

A car drove along the pedestrian street with people unwillingly moving aside. Line put down her half-empty glass of coffee and watched it cruise up to the kerb on the other side of the street and come to a standstill. The man who stepped out gazed across at them. It was her father.

7

Wisting waited until Hammer left the car before crossing the street. He only just caught sight of Line at one of the tables outside *The Golden Peace* before the man at the adjacent table stood up. Pulling his skip cap further down over his face, he shoved Maja's pushchair aside and headed off, walking at top speed.

They could not see his face, but his height, age and narrow shoulders matched Aron Heisel's description. He must have realised they were policemen simply from their demeanour, as their watchful awareness of their surroundings betrayed them, at least to anyone on the lookout.

'Hey!' Wisting yelled, following the man who had now turned his back on them. 'Wait a minute!'

The man quickened his pace, seemingly making for a motorbike parked with a helmet hanging from the handlebars. When Wisting called out again, he changed his mind and sprinted in a different direction.

'Stop!' Wisting shouted. 'Police!'

The nearest bystanders turned and stared. Stealing a quick backward glance, the man jostled some youngsters aside and ran on. Wisting dashed after him, his shirt riding up at the waist and flapping around him.

The man ran off down Dronningens gate and took the first side street to the right, already lost in the bustling crowds when Wisting turned the corner. He caught a glimpse of his skip cap and white T-shirt and forced his way through in pursuit. The man pushed recklessly forward past families with young children and other pedestrians. He tripped over a bike with stabilisers and fell, but scrambled to his feet right away.

27

At the next street corner he turned right and ran towards the quays before taking a sharp left and darting across a children's play park, stumbling again while looking back over his shoulder. Wisting caught up with him at the waffle stall. He grabbed him by the arm, but the man pulled back so violently that Wisting was flung head first against a lamppost. A shudder coursed through his body and he felt blood running down his cheek. The man fled along the quayside.

Wisting did not see where Nils Hammer came from, but he suddenly plunged in from one side, throwing himself at the man and knocking him off his feet, over the edge of the quay and into the water. Hammer almost followed, but regained his balance and remained on dry land.

Several customers at the nearest outdoor restaurant stood to watch what was going on. For a moment it looked as if the man intended to swim out, but he shook his head in resignation and grabbed his skip cap as it floated off. Three strokes brought him back to the quayside where Wisting and Hammer hauled him out.

'Aron Heisel?'

The man nodded, leaning forward with his hands on his knees, letting the water drip.

'Why did you run off?' Hammer asked.

Aron Heisel took a deep breath and sighed loudly, but did not answer.

'We need to talk about Jens Hummel and his taxi,' Wisting said.

'It was just sitting there.' The man sounded discouraged. 'I don't know any more than that. It was just sitting there.'

A patrol vehicle drove towards them. Hammer waved it over and curious onlookers moved aside. 'Take him in and see that he gets some dry clothes,' Wisting ordered.

'I haven't done anything wrong,' Heisel protested.

'We can discuss that later,' Wisting said, touching the side of his own head. Blood soiled his fingers and he could already feel a substantial swelling. One of the uniformed officers opened the rear doors of the patrol wagon and ushered Aron Heisel inside.

'He can sit and wait for a while,' Hammer said.

Wisting agreed. Waiting would advantage whoever was going to ask the questions. 'I want to go back to the barn,' he said, watching the police officers close the door on Aron Heisel. 'I think the car will give us more answers than the guy in there.'

8

Line put down her empty coffee glass.

Maja had grown restless. She was reluctant to sit in the pushchair, but would not settle on her mother's lap either. She wriggled like an eel and began to whimper.

'She's tired,' Sofie explained. 'I need to take her home so she can have a nap. Would you like to come?'

Line scanned the direction in which her father and Nils Hammer had disappeared. It did not look as if they would be back soon. She wondered what it had been about, but could ask this evening when he popped in to see her. 'I'd like that,' she answered.

Sofie put Maja back into the pushchair and manoeuvred it between the chairs and tables.

The walk took no more than five minutes. The Mandt house was located beside what was known as the Water Pump Park, because there was an old village pump among the massive birch trees. People in the past had come to fetch water, wash their clothes and hear the latest news. Now a photographer was there photographing a young couple.

The main entrance was at the rear of the house. Sofie opened the door before lifting Maja from her pushchair and Line followed them inside. They were greeted by a scent of green soap, and the white-painted wooden floor shone. Boxes not yet unpacked were stacked against the walls.

'There's not much sorted out yet,' Sofie said, kicking off her shoes. She showed Line into the living room and opened the doors to the glass verandah that overlooked the park. 'I'll be back soon,' she said, disappearing into the kitchen with Maja on her arm. 'Make yourself at home.'

30

Line surveyed her surroundings, feeling slightly envious. This house was larger, brighter and airier than hers. The ceilings were high and heavy beams gave an impression of elegance. The bohemian furnishings that Sofie had brought with her from Oslo failed to fill the room and did not seem entirely appropriate for its grandeur. Sofie appeared in the kitchen doorway. Maja had been given a bottle.

'It's so lovely here,' Line said.

'Come upstairs with me,' Sofie suggested, 'and see the first floor while I put Maja down for her nap.'

The staircase was worn, and several of the treads creaked under their feet. The air up here was stuffier and hotter. Sofie went into the first room on the left, opened a window and laid Maja down in a cot at the wall. The youngster kicked her legs before giving her full attention to the bottle of milk her mother had heated.

Sofie closed the door softly behind her and showed Line round. Most of the rooms were empty, but they were large with broad pine floorboards, faded wallpaper and deep window ledges with latticed windows.

'Workmen are coming next week,' Sofie explained. 'I want to paint the ceilings and paper the walls, but apart from that there's not much needing done.'

Line pointed at a door that stood slightly ajar.

'And then I need to renovate this bathroom,' Sofie added as she opened the door on a room with a toilet bowl, a cracked wash hand basin with flecks of rust around the drain where the tap had dripped, and a massive old bathtub. There were no windows and dampness had caused the floral wallpaper to peel.

'Big job,' Line commented.

'There was money in my inheritance,' Sofie said. 'And there's no rush. There's an almost new bathroom in the basement.'

'So there's a basement as well?'

Sofie headed for the stairs. 'It's huge and empty,' she said. 'Except for an old safe that I can't shift.'

'Why not?'

Sofie lowered her voice as they passed the child's bedroom. 'It's too big. You'd almost think it was installed in the basement before they built the house.'

'But why do you want it removed?' Line asked, following her downstairs. 'It's a good idea to have a safe.'

'I don't have the key,' Sofie told her. 'And it's locked.'

'Locked?' Does that mean you don't know what's inside?'

'Not a clue. Come and I'll show you!'

Sofie crossed to the basement door, opened it and switched on the light. The sudden draught from below fluttered the papers lying on a chest of drawers in the hallway.

Line led the way. There was a hint of the same dank odour down here as in her own basement, like damp clothes left lying too long. She peeped inside some of the rooms in the basement corridor and shivered with the cold. The safe was at the far end. Sunlight slanted across the floor from a window high on the wall. Line stood where it hit the rough wall and pressed her hand on her stomach.

The safe was really massive. They must have been only just able to negotiate its bulk through the doorframe, not to mention carry it down the stairs. She moved forward and pushed aside the little metal cover in front of the keyhole. 'Have you searched for the key?' she asked, looking round the room.

Sofie shook her head. 'I haven't, but I hired people to clear the house and they didn't find it.'

'It must be here somewhere.' Line stood on tiptoe, sliding her hand along a water pipe that ran along the ceiling without finding anything. At the top of the exterior wall, a ventilator was fitted, but the vent was too high to look inside. Instead she thrust in her fingers and rummaged blindly, picking up only dust and balls of fluff. Laughing at herself, she apologised for taking liberties. 'I'm just so inquisitive,' she said. 'What do you think might be inside?'

Sofie was quiet for a moment or two before she replied. 'It's probably empty.'

'Of course, you can always get someone to drill it open or

something like that. A locksmith could do it. I know someone who works on that sort of thing.'

'I'm not sure if I really do want to know what's in there, if anything. Whatever it is, it's bound not to be anything good. It's a secret the Old Man took with him into death, and that's where it might as well stay.'

'How did he die?' Line asked.

'He fell.' Sofie stood beside a dark stain on the concrete floor. 'On the stairs here,' she said, pointing. 'He fell downstairs and lay dead on the floor for a few days before someone found him.'

Line stared at the steep stairs.

'Do you think it strange?' Sofie asked. 'That I'm willing to live here?'

Line shook her head. 'A man died in my house too. Two, in fact,' she added, thinking of Viggo Hansen's father who had hanged himself in her basement nearly fifty years ago.

Sofie chuckled. A burst of hesitant laughter that grew heartier when Line joined in. 'I've actually not given it much thought, that he died here,' she explained, climbing the stairs. 'More about all the bad things he did while he was alive.'

Line followed, her interest aroused. There was a story here. She was on leave from her job as a journalist with the *Verdens Gang* newspaper and, strictly speaking, had no plans to go back. She hoped to use the period of leave to finish writing the manuscript of a book she had embarked on a few years ago, and her longer-term plan was to make a living as a freelance writer. What she liked especially about her work as a writer was the opportunity to tell a compelling story, and now she could discern the outline of one. She held back her questions.

Sofie rattled glasses in the kitchen as Line waited in the living room. An enormous bookcase had been assembled but most of the books were still packed in cardboard boxes on the floor, marked alphabetically. A to E had been placed on the shelves, while the other authors awaited their turn.

'We'll sit outside,' Sofie suggested as she reappeared carrying two glasses and a jug of iced tea. Line followed her out into the small shady terrace at the rear of the house, where they were screened from both noise and prying eyes. A lofty rosebush with red blooms climbed the wall and spread out to the eaves. Sofie filled the glasses.

'What were the bad things your grandfather did?' Line asked.

'You've heard of him?'

Line nodded. 'I know he sold spirits. Smuggled spirits.'

'He took my mother's life.'

Line sat with the glass in her hand, unable to ask her friend to continue.

'When I moved from the town, it was because my mother was sent to prison. She had to take the punishment for something he had done.'

Line put down her glass, feeling how close they had grown in the short time since they met. 'You really must tell me,' she said.

Sofie crossed her arms and stared at the ground and Line realised this was something she was reluctant to discuss, but also understood that after a long time the need to talk can be irresistible.

'They called him the Smuggler King,' Sofie said, with a flash of anger in her eyes. 'As if there was something noble and honourable about what he did.' She shook her head and continued.

'He began in the sixties, when he worked as a stevedore at the quay. Got the chance to buy some cheap bottles from the crews of boats that came from Rotterdam, Bremerhaven and other European ports. He sold them on at a good profit, but cheaper than at the state monopoly store.

'A few bottles turned into cases. At some point he began to operate his own vessels, and hired the skippers of fishing boats to carry spirits and cigarettes across the Skagerrak.

'He was newly married at that time, so the money came in handy. Mum was born in 1964. Grandma died not long afterwards, so Mum was in a way born and brought up to it all. Eventually he began to import spirits overland as well. Lorries came from factories in Spain and delivered to depots all over the Østland region.'

34

'Wasn't he caught?'

'Not he. Some of the vehicles were stopped at the border. He lost a consignment occasionally, but always got off scot-free. Then he turned to other goods. First hash, which was easier to smuggle than bottles and drums of spirits, took up less space and gave a greater profit.'

Line had heard rumours and gossip. 'What happened to your mother?' she asked.

'Mum was on her own with me. My father is just a name I've heard. I've never met him and don't know where he lives. I've no idea even how he and Mum met. We never got round to talking about it. I was ten, or almost eleven, when she died.'

Sofie stretched out her arm and picked a rose from the bush flowering on the wall. 'It was a Saturday in late summer,' she continued, peeling off a petal. 'We were going to the Handelsstevn market and fair in Skien, as we used to do. There was a fairground and famous celebrities appeared on stage.'

Line had been there once, years ago.

'We lived in a small flat right down the street. Mum had an old Opel. She had a lot of trouble with it, and that day it quite simply would not start. We came here to borrow one of the Old Man's cars, as we'd done loads of times before. He wasn't at home, but his Volvo was parked outside. Mum let herself in, found the keys and left him a note.'

The back of the chair creaked as Sofie changed position. Her dark hair fell over her face and she brushed it away, smiling uncertainly.

'At Vallermyrene in Porsgrunn, we were stopped by the police,' she said. 'I don't know why. Maybe it was sheer chance; maybe they were keeping a watch on the Old Man and had his cars on a list. Anyway, the police car drove up behind us and switched on the blue flashing lights. Mum pulled in to the side of the road. They asked all sorts of questions and began to look around in the car. Under the seat where I was sitting they found three kilos of hash and one kilo of amphetamines.'

Line's mouth fell open. 'But she couldn't have known anything about it?'

'She got five years in jail. They regarded as aggravating factors that she had a young child with her and would not cooperate with the police.'

'But didn't she tell them what had happened?' Line asked. 'That she had just borrowed the car?'

'The Old Man denied having anything to do with it. He sacrificed his daughter to get away with it himself.'

'What about the note she had written? That would prove what she had told them.'

'The police never found a note. The Old Man must have burned it or torn it to pieces and flushed it down the loo.'

'So he just sat there and watched your mother get convicted even though she was innocent?'

'He hired expensive lawyers, probably to learn what the case documents said and how much the police knew about him. As far as he was concerned, she was a pawn to be sacrificed. The loss of the drugs was probably more of a blow than what happened to her.'

Line laid her hand protectively on her stomach. 'You said that he took her life, though?'

'Mum could not last more than a year in prison. One night she smashed a glass and cut the arteries in her arm. I visited her only once. It was a dreadful experience. It was one thing going behind those thick walls, but even worse coming back out again, leaving her inside.'

Sofie had picked all the petals off the rose. She placed them in a little heap on the tablecloth. 'What happened to you when your mother was sent to prison?' Line asked.

'The first few days I stayed here with the Old Man. There was talk of me staying permanently and I thought that would be fine. I knew all the children and had only a short walk to school, but he didn't want me. It was too much for him, he said. So I was sent to a foster home. I had three of them. First in Arendal, then Hamar and finally Oslo.'

A wasp perched on the rim of the glass jug filled with iced tea. Line waved it away.

'She wrote a long letter of farewell to me,' Sofie said. 'I

didn't receive it until I was grown up. It stated on the outside of the envelope that I was to get it when I was eighteen. She wrote about what had taken place, about how her father had betrayed her, and how she felt she had let me down. Then she asked me not to have anything to do with the Old Man.'

She brushed the rose petals off the table with an abrupt movement before she went on. 'It feels a bit wrong to sit here with this huge house. It's as if it ties me to him.'

'You mustn't think like that,' Line objected.

Sofie took a drink from her glass. 'What kind of relationship do you have with your mother?' she asked.

'She's dead too,' Line replied.

'Sorry.'

'It's okay. It'll be six years this summer. It was a car accident in Africa. She worked on a teaching programme for refugees. The car she was a passenger in drove over a cliff. Everyone died.'

'Do you miss her?'

'Yes, especially now. She was the sort of person who always gave good advice. I sometimes catch myself thinking I'll phone her when I've something special to tell her.'

'I know,' Sofie said, with a smile, peering up at the first floor where her own daughter lay sleeping. 'It's terrible to think that she won't get to see her grandchild, and that Maja won't know her grandmother. I've hardly any photos of her either.'

They sat for a while in silence. The sun had moved and they were no longer in the shade.

'My Dad's got a safe at home in the basement,' Line said, after a while. 'A fireproof safe. He uses it to store old photographs and negatives. Pictures of Mum.'

9

After manoeuvring the car slowly in front of the farmhouse, Wisting stopped and got out. Sunlight glittered on the corrugated roof, dazzling him. The crime scene technicians' vehicles had ploughed through the tall grass all the way up to the barn door. A patrol wagon with a team of officers had also arrived. Nils Hammer remained in the car, talking on the phone.

Espen Mortensen emerged from the barn wearing the obligatory white overalls used by crime scene examiners. The weeds reached almost to his knees.

Wisting was pleased to see him. Mortensen was a thorough and experienced crime scene technician with a keen eye for detail. A crime scene investigation is not merely concerned with finding physical evidence left by a perpetrator, but equally about interpretation. Experience had taught Wisting that the impression left by a perpetrator at a crime scene could also be discerned in the life he led. A tidy crime scene as a rule implied that you were looking for someone living a well-organised life. A chaotic crime scene, where the perpetrator had left a trail of obvious clues, could indicate someone whose existence was similarly confused and spontaneous.

Mortensen was proficient at reading such information. However, he did not draw hasty inferences or conclusions, but preferred to listen to other people.

'What do you think?' Wisting asked, glancing inside the barn.

Espen Mortensen pulled down his mask and let it hang below his chin. 'It's too early to say.'

'What's your initial impression?'

Mortensen cleared his throat: 'This isn't a crime scene,' he asserted firmly. 'Whatever happened to Jens Hummel, it didn't happen here. The way I see it, the car's been driven here and stowed in the barn by someone else.'

Wisting felt the sunshine spread its heat across his back. He had hoped for more. 'There is something, though,' he said. 'Hiding the car does reinforce the murder theory.'

'It's a starting point,' Mortensen said. 'A fresh starting point.'

The starting point for the investigation, until now, had been the last sighting of Jens Hummel and his taxi when he had dropped off a passenger outside the Grand Hotel in Storgata. Wisting pictured a map in his mind's eye. The distance from the town centre to the discovery site was barely eight kilometres, a short distance, and the rest of the stretch was sparsely populated. An agricultural landscape with individual farms and smallholdings set back from the road, and side roads leading to fishing lakes and clusters of holiday cottages. Somewhere on that short stretch of road, Jens Hummel had probably made his last stop. 'What about the technical side of things?'

'We'll tow the car into the garage for examination, and do the usual stuff: fingerprints and DNA. Maybe the taximeter and electronics can provide us with answers, although the telecoms data suggests that the taximeter hadn't been in use.'

Wisting nodded. That was part of the mystery. A taximeter could give approximately the same information as electronic traces left by a mobile phone, but only if it had been switched on.

Nils Hammer slammed the car door and approached them. 'We're getting two dog patrols,' he told them. 'They'll be here in half an hour.'

'Good,' Wisting replied. 'Who owns this place?'

Hammer waved his mobile phone in the air. 'We'll soon have the answer to that.'

Wisting surveyed the densely wooded terrain. 'There was half a metre of snow when Hummel disappeared,' he said. 'There aren't many places to hide a body here.'

'Well, he's certainly not in the barn,' Mortensen said, replacing his mask before returning to the building.

Wisting waded through the tall grass to the outbuildings. Fat bees buzzed peacefully round the wild roses. None of the outbuildings was locked. Wisting pulled open the door of the nearest and peered inside. Specks of sunshine danced on the floor. The blue sky was visible through holes in the roof. Apart from a pile of four used tyres in one corner, the space was empty.

'I've brought some officers to go door to door beside the main road,' Hammer said, following Wisting to the other outbuilding. 'Somebody may have seen something.'

Nodding agreement, Wisting peered through a window high on the wall of the second outbuilding. Dozens of flies were trapped in a thick spider's web inside; otherwise it was impossible to see much.

He went to the door and pushed the bolt to one side. The hinges creaked. Three outboard motors lay in the middle of the floor where the sunlight flooded in, and engine parts and tools were spread out on a workbench along the wall. Hammer's mobile phone rang. He fished it out of his pocket and remained outside as Wisting entered.

There was another door at the opposite end of the room. Even from where he stood, Wisting could see that it was locked. In the gap between the door and the frame he could see that both the latch and deadlock were engaged in the striking plate. Lifting a large screwdriver from the bench, he pressed it between the door and the frame. The timber groaned, but he managed to force the frame far enough to the side, breaking open the door without too much damage.

The room inside was in semi-darkness. He located a light switch and flicked it down, but nothing happened.

The only window in the room was covered with black plastic. In front of this, boxes of empty bottles were stacked, making it difficult to approach the window. He yanked off the plastic cover. A copious layer of dust whirled up and hung in the air.

A stainless steel machine sat at one end of the room. On either side of it there was some kind of conveyor belt, thick with dust. None of it had been used for some time. A carton of small bottle tops sat on the floor beside it. Wisting picked one up and read *Absolut Vodka* printed in blue lettering.

He dropped the cap into the carton and took a step back. The machine facing him was for capping and sealing bottles. They had investigated a few local cases of illegal activity with liquor in the nineties, without success, but information gleaned suggested that alcohol produced in factories in Southern Europe was being smuggled into Norway in plastic containers and barrels, bottled and furnished with false labels and lids.

Nils Hammer appeared at the door behind him.

'Have you found out who owns the farm?' Wisting asked.

'According to HQ, it belongs to someone called Trygve Marsten,' Hammer said. 'But the entire property is let out on a long-term lease.'

'To whom?'

'Frank Mandt.'

Wisting touched his neck with his hand. 'The Smuggler King,' he said pensively, scratching.

Nils Hammer had exchanged his phone for his snuffbox. 'He died last winter when he fell down his basement stairs.'

Wisting recalled the case. The conclusion had been that it was an accident.

Hammer lifted his top lip and slipped the snuff underneath. 'It happened round about the time that Jens Hummel went missing, of course.'

10

The air conditioning in the department was turned off after office hours, just one of the many savings initiatives. It was not necessary to spend money cooling an entire storey when there was no budget even to keep the detectives at work.

Wisting rolled his shirtsleeves above his elbows and opened his office window. The sky was hazy and white with swallows diving and soaring above the rooftops. He lingered for a moment, pressing two fingers on his temple. It had become badly swollen after his collision with the lamppost. Before summoning Aron Heisel for questioning, he wanted to look through what had been recorded about Frank Mandt.

Most of it was found in the electronic intelligence register, information Wisting recognised from previous meetings and projects. Frank Mandt was described as the organiser and kingpin for large-scale spirit-smuggling operations stretching far back in time. Informants had spoken of an enterprise that imported 21,000 litres of pure spirits every month. Distilled in Spain, it was cleared through customs labelled as tomatoes. In Northern Germany, it was divided into smaller consignments, smuggled into Sweden and then Norway. The profit could be as much as one hundred and fifty kroner for every litre delivered on to the illegal market in Norway.

A number of attempts had been made to expose the activity. Police and customs had cooperated in several counter-offensives, and some of the consignments had been stopped at the border, but they had not succeeded in linking them to Frank Mandt personally. More recent notes suggested that he was pulling out of the spirits scene. Now that the East European mafia had cut prices and taken over the market, intelligence suggested that Mandt had shifted his attention to narcotics.

The case file on his death was slim. The most substantial document was the report containing illustrations of Frank Mandt lying on the concrete floor at the foot of the basement stairs. He had been there for three days before someone called Klaus Wahl found him.

In a brief interview, Wahl had described himself as an acquaintance of Mandt's. They were in the habit of having a coffee together at the bakery every Friday, but on Friday 13 January, Mandt failed to turn up. He was seventy-nine years old, had diabetes and was prone to dizzy spells. Wahl became worried and paid a visit to his home. No one responded when he knocked, so he skirted round the house and peered through the windows. No sign of Mandt, and the house was locked with both cars parked outside. In the end Klaus Wahl smashed a basement window, crawled inside and found him as the photographs showed.

The post mortem report showed atlantoaxial fracture, several broken ribs, fracture of the right cheekbone and crush injuries to the skull, all consistent with a fall down stairs. The report could not establish anything definite about the time of death, but newspapers and post dating back to 11 January were piled up in the mailbox. The date of death was therefore fixed at Tuesday 10 January. Wisting glanced over at the desk calendar: four days after Jens Hummel's disappearance.

His mobile phone rang as he got to his feet to collect Aron Heisel for interview. It was Line, and he had promised to paint her living room ceiling this afternoon.

'I spotted you outside *The Golden Peace* earlier today,' she said. 'You looked busy.'

'Yes, it was a man we wanted to get hold of.'

'Did you catch him?'

Wisting's hand rose to his forehead again. 'Hammer got him,' he replied, shifting the phone across to his other ear.

'I'm calling because I've bought too much steak for the

barbecue,' she explained. 'Do you want to pop round and eat with me?'

Wisting strode down the corridor as he spoke. 'I'll have too much to do this evening,' he said, opening the door to the stairwell that led to the custody cells in the basement. 'I probably won't manage to get any painting done today either.'

'I did the living room ceiling this morning,' Line said. 'My next project is the wallpapering. It'll really take both of us for that.'

'You shouldn't have done that, Line,' he said, with a sigh. 'I did say I would do it.'

She ignored him. 'The wallpaper I ordered will arrive tomorrow. Do you think you'll have any time before the weekend?'

The phone connection deteriorated as he made his way downstairs. 'I'll *make* the time,' he said. 'Put some of the grilled steak aside and I'll heat it up when I get home.'

'I'll save it until tomorrow,' Line said, with no discernible change in her upbeat tone. 'It's not much fun barbecuing by yourself.'

'Okay then. I'll call in anyway, if it's not too late.'

Line ended the conversation, leaving Wisting, phone in hand, in front of the door into the cell corridor. He conjured up a vision of her, now very pregnant. The idea that he was going to be a grandfather made him feel elated. Despite the circumstances of the child's father, he knew he was looking forward to it. That Ingrid would not be there to experience the grandchild naturally put a damper on his happiness, but for the first time in ages he was looking forward to the future.

Distancing himself from his thoughts, he opened the door and ventured into the grey corridor. Aron Heisel was in Cell 8, the only person down here. The custody cells in the police station were almost never used now that a central remand centre had been established in Tønsberg. Some of the local cells had instead been pressed into service to store archived materials or for keeping evidence under lock and key.

Aron Heisel stood up. 'Sorry,' he said, looking at the swelling on Wisting's forehead.

'That's okay,' Wisting brushed him aside. 'We'll go up to my office.'

Heisel padded barefoot ahead of Wisting along the corridor. Someone had found him a pair of tracksuit trousers and a slightly too large sweater, and his sodden shoes were left outside his cell door.

Wisting waited until the man had settled into the visitor's chair before taking his seat at the opposite side of the desk. He spent some time on the practical details, ensuring the personal information they had on file was correct and running through the formalities. Heisel's eyes slid down to the desk, across to the window, and then to his hands, folded on his lap.

'Tell me about the taxi,' Wisting said.

Heisel shuddered, as if the direct question filled him with terror. Wisting had spent a considerable amount of his time listening to liars. The man probably had a lot to hide, but something nevertheless told him that his statement about the taxi 'just sitting there' might well be the truth. 'When did you discover it?'

'The same day the disappearance was covered in the newspaper. It must have been Thursday, last Thursday.'

Wisting leaned back, keen to hear more.

'I went into the barn to look for a lawnmower. The grass had grown high in front of the house. I let myself in and there it was. There was dust on the tarpaulin, so it must have been there for a long time.'

'When were you last in the barn?'

Aron Heisel changed position. 'Last summer. I actually live in Spain, but I'm in Norway for a few weeks every summer.'

'On the farm?'

'Yes.'

'Have you had any visitors there?'

'No.'

'Who owns the farm?' Wisting enquired, though he knew the answer.

'I don't know the owner's name, but an acquaintance of mine has it at his disposal. He lets me stay there for a couple of

45

months in summer in exchange for me looking after the place. I do some painting, cut the grass and that sort of thing.'

'Frank Mandt?'

Aron Heisel nodded. 'He died last winter. I don't know how the lease stands, but in any case I've got an agreement about living there over the summer.'

'Who lives there in winter?'

'No one, I think. Not as far as I know, anyway.'

'What did Frank Mandt use the farm for?' Wisting asked. 'Apart from letting you stay there for a couple of months in the summer, that is?'

Aron Heisel shrugged. 'I don't know. I think maybe he stores things there.'

Wisting picked up a ballpoint pen and slumped back in his chair. The discovery of taxi Z-1086 inside the ramshackle barn had certainly raised the Hummel case from 'held in abeyance' to a new level of complication. Through Aron Heisel, the disappearance had now linked to the network in which Frank Mandt had operated. It was therefore imperative to gain an overview of the different participants in that arena as well as their activities and roles. A real challenge, he mused, twisting the pen between his fingers. The intelligence dossier showed that this was a closed world which no one had managed to penetrate.

Aron Heisel tugged at the sleeves of his sweater.

'How did you know Frank Mandt?' Wisting asked.

'Through mutual acquaintances.'

Wisting sat up straight and threw the pen down on the desk. 'Listen to me,' he said. 'We know the farm's been used for storage and transfer of spirits, but that's not what we're interested in right now. We want to know how Jens Hummel's taxi ended up there. If you can't answer that, then you'll need to cough up the names of other people who've had access to the barn.'

A gust of wind made the curtains at the window billow out. 'I think I might be better to talk to a lawyer,' Aron Heisel said.

Wisting pushed the office telephone across the desk to him. That Heisel wanted to talk to a lawyer did not necessarily

46

mean he knew something or would come out with any confessions about the Hummel case. More likely he wanted to guard against incriminating others.

The defence lawyer's name was Reidar Heitmann and he arrived an hour later. He conferred briefly with his client in private before Wisting got a chance to ask further questions. Aron Heisel gave a detailed statement about when he had arrived in Norway and what he had been doing while in the country, but shied away from everything to do with Frank Mandt and his operations. Finally Wisting led him back to the cells, no wiser about Jens Hummel's fate.

11

One of Wisting's duties was to keep the Assistant Chief of Police up to speed about developments in major cases. After locking Aron Heisel into his cell and accompanying his defence lawyer out of the building, he took his notepad and a cup of coffee into Christine Thiis' office.

A shaft of evening sun shone through the window, catching the right side of her face as she glanced up. Wisting drew up a chair and sat down. The heat in the room pasted his shirt to his clammy back.

'The media know we've found the taxi,' she said.

This was to be expected as a tow vehicle had transported the missing taxi through half the town. Also, detectives were making door to door enquiries in the vicinity of the smallholding.

'What did you give them?' Wisting asked.

'A brief comment confirming that the car been found but Jens Hummel is still missing, and that a man living at the smallholding is helping police with their enquiries.'

Wisting's thoughts turned to Line. He had been abrupt when refusing her dinner invitation, saying nothing about what he was working on. Now she would read it for herself in some online newspaper or other. 'Somebody needs to talk to his grandmother,' he said. 'So that she doesn't learn about it from the newspapers.'

'I've told Torunn Borg to do that,' Christine Thiis said.

Torunn Borg had been appointed as family contact when Jens Hummel was reported missing. Wisting was happy to avoid continuous contact with families in criminal cases. The delicate balance between the formal police role and the need to present a human face was demanding. You had to offer a great deal of yourself, and it shifted focus from leadership of the investigation. It was a distraction.

'Did anything emerge from the interview?' Christine Thiis asked.

'No, and I don't think Aron Heisel knows anything about the disappearance.'

'We'll have to let him go.'

Wisting looked at her through narrowed eyes. 'I've booked transport to the remand centre.'

'His lawyer was on the phone before you arrived. We don't have any reason to hold him.'

'Can't we keep him until we've concluded the examination of the barn and the smallholding?'

Christine Thiis sighed, and Wisting could see from her expression that she was weighing up the legal arguments against the tactical considerations, the formal guidelines against his preferences and requirements. 'The most interesting thing about Aron Heisel is his connection to Frank Mandt,' he explained. 'It points in the direction of some kind of showdown in criminal circles.'

'Jens Hummel isn't a criminal. He's got a clean sheet.'

'So had Frank Mandt, but he's probably one of the people who've smuggled most of the spirits and narcotics to this country.'

Christine Thiis moved to avoid having the sun in her face. 'Have you heard anything from the technicians?'

Wisting glanced at his watch. Espen Mortensen had said that he and the other crime scene technicians would finish in and around the barn before eight o'clock. Now it was quarter past and he had still not returned. 'No,' he replied. 'They'll phone me if they find anything of interest.'

'And the door to door enquiries?'

Wisting shook his head. 'The smallholding is out of the way. Mandt and his people have stored, divided and transported spirits from there for years without anyone noticing anything. It's not to be expected that someone has spotted a taxi out there.'

His phone rang: Nils Hammer. He fixed a quizzical look on Christine Thiis' dark eyes and let it ring.

'Okay,' she said. 'We'll let him sit it out until the morning.'

With a smile, Wisting answered the call. 'The dogs have found something behind the barn out here,' Hammer advised. 'Are you coming out again?'

'What have they found?' Wisting asked, glancing across at Christine Thiis.

'I don't know yet. There's an old potato cellar here that the dogs have shown interest in. Mortensen and the technicians are going in now.'

Wisting got to his feet. 'We're on our way,' he said.

12

The police guard had been moved to the main road, and a recording van from the local office of the national broadcaster, *NRK*, was parked behind two other cars at the verge across from the weed covered track. Several journalists huddled together. Wisting dropped his speed, recognising one of them as the journalist who had penned the critical article about police work on the missing person case. A photographer raised his camera and directed it at him but Wisting looked away, gesturing towards an officer who was standing with his arms crossed. The policeman lifted the red and white plastic tape that blocked the turn-off and let them pass.

Wisting parked in the same place as before and stepped out. Christine Thiis shut the door on the passenger side and surveyed her surroundings. Hammer waded towards them through the tall grass beside the barn. Wisting looked at him enquiringly. Somewhere behind Hammer, a dog barked.

'We thought he might have been in there,' Hammer said, sounding discouraged. 'The dogs went completely crazy, but we were wrong.'

Christine Thiis stared past him to the trail through the high grass. 'Completely empty?'

'Not quite,' Hammer said. 'Follow me.'

The sun had vanished behind the forest fringes in the west, but the air was still warm. The back of Hammer's shirt was soaked with sweat and the damp patch between his shoulders changed shape as perspiration ran down his spine. The trail skirted the barn. Approximately one hundred metres out in the meadow, several people stood in a semi-circle and a police dog jumped as they drew near.

The potato cellar was a slight elevation in the otherwise flat landscape and almost impossible to see, its entrance in a hollow, a rotting door with rusty hinges and fittings held open with a stick.

'This has probably been a potato field,' Espen Mortensen said, using his right hand to indicate its scope. 'Before the refrigerator was invented, crops were stored in cellars like this. Moisture from the earth made it cool in summer and frost-free in winter. It would have been fortunate for us if a corpse had been hidden in here. It would have been like keeping it in a large fridge.'

Wisting hunkered down and peered through the dark opening. 'What did you actually find in there?'

Mortensen fetched a hefty flashlight from the equipment case and used it to point at the aperture. 'Take a look.'

Wisting crouched and entered and Christine Thiis followed in his wake. The air inside was pleasantly cool, and he was aware of the raw smell of earth from the floor as his eyes gradually became accustomed to the dim light. The walls were lined with stone, and there were timber beams in the ceiling. At the far end, the wall had collapsed and stones were lying in a heap.

'Over there,' Mortensen said, pointing with the flashlight. 'Just be careful where you put your feet.'

Wisting looked down, avoiding the white patches of plaster poured into footprints on the ground and now hardening. He had an idea what the dogs had found. The ceiling was lower in the farthest part, and he had to walk with his head bowed. Here, the wall had totally collapsed, but the stones were no longer lying where they had fallen. Instead, they had been piled up to form a cave concealed by a stone slab.

'One of the dogs is licensed as both a patrol dog and a narcotics dog,' Mortensen said, directing the beam at stacks of pale brown packages inside the hidden space.

'Narcotics?' Christine Thiis asked.

'Hammer thinks they're amphetamines,' Mortensen said.

Supporting himself on a stone, Wisting crouched in front of the hiding place. Each of the packages was the same shape and size as a pack of cigarettes and sealed with tape. If these were amphetamines, then each might weigh a quarter kilo. He tried to count them and arrived at a total of seventeen, but there were probably more, further back among the stones. In any case, it was one of the largest narcotics hauls they had made.

Retracing his steps, he squinted in the daylight. The discovery of narcotics was confirmation of a picture, the shadowy outlines of which he had begun to discern in the course of the day. Jens Hummel had disappeared in the fallout from other criminal activities.

13

His mobile phone rang as soon as he opened the front door at home. It was Suzanne. 'Did you find the taxi?' she asked.

'We found the barn,' Wisting replied. 'The taxi was there, just as your customer had said.' He flipped off his shoes. 'I'm glad you called,' he added, though he wasn't entirely sure whether this was because of locating the taxi, or just hearing from her.

'Are you still at work?'

'Just home.'

'Have you eaten?'

'Yes,' he answered, though that had been some time ago.

Suzanne paused for a moment before continuing: 'I wondered if I could pop in to see you, if that's convenient?'

'That would be fine.'

The atmosphere inside the house was stuffy after the long summer's day. He opened the terrace doors wide and managed to air the room before she rang the doorbell. It was strange. She had lived with him for more than a year, had her own key and come and gone as she pleased. Now she was a visitor.

'What happened?' she asked, touching the wound on his forehead.

'It's partly your fault,' he said, describing the arrest of Aron Heisel while leading her through the house.

She was wearing a dark green dress, loose on her slim figure. She stood at the terrace railings looking out over the town and fjord with anxiety obvious in her eyes. An enormous sail boat was making its way into the guest harbour. 'I was twelve years old when I saw the sea for the first time,' she said. 'We visited relatives in Karachi and they took us to the coast. The beaches had brilliant white sand, the water was completely clear and a shade somewhere between green and blue.'

Rarely did Wisting dwell on the fact that Suzanne came from a different country, with a very different background from his. 'For me, it's always just been there,' he said. 'Big and blue. I learned to swim the summer I was five.' A sea breeze rustled the leaves on the old fruit trees. 'I'll get something for us to drink,' he said, but all he could find was a half carton of apple juice. He poured it into a glass jug and filled it with ice cubes.

Suzanne had taken a seat by the time he returned. 'Did you find anything else?' she asked.

Wisting remained silent as he poured juice into a glass. 'I don't think he's alive, anyway.'

Suzanne picked up the glass but did not drink. 'Doesn't it affect you?'

'What do you mean?'

'"That he who fights with monsters should be careful lest he thereby become a monster."'

'That's from Nietzsche,' he said. '"And if you gaze long enough into an abyss, the abyss will also gaze into you."'

'It must affect you, standing face to face with death and evil as often as you do.'

Wisting knew that he was a different person now from when he first encountered death as a young constable. He had seen some of the worst aspects of human nature, but also some of the best. His job as an investigator had actually taught him very little about death, but he had learned a great deal about life.

'If it has affected me, then it's made me understand how fragile life can be. Death, pain and sorrow put things in perspective. We can become grievously ill, be injured in a car accident, or at worst fall victim to a serious crime. Life isn't just joy and happiness. Life is both good and bad, and sometimes it's hard and brutal.'

He took her hand, intertwining their fingers and holding tight. Her hand in his made him feel sentimental for a moment. He glanced at her encouragingly and shook their joined hands.

Suzanne smiled but freed herself. 'I think one of the girls in the café is stealing from the till,' she said.

Wisting straightened up. 'What makes you think that?'

'Something in the accounts doesn't add up.'

'Is there cash missing?'

Suzanne shook her head. 'I think she's smarter than that. The past few nights, there's actually been too much money in the till.'

Wisting nodded thoughtfully. He knew how it went. Customers who wanted to pay cash usually stood with their money ready while their drinks were mixed. Then it was a simple matter for the staff to pretend that the money had been rung up on the till but take it for themselves. The staff member would normally do a mental calculation of what he or she had omitted to ring up in the course of a shift, and remove the excess near the end of the working day. In that way, there would often be a positive difference in the cash.

'On Saturday there were forty-two vodkas rung up,' Suzanne continued. 'That's nearly two and a half bottles of vodka, but the stock had reduced by five bottles. That would tie in better with the same Saturday last year, when there were almost a hundred vodkas through the till.'

Wisting did the sums in his head. 'That's nearly five thousand kroner,' he reckoned. 'Do you know who it is?'

'I know who I trust and who I don't, but I think it's difficult.'

'You've got a suspect?'

'It's someone called Unni. She's cheerful and smart, but she makes a lot of mistakes in ringing up and returns, and it's always when she's on duty that it happens.'

Wisting sat deep in thought. It was always difficult for a boss to deal with a member of staff who was stealing. It was a minefield, both legally and emotionally. 'What sort of contract do you have with her?' he asked.

'She's one of the permanent employees. In autumn and winter she works every alternate weekend, but in summer she works almost more than a full-time post. I can't give her the sack on the basis of just a suspicion.'

'I know somebody who runs a security firm,' Wisting said. 'He has inspectors who can conduct a shrinkage check. You'll receive a professional report and help with any dismissal. You'll save the cost in a couple of evenings.'

Suzanne had already considered that. 'I'd hoped you could help me,' she said. 'You probably don't have time now, but I'd appreciate it if you could sit for an evening or two beside the bar and keep an eye on things, so that I can be quite certain before I take things further.'

'She most likely knows who I am. She won't try it while I'm there.'

'You've worked on surveillance. You can sit at one of the nearest tables and pretend you're busy reading a newspaper or something.'

Wisting put his hand round his glass, now damp with condensation, and raised it to his mouth. Suzanne did likewise and gazed at him over the rim. The fine laughter lines were gone from the corners of her eyes. She has no one else, he thought. A few friends, but no family or anyone who knew her as well as he did. No one she could go to with distressing or difficult problems. 'I can pay a visit tomorrow evening,' he said.

Something glinted in her nut-brown eyes. 'Thank you,' she said.

They remained there until dusk, when the boats still out on the water lit their lanterns. He accompanied her to the door and stood gazing after her as she drove off. It was now three minutes past midnight, and a chilly breeze stirred the air.

14

Line sat at the kitchen table with tea, toast and jam. The radio played light summer music and the local paper was open in front of her. The headline was yesterday's news, that the police had located Jens Hummel's taxi. There was nothing more than what she had read online the previous evening, but they had used different photographs. One of them was of her father with a uniformed police officer lifting the crime scene tape to let him through to the track and the smallholding where they had found the taxi. According to the newspaper, the police had searched the area until late evening.

She leaned towards the window and peered up at her father's house. He had arrived home late. She had not seen his car until she had gone to the toilet around two o'clock. Now he had already driven away. She opened her laptop to see what *VG* had written about the case: a brief report that referenced the local paper. In addition, they had spoken to Assistant Police Chief Christine Thiis.

Dagbladet had a special story further up the page, illustrated with a reader's photo of the missing taxi behind a tow vehicle, partially covered with a grey tarpaulin, making the photograph even more effective and allowing the journalist to speculate on what it might hide.

Line could feel her journalistic instincts quicken. The discovery site was situated only a few minutes' drive away. She knew people here and could find angles to ensure her own newspaper won the battle of the tabloids. All of a sudden, the baby gave a hefty kick inside her womb, and she gasped softly. It was the first time it had felt painful when the child moved. She sat with her hand on her stomach, waiting, but no more kicks followed.

The fine skin on her belly only trembled when the baby turned.

On the radio, they were playing a Swedish summer song, something about blue winds and water. She hummed along until the baby obviously found a comfortable position and settled quietly. She cleared the table, went into the living room and examined the newly painted ceiling. Before she could paper the walls, the frames around the windows and doors would need another coat, which she could manage by herself.

She opened all the windows and a warm summer breeze drifted in. The paint would dry in the wink of an eye.

She had finished the frame round the first window when her mobile phone rang in the living room. The number was unknown. Now that she had stopped submitting material to the newspaper, she seldom received calls from people she did not know. She wiped her fingers on her trousers before she answered.

'It's Sofie,' said the caller, 'Sofie Lund from yesterday. I found your number on the Internet.'

'Hi,' Line said cheerfully, sweeping her hair back from her forehead. 'Thanks for your hospitality yesterday. I really enjoyed it.'

'I've phoned for a locksmith for the safe,' Sofie explained. 'He's coming about twelve o'clock.'

'That's exciting.'

'I don't know anybody here. I'd hoped you might be here with me when he comes. I don't know what's inside, you see.'

'Of course I can,' Line said. 'I just have to finish painting some frames, and then I'll be there.'

'See you soon, and thanks.'

Line returned to the living room window and picked up the paintbrush, her thoughts transferred from what the newspapers were calling the Hummel Mystery to the old safe in the basement of the Mandt house.

*

15

The door to the conference room was open, and every eye on Wisting as he entered. He closed the door and sat at the head of the table, flanked by Christine Thiis. Also present were Espen Mortensen, Torunn Borg and Nils Hammer. Wisting would have preferred a larger number, but the most crucial thing was that he had a team of dedicated and hardworking investigators. He opened the meeting by summarising the previous day's events before asking Espen Mortensen to run through the work undertaken by the crime scene technicians.

Mortensen pulled a cordless mouse towards him and displayed a picture of the ramshackle smallholding on the overhead screen. 'We can start with the barn,' he said. 'We know it has been used by Frank Mandt since the nineties, apparently as a warehouse for his liquor operations. Among other things, there are pallets of empty plastic containers. Most are covered in dust, and it doesn't look as if it's been in use for a long time.'

'The spirits market has been taken over by East Europeans,' Hammer said, as photographs of the rooms inside the barn flitted across the screen. 'In recent years, Mandt has been more involved in drugs.'

'We haven't found any trace of Jens Hummel in these locations,' Mortensen said, 'but we are going to spend a few days in there and expect what we find will be linked to illegal activities.'

He showed them several more pictures, including of a room furnished as an office. Telephone numbers and names were jotted on loose sheets of paper on a desk. A fine layer of dust blanketed everything.

The next photo was of the vehicle. 'We've made two extremely interesting discoveries inside the taxi,' Mortensen said, moving a little cardboard box on the table in front of him. 'A couple of minor aspects first, however.'

Wisting's curiosity was growing, but he leaned back patiently in his seat. The work of the crime technicians was always fascinating. Every case reached a point where the technical and tactical lines of enquiry crossed, and at that point the solution might well be found.

Mortensen exhibited a picture from the car interior. The half-empty cola bottle was in the centre console and the mouldy, half-consumed baguette on the passenger seat, just as Wisting had observed when they first found the taxi. 'This matches the movements we mapped out last winter,' Mortensen said, presenting a picture taken from the CCTV footage at the 24-hour Shell station in Storgata.

Wisting recognised the image. It showed Jens Hummel standing at the cash desk with a bottle of cola and a baguette, about three quarters of an hour before he disappeared. They had used a segment of it to demonstrate both what he looked like and what clothing he was wearing when he went missing.

It was satisfying to see these two images side by side, the past fitting into the present. It felt as if a little piece of the jigsaw had fallen into place.

Mortensen made reference to the mileage, explained how the seats and the interior mirror were positioned, and showed some parking receipts that helped to draw a timeline to the point of disappearance.

The next picture was of the almost empty car boot, with a plastic bottle of windscreen wash liquid and an umbrella lying inside, but bare apart from those. 'We believe there had been a rubber mat in the boot,' Mortensen said. 'That is to say, we believe Jens Hummel was lying there and the mat was removed with him.'

Wisting leaned forward. The next image was a close-up of the exterior wall of the boot compartment, just to the left of the lock. Four consecutive dark marks had been identified, one of them slightly larger than the rest.

'That's human blood,' Mortensen said. 'We've found it in a

couple of places on the sides of the boot compartment, but not on the floor. Therefore we believe an injured person has been lying in the boot and the rubber mat was removed at the same time as he was.'

It had pervaded the case from day one, but not been articulated. Suddenly they were sure that the Hummel case was a murder enquiry.

'When can we confirm that the blood belongs to Hummel?' Hammer asked.

'In a few days. We have reference samples from his toothbrush. As soon as we have a DNA analysis from the blood in the car, we can run a comparison.'

'You said there were *two* interesting finds?'

'I've got the other one here,' Mortensen said, pulling across the small cardboard box he had placed on the table. Opening it, he drew out a transparent evidence bag containing a mobile phone. 'This was hidden under the steering wheel column,' he said. 'Jens Hummel had a mobile phone we knew nothing about. It's registered to a false pay-as-you-go account taken out more than two years ago. Registered to Ola Nordmann from Oslo,' he added, drawing air quotes with his free hand.

Nils Hammer swore aloud as he took the plastic bag out of Mortensen's hands. 'There's only one reason people have two mobiles,' he grunted. 'They're doing something they don't want anyone else to know about.'

Wisting rubbed the bridge of his nose. An increasingly clear picture was emerging that Jens Hummel had been involved in Mandt's narcotics trade and that there had been some kind of internal confrontation.

'That fits,' Torunn Borg said, leafing through one of the ring binders. 'We have several statements to the effect that he worked as a courier transporting prostitutes and narcotics, which tallies with all those long trips of his.'

'And that he turned off the taximeter before he went missing,' Hammer continued. 'He was going to a meeting and didn't want tracked.'

Wisting listened with his fingertips pressed to his lips. They had spent time and resources following up these rumours about both narcotics and prostitutes. When they had not provided any immediate results, they had progressed the enquiry on a broad front instead of delving deeper into this single lead. 'What can we get from the phone?' he asked.

Nils Hammer inspected the phone in the transparent bag, turning it one way, then another. 'If we'd had it a fortnight ago it might have given us the solution. After six months, the telecommunications companies delete their data. We won't get anything more out of it than what's stored on the phone itself.'

'That could still be a considerable amount?' Christine Thiis suggested.

Hammer agreed. 'Give me a few hours.'

Wisting gazed at the two pictures on the screen. 'What about fingerprints and DNA?'

'We have both, but the taxi has carried passengers for a number of years. The steering wheel looks as if it's been wiped clean, but on the roof above the passenger door we've found a partial palm print. It's not good enough to run through the records, but probably belongs to the last person who got into the car.'

Wisting jotted a few more notes and looked at Torunn Borg. 'What about the door to door enquiries?'

'The most interesting scrap of information is that we have the name of a tractor driver who had agreed to keep the track to the smallholding clear of snow during winter. The track must have been ploughed clear in order for them to drive the taxi all the way up there. He's coming in for questioning today.'

'Excellent,' Wisting said, before turning to the potato cellar. The narcotics haul that had fallen into their lap was something tangible, a chink they could explore and broaden out and bring more into the light of day.

'It weighed 12.4 kilos,' Mortensen told them. 'We've brought the drugs in for analysis, and it'll also be interesting to compare the soles of Aron Heisel's shoes with the prints on the earth floor.'

Wisting nodded and turned to Christine Thiis. 'I'm preparing a remand hearing,' she said. 'We'll charge him with possession and ask for four weeks' custody.'

The meeting dragged on for another half hour as they allocated assignments and discussed theories and possibilities, continually returning to the most central topic: where was Jens Hummel?

16

A fly landed on the massive safe. Line ran her hand over the cold steel and chased it away. The surface was rough and cracks scarred the pale green enamel.

'I don't like it down here,' Sofie said, folding her arms. 'Last night I heard noises.'

Line looked up at the pipes that ran underneath the basement ceiling, one of them covered with a fine layer of condensation. 'Maybe there's air in the pipes?' she suggested. 'We had that where I lived in Oslo. It bumped and banged and made all sorts of strange noises.'

'It's true there are lots of noises in old houses,' Sofie agreed. 'But it's not much fun being here all on our own, just Maja and me.'

Line straightened up, placing her hand on her bump. 'Do you believe in ghosts?'

Sofie brushed a fly away. 'It wouldn't surprise me if the Old Man haunted this place. That would be just like him.'

'I've got two dead men in my house,' Line said. 'Neither of them haunt the place. You've only got one.' Giggling, they stared at the big metal box in the centre of the room. 'It's going to be damaged if he drills into it. Are you sure there isn't a key somewhere here in the house?'

'It still hasn't turned up,' Sofie said.

Line took a few steps back and observed the safe from a short distance. 'Do you know whether your grandfather used it at all?'

'I didn't even know there was a safe here until the lawyer told me.'

'If he did use the safe, then the key must be in the house

somewhere. After all, he did die in here, behind a locked door. Didn't he have a bunch of keys?'

'All I got was a single house key. He had two cars, but they were sold without me seeing them.'

Three flies buzzed round the narrow basement window high on the wall. Sofie opened it to let them out and the sound of a lawnmower somewhere in the neighbourhood reached in.

'Perhaps you ought to change the lock?' Line suggested.

'What do you mean?'

'There could be stray keys. There were three keys when I took over my house.'

Sofie crossed the room and stood with her back to the wall. 'I can ask the locksmith when he comes,' she said. At that moment the doorbell rang. 'I hope he doesn't wake Maja.' She rushed up the basement steps with Line following.

The locksmith, in his late twenties, was tall and muscular, wearing work trousers with multiple pockets and a T-shirt as black as his hair, and carried a large toolbox. The T-shirt was like an extra layer of skin on his tanned body and concealed nothing of the strong physique underneath. Line and Sofie exchanged glances.

'I'm looking for Sofie Lund,' he said.

'That's me.' Sofie took a step back to let him into the house. 'I'm Atle.'

'Come in,' Sofie said. 'We have to go down to the basement.'

Atle placed the toolbox on the floor in front of the safe. 'It's an old *Kromer*,' he told them, 'German. Made some time in the thirties.' He hunkered down, with one hand on the safe door to support himself.

'Will it be difficult?' Line asked.

'Not terribly, but a bit tricky. Very few safes can withstand professionals with proper tools and sufficient time. This is really just a fireproof safe. The steel wall is not as thick as it looks, a thin steel plate over a layer of insulation material. But I do need some stronger equipment.' He got to his feet. 'Have you searched for the key?'

Sofie and Line answered in an affirmative chorus.

66

The locksmith smiled. 'I have to ask,' he said, holding his hands up as he backed out of the room. When he returned, he had brought an electric drill, a drill press with a magnetic foot and an extension cable. He attached the drill press at right angles to the steel door, mounted the drill and looked round for a power point. Sofie took the plug from his hands and pushed it into a wall socket.

'I'll drill a trial hole,' Atle explained, putting on protective glasses and earplugs. A deep, whining noise filled the room as the drill bit into the steel of the safe. Line put her fingers in her ears.

'I'll need to see to Maja!' Sofie shouted across.

Line nodded and went on watching the man on his knees on the floor. The hairs on the back of his hands were finer and lighter than the ones on his head; he had long fingers and narrow wrists. He was smiling to himself, as if he knew something no one else did. Or perhaps he just enjoyed his job.

The drill ate its way through the steel, millimetre by millimetre, until the pitch changed and he withdrew the drill bit. Line wrinkled her nose. 'What's that smell?' she asked.

'The metal overheating.'

'Have you drilled right through?'

Atle shook his head. 'That's just a peephole into the lock casing.' He removed the drill press and rummaged around in his toolbox until he found an instrument reminiscent of what doctors use when they examine the eye and retina. 'So I can see where I am,' he said, staring into the hole he had just made. 'Slightly down and to the left,' he muttered to himself. He took out a felt tip pen and made a mark on the steel door before attaching the drill press again. 'If I hit the right spot now, I can turn the lock round with a screwdriver.'

Sofie reappeared with a baby alarm in her hand. 'She's still sleeping,' she said. 'You don't hear the noise much on the next floor when the doors are shut.'

Atle glanced up at them. 'Are you ready?'

They both nodded and covered their ears until the drill was through.

'Have you done this before?' Line asked. 'Opened safes, I mean?'

'Lots of times.'

'What do you usually find?'

He shifted his position on the floor. 'As a rule, they're empty,' he said, peering into the new hole, 'but now and again there's something odd inside. Old cognac and art, but mostly keys, insurance papers, pictures and worthless old share certificates.'

'You can have it,' Sofie said, looking at Line.

'What do you mean?'

'If there's anything inside, you can have it.'

Atle looked up. 'I've also known them to contain money.'

Sofie shrugged and looked over at Line. 'Are you not reno-vating a whole house?'

Line would not have minded a more generous renovation budget, but knew it would be wrong to accept.

'You know what I think of the Old Man and what he left behind. I don't want it.'

Line shook her head. 'Me neither. If there's anything valu-able in there, you'd be better giving it to charity.'

'We'll see,' Sofie replied.

The locksmith moved the drill press to the other side of the keyhole and started on a new hole. He crouched over his equip-ment, deep in concentration, the tip of his tongue between his lips. Tiny beads of perspiration began to appear on his forehead. After half an hour, there were seven holes in the metal door.

'So,' he said, wiping his forehead with the back of his hand. 'That should do the trick.' He put a slim screwdriver into one of the holes and the inspection instrument into another. 'It's been in regular use. No trace of rust; tumblers easy to push.'

A fly landed on his forehead. He blew it away before the tip of his tongue slid out between his lips again and he focused his attention on the lock. 'I'll just turn a cylinder that pulls the deadbolt with it, and then it's done.' There was a dull thud inside the safe as something heavy fell into place. He pulled out the screwdriver, turned the handle and pulled the door open.

Line looked at Sofie. 'You do it,' Sofie pleaded. Line stepped forward and opened the door. It was heavy, but slid open easily.

The safe was kitted out like a cupboard, with three shelves and a drawer at the bottom. On the lowest shelf there were several thick brown envelopes with a few black notebooks. On the middle shelf, a stack of five black ring binders, and on the top shelf bundles of banknotes bound together with rubber bands. Line took one out and handed it to Sofie. They were five hundred kroner notes, fifty thousand in total, she estimated. There were similar bundles of thousand-kroner and two-hundred-kroner notes. In total, there must have been around half a million kroner.

She could not hold back her laughter and it infected Sofie, even though they both knew that the money had not been earned by any honourable means.

Atle filled out a work sheet with half an eye on the safe, as if the contents did not really concern him. He handed the sheet to Sofie to sign that the work had been completed. 'Don't give it all away,' he suggested, smiling. 'Enjoy yourself a bit.'

Line put the money back and discovered a key that must open the lockable drawer at the bottom. She left it lying while she escorted the man to the front door with Sofie. They could hear that Maja was awake, and Sofie brought her down to the basement.

'Shall we count them?' Line suggested, taking out one of the bundles again.

Sofie nodded and moved Maja to her other hip.

Line stacked the bundles on top of the safe as she counted them, arriving at a total of 480,000. 'There's something else in here,' she said, pulling an envelope from the back of the top shelf. Sofie craned her neck to look when she opened it. 'More money,' Line gasped, displaying the contents before emptying the loose notes out beside the bundles. Thousand-kroner notes, maybe as much as a million altogether. They seemed to be discoloured with red ink.

'The proceeds of a robbery,' Line whispered.

She had written about it in an article for the newspaper.

Cases used for transporting valuables and the cassettes in ATMs were secured with colour cartridges. When anyone attempted to open them illegally, the colour ampules were activated and the banknotes stained so that they became worthless.

'Put them back again,' Sofie begged. 'I need to give Maja some food.'

Line tidied away the money and picked up the little key. 'We haven't checked the drawer,' she said. The key turned without difficulty, and she used it as a handle to pull out the drawer. There was an object there, wrapped in a piece of grey fabric. Line lifted it out, placed it on the floor and unfolded the material. It was a revolver.

'I knew it we'd have problems if we opened it,' said Sofie. ' First money from a robbery and then an illegal weapon. We can't lock it up again either. The lock's destroyed.' Maja began to whimper.

Line lifted the gun and turned it over in her hand. The metal was dull black.

'Be careful,' Sofie said, holding Maja away. 'It might be loaded.'

'My father once took me to the firing range in the basement at the police station,' Line said, releasing the cylinder latch. There were cartridges in two of the six chambers.

'Let's chuck it in the water.'

Line shook the two cartridges into her open hand and pushed the cylinder back into place. 'I can take it with me. You did say that I could have whatever was inside the safe.'

Sofie frowned. 'What'll you do with it?'

'Hand it in. My father can take it with him. The police are always getting old guns handed in to be destroyed. It'll be completely anonymous. I'll just say that I got it from a friend who found it among her grandfather's belongings.'

'Okay, then.' Sofie grabbed a few banknotes from one of the bundles. 'But only if I'm allowed to treat you to lunch.'

17

Wisting had forgotten that the police station canteen was closed for summer. He went into the conference room and found a packet of crispbread that had been sitting for ages in the cupboard above the mini-kitchen. He helped himself to two of them and stood at the window eating them dry. A car with stereo at full blast passed in the street. He followed it with his gaze until it had gone by, crossed to the mini-kitchen again, turned on the tap and let the water run cold.

He felt restless. A great deal now suggested that Jens Hummel had lived a double life they had not managed to uncover in the initial phase of the investigation. They had been on the right track but, instead of investigating it further, they had widened the search. He could account for this with reference to pressure of work and lack of resources but, nevertheless, it had been a misjudgement and he would have to take responsibility.

He brought his glass back to the window. Since the time when he had patrolled the streets out there, he had become an experienced and respected detective. Now he wondered whether he was getting too old. At fifty-five he would soon be a grandfather, and was not impressed by what he saw around him. Organised crime was gaining ground, at the same time as the legal framework that constrained an investigation was becoming more complex, with stricter formal demands and increasingly more advanced and time-consuming investigative methods. In addition, there were fewer people to carry out the tasks.

He drank from the glass.

It was not merely crime that had changed in thirty-two years. It was also the attitude of society towards the police.

71

Previously, citizens came forward to tell what they knew and what they had seen. Now the police were met increasingly often by a wall of silence, even when seeking information that was absolutely peripheral to a crime. Fear had crept in. People did not want to get mixed up in anything, and were afraid to give information. Simultaneously, they had become more distant from one another and less concerned about what was going on around them.

Back at the kitchen sink he threw out the rest of the water. All this was probably just an excuse to avoid taking to heart the fact that society was changing and, with it, crime.

Nils Hammer appeared in the doorway, leaning against the frame. 'The phone gave us nothing,' he said, waving the plastic bag with the phone inside. 'Messages and calls must have been deleted continuously. There's nothing in the internal memory.'

Wisting looked at him. He had hoped that the phone hidden in Hummel's car would have brought them a step further. 'Isn't it possible to retrieve deleted messages? Like on a computer?'

'We can get someone to take a look at it,' Hammer said. 'But it's going to take time, and it's not certain that it will give us anything.' He put down the evidence bag on the conference table and shook the thermos to see if there was any coffee left before fetching a mug from the cupboard. 'I thought he'd turn up when the snow melted.'

In the hours after Jens Hummel's disappearance, but before he had been reported missing, there had been a light snowfall across the southern part of the Vestfold district. Tracks had been wiped out. 'Do you think Aron Heisel knows anything?' Hammer asked.

'Not about Jens Hummel, but I think he does know a lot about Frank Mandt and the narcotics trade, enough to know who had access to the barn, and who might have put the taxi in there.'

'Do you think he'll say anything?'

Wisting took out a mug for himself. 'I'm afraid we won't get any more out of him than you got out of that mobile phone.'

'Have you considered that we may have a missing link?'

'We have several.'

'I'm thinking of Frank Mandt. If he had still been alive we would have picked him up. No one would have put a hot taxi in his barn without him sanctioning it.'

'He'd never have told us anything.'

'I know that,' Hammer said as he walked towards the door. 'But it could have been an opportunity to catch him at last. There were twelve kilos of amphetamines out there. He would have been forced to answer for that as well.'

Wisting followed him with his coffee, along the corridor to his own office.

At four o'clock he gathered the investigators in the conference room again. Christine Thiis arrived directly from court, where she had petitioned to have Aron Heisel remanded in custody. 'He had no explanation with regard to the narcotics find, other than that he didn't know about it,' she said.

'Nobody will believe him on that point,' Espen Mortensen said, pushing two pictures across the table. One was of the sole of a shoe, the other a plaster cast. The patterns on the soles were identical. 'Aron Heisel has been inside the potato cellar.'

Wisting drew the two images towards him and examined them more closely.

'At last, a connection,' Nils Hammer said.

Mortensen took the photos back and exchanged them for three others from his folder. 'Since we're talking about shoes. This was found on the floor mat in front of the driver's seat and on the brake pedal in Jens Hummel's taxi.'

It looked like three torn scraps of paper, each about the size of a fingernail.

'What is it?' Wisting asked.

'Sawdust,' Mortensen said.

Christine Thiis pulled one of the images towards her. 'Where does it come from?'

'We don't know how long it's been there, but there are two obvious explanations. Either Jens Hummel has been somewhere that he's stepped on sawdust and trailed it with him into the

73

car or the murderer has done that when he hid the car in the barn.'

'Could the sawdust have come from the barn?' Wisting asked.

Mortensen shook his head. 'We haven't found any sawdust in the barn. This comes from somewhere else.'

Wisting sat up straight. 'We have, of course, charted Jens Hummel's movements for the twenty-four hours before he disappeared. I can't remember him being anywhere that he could have picked up sawdust on his feet and carried it into the taxi.'

'Where do you get sawdust, anyway?' Christine Thiis asked.

'At a planing mill, sawmill, joiners' yard or building site,' Torunn Borg said.

'Or a circus,' Hammer suggested.

Wisting used his pen to point at him. 'Undertake a charting exercise,' he said.

Torunn Borg had spoken to the snowplough driver. 'There wasn't very much to learn from him,' she said. 'The old farm track is in his field of operations. He's had an agreement with Frank Mandt for ten years to keep it clear of snow. On the night Jens Hummel disappeared he noticed that it started snowing about seven o'clock in the morning and was out clearing from nine o'clock until about three. The smallholding at Huken is approximately in the centre of his rounds, so he reckoned he'd been there at about twelve o'clock, but he can't recall spotting anything in particular. Probably he would have remembered if he had seen vehicles or people.'

The discussion round the table returned to the narcotics cache in the potato cellar. It made them feel optimistic. In narcotics cases, there was always a profusion of people involved: recipients, suppliers, couriers and pushers: a number of stages in the process and a number of occasions that could offer the police access to the case, in contrast to the prevailing situation in a murder enquiry.

After almost an hour they had marked out the way forward, and the meeting was drawn to a close. Wisting was on his own in his office when he received a message from Line, another invitation to her barbecue. The steak would not benefit from being kept any longer.

They were at the jittery phase in an investigation when a great deal hinged on waiting for answers. Answers from routine interviews and door to door enquiries, technical examinations, analysis results and everything else that comprised an investigation. He might just as well wait somewhere else, so he stood up and left the office.

In the car on his way to Line's, his thoughts drifted to the grandchild who was going to grow up without a father, unless Line met a new man willing to step into that role. When he looked back at himself as a father, he had to admit that his job in the police had cast a shadow over his personal life. Far too often, he had prioritised it before his family.

He parked outside his own house and walked the few metres to Line's. He tramped through the weed-filled garden and round the corner, where Line welcomed him with a hug. 'Will you see to the steak?' she asked, vanishing into the house.

He turned the pieces on the grill until she emerged again with a large bowl of salad. 'These look ready,' he said.

'I took a chance and put them on before you came,' she said, holding out a dish. 'I'm pleased you could find the time.'

'Me too,' he said, and took a seat at the table. 'Have you collected the wallpaper?'

'No, but it has arrived.' She helped herself. 'Do you think you'll have time to help me?'

'I'll *make* the time,' he promised again.

'Do you know anything more about what's happened to Jens Hummel?'

'Not really.'

'But what direction is it taking?' she asked. 'Could he have hidden the taxi in the barn and gone off to the Caribbean, for instance?'

'We don't believe he's disappeared voluntarily.'

'Who's the owner of the barn?'

'You're no longer working as a journalist,' he reminded her. Line pulled a face in return. 'We're talking about a disused smallholding,' Wisting said. 'Most of your colleagues have traced the owner through the property register, but he's been eliminated from our enquiries. He's rented out the place for years.'

They chatted some more about the case as they ate. Line did not manage to root out any details, only enough to understand that there had been a development. For dessert, she brought out a tub of ice cream. Wisting helped himself twice and sat slumped in his chair.

'I've got something here I'd like you to take care of,' Line said.

'What's that?'

Line went into the house and came back with something in a carrier bag that she placed on his lap. Wisting glanced down at it and lifted a length of grey fabric wrapped round a heavy object. He folded the material to one side and found himself looking at a revolver with an octagonal barrel.

'An old friend of mine from primary school found it when she was clearing up her grandfather's belongings.'

Wisting picked up the revolver, swung out the cylinder and checked that it was not loaded. 'Have you kept it long?' he asked.

'Just a few hours. It's probably not in the gun records. She wanted to throw it into the sea, but I suggested that you could send it to be disposed of properly.'

Wisting nodded. Guns continually turned up in connection with deceased person's estates. Shotguns, rifles, pistols and revolvers that the heirs did not want to keep and had little idea what to do with. 'It's a *Nagant*,' he said, '7.5 millimetre. Made in Belgium at the end of the nineteenth century.' He raised the hammer and heard a click when he pulled the trigger.

'Does it work?'

'Revolvers are extremely reliable. It works as well now as the day it was made.'

'What happens to weapons that are disposed of?'

'They're ground down in a metal mill and end up as nails.'

'That could make an interesting story,' she said.

'How so?'

'An old weapon is full of history. That one there has been through two world wars. It would be thrilling to tell the story of a weapon that ends up being turned into nails.'

Wisting wound the material round the revolver again. 'What is it they say?' he said, as he looked at the nails on the cladding of his daughter's house. 'History permeates these walls.'

Line grew enthusiastic. 'Isn't it true? I could sell it to *VG for Men* or something like that.' She began to clear the table.

'Was he in the military?' Wisting asked, returning the revolver to the carrier bag.

'Who?'

'The man who owned it. *Nagant* revolvers were used in both the army and the navy.'

'I don't think so,' Line answered quickly and lingered at the terrace door with the empty plates in her hands. 'I don't know why he had it, or what he used it for.'

18

Wisting locked the old revolver in the safe he kept inside a cupboard in his basement, moving a photo album to make room, pictures from when he and Ingrid had married one summer day thirty years ago. He leafed through the pages. They had celebrated in the Hotel Wassilioff in Stavern with their closest relatives. Both of his parents-in-law and his own mother had been alive, and even Ingrid's grandmother had joined them. The following day they had driven to Denmark and stayed in a tent at Løkken. It had rained for three days at a stretch, but it was one of his best memories.

One of the photos had been taken beside a church that over the centuries had become buried in sand shifted by the wind. The building had eventually been demolished and moved, and all that was left was the square tower protruding from the sand. He had taken the photograph, Ingrid standing with her hair soaked by the rain, laughing at him. She was several years younger than Line was now, but the resemblance was striking. Two months later, Ingrid became pregnant.

They had journeyed back there the summer that Line and her twin brother were twelve when the sand dunes were lower and more of the tower had become visible. A man explained that it had been built on a moraine foundation that had gradually been washed away by rain water and the waves that broke over the land. In time the ground below the church would disappear and the tower would collapse into the sea. He put the album back, wondering whether it was still in existence.

The wedding photograph had hung on their bedroom wall and he had removed it a few days after Suzanne spent the night with him for the first time. It had left an empty photo hook and a square patch darker than the rest of the wall, but neither of them commented. The framed photo was too large for the safe, so he had simply placed it edgewise inside the wardrobe. He had never thought to hang it up again, and wondered whether he should do so now, but decided to leave it. Maybe he could get Line to give him a hand with wallpapering the bedroom instead. He changed his trousers and put on a clean shirt before heading for town and *The Golden Peace*.

The café was half-full, music subdued so as not to disturb the chatter at the tables. The customers were a mixture of young and old, locals and summer tourists. Suzanne stood at one of the innermost tables, talking to a young couple. She gave him a quick nod to show that she had seen him, before looking away. He found a table at the wall where not many could see him, but where he had a good view of the bar counter and the till. He put a newspaper on the table and hung his jacket over the back of the chair before approaching the counter.

The girl who served him had a name badge with 'Unni' printed on it, the one Suzanne suspected of being the thief. Blond and cheerful, she wore her hair in a ponytail. Wisting asked for a cup of coffee and a slice of caramel cake and paid with coins. The girl picked them up, but before she had them in her hand, Wisting turned his back. He heard her ring up the till and the money being dropped into the drawer.

Two other girls were working, in addition to Suzanne and Unni. All kept busy, and it looked as if they stood at the bar, cleared tables and washed glasses without any fixed pattern.

He felt uncomfortable in the role of undercover restaurant detective, but peeked up from his newspaper every time Unni took a new order at the counter. One time it appeared that she had rung up the wrong amount on the till. A grey-haired man had given her a two-hundred-kroner note for a glass of beer. The cash drawer opened and shut several times before she managed to give him his change.

Suzanne swept past him a number of times without him looking up at her. His coffee had grown cold, but he gulped

79

it down and began to read an article about the holiday habits of Norwegians. One of the other girls removed his empty coffee cup. 'Nina' was the name on her badge. She seemed more bashful than the other two, and smiled shyly as she moved off.

When he finished reading the newspaper, he stood up and walked over to the bar, bought another coffee and lingered at the counter for a moment or two. Suzanne moved nimbly among the tables, smiling at her customers. She was beautiful, tall and slim, with silky coal-black hair.

His mobile phone rang. It was Christine Thiis. 'Is there any news?'

'Were you expecting something?'

'I'm really just passing on the question,' she said. 'I'm at the formal summer dinner with the Police Chief and the other police prosecutors.'

Three men at one of the window tables turned round, their eyes on Suzanne as she walked past with her arms filled with empty glasses.

'There's no news. I'd have let you know.'

'I know that,' Christine said, hesitating momentarily. 'He's critical.'

'Who?'

'The Police Chief. He took me aside and said he wondered whether you were up to leading the investigation.'

Wisting took his coffee back to the table. Ivan Sundt was newly appointed to the post and came from a position as an Appeal Court judge, lacking experience and understanding of practical police investigative work. 'Why does he wonder that?'

'He's caught up with that newspaper article, the one about Jens Hummel's grandmother.'

Suzanne passed his table. Wisting looked up at her and received a fleeting smile in return before she disappeared behind the bar counter.

'What answer did you give him?' he asked.

'That I have full confidence in you. I have complete trust that you'll solve this case.'

Wisting thanked her for the support. When he had ended the

conversation, he was left with a feeling that bothered him. He ought to be sitting in his office delving into piles of paperwork instead of playing private detective here, but stayed for another two hours. When he stood up to leave, he had spent almost two hundred kroner on coffees in the bar without observing anything to bolster Suzanne's suspicions. He was in the midst of what was in all probability a murder investigation, and felt that his time had been wasted.

He texted Suzanne from the car, promising to return another evening and wishing her good night. She responded with a brief *Okay, thanks* as he drove up in front of his house.

19

The morning meeting was informal and swiftly concluded. The night had not brought anything new to the case. The atmosphere was edgy, and those present were keen to make a start on the day's work instead of sitting sharing thoughts and theories. Wisting spent the rest of the morning preparing a fresh round of questioning with Aron Heisel. If nothing new cropped up from any other source, Heisel was all they had to progress the case.

Wisting did not like the psychological game involved in an interview. He had met the whole gamut of human emotions in the interview room, and knew to employ all of his knowledge of human behaviour as well as his professional expertise. It was a matter of being cunning, tactical and constantly retaining a good overview.

Every interview was different. You could not simply sit down and start talking, or follow a list of set questions. The interview must be built around the topics on which you want to shed light. First of all: gathering information on the man provisionally charged with possession of amphetamines. What sort of background did he have? What kind of circle did he belong to? Where had he been? What had he done? Who had he met? Only when that picture had begun to emerge could the conversation trawl to where a link to Jens Hummel might be found.

They had already discovered that Aron Heisel had both Norwegian and Spanish phone numbers. The Spanish number would take some time to access. The Norwegian number revealed nothing. They had also asked the Spanish police to search his flat in Marbella. The customs authorities had assisted by providing a record of his travels and the finance group had examined his personal finances. Simultaneously, they had checked his immediate family and other close relatives. Neither of his parents was living. He had an elder sister who was married and lived in Trondheim. His last registered employment was as a driver for a courier company in Oslo.

At eleven o'clock Wisting put the papers aside to go out for something to eat. Barely on his feet, he received a text message from Suzanne, short and to the point: *Shrinkage of 8 dl vodka yesterday. 2,000 kroner.*

It must have happened before he arrived, he thought. He had watched every single transaction across the counter. Every single sale had been rung up on the till. He was about to phone her, but an unknown number filled the display.

'This is Wisting,' he said.

'Reidar Heitmann here.' It was Aron Heisel's defence lawyer. 'I've just had a meeting with Heisel in prison and, as the situation stands, I've advised him not to give a statement.'

'Why not?'

The lawyer cleared his throat. 'Heisel is charged with a crime he knows nothing about. Besides, you'll have a hidden agenda in any conversations you have with him.'

'What do you mean by that?'

'Give over!' the lawyer fumed. 'Both you and I know that the narcotics case is not the most important issue here. Jens Hummel is what this is really all about and my client has already told you what little he knows.'

'We'd like to talk to him again.'

'That's out of the question as long as he has a charge hanging over him.'

'What are you telling me now, in actual fact? That he'll give us information about the Hummel case if we drop the drugs charge?'

Heitmann brushed him aside. 'You don't really have a case against him. What I'm saying is that as things stand, he doesn't want to answer any of your questions.'

Aron Heisel had every reason not to answer the police's

The old wallpaper had been removed and cracks and holes had been filled and sanded so that the surface was even and smooth. She began at the corner behind the door where any unevenness in the join would be hidden anyway. The first few lengths went well. She had chosen self-coloured wallpaper with a pale brown sheen, so she did not have to worry about the pattern matching at the joins. When she reached halfway along the wall, she saw that it had gone awry. The wallpaper had wrinkled and, in a number of places, tiny air bubbles had formed. When she finished the first wall, she had to admit that the result was not particularly successful.

She felt annoyed that she had embarked on the project on her own. Her father was more meticulous and had greater patience for such things. She made up her mind to wait with the remainder and was about to put the lid back on the bucket of paste when the doorbell rang. It was the first time she had received a visitor, and she assumed it was someone wanting to sell something or who had gone to the wrong address.

It was Sofie, rocking a pram in which Maja was sleeping soundly. 'Hello,' she said, with a broad smile. 'We were just out for a walk and thought we'd see if we could find where you lived.'

Line smoothed her hair back from her face. 'That's lovely! I need a break right now.' She leaned over and peered into the pram. 'We can wheel her round to the terrace at the back,' she said, taking hold of the handle. 'Then we'll hear her more easily if she wakes.'

She pushed the pram through the untidy garden to the rear of the house. 'Do you want to have a look?' she asked, opening the terrace door. Sofie followed her inside.

Line showed her round, both in the rooms that were finished and those that still had to be decorated. Afterwards they sat outside.

'I was actually on my way to the post office,' Sofie said, nodding towards a parcel wrapped in brown paper in the tray under the pram. 'It's the money. I decided to send it to an organisation that does preventative work against drugs.'

'You're walking around with one and a half million kroner in your pram? That you've decided to send in the post?'

'There's not more than one million. I only took the notes that were coloured. I read on the Internet that people who have accepted coloured notes can apply to *Norges Bank* to have them exchanged.'

'Someone's going to get a great surprise when they open their mail,' Line said. 'Have you had a look at any of the other things in the safe?'

The expression on Sofie's face changed. 'Not very thoroughly. Mostly letters and documents from lawyers and the police, but I did find this.' She produced an envelope from her bag.

Line took it and opened it. It contained a small bundle of photographs.

'They are of Mum and me,' Sofie said.

Line browsed through them. There was a photograph of a new-born Sofie in her mother's arms, one of her mother caressing Sofie's hair, and another in which they had their arms round each other. There were also photos of her first day at school, of birthdays and Christmas.

'Maybe he did care after all?' Line suggested, as she handed them back.

'Maybe,' Sofie said. 'There's a lot about him we don't know.'

'What about all the ring binders and papers? Maybe it will be possible to find out who he was and what he did if we read them?'

'I don't know if I want to or can be bothered,' Sofie said.

Line felt inquisitive all the same; it was the journalist in her. Sofie had offered her everything inside the old safe, but she could not bring herself to ask. 'Don't throw anything away. You might feel differently one day.'

'I'll see,' Sofie said, nodding. 'And just leave it in the meantime.'

21

At half past two on Wednesday 25 July, work on the technical examination of the smallholding at Huken was concluded.

Wisting brought Nils Hammer with him when he returned to conduct a tactical search, because while the crime scene technicians had looked for fingerprints, footprints, hairs, fibres and other physical traces, it was the investigators' task to search for notes, papers, documents containing names or other details, that could provide clues about who had spent time there and what they had been up to. It was possible that they might find something they could use in their next interview with Aron Heisel.

The place looked different, no longer so uninhabited and abandoned. The tall grass was trampled and flattened by vehicles, and tattered remains of crime scene tape fluttered in front of the wide barn door. Wisting stopped the car and stepped out. The silence was as before, with just a faint chorus of insect sounds in the warm air.

Hammer rattled a bunch of keys and let them into the main farmhouse.

The crime scene technicians had left their obvious marks behind: remnants of fingerprint powder on door handles and other natural points touched by human hands, and little notes were also dotted around, covered in letters and numbers.

The kitchen was unchanged: painted blue and messy with used plates, knives, forks and dirty glasses filling the sink. Empty bottles and other clutter were strewn across the worktops. The low, sleepy sound of flies buzzing as they circled the room. Wisting opened drawers and cupboards and riffled through the pile of papers on top of the fridge, but found nothing of interest.

The sparsely furnished living room lacked any personal touches: a worn settee and a coffee table, a dining table with matching chairs and a cabinet with a TV set. No pictures on the walls or books on the shelves. He went into the adjacent bedroom while Hammer examined the living room cupboards. The quilt lay crumpled at the end of the bed, and there were a few magazines and dirty socks and T-shirts lying on the floor. What seemed most interesting was a suitcase that had been pushed underneath the bed. Wisting hauled it out and opened it, but all it contained was clothes.

He opened the drawer on the bedside table as Nils Hammer called from the living room. The drawer was empty, but something in Hammer's voice meant he did not take time to close it again. Hammer was at the living room window. 'Someone's in the field,' he said.

Wisting could not see anything apart from metre-high weeds.

'It could have been an animal,' Hammer said, 'but it looked like a man walking in a crouched position in the long grass. He's gone now.'

They stood scanning what had once been a cultivated field, and suddenly a blond head popped up, just beside the elevation that marked where the potato cellar was located. Hammer swore and wheeled round. Wisting followed him out the door.

They took the path that had been trampled flat by the investigators in recent days, Hammer two metres ahead. The man they had spotted was heading for the edge of the forest. He stumbled but did not fall. 'Stop!' Nils Hammer shouted, following the drill. 'Police!'

The man continued for the trees, the vegetation so dense that he had to clear a path for himself. A flock of small birds, startled, flew off in all directions. It was the second time in a few days that someone had tried to flee from them.

Wisting was gasping for breath and felt his pulse rate soar. Twigs scratched at his face, making it difficult to see. After fifty metres, the terrain opened out among tall pine trees. The man they were pursuing increased his lead and found a path. Farther ahead, Wisting could make out the main road. A lorry slowed down and moved out to overtake a car parked on the hard shoulder.

Hammer increased his speed, leaving Wisting further behind until he tripped over a fallen pine tree and fell spread-eagled on the ground. As he lay, he watched the man launch himself into the waiting car. The wheels spun on the gravel, hurling tiny stones into the ditch as he took off.

Wisting scrambled to his feet and brushed down his clothes as Hammer sauntered back. 'Did you get the number?' he asked.

'Just saw that it was a Norwegian plate. PP-registered, I think.'

'Did you see what kind of car it was?'

Hammer shook his head. 'Some kind of silver-grey Asian model. They all look the same, you know.'

Neither of them spoke on the way back, both understanding what had slipped through their fingers. The narcotics find had not been released to the newspapers. Someone out there knew about the potato cellar and had visited the old smallholding after the police had finished their investigations to see whether they had found the hiding place. Whoever knew about the farm and the potato cellar might also know something about Jens Hummel.

22

Hammer and Wisting spent the rest of their working day searching though the farm buildings. They did not know what they were looking for, but understood they would recognise when they found it: a scrap of paper with a name, a phone number or a receipt. Something missing from the big picture, a detail that would reveal something they had no knowledge of at present.

Their efforts were in vain.

After work Wisting went to visit Line in her new house. They papered the rest of the living room and had dinner together. He refrained from commenting on the results of her earlier attempt at paper hanging, but assured her that it would all look fine when she had placed the furniture and hung some pictures. The late hours of the evening he spent at *The Golden Peace*, but again failed to find evidence that one of the staff was stealing from the till.

The days that followed dragged slowly. They went through the documents again. They read and reread the reports, and circulated them in the group. They conducted a fresh round of interviews and followed tip-offs. They shared ideas, thoughts and theories and analysed all possibilities, but nothing suggested they were on the verge of a breakthrough. A couple of footprints on the ground in the potato cellar left by the man who had escaped were the only new developments.

On Monday 30 July Wisting rose at half past six with a sense that something had changed, although possibly only the weather. For the first time in ages, the sea breeze hinted at something other than overheated air. Rain was not far off, but in the meantime the increased humidity made the heat feel more intense.

It was now a week since they had found taxi number Z-1086. Two hundred and six days had passed since Jens Hummel had disappeared. The vast majority of serious crimes were solved rapidly in the initial hectic days while the case was still splashed on the front pages. In other instances, it took slightly longer. Very few cases were never resolved.

At the morning meeting, Torunn Borg gave a report of the previous day's search in the area around *Tanumsaga*. They knew that the chances of Jens Hummel being found there were low, but three tiny pieces of sawdust on the rubber mat inside the taxi meant that the private sawmill had to be checked. It was the type of assignment that made it look as though the investigation was moving forward, though in fact it was routine and only likely to augment the piles of paperwork.

Wisting stood in front of the map on the wall. Coloured pins indicated the few fixed points they were sure of. Hatched areas showed where they had searched with dog patrols or used a line of officers to comb the terrain. His phone rang. He recognised the first digits and realised it was an internal number at *Kripos*, the national major crime unit. He sat at his desk and grabbed a pencil.

The caller introduced himself as Erik Fossli from the technical section. 'Normally we just send a report, but this was so unusual that I wanted to phone,' he said.

Wisting's grip tightened on the mobile phone. 'Let me hear it.'

'We've done test shots on the gun in the usual way. The bullet produced a result in the evidence records.'

'What do you mean?'

The policeman at the other end of the line gave a deep sigh, as if tired of having to explain something so obvious. 'All guns have unique markings inside the barrel that leave similarly unique impressions on any bullet that is fired. It can be compared to fingerprints.'

'Ballistics. I know all that, but what gun are you talking about?'

The explanation dawned on him the moment he asked the question.

92

'A *Nagant*, 7.5 millimetre,' the *Kripos* investigator replied. 'Handed in anonymously. Have you submitted several guns?'

'No, of course not, it's just that my thoughts were elsewhere.'

'We test fire all guns, no matter how they end up here. It's purely routine.'

'What case flagged up a result?'

'A murder case.'

Suddenly his mind was in turmoil, his thoughts in a whirl. It was Line who had brought him the revolver. According to her, it had come from the estate of an old school friend's deceased grandfather. He guessed that the friend lived in the vicinity, but had not questioned her closely about whom or where, just said that it had been handed in anonymously when he had passed the weapon on, as they normally did. It must either be an old case, from before his time, or else a crime committed beyond his jurisdiction. 'What case?'

'The New Year Murder.'

'The New Year Murder?' Wisting repeated. 'The case that's about to go to court?'

'The gun was never found. I tried to call one of the detectives in Kristiansand, but couldn't get hold of anybody. I'm sending them a copy of the report, and they will probably want to know how it got to you.'

Wisting drew circles on the notepad in front of him. The case had been called the New Year Murder by the newspapers. The victim was twenty-one-year-old Elise Kittelsen who, on New Year's Eve, had been killed by two shots in Kristiansand city centre. It had taken the police only fourteen minutes to apprehend the perpetrator. What Wisting recalled best was her photo. On her way to a New Year party, she had published a photograph of herself on social media before she left home. There was a special sense of drama about that. A vivacious young girl who takes a photo of herself only minutes before she is killed. Naturally, the media had printed that.

'How sure can you be that it's the same revolver?' he asked.

'As sure as we can be,' Erik Fossli said. 'Every gun is unique, but this has in addition characteristic wear and tear damage in the barrel. All bullets, both the ones that were removed from the girl in Kristiansand and the ones from the test firing, have identical surface marks.'

'I see.'

'I'm sending the gun for DNA and fingerprint testing. It's been more than six months since the murder, but they might find something.'

'They'll probably find my prints,' Wisting said, but he did not mention his daughter.

'You'll probably be registered in the system, so they'll exclude those. Besides, the killer's been caught, so it doesn't matter much. The most important thing is that the gun is off the streets.'

The circles on Wisting's notepad had grown larger, fashioned by his inner anxiety.

'I'll ensure that all the reports from here are sent directly to the enquiry in Kristiansand,' Fossli added. 'So you don't have to be a middleman. You've probably got enough on your plate with this Hummel case?'

'I certainly do,' Wisting said, thanking him, 'but I'd like copies too.'

'Yes, of course, you'll get those.'

After concluding some practical details, they rounded off the conversation.

Wisting slumped back, struggling to remember more details of the New Year Murder. The last thing he had picked up was that a prosecution had been initiated and the court case against the young perpetrator was imminent. Arrested in one of the side streets immediately after the homicide, he had already managed to get rid of the murder weapon. Now it had turned up, and it was Line who had brought it in.

23

Line had met Sofie and Maja for lunch every day at one o'clock. Rising early she got some household chores out of the way, but in the hottest hours it was pleasant to sit in the shade in Sofie's back garden. She preferred to continue with the renovation work in the late afternoon and evening.

As the birth approached, she noticed she was increasingly dreading it. Not only the actual labour, but also what would follow when she was left alone to care for a child. Her chats with Sofie eased her worries. Sofie could answer many of her questions, but their discussions also revealed that she was an insecure single mother who needed support.

Today the front door was open when she arrived, a vase used as a doorstop. Line knocked and shouted into the house. She stepped inside but was reluctant to call out again in case Maja was sleeping.

In the kitchen, half a melon and a large kitchen knife were lying on a chopping board. A jug of yellow juice and two glasses sat on the kitchen worktop. A bag of ice cubes had started to melt and a little puddle of water had formed beside it.

Line continued into the living room, where a radio was playing. The doors leading to the terrace were open, and gauzy white curtains were fluttering in the breeze. 'Hello?' Line said in a loud whisper, and popped her head round the door.

The table outside was set with plates, but the seating area was deserted. She went back inside and heard a noise on the stairs. 'The door was open,' she apologised when Sofie appeared. 'I just came in.'

'Have you read the newspaper?' Sofie asked, brushing past her into the kitchen.

'What newspaper?'

Sofie lifted her iPad from the kitchen counter, activated the screen and held it up. It was the front page of the *Dagbladet* online newspaper. The top story was headlined *Anonymous Million-kroner Gift may be Robbery Proceeds.* The story was illustrated with what had to be an archive photograph of stained banknotes.

Line took the iPad and read. The manager of the organisation *No to Narcotics* was the journalist's source. Three days earlier, the organisation had received a package containing in excess of one million kroner. Every single note was stained at the corners. There had been no information about the sender and the money had been handed to the police.

A detective from Oslo Police District confirmed that they had received the money, and that it most probably was the proceeds of a crime. Banks, post offices, armoured vehicles and cash machines were attractive targets for criminals, and at least a hundred million kroner was still unaccounted for following a series of robberies in the Østland region at the beginning of the noughties. The notes had been passed to *Kripos* for tests.

The press spokesperson at *Norges Bank* stated that the monetary gift could well be worthless to the recipient. The organisation could apply to have the money exchanged, but if the notes were linked to a robbery it would be out of the question. The *No to Narcotics* manager was disheartened, as the money would have been invaluable in their work countering the use of drugs by teenagers. Neither the police nor the manager would speculate about the identity of the sender. There had been no letter enclosed with the gift, and the place of origin was not recorded.

Line handed back the iPad.

'That was really stupid of me,' Sofie said with a sigh. 'I don't know what I was thinking. I should have burned the money. Now they'll find our fingerprints on the notes.'

'Are you registered?'

'What do you mean?'

'Are your fingerprints on police records?'

'No.'

'Then they won't find out that you were the sender.'

'You mustn't tell anyone!'

'No, okay then.'

'Do you promise? Don't tell anyone about the safe.'

'I promise.'

Sofie leaned against the kitchen worktop. 'How could the newspaper actually find out?'

'There are lots of possibilities,' Line answered, thinking privately that it was a good story, and that she would have liked to be the one who wrote it. It aroused readers' curiosity and generated a high number of clicks on the paper's Internet pages.

'It could be that the manager of the organisation went to the newspaper, but it's common for an occurrence like that to be talked about and the news would spread fast. Detectives talk to their colleagues. They pass it on to their wives when they come home, who in turn chat about it to their friends, and so on. Somewhere along the line there'll be someone who knows somebody who works for *Dagbladet*. Many of my best stories came about that way.'

Sofie began to slice the melon. 'My intention was to help, you know. Now it's just led to problems.'

Line picked up the bag of ice cubes, tore it open and poured what was left of them into the jug of juice. 'You've been a good help even if *Norges Bank* won't exchange the money. The news will spread, and *Dagbladet* will follow up. The organisation will get publicity and sympathy. People will give them money. If they're smart, they'll rush to get a fundraising campaign off the ground while the story is still in the media. People will be more generous the next time someone rattles a collecting can or sells flowers with the receipts going to *No to Narcotics*.'

Sofie stood motionless, holding the knife. 'Maybe I ought to send them some of the other money. The notes are still lying in the safe downstairs.'

'Can't you wait and see what happens? You have to think about Maja as well. The money might come in handy.'

97

Sofie put down the knife and took out a dish on which she arranged the melon slices. Line's mobile phone rang. It was her father. He did not usually phone her from work, not unless it was something really important.

24

Wisting would not say over the phone what it was about. He only told her that he needed to talk to her, and asked where she was. She offered to drive to the police station and, in the car, speculated about what could be so urgent. All she could think of was that it must have something to do with her brother. Thomas had trained as a helicopter pilot in the military and served in Afghanistan, among other places. At that time she had been worried about him and followed all the news reports. He still had four years to serve, but at present was not taking part in foreign operations.

She found a free parking space in front of the police station. The officer behind the counter phoned for her father, who came down and accompanied her to his office. He closed the door behind them and sat while Line took a seat on the opposite side of the desk.

'What is it?' she asked.

He sat in silence for a moment or two, as if unsure how to broach the subject, despite having had time to think about it. 'Who gave you that revolver?' he asked finally.

Line felt dizzy all of a sudden; a feeling of nausea spread through her. 'I told you,' she answered, touching her stomach where anxiety and foreboding were tying knots, 'an old school friend. It belonged to her grandfather.'

Her father's eyes bored into her. 'Can't you tell me who she is?'

'I've promised not to.'

Her father sat in silence. She had not told him about Sofie Lund at all, the times they had been together. She had kept that back. She did not quite know why, but it had something to do with Sofie's grandfather. 'Why do you ask?'

'All guns handed in to the police go through a ballistic examination. The bullets are routinely compared with bullets in both solved and unsolved armed crimes.'

Line gave a gasp before her father finished speaking. 'You got a match?' She was suddenly short of breath. 'From an unsolved robbery?'

'Something like that.'

Line sat thinking about the money in the safe. 'If I'd known it would be examined like that, I'm not sure I would have handed it in. It would probably have ended up at the bottom of the sea. I thought it would be anonymous.'

'How long had this friend of yours kept the revolver?'

'She found it the same day I brought it to you.'

'And when did her grandfather die?'

'Six months ago.'

She saw her father grow pensive. 'I'll approach this in another way,' he said.

Line waited. Her father looked out the window. 'Who was that you were with outside *The Golden Peace* last week? The day Nils Hammer and I chased the man who had been sitting at the next table?'

Line bit her bottom lip. If she wanted to keep Sofie as a friend she must not make trouble for her. All the same, it would not be possible to keep her secret from her father. 'Her name's Sofie, but she has nothing to do with the revolver. She found it when she was clearing out her grandfather's belongings.'

Wisting sat in silence for some time. 'This is going to come out sooner or later. The revolver was used in a murder.'

The words struck Line like a punch in the belly, making her sit stock still until the cramping pain passed. She took a few deep breaths. 'What murder?'

'The New Year Murder in Kristiansand. It has been solved, but the murder weapon was never recovered. If nothing else, the defence lawyer will be able to make a song and dance about it. I could be asked to explain to them how the gun was handed in. You could be summoned and you would be obliged to give a statement.'

100

Line groaned at the thought of how she had messed this up for both herself and Sofie. She no longer had a journalist's confidentiality of sources to hide behind.

'Speak to her,' her father suggested. 'It's better if you can get her to talk now instead of ending up with a summons.'

Line struggled to rise from her chair. Her body was hot and sticky and she felt unwell. 'What are you going to do?'

'I'll have to talk to the detectives with responsibility for the case.' Wisting stood up and approached her. 'Are you okay?'

'Yes, thanks,' she said, using the chair's backrest to support herself. 'I just suddenly felt so tired.' She concentrated on breathing slowly and deeply. 'It's fine,' she said, heading for the door.

'I'll come with you down to the car,' her father said, and walked ahead of her to the lift.

She assured him repeatedly that she would be all right. 'I just need to have a rest,' she said, as she sat in the car.

'Drive carefully.'

She nodded and glanced back at him as she reversed out of the parking space. He appeared just as exhausted as she did. His complexion was pale and his eyes troubled. She knew he was in the middle of a challenging investigation and felt a stab of conscience for having burdened him with further worries.

25

Wisting sat unmoving behind his desk. The weapon was the very crux of a murder case. As far as he could recall, the Kristiansand police had expended considerable resources searching for the gun, without success. Now it had turned up unexpectedly through Line.

He touched the keyboard space bar to bring his computer screen back to life and logged into the Population Register. Unsure whether he should follow through with his idea, he hesitated. It felt like investigating his own daughter. He could not remember anyone named Sofie, but the answer would be only a few keystrokes away.

He typed *Sofie* in the search field for first name, entered the same year of birth as Line, and restricted the search to the Larvik district. Vacillating, he finally pressed *Enter*.

The search produced three hits: *Nina Sofie Lund*, *Sophie Fladen* and *Sofie Hekkensmyr*. Only the first of these lived in Stavern. He clicked into the detailed picture and saw that she had reported moving from Oslo to Johan Ohlsens gate only a few days earlier, and that she had a daughter aged one. He remembered the pushchair parked between Line and her friend when they were seated outside *The Golden Peace*.

A note explained that Sofie Lund had changed her surname. That was not unusual for women when they married, but Sofie Lund was unmarried. Another keystroke revealed that her former surname was *Mandt*. Drawing closer to the screen, Wisting felt his heart skip a beat. He swallowed hard as the data register confirmed that Line's friend's grandfather was Frank Mandt.

26

Line stretched out on the settee in her newly furnished living room, too worried to relax. She perched her laptop on her stomach and stuffed a big cushion behind her back. The latest article said the case against the accused twenty-five-year-old was scheduled for Monday 6 August. She clicked into a summary. The alleged perpetrator had not confessed, but three witnesses had seen him flee the scene. In addition, gunshot residue was found on his hands, and a map of the attack area in his back pocket.

His criminal record also counted against him. He had several previous convictions for violence and narcotics crimes, and had been released on probation a few days before Christmas after serving nine months for threatening with a knife when stealing a handbag.

The actual killing was described succinctly. Twenty-one-year-old Elise Kittelsen, who lived in Kristian IVs gate, was going to a party at the home of friends in Tangen, a ten-minute walk. Outside the abandoned school in Kongens gate, she was shot and killed.

One of the witnesses was Terje Moseid, who described how he and a friend tried to save her, but could not staunch the bleeding. They had heard two loud bangs and seen someone running away, and their description led to a twenty-five-year-old suspect being arrested immediately afterwards.

The speedy resolution was something the police emphasised to the media. Their theory was that a robbery had gone wrong. The arrest could have been even faster if the perpetrator had not attempted to flee the scene. Two policemen had pursued him through the city centre streets and, for a while, it looked as if he had got away. He was found hiding behind a rubbish container.

Apart from that, the coverage contained the obligatory portrayal of the young victim. Two of the friends at the party were interviewed. A photograph that Elise Kittelsen had published on Facebook that same evening was used by way of illustration. The accused's lawyer had offered little other than that his client denied any involvement in the crime.

Line could feel the baby kicking, as if protesting at the location of the laptop. She shut the lid and carried it back to the table.

She had no idea how the gun had ended up in the safe, but it was certainly a problem now. Uneasy at withholding information from her father, she still did not want to let down her friend. Rolling on her side she used her arm for support, sat up and texted a message to Sofie, asking her if it would be all right for her to drop by, and half an hour later they were on the terrace in her garden.

The weather was sultry and still. Maja crawled on a rug on the lawn. Line was unsure where to begin. 'I don't think it was such a good idea to hand the revolver to the police.'

A shadow crossed Sofie's face. 'Why not?'

'They examined it. They do that with all guns that are handed in.'

Sofie picked at the cuticle on her thumb.

'I spoke to my Dad. They've test-fired it.'

'Why did they do that?'

'To check the bullet. They compare the markings on it with bullets from other cases.'

'My God!' Sofie grabbed the arms of her chair. 'Was it used in a robbery, the one the money came from?'

'I'm sorry for creating problems,' Line said. 'We should have done as you suggested and heaved it into the sea.'

'What did they discover?'

Line leaned forward. 'Someone was shot with it.' Somewhere nearby, a gull screeched. 'I'm really sorry.'

'And killed?'

Line nodded.

'Who?'

She took a deep breath. 'Have you heard of the New Year Murder?'

'I think maybe.'

When Line told her about how Elise Kittelsen had been shot and killed Sofie stood up and took a few steps. 'I know he did a lot of bad things, but murder?'

'No, no! It's not like that. They've charged a twenty-five-year-old with the murder. The trial begins in a week's time.'

Sofie sat Maja on her knee. 'How can they be sure it's the same revolver?'

Line shrugged.

'I don't understand how it can have landed up here in the safe,' Sofie said. 'Have you told your father where you got the revolver?'

'No. It's registered as handed in anonymously, but I said I got it from a school friend who found it when she was clearing out her grandfather's belongings.' She qualified herself slightly. 'I did tell him about you, though. Since he saw us together outside *The Golden Peace* he's going to put two and two together. We may have to give evidence.'

'There's nothing to give evidence about. We don't know anything more than that we found the revolver in the safe.'

Maja began to make a fuss.

'But we might have to give a statement to that effect,' Line said. 'If I'd known it would turn out like this, I'd never have given the revolver to my Dad.'

Sofie gave Maja a bunch of keys to chew. 'Don't worry about it,' she said. 'It's not your fault. It's the Old Man who's to blame, for all of it.'

27

According to Criminal Records, Harald Ryttingen had responsibility for the New Year Murder case. Wisting did not know him, but knew that he was in charge of the criminal investigation department at Agder Police District. He had heard him give talks at a few conferences and seen him interviewed in the media. He was an athletic man with raven-black hair who looked secure and self-confident in his job. He found his direct number and rang.

Harald Ryttingen answered apathetically, as if engrossed in something else, but focused when Wisting introduced himself. 'I've received the weapon report,' he said in the soft tones of the south coast. 'It changes nothing as far as our case is concerned.'

'I would think it raises a few questions,' Wisting said.

'The most important questions have already been answered. The perpetrator was arrested fourteen minutes after the crime. The Public Prosecutor has preferred an indictment. The court case starts a week from now.'

'Since the weapon was handed in here, I wanted to let you know we're happy to assist.'

'The weapon was handed in anonymously, wasn't it?'

'Yes, but we may be able to take a closer look at its origins.'

'You needn't bother. The investigation of the case is concluded.'

'Have you already spoken to the Public Prosecutor about that?'

Ryttingen avoided the question. 'Listen,' he said. 'This is our case. You don't need to make any further enquiries. The report we've received is more than enough.'

'It could be of interest to your case to find out how the

revolver ended up here,' Wisting said. This dismissive attitude was very different from how he would have handled a similar development.

'Illegal weapons change hands all the time.'

'The perpetrator must have thrown it away when he ran off or else passed it to someone. Have you looked at the possibility that he wasn't acting alone?'

'Listen!' Ryttingen's soft accent became sharper at the edges. 'We have three eyewitnesses and I have no intention of letting this pistol create problems for us in court.'

'Revolver.'

Ryttingen gave a loud sigh. 'It's my job to present the most solid and convincing case possible. I don't need anything that leaves room for doubt and confuses the judge.'

Wisting was about to protest. That was not what an investigation was for. On the contrary, it was to bring all the facts to light.

'I'm grateful for you getting in touch. We'll take care of it from now on,' Ryttengen said, bringing the conversation to a close.

Wisting had mixed feelings. Line would be pleased that the investigating officers were not interested in following up on the gun. In his own eyes though, from a professional point of view, this was a misjudgement, a decision he regarded with extreme scepticism.

Christine Thiis appeared at the door with her bag slung over her shoulder, so he understood that she was on her way home and wanted a final update before she left. A deep furrow became visible between her eyebrows when her eyes met Wisting's.

'Is something wrong?' she asked, stepping inside.

'I don't know.'

Christine Thiis pulled a chair from under the desk and sat down.

'It's not really to do with our case,' he explained, pushing the ballistics report across.

'Have you spoken to the police in Kristiansand?' she asked, after skimming through the papers.

'I've just put down the phone. They regard the investigation as done and dusted. The court case begins in a week, and they don't want us to do anything further.'

'There's not really much more to be done. It was handed in anonymously.'

Wisting replaced the document in its folder. 'It's not as if someone left the revolver on the steps outside and sneaked away. We do know a little about where it came from.'

Christine Thiis tilted her head to one side and held his gaze.

'It comes from a deceased person's estate,' Wisting said. 'It was among the possessions left by Frank Mandt.'

The air conditioning system in the ceiling switched off and its regular drone was replaced by silence.

'That's not unreasonable,' Christine Thiis said. 'We know that Frank Mandt was a central player in criminal circles in Østland. For an illegal weapon to end up in his hands is not really so strange.'

Nils Hammer came to the door with a cup of coffee and a notepad. 'What's not really so strange?'

Wisting repeated his explanation, still without mentioning Line.

'There are a few things here that are strange,' Hammer said. 'A murder weapon is hot. It's something you get rid of as quickly as possible.'

'The killer couldn't have done it any faster,' Wisting said. 'He was arrested fourteen minutes after the message was relayed.'

'I remember that. The National Police Commissioner bragged about it in an interview.'

'Somebody must have found it and brought it here.'

'Just from sheer curiosity,' Hammer continued, 'where was Jens Hummel on New Year's Eve?'

Wisting sat motionless for a couple of seconds before swivelling his chair and pulling out a ring binder marked *Electronic traces*. 'The taximeter was not in use,' he said.

'Isn't that a bit odd? A taxi that's not in service on New Year's Eve?'

Wisting extracted the printouts that showed Jens Hummel's

mobile phone use for the six months prior to his disappearance. They had gone through them before and spoken to everyone he had been in contact with, but it had not taken them any further.

His index finger slid down the columns to 31 December. Throughout that day the phone had registered at various base stations in Larvik. At around four in the afternoon the signal began to move southwards. It registered at a number of towns along the south coast until he sent a text message from Kristiansand city centre at twenty-eight minutes past six.

28

Nils Hammer enlarged the telephone printout on the screen. The investigators had been kept behind and were huddled round the conference table. 'We know that Elise Kittelsen was murdered in Kristiansand town centre at 19.21 on 31 December with a gun belonging to Frank Mandt,' he said.

'We don't know for sure that it *belonged* to Frank Mandt,' Mortensen said. 'It was found among his possessions after his death.'

'Okay,' Hammer agreed, 'but we also know that Jens Hummel was in Kristiansand city centre at 18.28.' He pointed at the data printout where the call was underlined in red. 'The next thing we know is that he receives a message when he passes Bamble at 21.34, on his return journey.'

'The stretch from Kristiansand to Bamble takes almost exactly two hours,' Mortensen said. 'That means he must have left Kristiansand just after the shots were fired.'

'Who sent the text?' Christine Thiis asked.

'We checked that out earlier,' Wisting replied. 'Apparently it was a Happy New Year message. A couple of the people told us they were not even aware they'd sent him a text. They had him stored and selected all their contacts as recipients. The messages sent out by Jens Hummel were also New Year greetings.'

'He did have another phone,' Espen Mortensen reminded them.

'There could be a connection,' Wisting said. 'Hummel was in Kristiansand when the murder was committed. His vehicle was found on Mandt's farm, and the murder weapon was among Mandt's belongings. It could all be down to coincidence, but if not – what is it?'

Torunn Borg got the ball rolling. 'Jens Hummel brought the gun to Larvik,' she suggested.

'Jens Hummel could be the murderer,' Nils Hammer said.

'But the murderer's already been caught,' Christine Thiis objected.

Hammer defended his theory. 'They might have arrested the wrong guy. If Frank Mandt was Jens Hummel's employer, he wouldn't have much problem obtaining a false passport for Hummel to flee the country.'

'You mean that Jens Hummel was a hired killer?' Christine Thiis said, unable to restrain a smile.

'And why on earth would Frank Mandt want to kill a twenty-one-year-old girl in Kristiansand?' Torunn Borg added. 'Besides, you're forgetting Hummel's blood in the taxi.'

'There could be other explanations for that,' Hammer said, looking at Mortensen.

'There were only minimal amounts,' Mortensen said. 'Hummel had driven the taxi for a number of years. Maybe he cut himself at another time and some of the blood rubbed off in the car boot, but I don't see Jens Hummel as any kind of professional hit man for Frank Mandt either.'

Theories and suppositions were tossed about. In one suggestion, Jens Hummel was an inconvenient witness who had to be liquidated; in the next he had no connection to the gun or the murder and had done nothing illegal apart from putting the money for a lengthy trip into his own pocket.

Wisting waited to be asked how he knew the revolver came from Frank Mandt's estate, and how it came to be handed in, but it did not come. Eventually the conversation ebbed to a close.

'We've overlooked a pertinent question,' Hammer said. 'Who was the passenger when Jens Hummel drove to Kristiansand on New Year's Eve? Frank Mandt himself?'

They left with a long list of unanswered questions. The sky outside had turned grey.

29

The rain arrived around seven that evening. Sitting on the concrete floor in front of the safe, Line glanced up at the basement window. It was not the sort of rain that would put an end to the dry spell, but a fresh, clean summer downpour that would wash the dust off the grass and leaves.

Sofie had asked if she would look through the remaining contents after they agreed it would be best to get them cleared out. First, they removed all the money and placed the notes in a plastic carrier bag that Sofie was going to hide somewhere in the house. The rest of the contents she left to Line. 'But we're not handing in anything else to the police,' she had said.

There were five black ring binders, several plastic folders, notebooks and envelopes in the safe.

The first ring binder appeared to contain everything to do with the house: insurance papers, valuation reports, architectural plans, instruction booklets, receipts and guarantee certificates. Some of that could be useful for Sofie, but otherwise was of little interest.

Line put that ring binder aside and opened the next. It was full of plastic pockets containing newspaper cuttings. She unfolded one. The paper was yellowed and the print faded. The article was from 17 August 1972 and the headline read: *Smuggler's Boat Boarded Near Jomfruland*. Customs officials had boarded a fishing smack seven nautical miles beyond Jomfruland. On board they had found 720 litres of spirits. The vessel had been towed in to Langesund, and the skipper, who had been on board by himself, was arrested.

There were two more clippings in the same pocket. One was a shorter article explaining that the fifty-eight-year-old skipper had admitted the attempted smuggling but, apart from that, refused to cooperate with the police. The last extract was a brief notice about a fifty-eight-year-old man who was sentenced to sixty days unconditional imprisonment for smuggling 720 litres of liquor.

Next was a story from 1976. A lorry loaded with cigarettes and several hundred litres of spirits had been involved in a traffic accident on route 22, near the Swedish border. The driver sustained slight injuries and was charged with smuggling.

Approximately every third year there were similar newspaper articles, placed in chronological order in the ring binder. It was a strange collection, and the only explanation Line could think of was that Frank Mandt had saved stories from the newspapers that somehow involved him, probably as the man pulling the strings.

She put that ring binder aside. Something hit the floor on the storey above her head. Maja burst into tears, and the boards in the ceiling creaked as Sofie crossed the living room floor.

The next two ring binders contained duplicate tax returns and other financial papers. Line's eyes opened wide. If Sofie was her grandfather's sole heir, she had become extremely wealthy. He was listed as having capital of fourteen million kroner, divided into bank deposits, shares and properties. Other papers suggested that there was still more cash. Printouts from the *Bank Julius Bär* in Zurich showed a series of deposits of several hundred thousand euros. Line had heard about Swiss bank accounts, but had never seen anything like this. There was no name or address listed for the account holder, only a number, *Relationship No. 0016.2426,* concealing the identity. All that was needed to access the money was a code word.

The next papers showed that Frank Mandt was registered as a one-man business with the stated aim of buying and selling real estate. There were copies of title deeds and transfer agreements going far back in time. At the very end of one ring binder was a collection of payments of winnings from the Norwegian Trotting Association, and *Rikstoto,* the Norwegian National Tote. She knew that this was frequently how criminals obtained

113

start-up capital. You could buy winning tickets at the racing tracks. It was a sort of win-win situation. The real winner could cash in up to twenty-five per cent more than the original winnings, and the buyer was able to launder money. Property investments were another way of letting black market money grow. You purchased a property at a low price because it was in need of maintenance, and brought in black market tradesmen before selling at a profit.

Frank Mandt had an almost obsessional sense of order.

The final ring binder contained police documents: witness statements and interviews of suspects. One of them referred to a man called Aron Heisel, who had been interviewed by the police in Halden on 6 June 2002, charged with importing 2,400 litres of spirits in plastic containers. He admitted his guilt, but would not give a statement about where the consignment came from or the identity of the intended recipient. Another recurring name was Per Gregersen. He had given a statement to the police in a case concerning marijuana smuggling and it looked as if the Hells Angels in Denmark were also involved.

Line went back to the ring binder full of newspaper clippings and found an article from the *Halden Arbeiderblad* dated 7 June 2002, which stated that customs officials had stopped a Volkswagen Transporter loaded with more than 2,000 litres of spirits. An older clipping from the *Fædrelandsvenn* wrote of a man who had been convicted of importing eight kilos of marijuana. During the hearing, he had refused to explain his relationship with the Hells Angels and the criminal motorbike fraternity in Denmark.

Frank Mandt had created an archive of operations that had gone wrong. Crazy, because the police might find it but, as he had been operating since the sixties without being caught, he had probably become quite self-confident. Anyway, the newspaper cuttings were no more than circumstantial evidence.

The police documents were from various districts. Although there were different investigators, lawyers' names were mainly the same. She doubted whether Mandt had obtained the case documents from anyone in the police, and guessed that they were copies of transcripts used by defence counsel. From her experience with organised crime, she knew that those who were arrested often demonstrated their loyalty towards their employers with copies of their police statements in which no names were mentioned.

Water trickled and poured through the gutters. It was painful to sit on the hard concrete floor. Her back was stiff and her bump made it difficult to lean forward. She changed her position and picked out one of the black notebooks. Full of figures, it was obviously some kind of accounting, but the rows of numbers had no headings. In some places dates were noted, and in others one or two letters were followed by a full stop, like the initials of a name. A detective in *Økokrim*, the police finance division, would probably be able to extract more from this than she could.

The envelopes were what Line was most curious about. Sofie had already retrieved photographs of her mother and herself, but there were still several more envelopes at the bottom of the safe.

The first was bulky and contained small cassettes. One of her most senior colleagues in the local newspaper had used similar cassettes in a miniature tape recorder instead of using pen and paper, much as she made use of the recording function on her mobile phone. They were marked with date and year, and there were more than twenty, but no player.

She put that envelope to one side and peered down at the next, which contained something resembling surveillance photos. Old and grainy, they had been taken at a distance. The subjects were two men walking along a pavement, one gesticulating as if explaining something to the other. The pictures reminded her of the famous photograph of the meeting between KGB General Gennady Titov and Arne Treholt, convicted of spying in the eighties.

The next envelope contained similar pictures but they had been taken in an industrial area. It looked as if the buildings and location were the photographer's focus. Another collection was in colour. Snapped abroad, with palm trees and exotic

115

flowers in the background, the people standing around did not seem to be aware that they were being photographed.

It was obvious that the pictures had significance. Counter-intelligence had become an important part of organised crime, with reference to both the police and other criminal gangs. The pictures were old, and there was no telling why Frank Mandt had kept them. Even though they could not tell Line anything at present, they bore witness to how he had built up his criminal empire. When she struggled to her feet and returned the contents to the safe, more questions than answers were running through her head.

30

When the alarm clock rang, Wisting had already been awake for half an hour, his thoughts circling around Frank Mandt's death. The last time anyone had seen him alive had been on Monday 9 January. The date of death was fixed as Tuesday 10 January, since that day's newspaper had been spread out on the kitchen table and the mail for subsequent days had not been brought in. He was unsure whether he recalled correctly, but in one of the photographs there was a detail that, given what had emerged in the past few days, might prove interesting.

He got up and padded into the bathroom. Dirty laundry had piled up behind the door. He must remember to switch on the washing machine when he came home.

He was in his office as early as half past six. Blue-grey clouds blanketed the sky, but they parted and let sunlight spill through from time to time. Rain from the previous night had already disappeared from the streets. It was going to be another warm day.

The Mandt file was still on his desk. He picked it up and thumbed through to the pictures of the kitchen table. Mortensen had taken a close-up of the local paper for Tuesday 10 January. The main story was a quarrel about salmon fishing rights in Lågen. The other photo was of the mailbox. Side by side, these two photographs were self-explanatory. However, it was the next image that had surfaced in Wisting's subconscious, showing the entire kitchen table. Beside the local paper and a coffee cup lay a pair of scissors and an edition of *VG* open at an article about the New Year Murder. On its own it didn't mean a thing, but it could be significant.

Until now, they had taken Jens Hummel as their starting

point and searched for a link to Frank Mandt without finding anything. Now they had to search in the opposite direction: did Frank Mandt have a connection to the missing taxi driver? For decades, the police had struggled to persuade anyone to talk about him and his criminal activity. He had ruled his people with an iron fist, but now he was dead. Maybe someone would be willing to talk?

The assignments had been divided between Torunn Borg and Nils Hammer. After the morning meeting, Wisting went to the toilet and splashed his face with cold water. His eyes cleared and he looked at his face in the mirror. There was still a hint of bruising on the right side, but the swelling had gone.

By half past eight, when most of the routine administrative tasks had normally been completed in all the police stations in the country, Wisting dialled Harald Ryttingen's number in Kristiansand and gave a brief account of the possible connection between Jens Hummel and the New Year Murder. 'I'd like a copy of your case material to see if there's anything that can be linked to our enquiry,' he said.

'I've already told you that our investigation is over,' Ryttingen said. 'All the material is with the Public Prosecutor who will lead the case in court.'

'I only need electronic access. So that we can link up to the case documents from here.'

'We spoke about that yesterday. We don't need any assistance from you.'

'I know that, but we're the ones who need assistance from you. You may be in possession of information of interest to our missing person enquiry.'

'I'll have to clear it with the Public Prosecutor. I'll contact you as soon as I've been in touch with him.'

Wisting moved the phone to his other ear. There was no need to obtain approval to give him the information. This could only be a delaying tactic. 'Who at the Public Prosecutor's office has this case?'

'I'll get hold of him,' Ryttingen said. 'You'll hear from me.'

With that, the conversation was over.

Ryttengen's unwillingness to accommodate interest from another police district was inexplicable other than that it would disturb a case they had long regarded as fully investigated. There was nothing Wisting could do but wait, time he spent in front of the whiteboard on the wall of the conference room where the whole investigation was mapped out. A timeline stretched back to 31 December and forward to today, with events marked with key words in various colours, supplemented by extracts from maps and photos from the crime scene technicians.

What is it we're not seeing here?

All cases had a hidden door. A concealed opening that only became visible when you looked at everything in the right context.

At twelve o'clock Wisting felt hungry and realised that he hadn't prepared a lunch pack. Taking his reflections with him he crossed the square to buy a hotdog and a bottle of *Farris* mineral water from the *Narvesen* newspaper kiosk. Scattered clouds were still hanging in the sky, but they were white and fluffy. He sat on a bench to eat and absentmindedly watched a group of gulls fighting over a morsel of bread. Never before had he spent such a long time on a case and been so far from a solution. Other cases had been complicated and difficult, but never had six months passed without more than vague outlines appearing. Maybe it was not the enquiry. Maybe he had grown old and was losing his grip.

The gulls flew off when someone sat at his side. Wisting wiped his fingers on a napkin and half-turned to the left. It was Christine Thiis. She smiled and handed him a *Krone* ice-cream cone. Although it was not the price that had given the cornet-shaped ice its name, Wisting could actually remember when it had in fact cost exactly one krone. 'Thanks,' he said.

She removed the paper from her own. 'You mustn't let it consume you,' she said.

'What do you mean?'

'Do you ever think of anything other than this case?'

Wisting folded his ice-cream wrapper without a word. The unanswered questions gnawed continuously.

119

'You need a break. It's like when you've mislaid your keys or something. You find them when you stop searching. The best way to resolve a case is often to take a break from it.'

'Of course, you're right,' he said.

Christine Thiis stood up. 'At my house, seven o'clock tonight. I'll give you something else to think about.' He looked at her. 'Some time off to eat. I'm fed up preparing food just for myself.'

Wisting wiped ice cream from his top lip with the back of his hand. Before he got as far as accepting, Christine Thiis had turned and gone.

31

Sofie was following a recipe she found on the Internet, putting strawberries, water melon slices and ice cubes into her new blender before pressing in the juice from a lime and letting Line sprinkle on some icing sugar. She attached the lid and switched it on. The blades at the bottom of the glass jug went into action, but stopped suddenly. Line glanced up at the ceiling light. 'The electricity's off. It must be a fuse.'

'The cupboard's in the basement,' Sofie said. 'Could you do it?'

Line descended the basement stairs and located the fuse cupboard at the end of the corridor. It was relatively modern with automatic fuses, but everything was covered with a thick layer of dust. Circuit number thirteen had blown. She flicked the switch back into place, but it blew again with a bang.

'Try turning off the dishwasher!' she shouted.

'Okay!'

Line connected the circuit again. This time the blender started up in the kitchen.

She was about to close the cupboard door when, at the base of the fuse cupboard, she spotted a little torch, a few screws, an RCD circuit breaker and some papers left by the installer, but also a key, partly hidden underneath a folded electricity bill. She lifted it out. It was long with a complex set of wards and bits. She stole a glance into the room containing the safe before taking the key upstairs with her.

'Sofie?'

Sofie did not hear her because of the noise from the blender, but switched off the machine when Line entered the room.

'Have you seen this before?'

Sofie came closer and took it out of her hands.

'It was in the fuse cupboard.'

'Do you think it's for the safe?'

Line grinned. 'There's only one way to find out.'

They went downstairs again. Sofie inserted the key into the safe and pushed. The lock itself had been damaged when the locksmith had bored through, but there was no doubt that it was the right key. She burst out laughing. 'I got the bill from the locksmith yesterday. It came to nearly four thousand kroner.'

'Oh my goodness!' Line said.

'That's the way it always is when you're looking for something. You find it when you stop hunting.'

Line tried the key in the lock for herself. 'At least *that* mystery's solved.'

They left the key in the lock and returned to the kitchen. Sofie took out a bowl of prawn salad and sent Line out on to the terrace with it.

Sofie's always the one who pays, Line thought. It gave her a stab of guilt, even though she knew her friend could well afford it.

After Line had bought her house, she had felt the pinch financially. She was well enough off, but the renovation had been more expensive than anticipated. It was going to be a challenge to pay the mortgage when she also had to look after a child on her own.

Maja's pram was parked in the shade of the leafy old trees. Next time she visited, she would bring something with her, Line thought. A cake, or something for Maja.

Sofie emerged from the living room with the glass jug in one hand and her iPad in the other. 'They've found out about it,' she said, looking up from the screen. 'The money was from a robbery in Drammen.'

Line got to her feet and Sofie handed her the tablet. *Dag-bladet* had broken the news. *Million-kroner Gift from Violent Robbery* screamed the headline.

Line skimmed the text. The police had discovered that several of the banknotes could be traced to a robbery on an armoured security van outside the Gullskogen shopping centre

122

in Drammen in 2005. Two *Securitas* guards were threatened with a revolver and a shotgun. One was knocked unconscious with the gun butt. The total proceeds of the robbery were almost eight million kroner, but among the cash was a case of banknotes ready to be inserted into a cash machine. The serial numbers on the banknotes had now been retrieved from the anonymous million-kroner gift.

No one had been arrested for the robbery.

'What will we do?' Sofie asked, sitting on one of the garden chairs.

'Nothing,' Line answered.

'What if the Old Man took part in it?'

Line clicked on a link to *Dagbladet*'s coverage of the case in 2005. 'I doubt that,' she said, without mentioning her impression that Sofie's grandfather was the brains behind many crimes. 'Remember he was already an old man by then.'

The newspaper article from 2005 did not tell her any more, other than that the robbery had been the seventh in the Drammen area in two years.

'Why did he keep the money in the safe?' Sofie asked.

'He might have received it in payment for something,' Line said. After they had found the money, she had read more about the subject. Although such money was marked, it was often used as a means of payment in criminal circles, but at ten per cent of its face value. Whoever bought the marked notes also took on the task of using them in slot machines or other places where banknotes were read by machine.

'Why didn't he just burn them? After all, they're not worth anything?'

Line sat down again and put the iPad on the table. 'That's not your responsibility,' she said. 'You can't feel guilty about something your grandfather did.'

'I know that, but I feel I ought to do something to make up for the terrible things he did.'

'The best thing you can do is to take care of yourself, and make sure that Maja here has a better upbringing and more stability in her life than you ever had.'

Sofie flashed her a smile as Line leaned over the salad bowl.

'Is it safe for me to eat shellfish?' Line knew the answer, but wanted to change the subject.

'Yes, of course, but you should be careful about prawns when you're breast-feeding so that the baby doesn't become allergic. Make the most of them now!'

Line helped herself to a generous portion and the conversation drifted to other topics: baby equipment, renovations and interior décor. Now and again, she had to force herself to concentrate on what Sofie was saying. Her thoughts constantly turned back to the contents of the old safe. The stained banknotes had been lying for years, but the revolver could not have been there for long since it had been used on New Year's Eve. Frank Mandt had died immediately after, and the safe had not been opened until they broke into it the previous week. The man who had used the revolver had been arrested just after the killing. During the last few days of Frank Mandt's life the murder weapon must have been conveyed here and locked in the safe. Something in this sequence of events seemed illogical.

A lawnmower started in the garden next door and woke Maja. They brought her inside and let her crawl around on the living room floor. An hour later, Line stood up to leave. Sofie wanted her to stay longer, but she had things to attend to at home.

The mowing of the neighbour's lawn was completed, and the old lady who lived there stood at the gate paying a young lad with his torso bare. She looked at Line. 'Have you moved in?' she asked.

'No,' Line said. 'I was just visiting.'

'You're Wisting's girl, aren't you? The one who writes for the newspaper?'

This was how it always went. Most people knew her father.

'I'm on maternity leave now,' she said, running her fingers over her bump.

The boy who had cut the grass hopped on to a bicycle and the woman took a few steps closer, obviously keen to satisfy her curiosity. 'Do you know the woman who's taken over the house?'

'We were at primary school together,' Line said, unsure how much she should tell her about Sofie's past. 'But then she moved away. We hadn't seen each other for years when I suddenly ran into her in the street. It's a beautiful house.'

'Yes, and we are pleased to have new neighbours.'

Line was about to round off the conversation by hoping she enjoyed the rest of the summer, but a thought occurred to her. 'Did you know the man who lived here before?' she asked. 'Frank Mandt?'

The woman shook her head decisively. 'We had nothing to do with him.'

Line took a few steps back towards the gate. 'Were you at home on New Year's Eve?' she asked.

'Both Christmas and New Year's Eve. Why do you want to know?'

'Was Frank Mandt was at home?'

'Yes, but we didn't speak to him.'

'But he was definitely at home on New Year's Eve?'

'I seem to remember that I saw him, but I don't think he had any visitors. Not that night at least. He kept himself to himself. I don't think he had any family.'

'What time on New Year's Eve was it you saw him, do you remember?'

'Our son came to visit with our grandchildren at about half past five. We'd invited them to come at five. It had started snowing, and it was difficult to park the car. Mandt didn't exactly make it any easier. He was outside clearing all the snow on to the street, but I didn't say anything. 'Why do you ask?'

'No particular reason, really,' Line replied, walking towards her car. 'I just wondered if he could have been somewhere else.'

32

At 15.15, electronic access to the New Year Murder was opened. Wisting printed out all the documents, filled a pot with coffee and began to read.

The first document was a call-out report that explained how the police had received a message about the shooting and what the first patrol to reach the crime scene found. The message had arrived via the ambulance central switchboard from a woman in one of the nearest flats. She had been in the stairwell when she heard two shots but, since it was New Year's Eve, she had not reacted with any great surprise. When she let herself out, she had heard a shout for someone to phone for an ambulance, and saw two men crouched beside a woman on the ground. A doctor who had by chance been passing had begun resuscitation attempts, but the woman was already dead. The police arrived before the ambulance.

Among the members of the public who had gathered on the spot were three men who were listed as witnesses. One had seen the incident, while the other two had heard the shots and seen the perpetrator flee. They had given a remarkably concurrent description that had been relayed over the police radio.

Wisting highlighted individual sentences and made notes in the margin, understanding that he would probably find answers to the questions he was raising further on in the documents.

The next report dealt with the arrest of twenty-five-year-old Dan Roger Brodin. Patrol car Kilo 2-0 was on its way to the crime scene when the police bulletin was put out. At the Ernst Hotel, they had spotted someone who matched the description and who changed direction and broke into a run when he saw the patrol car. The officers pursued him through several back yards but lost sight at the bus station. A short time later he was apprehended behind the rubbish containers at the *Color-Line* ferry terminal. He had the previously-mentioned map in his back pocket, suggesting to the police that he had planned in advance where to strike.

He was driven back to the crime scene where the waiting witnesses identified him as the killer. Wisting placed an asterisk in the margin.

This immediate confronting of witnesses with a suspect was unconventional but effective. Witnesses' powers of recall were at their best shortly after an incident, while they were still unaffected by the media and other influences, and doubt and uncertainty had not yet set in. Later, the value of their evidence could be reduced when a suspect was not picked out from a line-up, as in a photo identification parade when witnesses had a number of faces to choose from.

The crime scene report did not add much. In addition to the description of the murder victim there was a description of the location and factual information about the weather, wind speed and temperature. About thirty centimetres of snow had fallen in Kristiansand city centre, but most had been cleared away. The asphalt in the street where the murder victim was lying had been dry and bare, making it impossible to secure any footprints.

Wisting flicked through the folder of photographs. He had no need to study the details, but left it lying open at a map on which the crime scene was plotted.

The post mortem report described a narrow bullet track through the victim's back with large tearing injuries in the chest cavity, and another bullet track at the nape of the neck. The shot to the neck was described as causing death instantaneously, but the wounds in the chest would have been fatal in themselves. There was sooting around the entry wound in the neck, which indicated that the shot had been fired from a distance of less than one metre. It was estimated that the shot in her back had been fired from a distance of between one and three metres.

127

Wisting underlined the words 'back' and 'neck'. Then he found a Post-It note, drew a question mark and used it to mark the page. The New Year Murder had been described as a robbery that had gone wrong. The perpetrator had taken the victim's mobile phone, but her handbag had been left lying. The shots, however, seemed purposeful.

He refrained from looking at the photographs of the naked cadaver on the autopsy table, but scrutinised the two deformed, mushroom-shaped projectiles that had been removed from the body.

A lengthy report described the search for the murder weapon. Neither it nor the mobile phone had been found.

Wisting consulted the map as he read about which streets were searched using dogs, which rubbish containers had been rummaged through, and where they had used divers. They had even searched on house roofs, with the idea that the murderer could have thrown the gun up there.

The explanation given by the key witness left little doubt about what had happened. Einar Gjessing, like the victim and many of the other witnesses, had been making his way to a party. However, unlike many of the others, he had not yet started drinking and was sober when he witnessed the murder.

He had walked round the street corner where Holbergs gate intersects with Dronningens gate when he noticed the perpetrator and the victim. The woman had torn herself free of the perpetrator and he had pointed a revolver at her and fired two shots in rapid succession. The shots hurled her to the ground. The perpetrator had run towards him and passed at a distance of only a few metres. The witness ran after him but gave up after only a block, returning to the crime scene where two other witnesses had already arrived. Eventually there was a throng of people, including the doctor who declared that the woman was dead.

Einar Gjessing had been interviewed twice, giving statements on both occasions, the second the more detailed. His description of the perpetrator and his clothes was more comprehensive and he explained in greater detail where he had come from and how long he had spent chasing after the murderer. He qualified himself by saying that it had not all necessarily happened exactly as he remembered. The report was more than eight pages long, but some questions had not been posed, to Wisting's mind, as for example about whether either of the two had said or shouted anything.

The two other witnesses were friends of the same age, Terje Moseid and Finn Bjelkevik, who had been heading for the same party and seen and heard the same things: the shots, the woman on the ground and a man running from the scene. They had done their best to check her bleeding, but it had not been possible to save her life. They thought she was dead even before the doctor arrived on the scene.

The interview with the accused twenty-five-year-old was brief. Dan Roger Brodin, known as Danny, denied the murder and denied that he had anything to do with the crime. Most of the account of his questioning was him giving a list of his previous convictions. He had been released on parole on 22 December after having served a sentence for violence and misuse of drugs, among other things, and he lived in a council flat outside the city. On New Year's Eve he had been wandering around the centre of Kristiansand at a loose end.

Some of the questions and answers were reported as dialogue:

'Why did you run?'

'Because the police arrived.'

'And why did you hide?'

'So that they wouldn't find me.'

The interview was wound up after less than an hour. It was the only police statement that Dan Roger Brodin had given. In the next interview report, his defence lawyer declared that his client had nothing to add.

Wisting dipped more deeply into the bundle, where he found interviews that gave an impression of Brodin's background. His father had been out of the picture since before he was born. His mother had subsequently married and divorced twice, and she and Danny had moved around a lot. In the course of his first seven years of education, he had attended eight different schools. Arrested for the first time when he was thirteen, his mother lost custody and he became one of the Child Welfare Service's revolving door children. Until they gave up on him at the age of seventeen, he had been through three different foster homes, three Child Welfare and Youth Psychiatry Service institutions and four treatment centres. He had run away from most places and in others his behaviour was so challenging that he was thrown out for the same reason he had been sent there in the first place.

Witness statements about the victim constituted the next folder in the bundle. Elise Kittelsen was the youngest of three siblings. Her parents ran a shoe shop where she worked in the evenings and at weekends. She was in her second year at teacher training college and had a large circle of friends.

The interviews confirmed that she was a kind and pleasant girl. However, some of the investigators had made an effort to scratch below the surface. Her eldest brother had warned Elise several times that some of her friends were unsuitable. Some were involved with drugs, particularly an older boy with whom she had struck up a relationship. Few people would speak ill of the dead, but some of her many girlfriends confirmed that she had inappropriate friends and hung out with the wrong crowd. This did not alter the fact that Elise was an innocent victim and it was the glossy side of her that was reported in the media.

Finally, Wisting tackled the lab reports. There were traces of gunpowder on the accused's right hand and jacket sleeves. Blood tests showed that the victim had 0.08 per mille alcohol in her blood, which tallied with the empty bottle of pear cider in her room. Dan Roger Brodin had a per mille alcohol count of 1.79. In addition, traces of THC, the active ingredient in marijuana, were found.

Nothing appeared to have any connection to the Hummel case. The closest came with the questioning of two taxi drivers who had witnessed Brodin's flight through the streets, but he did not spot anything of relevance to their own missing taxi driver.

Suzanne took a deep breath. 'Is it too late, or could you call in tonight?'

'Now?'

'Only if it's convenient.'

He glanced at the time and then across at Christine who had gone inside to fetch coffee and a plate of cake. He wanted to stay, but could not find the right words to turn Suzanne down.

'Or you could come tomorrow.'

'I can come straight after work.'

She thanked him and apologised for phoning so late.

Wisting sat down again. He felt the need to explain who had called, and told Christine about the misappropriation of money from the till in Suzanne's café. A grasshopper began to sing, but the call had broken the ambience. Half an hour later he made his way home.

34

At seven o'clock in the morning the air was already humid as Wisting drove to the police station. Far out at the mouth of the fjord, the sky was crumpled with dark-blue clouds. It would rain before the day was over.

The regular morning meetings became more difficult with each passing day. The investigators had their assignments, but their enquiries did not take the case any further forward.

'The challenge is to get somebody to talk,' Hammer said. 'Frank Mandt has run his operation for decades without any of his associates squealing.'

'Maybe it'll be easier now he's dead,' Christine Thiis said.

'Maybe, but these folk aren't exactly known for helping the police.'

Chairs scraped and the conference room emptied. Wisting sorted his papers and, last to rise from the table, found Christine Thiis waiting for him at the door. 'Thanks for yesterday,' she said, smiling.

'Thank you for your hospitality.' He searched for something pleasant to say about the previous evening but, before anything came to mind, she had disappeared into her office.

Wisting headed for his own office and called in Nils Hammer. 'I want you to come with me to see Klaus Wahl,' he said. Hammer moved a toothpick from one corner of his mouth to the other. 'He's in Frank Mandt's circle, one of his closest friends. He was the one who found Mandt dead in his basement.'

'What else do you know about him?'

'Not much. He's seventy-four and used to work in a haulage

company that deals with container freight; clean sheet. A widower since 2002, he lives in Blokkhusveien.'

Hammer stood up. 'Then we'll go there, eh?'

* * *

The blocks on their pillars were highly visible on the heights around Stavern. Built at the end of the eighteenth century as combined observation posts and firing positions, they were part of the fortifications surrounding the town. The road that had been named after the blocks was in Ausrød, outside the town centre. Klaus Wahl lived in a detached house tucked tidily into the hilly terrain.

A short old man with silver hair was standing by a dismantled lawnmower with a spanner in his hand when they drew up. His white legs were inside a pair of shorts that were far too wide, and he had a cigarette in the corner of his mouth.

As they got out of the car he greeted them with a brief nod.

'Klaus Wahl?'

'Who's asking?'

Wisting and Hammer introduced themselves. 'It's about Frank Mandt,' Wisting said.

A contraction was noticeable round the old man's eyes. 'He should be left to rest in peace,' he said.

'He will be,' Wisting said, 'but he's left a few traces behind.'

Wahl did not speak.

'You found him?' Hammer asked.

'He'd been lying for a few days by then. I've told you all this before.'

'You were in the habit of meeting up at the bakery?' Wisting asked.

'He had diabetes and often had dizzy turns,' Wahl said. 'When he didn't turn up, I went to his house. He had fallen down the basement stairs. That's how it was.'

Wisting pointed at some chairs and a table underneath a parasol in front of the house. 'Can we take a seat?'

137

Klaus Wahl followed with some reluctance. 'He had given up all that spirits stuff, you know,' he said when they sat down. 'Pulled out completely. He was nearly eighty.'

'He still had a smallholding out at Huken,' Wisting said.

'He hasn't been out there for years.' Frank Wahl grabbed a lighter from the table.

Wisting gazed at him as he flicked it and lit the cigarette that was still hanging from the corner of his mouth. 'Jens Hummel's taxi was found out there.'

'I read the newspapers.'

'Do you know if they knew each other?'

Wahl picked a flake of tobacco from his bottom lip. 'He sometimes took a taxi.'

'What about Aron Heisel?' Wisting asked. 'He lived there when he wasn't in Spain.'

Klaus Wahl let the tobacco smoke ooze slowly out through his nostrils. 'I've never been involved in any of that stuff,' he said. 'That wasn't how I knew Frank Mandt. We did some monkey business together almost fifty years ago, when we worked down at the quay. We were young. For me, it was just a short spell, but Frank was more reckless. He took chances that I wasn't willing to.'

'But you kept in touch?'

'It's a small town. It was more that our wives were friendly. They had known each other since primary school. We just tagged along, and once they were out of the picture we went on meeting.'

Wisting made another attempt. 'What do you know about Aron Heisel?'

'He was an assistant, a message boy. But I don't intend to sit here telling you all this. He can do that for himself if he wants.'

Wisting and Hammer had agreed in advance to keep the meeting informal. Each leaned back and crossed his legs. In circles such as Frank Mandt's it was easier to persuade people to talk outside of an interview room, without what was said being written down or recorded on tape.

'Who took over?' Hammer asked.

Klaus Wahl stared at him in silence, as if he had not understood the question, or else thought Hammer should have known better than to ask.

'You said that Frank Mandt had given up,' Hammer said. 'Pulled out. Who took over, then?'

Taking what was left of his cigarette out of his mouth, the old man pinched the glowing tip between his thumb and forefinger to extinguish it. 'I don't know that anyone took over.' He tossed the butt under a bush covered in lilac flowers. 'When he got diabetes, he gradually stepped down.'

'There were twelve kilos of amphetamines out at Huken.'

'Aron Heisel has probably got an explanation for that.' Wahl picked up the spanner from the table. Wisting took that as a sign that the conversation was drawing to a close. It was obvious that the man did not want to say anything that might tarnish his deceased friend.

'To me he was a genuine bloke.' Klaus Wahl got to his feet. 'I don't know what you've heard, but I wasn't alone in that opinion. Maybe there weren't so many people at his funeral, but there were certainly loads of flowers.' He spat as he strode back to the lawnmower, his eyes on Wisting's as he crouched over the motor parts again.

There was something elusive in his look, as if he was using his eyes to tell him that he knew more than he was willing to admit.

Hammer drove on the return journey. Wisting sat beside him and reviewed the conversation. He had a feeling there was something hidden in it, and tried to analyse the man's answers in an effort to find a way forward. Suddenly something struck him. He did not know if Klaus Wahl had wanted his look to convey a message, but the idea was worth following up anyway.

'Turn in here!' he said to Hammer, pointing at a side street.

Hammer parked the car outside the florist's shop, *Stavern Blomstermakeri*. Frank Mandt's house was located on the other side of the Water Pump Park. Although it was surrounded by a tall hedge that screened it from view, they could see a couple of open windows on the upper storey.

'What are we going to do?' Hammer asked, following Wisting from the car.

'The florist's,' Wisting replied, going inside without further explanation.

It was a long time since Wisting had been in the shop, but the woman behind the counter looked as if she recognised him. She was decorating a wine bottle with flowers, putting it aside when they came in.

'It's about flowers for a funeral,' Wisting said.

'I see.'

'Frank Mandt's funeral, to be more precise,' Wisting said, adding that it was in connection with an investigation. 'He died in January. Did you deliver any flowers to it?'

The woman produced a blue ring binder from the shelf. 'I did take some flowers there,' she confirmed, 'but there weren't many. There were no relatives or close family, but I think I may have done the decorations.'

She leafed through the folder. 'The estate paid for the coffin decorations and a wreath, and then there were a few simple bouquets and condolences ... and, yes, of course, there was also a huge centrepiece ordered through *Floragram*. That was to be flowers to the value of five thousand kroner. I mean, a coffin decoration usually costs half that. It was almost a bit too over the top.'

'Who ordered it?' Wisting asked.

The shopkeeper hooked on a pair of glasses hanging round her neck. 'Let's see,' she said. 'It was someone from the south coast, anyway. The order was placed at *Floriss* in Markens gate in Kristiansand. It was to have PG on the condolence card, but I've got the whole name and address here somewhere.'

She ran her finger down the page as she searched: 'Phillip Goldheim.'

The name was unknown to Wisting. 'Can I have a copy of those papers?' he asked.

The woman removed them from the ring binder and ran them through an old fax machine. The resulting copies were paler than the originals but legible. Wisting folded them and took them to the car. The wind had picked up and the dark clouds had moved farther inland.

As Hammer drove off, Wisting took a second look at Frank Mandt's house. It was only natural that the people who had been in his circle while he lived would also be around when he died, he thought, flicking through the flower orders with satisfaction. Klaus Wahl had bought a bouquet for 395 kroner with the words *Thanks for everything* on the card, while the legal firm Krogh & Co had spent 750 kroner on a floral tribute.

'What did it say on the card with the big flower arrangement?' Hammer asked as he turned out into Larviksveien.

Wisting produced the copy of Phillip Goldheim's receipt: '*With respect.*'

35

Phillip Goldheim was a confident-looking man in his forties with slate-grey eyes and long hair pulled back into a ponytail.

His face filled the entire screen on Wisting's computer. There was something penetrating about his gaze, as if he wanted to read the thoughts of the policeman who had taken the photograph. Wisting shuddered slightly and leaned back a little so that Hammer and Christine Thiis could also study the man who had given Frank Mandt such an outstanding floral tribute.

The printout from criminal records showed two minor convictions for violence and a longer sentence for the import of eight kilos of marijuana with a well-known Hells Angels leader from Denmark also implicated.

He was originally called Per Gregersen, but after his release from prison in 2002 had changed his name to Phillip Goldheim. He began by importing cars, did well and invested in shares. The gift of the gab and his ability to juggle loans and current accounts via established businessmen eventually made a successful financier of him. The money he earned, he spent like water. It went on luxury cars and new business ideas. Among other things, he established an import company for snuff that quickly went bankrupt. On his many holiday trips he stayed at the best hotels in Europe: the Arts in Barcelona, the Ritz in Paris, and the Don Pepe in Marbella. His wardrobe increasingly comprised hand-tailored Italian designer clothes, and he decked himself out in expensive watches and gold rings.

The police in Kristiansand suspected that his successful business interests were built on the proceeds of crime and that his operations involved laundering drugs money. Local police had initiated an investigation with the code name Mister Nice Guy.

A great deal of work had gone into tracking Phillip Goldheim's finances, but had not succeeded in breaking through the confusion of loans, current accounts and creditor exchanges. Many of the investments were undertaken in countries such as Spain and Brazil, where foreign investment and property companies administered the income.

The old slogan 'follow the money' did not seem to have paid off so, instead, the investigators followed a different lead. It was obvious they had an informant close to Phillip Goldheim, someone who might put the police in position the next time he was about to receive a narcotics consignment.

Last autumn the information from this source had started to become more specific, but suddenly it came to a complete halt. Was it coincidence that this had happened at the same time as Frank Mandt had died?

'*With respect,*' Christine Thiis said out loud. 'How should we interpret that?'

'Good question,' Hammer said. 'Were they business partners, or was Mandt a competitor he respected?'

Wisting was uncertain how to tackle the new information. From what he was able to read, it seemed that Goldheim had been a key person in the criminal fraternity in Sørland, as Mandt had been in the Østland region. The connection between them was demonstrated by the flowers.

The first raindrops struck the window as Torunn Borg and Espen Mortensen entered his office, each carrying a cup of coffee. Wisting saw no reason for them all to move to the conference room.

'Okay,' he said. 'What do we know about Frank Mandt that we didn't know this morning?'

'The only family he has is a grandchild and great-grandchild,' Torunn Borg said. 'His grandchild is called Sofie Lund.' Wisting picked up the ballpoint pen from his desk and twined it through his fingers. 'I couldn't find a phone number for her, so I went out there, she lives in her grandfather's house, but there was no one at home.'

'Have you checked her out?' Hammer asked.

'All we have are two domestic disturbance incidents when the police were called out while she was living in Oslo with her child's father. It's obvious he wasn't very kind to her.'

Wisting nodded, keen to continue, but Torunn Borg continued. 'I spoke to the neighbours. They told me that Frank Mandt was at home on New Year's Eve. At least, he was out clearing snow that afternoon.'

'Then he wasn't in the taxi with Jens Hummel when he went to Kristiansand,' Hammer said.

The rain outside grew louder as the investigators presented their findings of that day. Nothing of what they had unearthed pointed to a connection between Frank Mandt and Jens Hummel. It seemed as though there was an element missing, a crucial part.

Torunn Borg remained seated after the others had left the office. 'We aren't the only ones to ask the neighbours where Frank Mandt was on New Year's Eve,' she said.

'No?'

'Line has asked them the same question.'

Wisting grabbed the pen again. In the distance he could hear the sound of thunder. 'She and Mandt's granddaughter went to primary school together,' he said, clearing his throat. 'They met each other again by chance this summer, after nearly twenty years.'

'So the revolver wasn't handed in *completely* anonymously?'

'It was Line who brought it,' Wisting admitted. 'Sofie Lund had found it among her grandfather's belongings and wanted to throw it in the sea. I'll ensure that they come here tomorrow, both of them. Then we can get an official explanation.'

Torunn Borg lingered for a moment before leaving.

Wisting leaned forward, resting his arms on the desktop as he listened to the rain on the window ledges outside. The phone rang.

The man who called introduced himself as Ragnvald Hagen from the *Kripos* fingerprint section. Wisting's grip tightened on the receiver. A direct call from the fingerprint section normally meant that they had found a match. 'Do you know about the story of the robbery gift?' Hagen asked.

'Robbery gift?'

'It's been reported in the newspapers,' Hagen explained. 'The organisation *No to Narcotics* was sent an anonymous donation of a million kroner last week, but the money was stained. The serial numbers have been traced to a robbery on an armoured van in Drammen in 2005.'

A thunderclap made Wisting glance outside, where rain was pouring down in torrents.

'We've had the banknotes here for examination. We found several fingerprints on them, but there's one repeated loop pattern in particular. That's why I'm phoning you. The print belongs to Aron Heisel, the man you have in custody.'

At last Wisting was able to use his pen to some good purpose. 'The money was from a robbery in 2005, you said?'

'Yes, two security guards were attacked outside a shopping centre in Drammen. Heisel must have been in contact with the money after it disappeared from the armoured van.'

'And the money turned up recently, as an anonymous gift?'

'Yes, sent in the post.'

'Do you know where it was sent from?'

'No, that was impossible to track down. They've stopped using place names when they frank the mail.'

Another peal of thunder made the ceiling light flicker.

'Copies of our reports will reach you in the usual fashion,' Ragnvald Hagen concluded. 'But it is such an unusual case that I wanted you to know about it at once.'

Wisting thanked him and hung up, unsure whether what he had just learned could progress their enquiry or if it was simply another bewildering element, but he had a strong suspicion about where that money had come from.

36

Line turned on the bathtub tap and poured in plenty of bath salts. She had not yet tried out the big new bath, having contented herself with the shower, but now dark clouds and heavy rain encouraged a relaxing soak.

She stripped off and switched on the washing machine while the tub slowly filled, dimmed the light and lit a scented candle before stepping in. She lay back with a deep sigh of gratification. All she had to do for the next half hour was relax. The foam was scented with cinnamon and vanilla. The baby kicked, reminding her of the approaching birth, and she blew away the bubbles that covered her bulging stomach.

Every day that passed increased her sense of dread, a kind of fear that she had never known before. She was afraid of the pain, afraid of how long labour would last, afraid she would not cope, afraid she would not reach the hospital in time, afraid of the cutting, tearing, and that something might be wrong with the baby. She had no control, and had to face it entirely on her own. This last point was the most terrifying of all.

Submerging herself further she closed her eyes and emptied herself of all thoughts, immersed her head and held her breath for as long as she could.

The house was silent. All she could hear was the rain falling outside and the low thud of the washing machine, and she regretted not having put on some soft music. She stretched out for the sponge, but a noise made her pause. It sounded like the front door opening. She had thought to lock it when she was in the utility room, but it had slipped her mind again. She listened intently, certain that she could hear footsteps, certain that someone had come in.

'Hello!' her father called out in the hallway.

'I'm in the bath!'

'Your doorbell's not working.'

'I know.'

'Will it be long till you're out?' he asked through the door.

'Why?'

'I need to talk to you. I'll see if I can work your coffee machine in the meantime.'

Line leaned forward and pulled out the plug. 'Just give me a few minutes.'

It had to be something important since he hadn't offered to go home and come back later. She rinsed her hair, massaged in some shampoo, rinsed again and repeated the process with conditioner before stepping clumsily out of the tub. She picked up a towel and dried herself before throwing on a dressing gown and going out.

Her father was standing in the living room with a cup of coffee, studying the freshly painted window frames. His shoulders were soaked with rain. 'You should lock the door,' he said.

'Everything's fine, including me and my bump. I'm just not looking forward to the birth.'

A look of concern passed over his face which he banished with a smile. 'It'll be okay,' he reassured her.

She understood that he too was thinking of her mother, and how much simpler it would have been if she had been there. 'Promise me you'll be with me when the time comes,' she said, her stomach contracting at the mere thought. 'That you'll come with me to the hospital.'

'I promise.' He changed the subject. 'You've made a grand job in here.'

While she had been decorating, all her living room furnishings from Oslo had been stacked at one end of the room. Now they were in their rightful places she was not entirely happy with the result herself. 'This living room is bigger,' she said. 'I'll need more things eventually.'

'This is a good start.'

Line raked her fingers through her wet hair. 'Why are you here?'

147

'It's about the Hummel case,' he said, taking a few steps towards her. 'You know that his taxi was found in a barn out at Huken?'

'Yes, and that you discovered a large consignment of narcotics out there.'

'Frank Mandt had that barn.'

Line frowned, and a couple of drops of water fell from her forehead. 'I thought it belonged to a local farmer.'

'It's true that a local farmer owns the smallholding. Mandt had an agreement for a long-term rental, but hadn't been there for a long time.'

'Do you think he had something to do with it?'

'He has had some role in it, but he always stayed behind the scenes. I doubt whether he's had anything directly to do with the disappearance.'

Line folded her arms, making an effort to reconcile what she had just learned with what she already knew about Frank Mandt. 'He was at home on New Year's Eve,' she said.

'Yes, while Jens Hummel was in Kristiansand.'

Line sat down, her stomach pressing against her ribs. 'How does it all hang together?'

Taking a seat opposite her, Wisting admitted he did not know. 'But you and Sofie will have to come to the police station tomorrow and give statements about the revolver. I'm sorry, but I've kept you out of it for too long already.'

'Of course,' she said. 'Sofie's prepared to do that.'

'How did you find the revolver?'

'It was inside a safe, the only thing left in the house when Sofie moved in. There was no key, so she hired a locksmith to drill it open. I was there at the time.'

'The revolver's been locked in there from the time that Frank Mandt died until you opened the safe last week?'

'More than likely. I came across the key in the fuse cupboard yesterday.'

'What else did you find in the safe?'

Line had promised Sofie she would not tell anyone.

'Was there any money in it?' he asked, before she had overcome her reluctance.

Line felt herself blushing.

'Stained banknotes?'

'I promised Sofie I wouldn't say anything. There were enough problems with the revolver.'

'Did it contain anything else? Something that might have some relevance for the case I'm working on?'

'Photographs and personal papers.' It wasn't a downright lie, but she knew too little of the Hummel case to judge whether there was anything in the safe that might be of interest to the investigation. 'Have you anything at all to go on? Did you find any clues in the taxi?'

'He had a mobile phone with a fictional subscription hidden under the dashboard,'

Line struggled to find a comfortable position. She put a cushion in the small of her back.

'All the numbers and messages were deleted,' Wisting said.

'What about the itemised usage data?'

'That information's also gone.' He flung out his hands in a gesture of despair. 'All phone data is erased after six months.'

'So what's the connection between Frank Mandt and Jens Hummel?'

'We haven't succeeded in finding one, apart from the taxi being found in Frank Mandt's barn.'

'What does the guy in custody have to say?'

'Nothing. He refuses to give a statement.'

'Technical traces? Have you as little to go on as the newspapers suggest?'

'I don't want you to bring this to light.'

'I'm on leave.'

Wisting knew that she would not pass on information that the police did not want to divulge. 'Jens Hummel's blood was found in the boot,' he told her.

'So he was murdered?'

'That's the theory.'

'What about traces left by the perpetrator?'

Wisting got to his feet and stood in the middle of the room with an anxious look on his face. 'All we have is some sawdust.'

'Where did that come from?'

'That's what we're wondering too. We're checking sawmills and joiners' workshops, but so far they haven't led anywhere.'

Line took hold of the armrests and levered herself out of the chair. 'I can make some food later,' she said, tightening the belt on her dressing gown. 'You can drop in and have something to eat.'

'I'm going to call in on Suzanne,' Wisting said. 'One of her employees has been stealing from the till. She was caught red-handed yesterday and Suzanne wanted a chat about it.'

At the front door Line watched as he strode, head bowed, through the rain to his car. She was fond of Suzanne and had been sorry when the relationship came to an end. Her father needed a focus in his life apart from work, so it was good for him that they still stayed in touch.

37

Wisting had not visited Suzanne's loft apartment above the café before. A steep staircase from the backyard of *The Golden Peace* led him to a creaking door and into an attractive flat with painted floors and sprigged wallpaper.

Moving aside a throw and a cushion he sat on a leather chair. Roof windows usually let in more light, but the sky was covered in grey-blue storm clouds. To compensate, Suzanne had lit candles and arranged them on the table. She fetched coffee and a plate of Wisting's favourite caramel cake from the simple kitchenette. 'It wasn't her,' she said, taking a seat.

'Hmm?'

Suzanne poured coffee into his cup. 'It wasn't the one I thought it was. Unni. It was one of the other girls.'

'Which one?'

'Nina. She was working both evenings you were there.'

A shorthaired blond girl who had seemed more withdrawn than the others.

'I was so sure it was Unni,' Suzanne said. 'She made so many mistakes when ringing up the till, but I realise now that she's just a bit confused about the cash register.'

'How did she manage it?' I watched them all closely and didn't notice any irregularities.' Wisting noted that the coffee was better than in the café.

'It was quite simple, the cash register has a function where you can enquire about price. Instead of registering a drink as a sale, she keyed in *price enquiry*. Then the amount comes up on the display, and it looks identical to the customer.'

'But she put the money in the till?'

'She's given a full explanation. Whenever she started her

151

shift, she would put a handful of peanuts in her right trouser pocket. Every time she pretended to ring up the sale of a particular drink, she moved a peanut to the left-hand pocket. Towards the end of the evening, she counted them up, so it was just a matter of calculating how much she could take out of the till without it being noticed.'

'Crafty.'

'She's admitted it all, signed a letter of resignation and says she'll pay me back.'

'Then at least you'll avoid any further problems.'

A bolt of lightning split the dark sky, followed by a clap of thunder. Suzanne stood up and pulled out the plugs from the television and computer. Remaining on her feet, she touched her hand to the back of her head and straightened her hair, piled up in a topknot. Wisting recalled how she used to let down her hair before they made love, her teasing smile that appeared as her hair danced around her shoulders.

'How's the Hummel case going?' she asked, sitting down again.

'I don't quite know.'

'I'm pleased you had time to help me.'

'I may be slightly out of training when it comes to surveillance operations.'

'All the same,' she replied, returning his smile. 'I'm glad you spared the time.'

They continued chatting, the way they used to when she had been living with him. About people they had met, books they had read since they'd last seen each other, and films they hadn't got round to seeing.

In mid-conversation, there was a power cut. Neither of them commented on the darkness, but they continued to sit in silence. The candle flames reflected in her eyes and cast flickering shadows around the room. Her face looked slightly different in the dim light. All of a sudden she looked sad and pensive, almost as if she were weeping.

She held out her hand and put it in his. Wisting remembered what it had been like to wake with her by his side every morning, and realised that he had let her go too easily. For a long time there had been only one woman in his life and after she, Ingrid, died he could not imagine a space for anyone else. Suzanne had entered his life quite unexpectedly, and taken part of it with her when she left.

Suzanne cleared her throat, about to say something, when his phone rang somewhere in the depths of his trouser pocket. It was Christine Thiis. 'Are you at work?' she asked.

'Why do you ask?'

'Haven't you heard? 'They've found Jens Hummel.'

38

Slanting rain battered the car bonnet. The windscreen wipers whined, smearing water and dead insects across the glass.

The body had been found on Brunla farm, a sizeable landholding northwest of Stavern with a farm whose history stretched back to before the Viking period. The farm and surrounding land had passed from one prominent family to another, with the land parcelled off and the farm eventually falling into disuse. In the mid-seventies, a major riding centre had been established there. Wisting had taken Line a few times before she discovered that horse riding wasn't for her.

He turned off the main road. Some of the rainwater had turned to vapour where it came into contact with the warm ground, shrouding the estate in a grey mist. The courtyard in front of the main building was so muddy the car slewed from side to side. Wisting followed the tracks of larger, heavier vehicles round the barn to where the horses were stabled.

Three patrol cars and a large tractor were parked at the rear of the enormous stable. In addition, Espen Mortensen had arrived with the crime scene van. Mud gurgled under his feet as Wisting stepped into the rain.

The barn was in need of a coat of paint, and weeds grew along the white cellar walls. Plaster had fallen off and several of the windows were broken. The roof tiles had loosened and one rone pipe hung loose so that water gushed down the wall. Police officers were huddled in a semi-circle round what was left of a dump of horse manure.

The tractor's engine was running and the scoop was raised. Rain fell like shining threads in the glow from its headlights. Wisting breathed in the damp air and wiped the rain from his face.

The corpse was lying beside the mottled, stone wall, still half-covered in sawdust and manure. Somewhere inside the barn, a horse whinnied. Another one answered, slightly farther away.

The decomposing remains were being washed clean by the rain. Much of the body had gone. Tracks and traces of rats marked the manure pile and the neck and head looked as if they were picked clean of flesh. In certain other places on the body, there were only a few dark bones protruding.

Wisting approached the nearest police officer and nodded without saying anything in particular, trying to form a picture of what had happened.

The taxi with Jens Hummel in the boot compartment had driven round the barn, stopped beside the manure pile and perhaps reversed into place. Hummel had been lifted out and horse manure shovelled over him. One man could do it by himself.

'Who found him?' Wisting asked.

'The stable master,' one of the policemen said. A man in overalls was sheltering from the rain at the top of the barn ramp. Wisting positioned himself in the door opening beside him. The horses inside the barn turned to look at him from their stalls, pricking up their ears.

The stable master was a tall, slim man in his fifties. 'He's been lying there for a long time,' he said, without Wisting having to initiate a conversation. 'Since early last winter.'

'You're probably right.'

'We're spreading muck on the fields. We don't always clear it all, but just before Christmas I scraped away almost all of it. I took a few more scoops when the snow began to disappear in March, but never so deep as I did today, not since last December.'

Below them, the uniformed officers were closing off the area while Mortensen set up a crime scene tent. He was faced with a laborious task. It was one thing to bring out the body, but something else entirely to examine the surrounding area in minute detail.

'What does it look like out here in winter?' Wisting asked.

'I clear the area round the stables and up the barn ramp, all the way to the dunghill. You can drive all the way up.'

'Who could have put him there?'

The stable master shrugged. 'Anybody at all. There's nobody here after ten o'clock at night, except when one of the girls decides to sleep over.'

Wisting peered into the stable, where the air was warm and oppressive. He saw a few dirty pigeons ensconced high under the rafters. 'Wouldn't you have to be familiar with the place to think of hiding a body here?'

The stable master looked Wisting straight in the eye. 'I've no idea what has happened, but there's one thing I'm sure of. Nobody here at the stables has done this.'

The horses were restless. A crowd of curious onlookers had gathered outside the barriers, watching the police at work: three young girls in riding boots, a man with a dog, and two boys on bikes. They moved back when an unmarked police car lurched over the boggy ground. Nils Hammer was behind the wheel with Christine Thiis in the passenger seat.

Heading down to the discovery site again, Wisting, together with his two colleagues, squeezed into the crime scene tent. The warm odour of manure and urine filled the air, but now they could also smell the corpse.

'Can you tell us anything?' Christine Thiis asked Mortensen.

'It's Jens Hummel, obviously. It all fits. Both the time perspective and what's left of the clothes he's wearing.'

'And the sawdust,' Hammer said, kicking the ground.

'They use the tractor to spread the manure over the fields,' Wisting said. 'The last time they emptied the dung heap was in December, before the snow came.'

'How far is it from here to the farm where we found his taxi?' Christine Thiis asked.

'Less than two kilometres.'

'We should have thought of that,' Hammer said. 'How many places can you hide a body in the middle of winter, and at the same time bring sawdust into the car on your feet?'

Wisting felt they could not blame themselves for not having

found the hiding place earlier. 'We didn't think of it,' he said. 'But the murderer did. What does that tell us? Is he familiar with this place? Has he been here before? Does he live in the vicinity? Does he have a horse stabled here? Or was it just a place he came across by chance?'

There was a host of questions. Only a few days of routine work might provide the answers.

Mortensen readied his camera. He was going to be here all night. The entire cordoned area would be combed in all directions, almost like a farmer ploughing his field, before he could be certain that nothing had been overlooked.

Wisting pulled his jacket together at the neck. 'I'm finished here,' he said.

'I'll sit with you on the way back,' Christine Thiis offered.

39

Next morning, Wisting took the inland road from Stavern to the police station in Larvik. Along the way, he revisited the discovery site at Brunla farm. It had stopped raining during the night. The clouds had drifted away, and the morning sun had already dried the mud to some extent.

Trudging across the restricted area, he found Espen Mortensen sitting beside the open sliding door of the crime scene van, a thermos flask by his side, chewing on a baguette. Birds were singing in the trees, and the first of the stable girls was on her way up the ramp.

'Long night?' he asked.

'It's nearly over,' Mortensen replied, taking out a cardboard beaker. He filled it with coffee from the flask and handed it to Wisting.

'Are you any the wiser?' Wisting asked.

'He was shot.'

The coffee was hot. Wisting waited for it to cool, nibbling the edge of the beaker.

'The undertakers took him away about five o'clock. He should be lying on the autopsy table in an hour or so, but as far as I could see, he'd been shot twice from behind.'

The technician stretched out for the camera in a bag at his back. 'The body wasn't in too bad a state, considering. In earlier times, they used sawdust for insulation and preservation.'

He located a photograph on the camera display and held it up to Wisting. It showed the back of a skull with an opening the size of a krone coin. The wound was surrounded with bone splinters and filled with an indeterminate viscous substance. Mortensen searched through the images until he found a

158

picture showing a rip in the discoloured jacket, approximately in the middle between the shoulder blades. 'Reminds me of an execution,' he said.

Wisting drank his coffee with flies circling in the air around him. 'Anything else?' he asked.

Mortensen edged round the van with Wisting following in his wake. 'The wallet in his back pocket,' Mortensen said, picking up a bag from the floor of the van. The wallet was of black leather and swollen at the corners. The contents had been removed and distributed into other bags. Wisting lifted the one that contained his driving certificate. The plastic on the taxi permit was blistered, but the name to which it had been issued was completely legible: Jens Hummel.

'Is there anything here that might tell us more?' Wisting asked. One of the other bags contained a few banknotes.

'Just the usual. Bank card, driving licence and old receipts.'

A horse neighed in the stable behind them. 'Did he have anything in any of the other pockets?' Wisting asked.

'I've only done a superficial examination. They'll do it more thoroughly in the course of the post mortem.'

Wisting pointed at a box of small brown envelopes marked with individual numbers. 'What's this?'

Mortensen picked up the box. 'Chewing gum. Most likely they don't have anything to do with the case. We found more than twenty lumps. Probably the stable girls have spat them into the sawdust and cleared them out with the horse manure.'

Two girls with high boots, each leading a horse down the ramp, loitered at the foot, whispering together, before they swung up into the saddle and trotted off towards one of the paddocks.

Chasing a fly away, Wisting crumpled the cardboard beaker and discarded it in a rubbish bag already full of used disposable gloves and other protective gear. 'Go home and get some sleep,' he advised Mortensen, stealing a final glance at the finds. 'None of this requires an urgent report.'

159

40

The media splashed the story. Christine Thiis supplied factual information about how the body had been found, and explained that they needed to wait for the result of the post mortem to establish the cause of death and the victim's identity. How certain the police were that the body was Jens Hummel was something she manoeuvred around by saying he was the only male reported missing in the district.

Wisting took out the newspaper featuring the interview with Jens Hummel's grandmother in which she called for answers from the police about what had happened to her grandson. He would not simply leave of his own accord. He was thoughtful and caring and she had difficulty believing that anyone would wish him any harm. A kind boy with a generous heart, he had a pronounced sense of fairness.

It was always a challenge to provide family and close relatives with information before the newspapers got their hands on it. Jens Hummel only had an eighty-three year old grandmother who, fortunately, did not have access to the Internet, but news of the discovery would soon reach her. It was only right to let her know immediately.

Erna Hummel had given a statement early in the investigation, before they learned of Jens Hummel's trip to Kristiansand on New Year's Eve. They would have to ask her what she knew about that evening. At the same time, she had mentioned things in the newspaper interview that had not emerged in the police questioning. The way she characterised Jens Hummel supported a tenuous theory that Wisting was not yet willing to share with others. He invited Torunn Borg to accompany him on the visit to Hummel's grandmother in the nursing home.

There is no standard procedure for breaking news of a death. It depended on the situation and circumstances. Wisting leaned back on the green velour settee and listened as Torunn Borg led. One of the nursing home staff was also present. Torunn Borg used simple words, but imparted the information in a truthful and solicitous manner. Erna Hummel had been prepared and accepted the news with apparent calm, though it seemed to take the wind out of her sails.

The old woman had lost many friends and relatives in the course of her life, Wisting realised. First her own children, and now she had outlived her only grandchild. She had no one else. She looked down at her hands in her lap, at the wrinkles and liver spots and dark-blue veins that marked her skin. Her fingers trembled as she fumbled with a handkerchief.

Wisting assumed control of the conversation. 'We've found out a bit more since the last time we met,' he said. 'We think that Jens may have had a connection to a man called Frank Mandt, and that this might have something to do with the case.'

Erna Hummel raised her eyebrows, as if concentrating hard. Her glasses slid down her nose. 'I don't know that name,' she said, reaching out for a glass of water on the table.

'What about Phillip Goldheim?'

Erna Hummel raised the glass to her mouth as she searched her memory. Her hand shook and some of the water spilled and ran down her wrist, along her arm to her blouse. 'I don't know that name either.'

The care assistant helped her to put the glass back on the table.

'He lives in Kristiansand,' Wisting said. 'Do you know if Jens knew anyone down there?'

'No, she decided, shaking her head.

'The last time he was down there was on New Year's Eve.'

'Then he was working,' Erna Hummel said. 'He always drove when the others wanted time off. He took it on himself. Christmas and suchlike. New Year's Eve as well. He visited me the next day.'

'On New Year's Day?'

161

'He brought me some cake. We sat here and ate it.'

'What did he talk about?'

'I don't really remember. Maybe we talked about the year that had gone by. I don't know. We listened to the Prime Minister's speech, but he mostly sat there using his phone.'

'This could be important,' he said. 'Do you know who he was speaking to?'

'He wasn't speaking to anyone. He was reading the news and that sort of thing. He could do that on his phone.'

Torunn Borg interjected. 'Was there anything special in the news that he was interested in?'

Erna Hummel folded her hands on her lap. 'No, but he was obsessed with all the injustice in the world. The Prime Minister talked about that as well.'

Wisting pondered whether to ask her about the New Year Murder, but it was a leading question and would probably unsettle her. 'I understood he was like that,' he said instead. 'Kind and with a sense of justice.'

'He took after his father,' she said. Wisting could see from her eyes that she was thinking back to the past. 'They wouldn't let him into the football team because of it. He was good at playing football, but if the referee made a mistake and gave his team the ball when it was wrong, then he would say so and let the other team have it.'

Wisting searched for the expression Erna Hummel had used in the newspaper interview. 'He had a generous heart?'

'He was a kind boy. His mother took him once to the toy-shop. He had wanted a fire engine with lights that flashed and a ladder on the roof. He'd got some money from me, but he'd saved most of it himself. When they went into the shop, there was one fire engine left. When they were about to pay for it, another boy came in with the same purpose in mind. Jens felt so sorry for him that he let the other boy buy the fire engine instead.'

She stretched out for the glass of water again. 'His father was like that too, naïve and kind to a fault. He couldn't say no to anybody. That's not always a good quality.'

162

The care assistant took the glass out of her hands as Erna Hummel let her eyelids close and gave a deep sigh.

'I think that's maybe enough now?' the carer said. 'Erna usually has a nap about this time.'

Wisting nodded and rose from his seat.

'You must come back,' Erna Hummel requested. Her voice had grown rough and raw in the course of the conversation. 'You must come back and tell me what really happened.'

'We'll do that,' Wisting promised.

41

The provisional post mortem report arrived at 14.30. The corpse had not yet been identified but was described as a man between thirty and forty years of age. The cause of death accorded with Espen Mortensen's conclusion. It was surmised that the shot in the back had hit him first, striking the spine and shredding nerves and muscles, but had probably not been fatal. The second shot had entered the lower part of the parietal bone and exited through the roof of his mouth. It had destroyed large parts of the brain stem and caused instantaneous death. The time of death was estimated as between four and eight months ago. A more formal date would be established when the deceased had been identified via DNA analysis. In practice this meant that 6 January, the day he disappeared, was the date that would be carved on Jens Hummel's gravestone.

The most interesting aspect of the report was noted last. A bullet had been found in the chest cavity. No more detailed description was given, but it had been passed to the *Kripos* representative at the autopsy. Wisting flicked through his notes and found Erik Fossli's name, the ballistics expert who had phoned from *Kripos* to tell him that the gun he had handed in was a murder weapon.

Fossli showed immediate interest when Wisting introduced himself. 'Is there any news about the revolver used in Kristiansand?' Fossli asked.

'I don't know, but we've conducted a post mortem today.'

Fossli had obviously read that day's newspapers. 'The taxi driver?'

'Most probably. He hasn't been identified yet, but a bullet was found in his body.'

'What kind?'

'I don't know any more than that, but it's on its way from the Forensics Institute to your department. I'm just phoning to ask how quickly you can take a look at it.'

'I understand. They take so much time on the admission formalities here. Registration and request forms have to be filled out in triplicate before they are sent through the internal mail. I'll go straight up to the boys in the ID group and find out who was at the post mortem and get the bullet from him myself. You'll probably hear from me by tomorrow morning.'

Wisting thanked him, rounded off the conversation and lingered with the phone in his hand. The Hummel case was now officially a murder enquiry. He considered phoning Ryttingen in Kristiansand to even the score a little for his arrogance, but restrained himself. The court case would begin on Monday.

42

Line sat in the sunshine outside the police station. Sofie's interview was taking longer than hers. They had arranged in advance what they were going to say. It wasn't so much a matter of lying or withholding information, but of leaving out some details. Frank Mandt's safe contained documentation about his criminal activity and contact network. Even six months after his death, the information would be of interest to the police, but Sofie was reluctant to let them have it. It was not that she did not want to blacken her grandfather's name, but that she feared what might follow. Her grandfather had inflicted enough pain and sorrow on her while he lived. He would not be allowed to do it after his death.

Line understood, but at the same time felt slightly disloyal towards her father.

They had agreed to talk about the revolver and the discoloured banknotes, which Wisting knew about already. If the police asked to examine the remaining contents, Line would answer that this was up to Sofie, while Sofie would tell them that she had got rid of it all. That was actually a lie. The papers were still inside the safe.

The question had not been asked of Line. The investigator was mostly concerned about getting what they already knew down on paper.

She glanced at the tall brick building. Her father was inside somewhere, pursuing Jens Hummel's killer. It appeared that he believed there was a connection between the two cases. She had not spoken to him since the discovery of the body, and had no wish to visit him now.

In her job as a crime reporter she had covered several enquiries

166

in which she had written about suspects who had coordinated their statements. As a rule, it meant that they had something to hide. At least that was how it had to be interpreted, that they had lied to the police. The complicity damaged the investigation, but finally implicated the conspirators when they were caught.

The entrance doors of the police station slid open and Sofie came out with Maja in her pushchair.

Line stood up. 'How did it go?'

'Okay, but it wasn't pleasant. They asked all sorts of questions about the Old Man, just as if I was expected to have known him. I couldn't really answer any of them.'

'Shall we find a café?' Line suggested.

'Great idea.'

They walked towards the square. Sofie received a phone call and, when Line took charge of the pushchair, it occurred to her that she was looking forward to pushing her own pram. Maybe she ought to buy one under Sofie's guidance.

Line steered the pushchair into the backyard of what had once been a glazier's workshop with Sofie a few metres behind, talking into her mobile phone. She chose a table where the pushchair could sit in the shade beside them. Sofie ended her conversation and sat opposite. 'That was my lawyer,' she said.

'Have you engaged a lawyer?'

'Not because of this,' Sofie said, waving her hand in the direction of the police station. 'I have to go to a meeting in Oslo next week about parental rights and access. Could you look after Maja for me? I don't want to take her to a meeting like that.'

'Of course,' Line said, beaming.

A waiter appeared. Sofie took the menu. 'Did they tell you any more about what this is all about? I mean, you've worked on things like this for the newspaper and know something about how the police think.'

Line waited until the waiter had left. 'I think what they have in mind is that there might be a connection between the New Year Murder and the Hummel case.'

167

'How's that?'

'The murder weapon from Kristiansand was found in your grandfather's safe, and Jens Hummel's car was found in his barn.'

'Maybe it has something to do with Phillip Goldheim?' Sofie said, studying the menu.

'Who?'

'Didn't they ask you about him?'

'No, who's he?'

'A guy down in Kristiansand. They wanted to know if the Old Man knew him, but I couldn't say. I've neither heard nor seen that name before.' Her gaze slid back to the menu. 'Have you?'

Line shook her head.

'I think I'll have the chicken salad.'

Line put down her menu. 'Me too. When was it you needed a babysitter?'

'On Tuesday.'

43

Wisting lifted the coffee jug before the machine was finished. Water spat out and sizzled on the hotplate while he poured coffee into his cup. He had a slight headache, as usual when he had too little sleep.

Christine Thiis came into the conference room. He raised the jug and asked if she would like some, but she shook her head. 'I have the Police Chief in my office. He wants to talk to you.'

Wisting followed her into her office at the end of the corridor.

Chief of Police Ivan Sundt remained seated and greeted him with only a nod. His office was in Tønsberg together with the rest of the district's administration and management. Only occasionally had he made the half-hour trip to the police station in Larvik.

Sundt was the seventh police chief Wisting had worked under. Introduced as a leader to face the force's social challenges and future change, one of his first actions had been to reorganise internal resource from criminal investigation to community policing. Wisting understood the need for a more visible and accessible force, but his personnel numbers were undermined when every lead had to be checked with accompanying paperwork.

'I came to hear how this Hummel case is going,' the Police Chief said. 'It was unresolved when I started in this post, and so it remains six months later.'

Wisting sat in the vacant chair, holding his cup in his hand. 'It's been one of the most challenging cases we've ever had.'

'The body's been found. Isn't that what you've been waiting for?'

'That does give us some answers, but also a few more questions.'

'Do you have a suspect?'

'Not as things currently stand.'

'A lot of people are starting to become impatient,' he said. 'Myself included.'

'We're waiting for the lab results following the post mortem and examination of the crime scene,' Wisting said. 'I'm hoping that the next few days will bring some progress.'

The Chief of Police stood up as if to indicate that he had said all he intended to. 'The court case against Dan Roger Brodin begins in Kristiansand on Monday. I understand you've been snooping around in their case documents. Whatever steps you take in your own enquiry, don't do anything to screw up the case down there. It's fully investigated and stands as an example of good, speedy and effective police work. Don't meddle unnecessarily in that enquiry.'

Wisting also got to his feet, still holding his coffee cup. 'There are a few unanswered questions . . .'

'There are always questions that we don't find answers to. I've been an Appeal Court judge for almost twenty years. Hypothetical doubt is not desirable in a courtroom. Don't do anything that might give grist to the defence counsel's mill.'

Wisting remained on his feet, gazing after him when he left. His coffee hadn't even had time to go cold.

44

The phone call from the ballistics technician at *Kripos* came immediately after eleven o'clock and was succinct. The gun that killed Jens Hummel was the same one that had been used in the New Year Murder.

Wisting gathered the investigators in the conference room, without telling them what it was about. He closed the door behind the last to arrive and flicked the switch that turned on the red light outside.

The others were seated, but Wisting stood, his legs astride behind his chair at the end of the table, like a sea captain about to change course. 'We're faced with an entirely new situation,' he said. 'We've found the gun that killed Jens Hummel.'

His words were met with puzzled looks. Wisting gave a brief account of the new test results that left no doubt that Jens Hummel and Elise Kittelsen had been murdered with the same gun, sitting again as conversation broke out round the table.

Elise Kittelsen was a random robbery victim and the perpetrator had already been caught. The Hummel case appeared to have links to organised crime. The victim in their case had been in Kristiansand at the same time as Elise Kittelsen was murdered.

'It could be as simple as that Jens Hummel found the weapon after the perpetrator threw it away,' Torunn Borg suggested. 'In that case, he would not be the first person to be murdered with his own gun.'

Christine Thiis glanced at Wisting, as if to remind him not to muddy the Kristiansand waters. Wisting did not feel convinced, but had to concede that Torunn Borg's theory was one that the legal system would find acceptable.

171

'If he was killed with his own weapon, that does not bring us any closer to the murderer,' he said, pushing the ballistics report across the table. 'The question that remains is: what was Jens Hummel doing in Kristiansand on New Year's Eve?'

Nils Hammer browsed through his folder. 'I think it may have something to do with Phillip Goldheim. The police in Kristiansand have collected a lot of material on him. I'm working to put it in order.'

'Good,' Wisting said. 'We should really concentrate on him.' He leafed through to a blank page in his notepad. 'Apart from that, is there any news from Brunla farm?'

'We're beginning to get an overview of everyone who had a horse in the stable there in January, or who had some other connection to the farm at that time,' said Torunn Borg. 'We have spoken to a few, but I doubt whether that's going to give us anything.'

The meeting went on for another half hour with discussions about links and connections. Fresh assignments were allocated before the meeting broke up, when Wisting returned to his own office and closed the door behind him. He knew that the police in Kristiansand had received the report about the comparison of the bullets in the two cases and had hoped that Harald Ryttingen would have phoned. Now it was Wisting who called him again.

He used his landline, which rang for some time. When Ryttingen finally took the call, he answered in an abrupt, toneless voice.

'I assume you've received the ballistics report,' Wisting said.

'Yes,' Ryttingen said.

'Have you any opinion about how this is all connected?'

'We've had this conversation before. There is no connection.'

'The same murder weapon was used in both crimes.'

'Those are just extraneous circumstances. It doesn't mean the two cases are connected.'

'I have a problem understanding what actually happened,' Wisting said. 'You have a fourteen-minute window of opportunity from the time the murder was committed until the

172

perpetrator was apprehended. In the course of that time the weapon changed hands, and a short time later it was used in another murder case nearly two hundred kilometres away.'

'No, the window of opportunity was much greater. It could have been found and picked up at any time in the course of the next few days.'

The police in Kristiansand had searched for the murder weapon throughout the night and during the following days. The map accompanying the report lay on the desk in front of Wisting with the search areas shaded in various colours. Nowhere had been overlooked. 'But where did he get rid of the gun?' Wisting asked.

'The same place that he disposed of her mobile phone.'

Wisting drew the map towards him. 'There are just so many unanswered questions. Have you contemplated postponing the court case?'

The question was greeted with a snort. 'We have irrefutable evidence in this case,' Ryttingen's voice rose. 'The perpetrator was caught just beside the crime scene, only minutes after the murder. Three eyewitnesses have pointed him out, and he had residue from the murder weapon on his right hand. In addition he had in his possession a map of the area. This case has run smoothly from the very first moment. Now it's going to run equally quickly and effectively through court. Hopefully, this can correct some of the impression the public have of an incompetent police force lacking in application.'

Wisting realised that this was a direct criticism of his handling of the Hummel case.

'What is it you want, actually?' Ryttingen asked.

'I want access to your null and void documents,' Wisting replied, 'the tip-offs and intelligence information.'

'Do you think we're hiding something?'

'I want to look at the information from our point of view and with my own eyes.'

'You think we've overlooked something? That you'll see something we didn't? Is that what you're saying? That you're better than us?'

173

'I just don't want to leave anything untested.'

Ryttingen gave a deep sigh. 'The information you're asking for is not stored electronically. It's in ring binders. I can get someone to copy them and send them to you next week.'

'I can come down and have a look at them,' Wisting suggested. The other end went quiet. 'Anyway, I want to come down and talk to him.' Wisting took out the photograph of the young accused.

'To whom?'

'Dan Roger Brodin.'

'Forget that. He's our man.'

'He's my witness,' Wisting said patiently. 'He's the last person we know was in possession of the gun that killed Jens Hummel.'

Harald Ryttingen was obviously irritated. 'Wisting, I thought you'd been instructed not to do anything to screw up this case?'

Wisting sat back. That was the same expression that the Chief of Police had used. There must be talk behind the scenes.

'Do you really think he'll tell you anything?' Ryttingen said. 'He denies having anything to do with the crime. How could he then tell you what he did with the revolver? That would mean he has to admit having used it. Do you think he'll confess to the murder just because you're the one doing the asking?' He snorted again. 'You're wasting your time. Dan Roger Brodin has refused to cooperate with the police from day one. But . . . by all means. Good luck!'

45

Line opened the double terrace doors and let sunlight into the living room. Standing with her back to the garden, she folded her arms. It had taken longer than she had estimated, but now, at last, the living room was completely redecorated. Her back was aching and she realised that she had perhaps taken on too much. She had not actually expected to receive much help from her father, but he had turned up whenever he could.

She put one hand on her belly. The movements were different now. The baby had become quieter, as if there was not much space left and it had become more difficult to move about in there.

The rest of the renovations would have to wait until after the birth, she thought. It was fast approaching and the nervousness she had felt at the beginning of her pregnancy was creeping back. There was nothing to be afraid of, the midwife had told her. Babies are born every single minute all round the world. However, for Line and all other first-time mothers, it was a completely new experience. Actually, she knew what scared her most. The actual labour was one thing, but the responsibility of being a single mother was even more frightening.

'Hello!' she heard her father shout from the front door.

'Hi,' she said, and went to greet him. 'Have you time to visit?'

'I brought some batteries for your doorbell,' he said, taking down the apparatus from above the front door, where it left a faded shadow on the wall.

'Have you time for a cup of coffee as well?'

'Yes, please,' he said. The batteries had leaked acid and were covered in a greyish-white coating. He picked up a screwdriver and began to scrape it clean.

'Is it a long time since you had a visitor?' he asked, blowing away the loosened verdigris.

'Luckily for you,' Line said, 'I think I have some ice cream cake left as well.'

She took out the ice cream and switched on the coffee machine. Before it was ready, she heard ringtones in the hallway.

They sat in the kitchen and chatted about the renovations until her father changed the subject. 'Have you spoken to Sofie today?'

Line shook her head. 'I'm going to see her this evening. Why do you ask?'

'I read your police statements.' Line had anticipated that. 'They were fine. Thanks for persuading her to come with you.'

'She totally dissociates herself from her grandfather and everything he was involved in,' Line said, going on to relate the story of how Sofie's mother was arrested with her grandfather's stash of drugs in the car. 'He let her take the rap. It ended with her mother committing suicide in prison.'

Absorbed in thought, Wisting sat with his spoon in his hand.

'Your ice cream's melting,' Line said. 'What are you thinking about?'

'Dan Roger Brodin.'

'Who?'

'The man charged with the New Year Murder. The court case begins on Monday.'

The name of the accused had not been publicised, but she had heard it at the newspaper office before she had left on maternity leave.

'I thought so,' Line said. 'We covered it extensively at the time.'

Wisting produced a folded sheet of paper from his back pocket. 'I've got something that might be of interest to them.'

Line recognised the *Kripos* logo on the paper he put down on the table. He placed his hand on it as he got to his feet. 'No need to say where you got it.'

'What is it?'

He did not answer, but instead moved abruptly to the door. 'Thanks for the coffee, and the ice cream cake.'

'Are you off already?' Line sat at the table, perplexed, while he made his way out. Then she drew the document over. It was a report from a specialist in the technical section at *Kripos* and had to do with the comparison of bullets. The technical details and descriptions confused her, but the contents were familiar. The bullet from the weapon used in the New Year Murder came from the revolver she had handed in to her father. She already knew that, but there was more. The bullet from the test firing of the gun that had been handed in was also identical to a bullet from case number 10899421 – the murder of Jens Hummel.

Line blinked and suddenly felt cold. Thoughts and questions raced through her head, and she wished her father had not left in such a hurry. She read the report one more time to be sure that she had understood the conclusion. However, it was unmistakable. The gun from the safe in Sofie's basement had been used in two homicides.

She stood up and began to clear the table. Her father had never given her information in this way before, but that was probably why he had come. It hadn't only been about the doorbell.

46

Carrying a pot of coffee into his office, Wisting immersed himself again in the Kristiansand murder documents, cross-checking names of witnesses and others against criminal records. Several of Elise Kittelsen's friends had a connection to the drugs scene in the city, and one who had given a statement was called Julian Broch. Some had described him as Elise's boyfriend, but he had described them as 'just good friends'. He had been previously sentenced for fraud and selling narcotics.

It gradually became clear that Elise Kittelsen had been on the periphery of a criminal environment, but there were no links to central figures such as Phillip Goldheim. Nothing suggested that she was anything other than an innocent victim.

At five to four, Christine Thiis entered, exactly one hour and forty minutes after he had left Line. 'VG phoned,' she said, sitting in the spare seat. 'They know about the revolver. That it was used in both murders.'

Wisting leaned back in his chair and fixed his gaze on his half-empty cup of coffee. 'Such things have a tendency to leak.'

'It looks as though they have access to the report.'

'It's not information we'd be able to withhold. The court case begins in Kristiansand on Monday. The police down there have obviously been required to familiarise the defence lawyer with the report.'

Christine Thiis shook her head despondently.

'What did you tell them?' Wisting asked.

'As little as possible. I confirmed it was the same weapon, and that it had been handed in after the death of the owner.'

'I don't suppose they contented themselves with that?'

'I had to tell them that the revolver had been kept in a safe since the owner died in January, and that it had only been found now.'

'Did you tell them about the robbery proceeds in the safe?'

'They wanted to know if anything else had been found in the safe. I told them that the police had only received the revolver.'

Wisting turned to his computer screen and clicked into the *Verdens Gang* online edition. The story had not been published yet. If they felt certain of being the only ones in possession of the news report, they might wait to print it in the paper edition the following day.

Christine Thiis stole a glance at his notes. 'What are your plans?'

'I'm going to Kristiansand early tomorrow morning.'

A furrow appeared at the bridge of her nose, as usually happened when she was sceptical. 'What are you going to do there?'

'Harald Ryttingen has given us access to the null and void documents,' he said, without telling her how he had achieved that. 'I'm going to go through the list of tip-offs.'

She said no more, but a movement of her head suggested she wanted to hear more.

'And I'm also going to interview a witness,' Wisting said.

'What witness?'

'Dan Roger Brodin.'

The furrow at the bridge of her nose disappeared as her eyes opened wide. 'The killer?'

'He's the only one who knows what became of the murder weapon. Only he will know of the connection to our case.'

'If there is a connection.'

'We can't leave that possibility untested.'

'Do you think he'll tell you anything?' she asked. The furrow was back. 'Do you think he will want to talk to you at all?'

Wisting pulled the coffee pot towards him. 'I've left a message on his lawyer's answering machine. I expect he'll phone me back as soon as he's read *VG*.'

Christine Thiis rose to her feet. 'I'm coming with you.'

179

47

It was Friday afternoon, and the usual sounds of phones ringing and office doors opening and closing gradually died away.
Slowly but surely the police station emptied of personnel. Wisting remained bowed over his case documents for another few
hours, but did not find any more answers.

At seven o'clock, he got into his car and drove out from the
backyard. On the seat beside him lay a map he had prepared of
Kristiansand's city centre streets and a printout of the statement
given by Finn Bjelkevik, one of the three main witnesses to the
New Year Murder. He lived in Sandefjord and had celebrated
New Year in Kristiansand. Wisting keyed in his address on his
GPS system and learned that it would take twenty-two minutes
to drive to his home.

According to the papers, he lived with his parents. It was not
certain that he would be there now, but a face-to-face meeting
was always better than a phone conversation.

Wisting drove down Prinsegata and took a left turn at the
traffic lights in Storgata. The summer evening was warm and
still, and he wound down the car window, listening as music
drifted in from one of the quayside restaurants. Finn Bjelkevik
and his friend had arrived on the scene immediately after the
shots were fired in Dronningens gate, and had seen Dan Roger
Brodin run from the incident. His statement had taken up less
than two pages.

Experience had taught Wisting that there were always details
and nuances in a witness's observations that had not been committed to paper: words that had been said, the order of events,
movements, reactions and thoughts. Although not everything
that happened appeared in black and white on an interview form,

180

Wisting had no expectations that a conversation with Bjelkevik would add anything new. His statement contained more than enough to convict Dan Roger Brodin of the murder. He was the nearest thing to an eyewitness you could get. He had heard the shots and seen Brodin flee the scene with a revolver in his hand. It was the revolver that Wisting wanted to know about most.

Satnav led Wisting into a well-maintained residential area on the west side of the Sandefjord Fjord. The house, a two-storey timber villa with rose bushes climbing the walls, was situated at the end of a cul-de-sac right down at the water's edge. He turned into the monoblock courtyard. Before stepping out of the car, he used his mobile phone to check the *VG* web pages. The news was now the top story, illustrated with a picture of Elise Kittelsen. The report had been broken less than seven minutes earlier. He began to read as a woman in her fifties emerged on to the steps.

He put the phone back in his pocket and approached her. It was Finn Bjelkevik's mother. He explained that his visit was related to the murder her son had witnessed.

'A dreadful business,' she said. 'I'll be glad when the court case is over.'

'Is he at home?'

'In the back garden.' She ushered Wisting through the house.

Finn Bjelkevik was standing beside the barbecue. From his reading of the case papers, Wisting knew that he was twenty-two. He was tall and sinewy with short sandy hair and glasses. At one end of a table, a girl of around the same age was seated. An older man arrived from a jetty down at the water's edge with a longhaired dog ambling behind him.

The mother explained who Wisting was and Wisting shook hands with them in turn. The girl was Finn Bjelkevik's girl-friend. The man with the dog was his father. Wisting guessed that none of them would have read the latest news and saw no reason to pass it on.

'Will you eat with us?' the father asked, glancing at the grill. 'There's more than enough.' The aroma of sizzling meat hung in the warm evening air.

'No thanks,' Wisting replied. 'I won't take long. I just want to go through what happened on New Year's Eve one more time.'

Finn Bjelkevik handed the grill fork to his father. 'I spoke to Ryttingen on the phone earlier today. We went through all of it then.'

The mother handed Wisting a glass of *Farris* mineral water with ice cubes. 'Thanks,' he said, smiling.

'We talked about how important it was that I appear absolutely certain,' Finn Bjelkevik continued. 'That I don't leave any room for doubt in court.'

Wisting had often prepared witnesses. Most of them had little or no experience of a courtroom. It was mainly a matter of making them familiar with practical details, such as where they should stand, where the prosecuting counsel would sit, where the accused would be and what the judge would ask about. He had never instructed witnesses about what they should say. He reminded them that it was important to express themselves with precision but, unlike Ryttingen, he usually asked them to leave room for doubt if they felt unsure.

They distanced themselves from the others, down at the edge of the fjord. 'Are you in doubt about what happened?' Wisting asked.

'Not really.'

Wisting paused, taking a drink from his glass. 'What do you mean by *not really*?'

'It all happened so fast, you see,' Finn Bjelkevik explained, continuing down to the little private jetty. 'I didn't manage to see much, but then of course they turned up with the killer in their car just afterwards.'

'Did you recognise him?'

The young lad picked up a stone and threw it into the sea. 'Right away.'

A gull took off from a spar buoy out in the sound. 'You're not in the courtroom now,' Wisting said. 'You don't need to be so positive.'

'I'd had a lot to drink. Terje got a better look at him than I did.'

'How much had you had to drink?' This was one of the questions that had not been posed during the official interview.

Finn Bjelkevik shrugged. 'I don't know,' he said. 'Six or seven beers, maybe, but I sobered up on the spot, you know. I mean, it was such a shock. A woman was shot and killed right in front of us.'

'Can we take it all one more time?' Wisting asked. 'What actually happened?'

The young boy sighed and glanced at his girlfriend. 'Well,' he said, composing himself. 'We'd been at Terje's house. He lives in Lund but we were going on to see a friend of his in the city. We walked around, just messing about and drinking. Terje had a rucksack with some beers and a little wine. We stopped so that I could fish out a couple of bottles from his bag. That was when we heard the bangs. Two sharp shots. First of all I thought it was fireworks, since it was New Year's Eve, but it was sort of different. I turned in the direction of the noise. The girl was already lying on the ground. I hadn't noticed her earlier, but she'd been walking towards us. The guy who shot her took a couple of steps back while he stuffed the gun into the waistband of his trousers. Then he turned on his heel and took off.'

Finn Bjelkevik threw out his arms as if to emphasise that this was the whole story.

'What happened after that?'

'We stood rooted to the spot for a couple of seconds. Then we looked at each other and ran over to her, but she was already dead. I lifted up her head to try to make contact, but it was as if there was nobody there. Her eyes were completely empty, and there were clots of blood coming out of her mouth. It was impossible to stop it.'

Wisting did not say anything.

'More people turned up,' Finn Bjelkevik said. 'First of all, the guy who ran after the man who'd done the shooting. I don't know if he was thinking of trying mouth-to-mouth resuscitation and that kind of cardiac massage thing or what, because he turned her on to her back, but it was completely hopeless.

Right after that, someone came who was a doctor. He said there wasn't anything more we could do.'

His voice had grown fainter as he spoke, and Wisting realised that telling the story again was like tearing open an old wound.

'The police arrived almost at once. It was all just chaotic. Terje and I sat in the back of a patrol car and waited. We listened to everything that was going on through the police radio. How they ran after the murderer and managed to catch him.'

Wisting stood, lost in thought. Most of what Finn Bjelkevik had told him he had already read in the case documents. He was not entirely sure what he had anticipated. 'The man who'd done the shooting . . . ,' he began, fumbling for a way to continue the conversation.

'Yes?'

'Could you describe him again?'

'A black, turtle-neck sweater with something written on it, a grey windcheater, dark trousers and blue trainers.'

Wisting nodded. On Dan Roger Brodin's sweater, the word *Magic* and the line drawing of a bird were printed.

'Had you seen him before?'

'No, but I'm not from Kristiansand.'

'What was the distance between you?'

The young man shrugged. 'We were standing outside an exercise studio or something like that. She was lying on the ground near the entrance to the school playground.'

Wisting was not familiar with the street layout. 'What would that mean?' he asked, pointing towards the jetty. 'Such as from here over to the boat?'

'Something like that.'

Approximately thirty metres. 'What were the light conditions?'

'It was fairly dark.'

'Were there streetlights?'

'There was a streetlamp almost exactly where she fell, but there was no light from it. The light came from the windows on the other side of the street.'

'Did he have anything with him?' Wisting asked. 'Was he carrying anything apart from the revolver?'

Finn Bjelkevik shook his head.

'Did he say anything?'

'Not a word.'

Wisting went on asking routine questions to which he had not found answers on the interview form. Most of the questions had, of course, already been posed, but the replies had been considered of such little interest that they had not been recorded. He did not make any notes either.

Little that was new had emerged, but all the same there was something about the conversation with Finn Bjelkevik that grated. Somewhere in the conversation, something had been said that unsettled him. He just could not quite isolate what it was.

48

Line sat with her laptop on her knee, having placed a cushion underneath so that it would balance securely. It had been a long time since she had logged herself into the newspaper's data system. The dashboard showed at any time how many people were on the web pages of *VG*'s online edition and showed that the murder weapon story was the most popular by far. Published not much more than two hours ago, it had already received more than 250,000 hits, more than most of her stories.

The newspaper spread was linked to the New Year Murder. Above an image of Elise Kittelsen they had placed the headline: *Mystery Murder Weapon Used Again.*

She would have to pretend to Sofie. She could not tell her that Wisting had given her the information, but as soon as the story was published she had phoned. She was afraid that Sofie would be angry as it was she, Line, who had persuaded her not to get rid of the revolver, but instead to hand it in to the police.

Sofie's reaction had not been as anticipated. She had sighed disconsolately, as if she constantly expected bad news, or else she simply did not understand how dramatic the story was. Perhaps she was just tired.

Line did not like words like mystery, puzzling and inexplicable being used in headlines to arouse curiosity and attract readers, but all three were totally apt when used to describe the revolver. Curiosity had driven her to examine the ring binders and notebooks in the safe, confirming what Sofie had already said, that her grandfather was a criminal, though his activities were on a larger scale than even Sofie had ever guessed.

She typed Frank Mandt into the search field to see if any of the journalists had saved the name in background material. The search produced one result. The name appeared in a folder with notes in connection with a series of articles on organised crime printed several years earlier. The journalist's name was Geir Hansen. She had only been on nodding terms with him. He had subsequently resigned and gone to work in the information department of some government enterprise or other.

She located the paragraph in which Mandt was mentioned.

Frank Mandt from Vestfold may have a central role. He is an older man who is best known for the import and sale of illegal spirits. Probably on his way out.

The short note with key words did not make her any the wiser. It was obvious that the journalist had a source inside the criminal fraternity, but the note did not mention any sources or basis. She struggled to remember some of the names she had seen in the ring binders in the safe. One of them was rather unusual, Aron Heisel.

She keyed it into the search engine. It came up with a number of references, and one of the case logs linked to his name was only a few days old. She frowned when she realised that it was in connection with the narcotics seized from the farm where Jens Hummel's taxi had been found. Her father had not mentioned his name, but Aron Heisel must be the man remanded in custody who refused to answer any of the police's questions.

The case log did not contain much more than had been summarised in print, apart from the name of the accused. The last time Aron Heisel had been mentioned was in connection with a major smuggling enquiry in Østfold three years previously, in which he had been picked out as one of several suspects, but not convicted.

One of the other names she recollected from the safe was Per Gregersen. It turned up in background material for the series of articles about organised crime together with Frank Mandt's name, and was mentioned almost incidentally in another paragraph: *Phillip Goldheim's original name was Per Gregersen.*

She scrolled up to read the entire section summarising the source's information:

Phillip Goldheim. Released after a lengthy sentence for drugs offences in 2002. Earlier he had worked closely with Hells Angels. Keeps a low profile. Laundering of drugs money. Built himself up as an investor. Purchase and sales of real estate. Vehicle imports. Shares. Shift to financial crimes. Fraud – use of shell companies, front men, false accounting. Still big in amphetamines. Major player in Sørland. Ambitions to become even more powerful. Network little known.

With a few more keystrokes she arrived at his photograph, taken during his last court case. He was neatly dressed in shirt and blazer, but a thick ponytail and ring in one ear suggested that this was not his everyday attire.

The doorbell rang before she managed to check whether the newspaper had any further information on Phillip Goldheim. Before she could get to her feet her father called her from the hallway. She answered, closing the laptop and setting it down on the table, and struggled to her feet to meet him.

Wisting stood with his shoes on in the doorway between the hall and the kitchen. 'I just wanted to let you know I'm going away this weekend,' he said.

'Where to?'

'Kristiansand. I'm setting off early in the morning.' He stole a glance at her stomach. 'Is that okay with you?'

Line nodded. 'Will you be away long?'

'Just till Sunday.'

Line stepped aside and used the kitchen table to support herself. 'How does this hang together? This information about the gun?'

'I don't know. That's why I'm going down there.'

'Has it created problems for you? The article, I mean.'

He smiled and shook his head. 'What creates problems is when somebody tries to keep things hidden. How did Sofie take it?'

'Fine.'

'What about you? What do you think?'

188

The thought that she had held a gun that had taken the lives of two people made her feel queasy. She changed the subject. 'Are you travelling alone?'

'Christine Thiis is coming with me.' He looked again at her bump. 'Call me if anything crops up.'

'Be careful.'

'You too.'

49

Wisting woke before the alarm clock and listened to the distant screeching of gulls before getting up.

The arrangement with Harald Ryttingen in Kristiansand was that a detective would meet them at the police station down there at ten o'clock. The drive from Larvik to Kristiansand took two and a half hours. That would give him plenty of time.

He spread jam on a slice of bread and sat at the kitchen table, eating as he watched the sky brighten and turn a clear summer blue.

It was not the gulls' screeching that had wakened him, but thoughts of the New Year Murder case. With the exception of the vanished murder weapon, it appeared a straightforward business that had progressed to a speedy, simple resolution. It had almost gone too quickly. The perpetrator had been apprehended before Ryttingen or any of the other investigators had been roused. When they first reported for work, they had merely followed the lines on which the enquiry had already been steered.

Wisting placed his empty cup and plate in the dishwasher before heading for the bathroom, where he shaved and took a shower before packing an overnight bag. Immediately after seven o'clock, he picked up Christine Thiis from outside her house.

The road was deserted. Neither of them said much. During the hours of morning, Wisting tried to think differently from the investigators in Kristiansand and had possibly arrived at a logical explanation for how the revolver had ended up in Larvik. However, it was premature to share his thoughts.

Outside the car, signposts with the names of small towns

on the south coast whizzed by: Risør, Tvedestrand, Arendal, Grimstad, Lillesand. Just after half past nine they turned off for Kristiansand. Before they drove to police headquarters, Wisting wanted to see the place where Elise Kittelsen had been killed. He manoeuvred through the grid system of streets to Dronningens gate.

Reading the documents he had not quite understood that she had been murdered outside the abandoned school in Kongens gate, though the address of the crime scene was Dronningens gate. Now he understood it better. The entrance to the school was located in Kongens gate, but the schoolyard faced out towards Dronningens gate. Elise Kittelsen had been shot in front of the opening in the wall around the playground. The case papers suggested that the perpetrator had been hiding there waiting for a prospective victim.

Wisting rolled slowly past and parked outside the exercise studio where Finn Bjelkevik had told him he and his friend had been standing when the shots were fired. He stepped out of the car and looked at the spot, recognising the street scene from the folder of photographs. The difference was that the pictures in the folder had been taken at night, with artificial illumination from floodlights and a few patches of snow on the pavement, whereas now the sun was shining and green leafy branches were hanging over the schoolyard wall.

Christine Thiis stood by his side. A young boy on a scratched skateboard rolled past them, wheels rumbling on the asphalt.

The distance to the spot where Elise Kittelsen had lain was about thirty metres as Finn Bjelkevik had said. As they walked forward to the crime scene, birds took off from the treetops. The old school buildings behind the wall looked empty and, in the schoolyard, they could see the outlines of a handball court, even though the vast empty space was now used as a car park.

Wisting stood where Elise Kittelsen had lain. From there he identified where the three witnesses and killer had been. Terje Moseid and Finn Bjelkevik had been walking towards her. Dan Roger Brodin had come out of the dark playground with the revolver raised. Einar Gjessing had come round the street corner twenty metres behind only seconds before the shots were fired.

Wisting took a side step and changed role. He raised his right arm and cocked his finger and thumb, as if holding a gun. Adopting the role of the killer, but instead of running, he walked with determined steps in the direction Brodin had run off. At the corner of Holbergs gate, he had passed Einar Gjessing who took up chase. His onward getaway had passed a music shop and diagonally crossed a small square that the case papers had called Olav Vs plass, and on down to Østre Strandgate where Einar Gjessing had abandoned pursuit.

The simple reconstruction was useful, but did not provide a different picture of the chain of events from that outlined in the reports.

At ten o'clock exactly they parked in front of the large police headquarters nearby in Tollbodgata. Stepping from the car, Wisting put his head back and peered up at the nine-storey-high concrete building. The two top floors belonged to the prison service and contained forty-four jail cells. Dan Roger Brodin was incarcerated in one of them.

They reported to a young uniformed police officer behind a glass window and, five minutes later, a man emerged from the lift to take them up to the criminal investigation department.

The detective was called Ivar Horne. Wisting recalled the name from the case papers. Scruffy, dressed in denim jeans and a white T-shirt, with unruly hair and stubble on his chin, his appearance contrasted with the tidiness and reliability of his reports.

'The documents are ready for you,' Horne said, leading them along a grey corridor. In one of the offices they passed, an investigator behind a computer screen did not look up. Slightly farther along the corridor, they heard the sound of a radio. Apart from that, the section was silent.

'Here,' Horne said, pushing open a conference room door. Three cardboard boxes were in the middle of the table, crammed with ring binders.

'I worked on that case myself,' he said as he headed for a

192

kitchen worktop at the far end of the room. 'What is it you're actually looking for?'

'A connection to Jens Hummel's murder,' Wisting said, picking up a blue ring binder marked *Interviews – drugs scene*.

Ivar Horne opened a cupboard above the sink and took out three white coffee mugs. 'What kind of connection?'

Wisting put down the folder, drew out a chair and sat down. Christine Thiis chose a seat opposite. 'These two cases are connected somehow,' Wisting said, 'in that the same weapon was used.'

Ivar Horne lifted the coffee pot off the machine and looked at them quizzically. Wisting nodded. 'In addition, there are other, slightly more tenuous connections.'

The local detective poured coffee. 'Such as what?'

'Firstly, we know that Jens Hummel was in Kristiansand on New Year's Eve. Second, an interesting name has cropped up in our enquiry. A man from Kristiansand.'

Ivar Horne returned the coffee pot to the machine. 'Who's that?' He took a seat at one end of the table.

'Phillip Goldheim.'

'PG?' Horne asked with raised eyebrows.

Wisting nodded.

'Yes, well, that is an interesting name,' Horne said, 'that I don't think you'll find in any of those folders.'

'What do you know about him?' Christine Thiis asked.

'He's mainly involved in the import and sales of narcotics under cover of different types of legal activity. He has operated for a number of years. We've made a few attempts to catch him, and were close on his heels six months ago.'

'What happened?'

'I don't know,' Horne said. 'We had an informant who pulled back and shut up. Most of it had been built round him. He was in a position to tell us about the next consignment and how we could link Phillip Goldheim to it.'

'Project Mister Nice Guy?'

'No more Mister Nice Guy,' Horne said, beaming.

Wisting lifted his mug to his mouth. 'You say that this took

193

place six months ago. When was this consignment actually supposed to arrive?'

'In the middle of January. The project was left in abeyance when we lost the informant, but now it's up and running again. We're carrying out a surveillance operation on him now.'

Wisting drank his coffee. The information police obtained from inside criminal circles was important. Informants usually played a major, crucial role in solving serious narcotics cases, a concealed method that neither courts nor defence lawyers were aware of, which could be a dangerous game. Informants had to violate the trust of people on whom they had information, and no one likes traitors. Mere rumour that someone had talked to the police could lead to reprisals. The safety of informants was crucial, and therefore it was an unwritten rule that police colleagues never revealed the identity of a source, even to one another.

Ivar Horne got to his feet, still holding his mug of coffee. 'I'll not detain you any longer,' he said. 'I'll be in the office across the corridor if you need anything.'

50

Wisting crossed to the kitchen worktop and refilled his mug. He had felt uncomfortable in his phone conversations with Harald Ryttingen, almost as if mocked and ridiculed. The detective who had met them now, on the other hand, had been extremely obliging and pleasant.

'Where do we begin?' Christine Thiis asked, bending over a cardboard box.

'Anywhere you like.' Wisting selected the ring binder of interviews of people involved in the drugs scene. It contained identical forms on which people involved in the narcotics milieu had given quick, informal statements about what they knew of Dan Roger Brodin. Detectives on the streets had filled out the forms by hand.

Wisting skimmed through the first few. What the police were obviously looking for was whether anyone had seen Brodin with a gun. The weapon was the loose thread in the case, and if anyone gave evidence that he had access to a gun the case against him would be considerably consolidated.

Several of the people interviewed did not know who Dan Roger Brodin was. Others had not seen him for a long time. Those who knew him described him as a pleasant boy and said that they could not comprehend him doing this.

Wisting's phone rang when he was halfway through, an unknown number. 'This is trainee lawyer Olav Müller,' the man said. 'I represent Dan Roger Brodin.'

He grabbed a pen and jotted down the name. In the case documents and newspaper coverage, it had been a celebrity lawyer who had fronted the case. 'I thought Kvammen was defending?'

'I'm working with Kvammen,' the trainee lawyer said. 'He was prevented from doing it. I've taken over the main responsibility and am going to be representing Brodin in court.'

'I see,' Wisting said. The star counsel now regarded the New Year Murder as a lost cause and had relegated Brodin's fate to a proxy.

'Thanks for returning my call.'

'You wanted to talk to me?'

'Yes, that is to say, I'd like to talk to Brodin.'

There was silence at the other end of the phone. Wisting waited for a reply to the effect that Brodin was not willing to give a statement to the police. 'Was it you who found the murder weapon?' the lawyer eventually asked.

'It was handed in to us. Tests showed it had also been used in our case.'

'Do you suspect Dan Roger Brodin of that murder as well?' Müller knew that Brodin had been in custody when Jens Hummel was murdered and his tone was slightly sarcastic.

'I suspect the case against Brodin is not exactly as the police in Kristiansand would like it to be,' Wisting replied.

'What does that mean?'

Wisting glanced at Christine Thiis, listening with a ballpoint pen in her mouth. 'It's too early for me to go into details,' he said. 'But there are obvious shortcomings in the investigation.'

'Brodin doesn't know any more than he has already stated. He wasn't the one who shot Elise Kittelsen.'

Wisting shifted in his seat. He would have to go further in his efforts to persuade Olav Müller to give him permission to meet his client. 'I'm working on a murder case with an unknown perpetrator. If what your client claims is true, then there could be a closer connection than simply that the same gun was used.'

'You mean that it could be the same perpetrator?'

'I mean that it's important for me to speak to Dan Roger Brodin.'

On the other side of the table, he heard a crunching sound as Christine Thiis chewed too hard on the plastic pen.

'I'm going to meet him in prison at three o'clock this afternoon,' said Müller. 'You can come with me then.'

Wisting's face lit up. He thanked him before hanging up.

Christine Thiis took the pen out of her mouth. 'Do you believe that?' she asked. 'That there's a closer connection between these two cases than the coincidence of the same gun being used?'

Wisting gazed at her, wondering if he should tell her what he thought about the connection between the two cases, but decided to leave it. 'I don't believe in coincidence,' he said.

51

Light from outside filtered through the venetian blinds, throwing shadow stripes on the conference table. Wisting and Christine Thiis sat on opposite sides, working their way through the ring binders, the silence between them broken only when one of them turned a page.

The papers were smooth and stiff, as if no one had leafed through them before or shown any interest in their information. At the corner of his eye, Wisting noticed when she made a note and sat with pen poised on her lower lip. 'Have you got something?' he asked.

'It's a tip-off from an employee in McDonald's in Markens gate. The guy who works there knows Dan Roger Brodin from junior high school. They were in the same class until Brodin moved away.'

'Yes?'

'He was working on the morning of New Year's Eve and remembers Brodin coming in to buy a hamburger. It was memorable because at first Brodin wanted to pay with a thousand-kroner note. They didn't have change.' She glanced down at the note again. 'There were more thousand-kroner notes in the bundle he stuffed back into his trouser pocket.'

Wisting leaned back in his chair. 'That seems unlikely.'

'It certainly doesn't chime with him robbing someone a few hours later. Maybe he's confused about the date?'

'What's his name?'

'Mathias Gaukestad.'

Wisting took out the ring binder of official case documents. He could not recall seeing that name before, nor could he find it on the list of witnesses. 'He hasn't been interviewed,' he said.

'Shouldn't he have been?'

Wisting did not answer. Instead he thumbed through to another document, the report of Dan Roger Brodin's arrest, where the time and place of his capture were stated, together with what clothes he had been wearing, and what possessions had been removed when he was searched in the custody suite. However, one detail had slipped past the radar. 'He had a total of 643 kroner on him when he was taken into custody,' he said. 'Something doesn't add up here.'

'What happened to the rest of the money?'

'Not only that. The entire case is built on the theory that this was a robbery that went wrong.'

'He was found guilty before of bag snatching and using a knife to threaten victims.'

'Those were instances when he was desperate to get money for drugs or needed money fast to repay debts to people threatening to kill him,' Wisting said. 'But that wasn't the situation on New Year's Eve. 643 kroner would have been enough for a fix that day and the next.' He indicated the ring binder open in front of her. 'He'd had more money earlier in the day.'

'So why haven't they followed up this information?'

Wisting closed the folder of case documents. 'Because it doesn't fit their theory.'

'Do you have a different theory?'

'Could Mathias Gaukestad have been mistaken?'

'What should we do?'

Wisting tore off a Post-it note, leaned over the table and attached it to the tip-off form in front of her. 'Continue,' he said, turning back to the forms detailing the individual interviews.

Five minutes later, he found something to support the witness in McDonald's. A girl of the same age involved in the local drugs scene said the same as the others, that she had never seen Dan Roger Brodin with a gun. In answer to the routine question about when she had seen him last, she replied that it had been at the *Amfisenter* shopping mall in Vågsbygd outside the city centre, two days before New Year's Eve. One sentence

199

referred to him having treated her at the *Kafé Seblis* on the first floor.

Wisting passed this information to Christine Thiis. 'It looks as if he had money after all,' he commented, tearing off another Post-it note. He attached it and continued to peruse the folder. Another girl from the local drugs scene, Leni Dyste, confirmed this. Her answers had only been noted as keywords on the form. Wisting read them aloud: '*Known Danny for years. Never seen/ heard anything about a gun. Saw him last, day before New Year's Eve, outside library. Had lots of money from a "job". Was to get more where that came from.*'

'What sort of job?' Christine Thiis asked.

'There's nothing more here,' Wisting said, checking for Leni Dyste's name on the witness list. 'She hasn't been formally interviewed either.'

Ivar Horne entered the room with an empty mug. 'Find anything interesting?' he asked, making for the coffee machine.

Wisting responded with an evasive 'Nyeah'. What they had found so far was flimsy and had no direct relevance to their own case.

'I don't think you'll find very much,' Horne said, filling his mug with coffee. 'It's a solid case.' Leaning against the kitchen worktop, he fixed his gaze on the boxes. 'What's ironic is that the main witness actually shouldn't have been there.'

'What do you mean?' Christine Thiis asked.

'Einar Gjessing,' Horne said. 'The guy who ran after the killer. He should really have been inside.'

Wisting leaned back, wanting to hear more.

'The finance group has been working on him for nearly a year,' Horne continued. 'I don't know much about that kind of thing, but he started a company involved in microcredit. Some sort of Internet-based lending company. It was called *P2P*, short for "person to person". The idea was that he arranged loans directly between individuals. Instead of putting your money into an ordinary bank, you made it accessible on his Internet pages to people who might not be able to obtain loans by the usual means. High interest rates and hidden costs for the person who needed the money, and huge risk of loss for the person who lent it. The only person who made any money out of it was Gjessing himself, of course.'

Wisting nodded. He had read about new operators who offered quick cash loans without security.

'It was the Financial Supervisory Authority who reported him, because he did not have a licence to run credit activities. He was accused of tax evasion, insufficient accounting procedures, fraud, money laundering and a few other financial crimes. Pretty comprehensive, with high prison tariffs.'

'Fraud and money laundering?' Wisting repeated.

'Yes, or participation in money laundering. Not all the money that ended up in his lending capital came from legal activities.'

'So your main witness has been convicted of fraud?'

Ivar Horne took a step forward and waved his coffee mug over the conference table. 'No, that's my point, you see. He was never convicted. Most of the charges were dropped.'

'What happened?'

'Harald Ryttingen was what happened.'

'Ryttingen?'

Ivar Horne's smile grew even broader. 'You know him,' he said, moving his mug to his other hand. 'At least you've spoken to him. He doesn't like to lose. Doesn't like to go into court without having a case all sewn up. The *P2P* case was complicated, with a host of reluctant witnesses, especially when it came to the money laundering part. A lot of resources and prestige had been tied up in it, but the outcome was far from certain, and so they entered an agreement. Einar Gjessing admitted the minor charges and received a lesser penalty than if he'd been convicted of everything. At the same time, we spared the courts months of work.'

'What was he convicted of in the end?' Christine Thiis asked.

'Something about not having a licence to operate and market financial services, and breach of tax regulations. He got six months, half of which was suspended and he was out before Christmas.'

The sound of a police siren reached them. Ivar Horne crossed to the window and looked out. 'Many of us here at the station thought it was blameworthy,' he added, turning to face them again. 'But the most important thing, of course, was to make sure Einar Gjessing's company was wound up. The ironic thing is, though, that if Ryttingen had done his job that time, then he wouldn't have a key witness now.'

'There are three eyewitnesses,' Christine Thiis reminded him.

'Yes, that's true,' Horne replied. 'But Gjessing was the only one who was sober, and the one who saw the perpetrator best. Brodin ran right past him.'

Wisting refrained from commenting on the professional abilities of the leader of the department he was visiting, and decided to change the subject. 'Do you know where we can get hold of Leni Dyste?'

'You can't, I'm afraid,' Horne answered quickly. 'She's dead. Took an overdose in May. Why do you ask?'

Wisting recounted the conversation one of the investigators had had with her the day after the murder.

'I hadn't picked up on that,' Horne admitted, reading the interview form for himself.

'Why would he attempt a straightforward robbery if he'd just done a well-paid job and there was more money where that came from?' Christine Thiis asked. 'And what became of the money?'

'Money doesn't last long in those circles,' Horne replied. 'But in this particular case, there's a logical explanation.'

'What's that?'

Horne was on his way to the door. 'That he spent it on a revolver.'

52

At two o'clock, Wisting rose from the table. 'We need a break,' he said, rubbing his dry eyes. 'I'll try to have a few words with Einar Gjessing before I meet Brodin in the prison.'

Christine Thiis leaned back in her chair. 'We'll have to eat,' she said, getting to her feet. 'I'll come with you.'

Ivar Horne appeared at the door again. 'Finished already?'

'Just a short break,' Wisting said. 'How long will you be here?'

'Ages.' Horne presented his business card. 'Call me when you're back and I'll come down and let you in.'

The car had overheated in the sun. Wisting switched the air conditioner to full blast and adjusted the vents so that air was blown directly at them. He flicked through his notebook, found the main witness's address and keyed it into the GPS.

Gjessing lived only a few minutes away from police head-quarters, in the Lund district on the other side of the Otra River. En route they stopped at a grocery outlet and bought a hotdog each. They sat down on a bench outside to eat.

'I'll go to the prison by myself,' Wisting said. 'Two members of the police force might be too much for him.'

Christine Thiis agreed. 'I can continue with the ring binders.'

They finished eating and got into the car again. The GPS led them on past old timber houses and down to an enormous apartment complex beside the river. They parked in the visitors' car park and walked along the rear of the building until they located the right entrance. Einar Gjessing was the top name on the doorbell panel. Wisting put his head back and peered up at the penthouse flat that was bathed in glorious sunshine.

'He must have made some money playing at bank managers,' Christine Thiis said as she rang the doorbell.

They stood waiting. A man with a dog walked by on the footpath. She tried the doorbell again and Wisting looked at his watch. 'We'll go and check in at the hotel,' he suggested. 'Then we can try him again tomorrow.'

A man in dark sunglasses and a white, short-sleeved shirt approached them as they turned to go back to the car. He took out a bunch of keys and headed for the door.

'Einar Gjessing?' Wisting asked.

The man took off his glasses. 'Who's asking?' he replied, smiling.

Wisting introduced himself and explained who Christine Thiis was. 'It's to do with the court case that starts next week,' he said.

'What about it?' Gjessing asked in a rough south-coast dialect. An irritated frown crossed his face.

'I know you've been over this many times, but do you have time to answer a few questions from us as well?'

Sighing, Gjessing inserted the key in the lock. 'You can come up with me.'

Two minutes later they were sitting at a table on the sunny roof terrace with an outlook over the city and the old fortress on Odderøya Island.

'You said you came from the Vestfold police?' Gjessing asked, setting glasses and cans of cold drinks on the table.

'We're investigating a different case,' Wisting said, going on to explain the connection between the New Year Murder and that of Jens Hummel.

'I read about that,' Gjessing said, hoisting a parasol before he sat down. The shade brought welcome relief.

Christine Thiis sat forward, perched on the edge of her chair. 'Can you tell us what happened on New Year's Eve?' she asked.

'I expect you've read my statement to the police? There's not much more to say than what's in that. I was on my way down to the Strand Promenade. Some friends had hired a function

204

room and I was walking along Holbergs gate and across the intersection at the old junior high school.' He paused to pick up a can of lemonade. 'You know what happened then.'

Christine Thiis accepted with thanks when he held up the can and offered to share. Wisting took one of the other cans and opened it.

'First of all, I thought it was just a couple having a quarrel. There's such a lot of that on New Year's Eve. Loads of people drinking, and loads of people quarrelling. The man had grabbed her arm, the one that was holding her bag. She pulled free, and that was when I saw the revolver. She'd already turned her back on him and started to run when he pointed it at her. A spurt of flame came out of the muzzle when he fired.'

Einar Gjessing put down his glass and made the shape of a gun with his thumb and index finger. 'Two shots,' he said, imitating the sound as he jerked his hand back. 'She fell on the ground. The man turned and ran towards me. I got such a shock that I just stood there. He ran past me. I didn't know what to do, so I ran after him, but I was wearing slippery shoes. I slid and fell a couple of times and he got away from me. So, I ran back to where it had happened instead, but by then it was already too late. Even if I had run over to her at once, there wouldn't have been anything I could have done. Besides, other people turned up.'

Wisting sat thinking, as if to create distance between the explanation Gjessing had given and the questions he was about to pose. 'When he fired,' he began, 'did he have the gun out, or did he pull it out after she had wriggled free?'

Einar Gjessing allowed for the same uncertainty he had voiced during his interview: 'It happened so fast,' he said, 'but I think he had it out the whole time. That he stood there threatening her with it, but I don't know whether that's just the impression I have, or whether that's how it actually happened.'

'Did you see what he did with the revolver?'

The man on the other side of the table flashed a crooked smile. 'Don't you think I would have told that to the police here in Kristiansand? It was one of the first things they asked me. They've been searching for it for weeks.'

'Of course,' Wisting said, returning his smile. 'I was thinking more of whether he ran off with it in his hand or stuffed it down his trousers or something like that.'

Einar Gjessing sat back and reflected. 'He had it in his hand when he ran past me,' he replied. 'I remember that very well, but afterwards he must have pushed it down his trousers because I remember him running with both hands free.'

'How far had he reached when you saw that his hands were free?'

'Not very far. To the fountain, I think.'

Wisting regretted not bringing a map, but remembered the fountain structure in the first side street. 'So he ran down the steps to Kongens gate,' Gjessing ploughed on. 'I didn't follow him much farther before I turned back.'

'How far is it from the place where he passed you down to the fountain?'

'Not far. Not much more than a hundred metres.'

'Could he have got rid of the gun along that stretch?'

'The police have looked for it.'

'I'm thinking about whether someone might have found it or picked it up before the police began their search,' Wisting said. 'Could he have thrown it away without you seeing that?'

'I doubt it.'

'You said you slipped and fell twice,' Christine Thiis reminded him. 'Where did that happen?'

'The first time was almost as soon as I started running. The next time was at the foot of the steps down from the square.'

Wisting waited for him to come to a conclusion himself.

'That fits,' Gjessing said, now slightly pensive. 'He could have got rid of it when I fell the first time. I glanced along Dronningens gate as well when I got up again, and saw that the two other witnesses were on their way over to the girl on the ground.'

'How far had he reached when you were on your feet again?'

'I guess he had a head start of fifty metres or so.'

'Did you see anyone else in the vicinity?'

Einar Gjessing shook his head.

'Vehicles?'

'There are usually a few cars parked behind the fountain, but I can't remember noticing any. Holbergs gate is a pedestrian street.'

'What about taxis?'

Gjessing shook his head. 'I would have remembered that. I had actually been looking for an available taxi.'

Christine Thiis sat up straight: 'You didn't see any taxis nearby?'

'No, you see, I had been to visit my mother up in Posebyen and had intended to take a taxi down to the Strand Promenade. There was a taxi in the street, right down from where my mother lives. The light on the taxi wasn't switched on, but there were no people inside so I tried to flag it down. It was only a matter of a kilometre or so, but it was a taxi from out of town, so the driver wasn't allowed to pick up passengers.'

Wisting glanced over at Christine Thiis. 'Where outside town did it come from?' he asked.

Gjessing shrugged.

'Exactly where were you when that happened?'

'I don't remember, but Mum lives in Tordenskjolds gate. It was probably a couple of blocks further down. In Skippergate, maybe, somewhere round there.'

'Do you remember what sort of car it was?' Christine Thiis asked.

'Not apart from that it was a taxi.'

'Colour?'

'Dark.'

'What did the driver look like?'

Gjessing shook his head.

'Well, you see, he only half-turned towards me when I opened the back door and sat inside. I've no idea what he looked like.'

'Glasses, beard, moustache?' Wisting asked.

Gjessing shook his head again.

207

'But it was a man?'

'Yes.'

'And he was alone in the car?'

'Yes, but it looked as if he was waiting for someone.'

Wisting felt sure that it had been Jens Hummel who had been waiting in the taxi. He was keen to know more, but could not hit upon any questions to bring them closer to an understanding of what Hummel had actually been doing that night. Instead he returned to the crime scene and asked the questions that had not been answered in his reading of the documents. 'Was anything shouted or said?'

'Elise shouted something,' Gjessing said. 'No or stop or something like that.'

Christine Thiis tilted her head to one side. 'Did you know the victim?'

Einar Gjessing cleared his throat and lifted his glass to his mouth. 'Elise Kittelsen?'

'Yes.'

'I didn't really know her very well, but I knew who she was. I didn't see who it was lying there. I didn't know that until the next day.'

'How did you know who she was?'

The sun had moved and was now shining directly in Einar Gjessing's face. He stood up and shifted the parasol to let them continue to sit in the shade.

'Through mutual acquaintances,' he said. 'She had a boyfriend who was a data analyst. He did some work for me a while ago, so I'd been introduced to her in the city once, but of course she was a lot younger than me.'

Wisting did not want to talk about Gjessing's company and what had led to him being charged and convicted. 'Tell me about what happened when you came back to the crime scene.'

Gjessing coughed. 'When I got there, there were only the two boys, but then it got chaotic with people coming from all directions. This doctor turned up and looked after the girl on the ground. The police arrived before the ambulance, but there wasn't much they could do. I told them where the gunman had gone, and what he looked like. They sent out a message and it didn't take long until they'd caught him.'

'They came back to the crime scene with him?'

'Yes, they wondered if I recognised him.'

'And did you?'

'Yes. He was sitting in the back of a patrol car. They asked me to take a look at him before they drove him to the station, to be quite sure.'

'And you were sure?'

Einar Gjessing picked up his glass again. 'Of course,' he answered. 'Who else would it be?'

53

The lift rumbled and shuddered on its ascent through the storeys. A young woman in a grey-blue prison officer's uniform greeted him. He handed her his police ID in exchange for a visitor's pass that he pinned to his breast pocket before she ushered him inside. A bunch of keys in her belt jingled as she walked. Halting in front of a massive wire grated door, she took out the correct key and let him in. The hinges squealed before the door slammed behind him.

In the centre of the wall, a red lamp shone above the door into a visitors' room. She knocked before opening. Two men were sitting inside. Trainee lawyer Olav Müller sat on a black leather settee beneath the window, wearing a pair of light, grey trousers and a white short-sleeved shirt. A document case sat by his side. Dan Roger Brodin had his back turned. His head was close-shaven and his shoulders narrow.

They stood up in unison. The lawyer held out his hand and introduced himself. Brodin greeted him silently. Behind them the prison officer locked the door. Wisting looked around and noticed toy-boxes on the floor, and that the carpet was patterned with streets and roads. Prisoners had children too.

'I've told Dan Roger what you said on the phone,' Müller said. 'That you're actually working on another case, in a different police district, where the same gun was used as in the case against him.'

Wisting pulled out a chair but waited until the others had resumed their seats before sitting down. 'That's right,' he said, telling them who he was and outlining the case.

Brodin stared at him while he spoke. His skinny face was tense. Serious.

'One way or another, the revolver was conveyed from Kristiansand to Larvik,' Müller summarised when Wisting stopped.

Brodin shrugged and began to pick at a scab on his lower arm. 'I don't know,' he said softly.

'What's your theory?' Müller asked Wisting.

'There are several possibilities,' Wisting replied. 'But the murder victim in our case was in Kristiansand on New Year's Eve. It's possible he's the one who took the weapon.'

Müller was making notes.

'Could he have been the one who shot her?' Brodin asked.

'We don't have any grounds for believing that,' Wisting said. 'But regardless of who did it, you were in the vicinity of the crime. The police arrested you only a few blocks away.'

'I heard the shots,' Brodin agreed. 'Or, I'm not sure, it could have been fireworks. There were loads of people letting off fireworks all evening. But it sounded like two clean shots.'

Wisting took out his thick notebook and the few case papers he had brought with him. What Dan Roger Brodin had just told him did not appear in any of the interviews. 'Where were you when you heard the shots?'

'Right up in Tollbodgata, I think,' Brodin answered.

Wisting pictured the map of the city centre in his mind's eye. Tollbodgata was parallel to Dronningens gate, where the shots had been fired. 'What were you doing there?'

The taciturn man facing him shrugged. 'Nothing.'

'What did you do afterwards?'

'After what?'

'After you heard the shots?'

'I just walked on.'

Müller interjected: 'Did anyone see you?'

'Probably. There were a few people out walking.'

'Anyone you knew?'

Brodin shook his head and went on picking at the wounds on his arms.

Wisting glanced across at the lawyer. He was too late, he thought. If he had really believed his client to be innocent, then this was a question he should have asked long ago. Now the

211

leads were cold. No one would remember enough to give him an alibi. 'Did you notice a taxi?'

'The guy who was shot in Larvik was a taxi driver,' Müller said, by way of support.

'I didn't notice anything other than the police car. It was probably on its way to the woman who was shot, but they turned when they saw me.'

'And that's when you ran?'

'Yes.'

Wisting had no wish to pry, but was bound to ask. 'Why was that?'

'Because they came after me.'

It was the same answer he had given in the first interview, when he had said that he had hidden so the police would not find him.

Müller cleared his throat: 'We've been through this with the investigators in the case. That wasn't what you were supposed to be asking about now.'

Wisting ignored him. A thought was beginning to take shape, and he leaned across the table. 'But why?' he repeated.

'I didn't want to go in again,' Brodin answered, gazing at the walls.

Wisting drew his chair even further forward. The young man facing him obviously did not understand the thrust of the question. 'Why would the police arrest you?'

Dan Roger Brodin looked in consternation at his lawyer and the bundle of case documents in front of him. 'I matched the description.'

Wisting nodded patiently. 'Yes, but you didn't know that then. So why did you run away if you hadn't done anything wrong?'

'I was out on parole, you see. I didn't want to go back inside again.'

Wisting leafed through his papers. 'You were released on probation on 22 December?'

Brodin nodded. The scab on his arm loosened and he wiped away a trickle of blood with the palm of his hand.

'The conditions for release were that you should abstain from all intoxicating substances?'

Brodin nodded again. Wisting produced the blood test results establishing that traces of cannabis had been found, and that he had 1.79 per mille of alcohol in his bloodstream when apprehended.

'So when you said in your statement that you ran away from the police because you were scared of being arrested, it was because you had broken the conditions of your release on parole?'

Brodin nodded again, as if it had been obvious to everyone from the very beginning. 'I'd just got out.'

The lawyer glanced across at Wisting's papers and produced the same documents from his own bundle. He opened his mouth to speak, but sat in silence.

The air was already hot and stuffy in the small room. Wisting looked over at the windows, but naturally they could not be opened. 'I need to ask you about something else as well.'

Dan Roger Brodin looked at his defence counsel, as if to obtain permission. Olav Müller nodded. Wisting sat back in his chair with the notes on his lap. He would have to take this step by step.

'Do you know someone called Mathias Gaukestad?'

The man accused of murder seemed confused.

'Yes?'

'In what way?'

'From junior high school.'

Wisting nodded. 'Do you know where he works now?'

'At McDonald's.'

'Do you remember that you were in McDonald's on New Year's Eve?'

Brodin hesitated. 'Maybe.'

'Mathias Gaukestad remembers you,' Wisting said. 'He says you tried to pay with a thousand-kroner note.'

It looked as if something had dawned on the young man. Müller thumbed through the list of witnesses. 'Where are you now?' he asked Wisting.

'This is from the log of tip-offs. You won't find it in your copy set.'

He turned to face Brodin again. 'Leni Dyste says the same thing. You met her at the *Amfisenter* in Vågsbygd a couple of days earlier. You had a lot of money on you and you treated her at the *Kafé Seblis*.'

'Leni's dead,' Brodin told him.

'I know that,' Wisting said. 'But she said you had been well paid for a job.'

The lawyer shifted in his seat. Wisting could see he was sceptical about drawing his client into a relationship that had anything to do with money. 'Does this have anything to do with the case?' he asked.

Wisting appreciated his reluctance to touch on a topic that could cast suspicion on his client, but Müller obviously did not understand the whole connection.

'You were convicted of robbing people before,' Wisting explained. 'This case also looks like a robbery, but the point is that you did not have any obvious reason to rob Elise Kittelsen if you had already been well paid for a job.'

Both the defence lawyer and his client sat in silence.

'Can we take a break?' Olav Müller requested, getting to his feet. 'I need to have a private chat with Dan Roger.'

Wisting agreed. The thought that had struck him had obviously also struck the lawyer. The job Dan Roger Brodin had been paid for might well have been the murder of Elise Kittelsen.

54

When the defence lawyer pressed the button on the intercom beside the door, there was an immediate buzz on the loudspeaker. 'Guard speaking.'

Müller explained the situation and the need to let Wisting leave the room. It took some time before they heard keys rattling outside and a different prison officer opened the door. Wisting followed him to a break room where he was offered a cup of coffee. He had really had more than his fill, but accepted with thanks mainly to pass the time.

'Did he say anything more?' the prison officer asked as he handed Wisting a cardboard beaker.

'He was a bit more forthcoming.'

'He hasn't confessed, has he?'

Wisting smiled and drank his coffee instead of answering.

'Most of them here are innocent, of course,' the officer said with a nod in the direction of the board where the names of the inmates were listed. 'Even when the opposite has been proven.'

Wisting crossed to the window. The city outside had more than double the number of inhabitants than his own town. He was a stranger here. All towns and cities have their own pulse, their own personality, with which it took time to become familiar. Kristiansand seemed to be a quiet, almost sleepy city, but here too there were currents below the surface. Here too crime was on the march, more complex and organised, crossing all borders, than ever before.

'This is the first time he's had anyone to see him since the date for the court case was fixed,' the prison officer said, sitting on a deep settee.

'Who is it who comes to see him?'

'Mainly lawyers or someone from the prison visiting service.'

'No family or friends?'

The prison officer shook his head. 'I don't think he has so many. His mother was in here a couple of years ago. I don't expect she'll come back again of her own free will.' He leaned over the table and drank his own coffee. 'But come to think of it,' he went on, 'he visited her. One hour every Wednesday. You could almost set your watch by him.'

The radio on his belt crackled. The officer fumbled to release it and gave a confirmatory reply before glancing over at Wisting again. 'I think this is the fourth or fifth lawyer who's been here. He's not even really a lawyer yet, just a trainee. Of course, it's not unusual to have a change of lawyers, but it's usually at the client's request.'

Wisting nodded. Hijacking clients was a known problem. All of the legal firms wanted court cases that gave them publicity. Individual lawyers used their own clients to put in a good word for them among those remanded in custody, so that they could acquire a larger circle of customers.

'They usually want Kvammen, Elden, Meling or some other celebrity lawyer when they're arrested,' the officer added. 'But when the case is no longer in the public eye, then it's the lackeys that turn up.'

Wisting turned again towards the window. Four different lawyers from the same office meant that Dan Roger Brodin was no longer of any interest to them. The New Year Murder was a lost cause in which all sympathy lay with the victim. The radio crackled again. The two men in the visitors' room were ready.

Wisting threw the rest of his coffee down the sink and discarded the beaker in the rubbish bin before following the prison officer back along the grey corridors.

Dan Roger Brodin and his lawyer were sitting in the same places as before. It was impossible to read anything in their faces. Wisting thanked the officer who had accompanied him, entered the room and sat down. The door was locked behind

216

him. Olav Müller gave his client a brief nod. 'Tell him about the money,' he said.

Brodin swallowed noisily. 'I stole a container,' he said, eyes fixed on the table.

Without uttering a word, Wisting waited for him to elaborate.

'It was a theft to order,' Müller explained when nothing further was forthcoming. 'A container full of fireworks. He got ten thousand kroner for the job.'

'It was in the newspapers afterwards,' Brodin informed them, picking at the sores on his arms again.

Wisting looked over at Müller and back to Brodin. 'You're aware that for this to have any value as evidence in court, you'll have to tell us who gave you the money?'

Brodin shifted in his seat. 'I don't know his name. It was somebody else who gave me the job.'

'And who was that?'

'Somebody called Stikkan, or at least that's what he's known as.'

Wisting sat back. The theft had nothing to do with his case. It was a circumstance Brodin and his defence counsel were obliged to ask the Kristiansand police to investigate more closely if they wanted to use it in court. 'How do you know him?' he asked nevertheless.

'He's from Arendal. We were in prison together once.'

A sunbeam had sneaked in through the window on the wall, catching Brodin in the face.

'He came with a big lorry, late on Christmas Eve,' he went on, moving away from the sunlight. 'He had a map with him, told me how I was to do it and where I was to deliver the lorry.'

'Did anyone see you?' Müller asked. 'Were you with anybody on Christmas Eve?'

'I was at *Shalam*.'

'*Shalam*? What's that?'

'It's a Christian organisation. They serve Christmas dinner to people like me.'

217

Wisting cast his mind back to his own Christmas dinner. There had been Line, his father and himself. The close family, but all the same it had felt empty and lonely. 'Weren't you at your mother's?' he asked.

Dan Roger Brodin shook his head. 'It didn't suit.'

'Did anyone see you taking the lorry? Are there any witnesses who can confirm your story?'

'No, it happened after that. Late at night. There's nobody out at that time, late at night on Christmas Eve.'

'What did you do with the money?'

'Spent it.'

'On what?'

'All sorts of stuff. Paid off some debts and that kind of thing. Most of it was gone in a couple of days.'

'You had 643 kroner on you when you were arrested.'

'I took some of the fireworks as well. Sold some on the side.'

Wisting sat lost in thought, turning over in his mind whether what had now emerged had any significance. There were witnesses who could confirm that Brodin had money over the Christmas period, but even though his lawyer should get hold of Stikkan and get him to confirm the story, it did not mean anything other than a slight shift in relation to the question of guilt. There were still three eyewitnesses to the murder.

'That was why I ran off,' Brodin added.

'What do you mean?'

'It wasn't just that business about being out on parole. I'd just lit a barrage and tossed it into a rubbish container. It made a huge bang when it exploded, and sprayed green and red all over the place.'

Müller leaned forward: 'Where was this rubbish container?'

'At the bus stop outside the *Kiwi* supermarket,' Brodin replied. 'It went on fire, so I ran away.'

'Was there much damage?'

His client shrugged, not seeing or understanding where the lawyer was going with the question. If anyone had reported damage and the fire brigade had been called, he might have something like an alibi. At least, something to disturb the police's timeline.

'How long after that did you hear the shots?' Müller asked.

Brodin answered in his usual fashion, with a shrug of the shoulders.

'Five minutes?' the lawyer suggested.

'A bit more than that.'

Wisting leaned back again, observing them both. Dan Roger Brodin picked distractedly at the scabs on his arms, while the trainee lawyer tried to extract as much information from him as possible. However, though there should be a report of a burnt-out rubbish container somewhere, it would not be of much value in the forthcoming court case. The defence counsel would accentuate how illogical it was for Dan Roger Brodin to be playing with fireworks only minutes prior to a brutal robbery, while the prosecutor would claim that the story about the rubbish container could have its origin in something Brodin had seen on his way to the crime scene and which he only now had incorporated into his own statement.

'Did you have any more fireworks?' Müller asked.

'I had a little store. There were a few barrages left.'

'Where was this store?'

'In an electricity substation down by the Otra. There's a loose grating in an air space at the back.' A smile formed on Müller's lips.

'Could the fireworks still be there?'

Brodin heaved his shoulders. 'If nobody's been there, I suppose.'

The defence lawyer was enthusiastic. 'If the fireworks are still there, they reinforce your explanation. You weren't in the city centre to commit a robbery. You had money, and were about to earn even more by selling the stolen fireworks.'

Another scab on Dan Roger Brodin's arm loosened. For the first time, something had been said to spark his interest. 'Will they believe that? Are they going to believe me?'

'If we find the rockets.'

Müller took out a sheet of paper and asked his client to

draw a map that showed where the fireworks were hidden. The pen sped across the paper.

Wisting did not share Müller's optimism. The fireworks story was only a tiny counterweight to the prosecution's list of evidence. In the best case scenario, it had the ability to disturb and create some distraction from the otherwise extremely straight line of the prosecution's case, but these developments could also be used in the opposite direction. Dan Roger Brodin knew the city well, knew where he could hide a small store of fireworks. He must also know where he could hide a revolver so that the police could not find it but where other criminals could pick it up.

Müller grabbed his document case as if he had received a message that his time was up. 'Are you coming?' he asked, turning to face Wisting.

'Where?'

'To see if the fireworks are still there. I can't do it by myself. I need a trustworthy witness, and doubt whether anyone from the police here will show up.'

Wisting glanced at the time. The meeting with Brodin had not taken him any further on the trail of the gun, and there were still several hundred documents to examine.

'It'll only take a few minutes,' the trainee lawyer said, opening his document case.

'Okay,' Wisting agreed.

Olav Müller removed a sheet of paper from his case and handed it to Wisting before packing his case papers inside.

'What's this?' Wisting asked, but understood in a flash.

'Just some advance warning.'

It was a copy of a letter to the Public Prosecutor in which the legal firm requested that Chief Inspector William Wisting be summoned as a witness in the case against Dan Roger Brodin.

'But the court case starts on Monday,' Wisting protested. 'Do you think the Public Prosecutor will go along with that? It's short notice.'

'The murder weapon only turned up recently,' Müller replied. 'Besides, they won't allow a postponement. This is a prestigious case for the police to demonstrate their efficiency and energy. They'd actually have preferred to have the case called before summer.'

Wisting folded the letter. The defence lawyer approached the intercom system on the wall and reported that the meeting with Dan Roger Brodin was over.

55

Olav Müller lit a cigarette as soon as they were out on the pavement. He pinched it between his lips and studied the map Dan Roger Brodin had sketched. 'We might as well walk,' he said, pointing in the direction of the river. 'It's only a couple of blocks.'

Wisting agreed. A heavy, warm haze drifted above the asphalt, blurring the streetscape. 'Have you had many cases like this?' he asked.

Müller flicked some ash from his cigarette. 'What do you mean?'

'Murder cases.'

'Not on my own. I've a couple of months to go before I get my own practising certificate. This case will give me good experience of procedure.'

'You could have chosen a simpler case.'

'It would have been easier if he'd confessed,' Müller agreed. 'Or if there were some grounds I could plead. But we've been through that. He denies having anything to do with the killing.'

They walked on in silence. The buildings on either side of the street were grimy with exhaust fumes and dust from the road. Wisting wondered whether the lawyer actually had any studied strategy. It was one thing to point out deficiencies in the police investigation and demonstrate weaknesses in the evidence but he would have to present an alternative explanation to the court. In practice, it was not sufficient to sow doubt. If anyone were to believe in his client's innocence he would have to present an explanation that made sense of all the evidence and provided an alternative interpretation. Above all, he should also be able to finger an alternative perpetrator.

'It's going to come down to the assessment of sentence,' Müller said, as if he had read Wisting's thoughts. 'That's where I'll have something to contribute. He hasn't had it easy, you know.'

The rest of what he said was lost in the dust whipped up by a bus stopping to set down passengers, but Wisting understood that the strategy was psychological and depended on generating sympathy for the accused. Telling them that Dan Roger Brodin was a victim with a difficult childhood, and that he had never received any of the help or treatment he needed.

The street ended at a fenced-off children's playground, a small park and a jetty down by the river. A group of children were playing on the swings. Müller threw away his cigarette and checked the map Brodin had drawn.

'Down there,' he said, pointing at a grey brick structure underneath a silver birch. The walls were covered in graffiti. He pushed some branches aside and skirted round to the rear of the substation. 'Here's the grating!'

'You should take a photograph before we remove it,' Wisting suggested.

'Yes, of course.' Müller took out his mobile phone and held it up. A beer can had been crushed and pressed between the metal bars on the grating. More rubbish was lying on the ground. Wisting prodded a used syringe with the tip of his toe.

The trainee lawyer inserted his fingers between the bars and rocked the grating. Plaster loosened at the corners. 'It's off,' he cried triumphantly as he tugged it out.

Wisting drew closer.

Müller put the grating aside and used the torch on his mobile phone to light the space inside. It was no more than thirty centimetres deep, but had been hollowed out in both directions. He pointed the light first in one direction, then the other. There was nothing to be seen.

56

A pizza box had appeared on the table in the conference room at police headquarters. Christine Thiis laid aside a ring binder when Wisting entered. 'How did it go?' she asked.

Wisting took a slice of pizza. 'He doesn't know anything about the revolver. At any rate nothing he wanted to tell me.' He sat down and told her about the theft of the fireworks.

'A criminal alibi!'

Wisting agreed. It had happened before, that an accused was acquitted of one offence because he had committed another at the same point in time. 'It's not an alibi though,' he said. 'He had time and opportunity to do both.'

'But do you believe him?'

'If we had found the rest of the fireworks where he said he had hidden them, then that would have supported his story.' Wisting shrugged the way Dan Roger Brodin had done for the entire duration of their interview. 'Either somebody has found them, or his story doesn't add up.'

'But it does add up that the theft was committed in the way he said?'

'He said it had been in the newspapers. He could have hit on the idea there, but I don't see any reason for him to come up with a yarn that doesn't place him farther away from the crime scene.'

Christine Thiis turned to her laptop and tracked down the online version of the local newspaper. Wisting read over her shoulder as he ate. Fireworks worth more than 100,000 kroner had been stolen from a container in Lund. It had been parked with no identification marks or direct access, so the police assumed that the perpetrators had known where it was and what it contained. 'Have you seen the map?'

'What map?'

Wisting wiped his fingers and leafed through the documents. 'Ryttingen stated in a newspaper interview that the attack on Elise Kittelsen had probably been carefully planned. Brodin had a map of the crime scene in his trouser pocket.'

He found what he was looking for, an evidence report with a list of the items the accused had on his person at the time of his arrest. *Map of crime scene* was entered as evidence item A-3, found in the accused's right back pocket. 'That map.'

She shook her head.

'It must be in this ring binder here,' she said, pulling out a slim green folder marked *Evidence – copies*.

The folder functioned as a practical reference book for the investigators. All the documents were copied so that the personnel working on the enquiry had no need to sign out evidence from the store room every time they wanted to look again. The same applied to receipts, memos and keys or other small articles that could be placed on the glass plate of a photocopy machine.

Christine Thiis thumbed through to the map, the kind you came across in hotel receptions and could tear off a pad. The copy had obvious creases and stains where it had been folded.

'Is anything marked off?' Wisting asked, studying the grid pattern of streets with her. The original had presumably been in colour and A3 format. The map they were faced with was in black and white and had been scaled down to A4 to fit the size of the folder.

'Doesn't look like it.'

Wisting removed the map. 'It says in the report that it's a map of the crime scene, but this is of the whole city.'

He folded the sheet in the same way that the original must have been folded. On the part that was turned out, the streets ran parallel to one another, and the site outside the disused school where Elise Kittelsen had been murdered lay roughly in the middle. When he turned it the other way round, the district of Lund, where the fireworks had been stolen, was approximately in the centre. 'This could be the map he got from Stikkan.'

225

'Stikkan?'

'The guy who gave Dan Roger the job. He pointed out the location of the container on a map for him.'

'What does he say about the map in his interview?'

Wisting took out the ring binder with the case documents and flicked through to Brodin's statement.

'The accused was shown the map found in his right back pocket, evidence item A-3,' he read aloud. *'He explains that he has had it for a while, but had forgotten about it. Does not know where he got it.'*

'It does actually seem more logical that someone has pointed out a burglary site for him on the map rather than that he has used it to plan an attack,' Christine Thiis said.

Wisting closed the ring binder in front of him and sat absorbed in his thoughts.

'What do you think?' she asked.

He hesitated before answering. At the back of his mind he had held a thought for some time that he had been afraid to share with others. Now the time was ripe.

'I think Dan Roger Brodin is innocent,' he said in a subdued voice, gazing at Ivar Horne in his office across the corridor. 'I think they intend to send an innocent man to court.'

It looked as though Christine Thiis was in two minds whether to believe that he meant what he said, or that he was joking.

'The map may prove nothing,' she said. 'But there are three eyewitnesses, and he had residue from the murder weapon on his hands.'

'Did he?'

She rolled her eyes. 'Well, it says so in the reports.'

'It doesn't say that it's from the murder weapon.'

'No, of course not. But gunpowder residue is gunpowder residue.'

'Exactly,' Wisting agreed. 'I think the gunpowder on Brodin's hands could have come from the fireworks, and not from the murder weapon.'

She sat with her mouth half-open. As the logic of this alternative explanation dawned on her, she slumped in her chair and exhaled slowly. 'Wouldn't there be different chemical components and compounds in gun residue as opposed to the gunpowder used in fireworks?'

'Probably,' Wisting replied. 'But that hasn't been checked. Anyway, they didn't have the gun to take reference samples from. Until now.' He stood up. 'Have you heard of ordeal by fire?'

'Yes,' she answered, though she did not understand what he meant. 'It's a tough, difficult trial.'

'But do you know where the expression originates?'

She shook her head.

'It's from an ancient Babylonian legal system. Ordeal by fire was a technique for establishing guilt. The accused person had to lick a red-hot spoon that had been drawn out of the fire, and the priest would examine the tongue for signs left there by the gods. Guilty or innocent? The wounds on the tongue were what decided, and that differentiated between life and death.'

He picked up the map and unfolded it.

'You would think that the judicial system had changed in that time, but it's still about interpreting signs and assigning meaning to what we see. It's not just a matter of police work. We judge and evaluate all the time, assess other people according to the kind of clothes they wear, what sort of car they drive, where they live, what level of education they have and their employment. Sometimes we're right, and other times we're wrong. Maybe we're wrong when it comes to Dan Roger Brodin.'

Christine Thiis got to her feet and took the ring binder of tip-offs from one of the boxes on the table.

'Then maybe this will be of interest,' she said, flicking through to the appropriate page before presenting it to Wisting. It was a form for telephone tip-offs, dated 2 January. In the column for name, *Anonymous* was entered, but in the next column, a phone number was listed. In the field for tip-offs there was only one sentence: *You have arrested the wrong man.*

It was inane, an empty assertion, and most investigators would not even have gone to the bother of jotting it down, far

227

less holding on to it. Probably it had been a conscientious office employee who had taken the phone call, or an inexperienced police trainee.

'It was phoned in from Larvik,' she said, pointing at the column with the phone number, a landline.

'Have you checked it?' Wisting asked.

She returned to her laptop and keyed in the eight figures. 'Unlisted.'

'Put Hammer on to it.'

'But we still have three eyewitnesses,' she said.

Wisting pulled out a chair and flopped down in front of the boxes of case papers.

'I know that,' he sighed. 'But if we're going to solve our own case, we'll have to solve this one first.'

57

With a dull headache grumbling behind his eyes, Wisting pushed the papers aside, crossed over to the worktop and took a glass from the cupboard and turned on the tap.

False testimony could be found in every case, was what ran through his mind as he let the water flow. Not because anyone consciously wanted to lie to the police, but because someone thought they had seen something they actually had not. Witnesses confused imagined events with factual ones. The memory was affected by previous experience, what other people said and the way questions were asked. Even if you were present, important things could have slipped your attention. It was normal. The human brain was not designed for detailed recollection, and in an interview situation you were usually faced with unrealistic expectations of what you had committed to memory.

As an investigator, it could often be difficult to know what to believe. The witnesses who were most credible were usually the ones who spoke well for themselves and appeared certain. Poor vocabulary and incoherent presentation had a certain effect on trustworthiness, but trustworthiness was not the same as reliability. He filled his glass and drank deeply, the cold water clearing his head.

Christine Thiis peered up from the bundle of papers facing her.

'Have you seen that film with the gorilla?' Wisting asked.

'*King Kong?*'

He laughed. 'No, I'm thinking about witness psychology. There's a film of a basketball court with five players in each team. They showed it at a course I was on. Before they start the film, you are told to count how many times the players in white throw the ball to one another. In the middle of the game, a man in a gorilla costume comes on to the pitch. Afterwards, there are no questions about how many passes there were, but whether anyone noticed anything else. Very few people have spotted the gorilla.'

Christine Thiis was unsure why he had told this story.

'It demonstrates how unobservant we are. That something quite crucial can be missed because we are engrossed in something else.' He sat at the table again. 'And that's mainly how it is when we are preoccupied.'

She put the end of her pencil in her mouth. 'People have sharp memories when it comes to dramatic situations. I don't think the witnesses in this case were concentrating on anything other than what was happening right in front of their eyes.'

Wisting did not respond.

'What are you thinking about?' she asked.

'About a mail coach that was robbed in France at the end of the eighteenth century. There were dozens of eyewitnesses, and seven people were recognised. They were convicted and hanged for the robbery, all of them, even though none of the witnesses had seen more than five perpetrators.'

Christine Thiis shifted the pencil to the other corner of her mouth. 'You mean that all three witnesses in this case could be mistaken?'

Wisting placed the three witness statements side by side on the table in front of him.

'They're too alike,' he said, lifting the picture of Dan Roger Brodin when he was arrested. A skinny, ungainly young man with scared eyes.

'All three witnesses have described him in almost identical fashion,' he went on. 'If it's the same interviewer who is talking to all the witnesses one after another, then he might transfer aspects and descriptions from one witness to another, but these three have been interviewed by three different investigators. Nevertheless, the descriptions agree.'

230

'From my point of view in the courtroom, that's a dream situation.'

'But what you dream of is not normally true. Even if three people have seen the same incident, they have three different experiences of it.'

She stood up, skirted the table and stood by his side while she read the descriptions given by the three eyewitnesses. Wisting knew them by heart. The perpetrator had a Nordic appearance, was about twenty-five, approximately five foot nine, slim with short, blond hair and dressed in a black, turtle-necked sweater with writing on the front, a grey windcheater, dark trousers and blue trainers.

'I see what you mean,' she said. 'The two friends had time to talk to each other before they were interviewed. They were seated in the back of a police car and could have influenced each other.'

Wisting looked again at the statement given by Terje Moseid, of the two friends the one he had not made contact with. 'I think I want to talk to him as well, before we pack it in for the day.'

'Shall I come with you?'

'Please do.'

Wisting took another slice of pizza on the way out. Ivar Horne glanced up from his desk on the opposite side of the corridor.

'We'll be back,' Wisting told him. 'Will you be here until late?'

'Just call me when you want in again. We've got a surveillance operation on a mutual acquaintance of ours, so I'll be here until he's gone to bed for the night.'

'Phillip Goldheim?'

'The very one. Mister Nice Guy himself.'

Wisting was going to ask what it was all about, but was interrupted by Christine Thiis' mobile phone.

'Hammer,' she said, looking at the display.

They walked towards the lift. She answered in monosyllables and ended the conversation as the lift doors opened. 'He's traced that 331 number. The phone box at the railway station.'

Wisting gazed at the ceiling as the lift descended. 'So somebody phoned from a phone box in Larvik to tell the investigators in Kristiansand that they'd arrested the wrong man,' he said, unsure how much weight they should attach to that.

'I didn't think there were phone boxes any longer.'

The lift stopped and the doors slid open. Two uniformed policemen stood discussing something with a bare-chested man in the corridor. They walked past them in silence and headed for the car. When they were seated inside, Christine Thiis voiced what they were both thinking. 'If Brodin is the wrong man, then who is the guilty party?'

Wisting cast his eye over the huge police headquarters. 'I don't know,' he said. 'But we don't have much time to find out.'

58

This time Wisting phoned first, to make an appointment with the third witness. The number was listed among the personal details given on the interview form. Terje Moseid answered after the third ring, wind and engine noise in the background. Wisting introduced himself and explained that it had to do with the court case starting next week. 'Do you have time to meet me for a brief chat?'

'I'm on my way in with my boat now.'

'Where are you tying up?'

'In Tresse.'

Wisting knew where that was. Tresse was the city's party locale, in the middle of the Strand Promenade.

'We can be there in ten minutes.'

'That's not actually very convenient,' Moseid said.

'It'll be quickly over and done with. I'll meet you at the harbour.'

Before Moseid had time to protest, Wisting had turned on the ignition and moved off.

The sun was low in the sky, and the shadows of the boat masts stretched far inland. Wisting drove to the quayside and stopped the car. Four or five young people were on their way ashore from a V-shaped boat with a massive engine. Christine Thiis put on her sunglasses. Wisting followed her out of the car and went to meet the group.

'Terje Moseid?' he asked, looking at a young man with whitened teeth and suntanned complexion.

'That's me.' Moseid moved his bag to his left hand to facilitate a handshake.

Wisting introduced himself and presented Christine Thiis. Moseid asked the others to go over to the car and wait.

'The murder weapon has turned up,' Wisting said, 'which opens up a lot of new questions.'

'I saw that in the newspapers.' Moseid put down his bag.

'I wonder if we could go through it all again. If you can tell me what you saw and did that evening.'

Moseid glanced at his friends. 'I don't know anything about the weapon,' he said. 'I didn't see anything other than that he ran off with it.'

'Can you take it from the beginning?'

Moseid sighed and began a well-practised statement. He had apparently not only repeated it to the police in his hometown, but also to his family and friends. Wisting listened without interrupting. The statement was detailed when it referred to the blood and what he and his friend had done to try to save the life of the woman who had been shot, but vague about the perpetrator and the direction in which he had fled. 'Most of my attention was on her,' he said.

'Can you describe him?' Christine Thiis asked.

One of the boys over at the car shouted a message. Terje Moseid used his hand to indicate that he had heard it. Then he rattled off the same description that had been written on the interview form. 'Afterwards they drove him over,' he concluded.

'You recognised him? Can you confirm that?' Christine Thiis asked.

'Of course it was him. It all went so fast, all of it. But it was him. The police had caught him, you see. He sat there in handcuffs and all that. Tall and thin, with the same clothes.'

'Did you talk to each other when you sat waiting in the back of the police car?' she asked. 'Did you discuss what you had seen and experienced?'

'Of course, but we mostly sat listening to the police radio. They were chasing the guy through the streets.'

A mild sea breeze sent ripples over the water, making the tall oak trees whisper as the leaves rustled.

A thought occurred to Wisting. Terje Moseid's description of the perpetrator had been given according to the formulation used by police when reporting a missing person. He was described by gender, ethnicity, age, height, body type, hair and what he was wearing. The clothing was described from the inside out, from top to bottom, completely according to the textbook, with the clothes underneath before the outside layer, and the clothes at the upper part of the body before the lower part, down to the footwear. 'You didn't answer my question.'

'What question?'

'Did you recognise him when the police drove there with him?'

'Not really,' Moseid admitted. 'But he answered the description.'

Wisting took a step forward. 'What description?'

'The one they relayed on the police radio. They repeated it twice.'

A nerve on Wisting's temple began to pulse. He took out the copy of the police interview and showed it to the young man facing him, pointing out the paragraph containing the description.

'When you say that the perpetrator has a Nordic appearance, is twenty-five years of age and wearing a black, turtleneck sweater with writing on the front, it's not because you've seen that, but because you heard the description on the police radio?'

Terje Moseid threw out his arms. 'That was what he looked like. I saw that when they drove up with him. They caught him just nearby.'

Wisting lowered the papers. 'But was that what the man who fired the shots looked like?'

Terje Moseid picked up his bag and began to walk towards the car. 'That's what I'm standing here telling you,' he said, shaking his head glumly.

'No,' Wisting said, blocking his path. 'You say the man the police arrested fitted the description you heard on the police radio, but was it the same man that you saw?'

Moseid peered down at Wisting's forefinger pointing at his chest. The interview printout was crumpled in Wisting's hand. 'I've already said that I didn't see him very well. That other guy saw him much better than we did. He ran right past him. He even ran after him. He was the one the police spoke to when they sent out the description.'

Gulls were squawking in the harbour behind them.

'Okay, then,' Wisting said, letting his hand sink. 'Thanks for your assistance.'

Terje Moseid looked at him in confusion before slinging his bag on his back. 'It's only in the movies that police arrest the wrong person,' he said, heading towards his waiting friends.

'This changes the whole case,' Christine Thiis said, removing her sunglasses.

Wisting looked directly into her eyes. 'There aren't three eyewitnesses,' he said. 'There's only one.'

'We need to talk to the people responsible for this case,' she said. 'About this and about the fireworks.'

'Not yet,' Wisting replied, noting how reluctant he felt to speak to Harald Ryttingen. 'We need an alternative answer first. We must be able to point to someone else.'

59

The balmy summer evening covered the city like a soothing blanket. People who were out and about moved slowly through the streets of the city centre. At an intersection, Wisting braked for a dog that sauntered on to the road, crossing the street with its tongue lolling and its tail down.

When the car moved off again, he noticed a *Kiwi* supermarket up ahead, with green rubbish containers on either side of the entrance, hard plastic of the type usually used in public places. One looked slightly cleaner and newer than the other.

The shop was still open. Wisting turned the car and parked at the pavement. 'I'll just go and see if it's true,' he said, pointing at one of the rubbish bins. 'If one of them was blown up on New Year's Eve.'

'I'll wait here.'

He left the key in the ignition. The air was filled with the smell of asphalt cooling after a long, hot summer's day. Only one of the checkouts was open. A young girl with lilac streaks in her hair was buying a frozen pizza, cola and potato crisps. Wisting waited until she had paid before approaching the boy at the checkout and showing him his police ID. 'I've a short but rather strange question,' he said. 'Do you know if one of the rubbish bins outside was damaged by fireworks on New Year's Eve?'

The boy looked at him oddly.

'Someone's supposed to have set off a barrage of fireworks in one of the rubbish bins.'

The boy shook his head. 'I've just got a summer job here,' he explained.

Wisting peered into the interior of the shop. 'Is there somebody else here who might know about it?'

'Karsten probably does. He's the shop manager. Do you want me to call him?'

'Yes, please.'

The boy pressed a button three times in rapid succession. Farther inside the shop, a bell rang. Wisting stepped aside and let a woman with a full trolley pass.

A man with glasses and a beard, dressed in the supermarket chain's green uniform appeared between the shelves. He looked round and made eye contact with Wisting.

'Police,' he said, showing his ID again. 'I'm wondering if one of your rubbish bins was vandalised on New Year's Eve?'

The shop manager looked past Wisting and out to the pavement. 'Why are you wondering about that now?'

'It's in connection with another case,' Wisting said. 'An unconfirmed detail in connection with a murder.'

The manager nodded his head, but did not appear to understand the link.

'The court case begins next week,' Wisting added.

'Yes, that's right,' the shop manager confirmed, adjusting some bars of chocolate on the nearest shelf. 'Some idiot or other lit a big barrage of fireworks and dropped it into the rubbish bin. It could have been really nasty.'

'Was the fire brigade called?'

'No, the fire died out by itself, but it made a good blaze for quite a while. The whole container was damaged, cracked and blackened with soot. I had to buy a new one. They cost nearly eight thousand kroner.'

'Did you report it to the police?'

'I filled out a form, but nothing happened. The excess on the insurance policy is ten thousand, more than the cost of the damage.' He glanced at the CCTV camera on the ceiling. 'I have pictures of the guy who did it, if you're interested?'

Wisting was more than interested. 'You have pictures?'

'In my office.'

He ushered Wisting past shelves of packets and tins of soup into a crammed office at the far end of the premises. Food that had gone out of date was stacked on the floor, as well as old newspapers and magazines. The walls were covered in notes about ordering procedures, emails from suppliers and unframed photographs of the staff. The breeze from a table fan fluttered the notices.

He sat behind a desk and moved a couple of unwashed cups. The computer screen was divided into eight squares, one for each camera in the shop. None seemed to be mounted internally, but one showed the customers as they entered. The push doors closed behind a young woman in a tracksuit, and Wisting could see the two green rubbish bins outside. 'The actual film has been deleted,' he explained, opening a drawer, 'but I have printouts.'

He took out a grey envelope and withdrew a bundle of colour printouts. The top one showed an inferno of light that the camera lens had difficulty coping with. The next two images showed the same blinding intensity.

'I took this myself in daylight,' he said, showing a photo of the damaged rubbish container.

The next picture showed the remains of the burned-out barrage of fireworks. At the bottom corner the manufacturer's name was legible. *Svea.* According to the article in the local newspaper, this was the same manufacturer as the fireworks stolen at Christmas.

'Do you have any pictures of the person who put the fireworks in there?' Wisting asked.

The manager leafed through the sheets and handed him the entire bundle that showed a man at the side of the container. The printouts had been produced on ordinary copy paper, and neither it nor the printer was of the best quality. Besides, the shot had been taken from inside the supermarket and out through the glass doors. The light above the entrance helped, but the image was not clear enough to identify the person.

Wisting flicked through to a picture that showed the perpetrator arriving with a box under his arm. Just a grey shape, but the physique reminded him of Dan Roger Brodin. In the next picture he was even closer to the camera and it looked as if he was walking with his jacket open. The sweater underneath had

239

an indistinct white pattern on it. Dan Roger had been wearing a black sweater with the drawing of a bird and the word *Magic*.

'Did you attach these pictures to your complaint?'

'It was a bit tricky to capture the right files from the computer, but I did write in the report that we had CCTV cameras.'

Wisting pondered this. 'Is the clock at the right time?' he asked. The time information in the top right-hand corner of the printout gave the date as 31.12, and the time was 20:09:09. Almost an hour after Elise Kittelsen was shot, which could not possibly be right.

'Not quite,' the manager said, peering at the computer screen. The digital clock top right showed 20:35:47. 'It's an hour out. We don't adjust it for summer and winter time.'

'But it's right now, in the summer?'

'Approximately, at least.'

Wisting took out his mobile phone. Linked to the Internet, it always showed the correct time. It was now 20:33. He waited with it in his hand until the numbers flipped over to 20:34. The time on the surveillance screen showed 20:36:11.

'Two minutes and eleven seconds fast,' he concluded, figuring out that if he made allowances for wintertime, the fireworks in the rubbish container had gone off at 19.07. Elise Kittelsen had been murdered at 19.21. The margins were tiny. It gave Brodin time and opportunity to be in both places, but made it more likely that he ran from the police because of the vandalism to the rubbish bin rather than the murder.

The shop manager sat back in his chair. 'What's this actually all about?'

Wisting did not want to go into any detail. 'We're charting a chain of events,' he said. 'Everything that we can place on a timeline is of interest.'

The manager seemed satisfied. 'Just keep the printouts,' he said, taking a business card from a pile under the computer screen. 'Phone me if there's anything else.'

60

The air in the conference room in police headquarters had cooled while they were out. Wisting took out the folder with the pictures taken of Dan Roger Brodin when he was arrested, and compared them with the CCTV image.

'I see why he didn't go to the bother of attaching these pictures to his complaint,' Christine Thiis commented. 'They're completely unusable.'

'It's impossible to see who it is,' Wisting agreed, 'but the possibility that it is Brodin can't be excluded. The height and frame match, and the clothes.' He pointed at the white script on his sweater and moved his finger to the unclear surveillance photo. 'There's something white here too.'

She picked up the printout. 'Isn't it possible to work on this somehow to improve it?'

Wisting shook his head. 'The original digital file's been deleted, and even if we had an electronic version, we would never produce an image suitable for identification purposes.'

'What do we do now?'

Wisting sat down. 'We need to look at this with a fresh pair of eyes,' he said, glancing at the case papers on the table.

'I thought we were the fresh eyes,' she remarked tersely.

'Yes indeed, but until a few hours ago, we also thought that Brodin was the perpetrator. The theory assumes that Elise Kittelsen was a random victim in a robbery that went wrong. If he wasn't the one who killed her, she might have been a specific target.'

'Why would anyone want to kill her?'

'I don't know,' he admitted. 'But that's the point. The investigators have looked at Brodin in depth and drawn a picture of a violent habitual offender, but we know very little about Elise Kittelsen. She went to college and wanted to become a teacher, she worked in her parents' shoe shop, was pretty and popular among her friends, that's about it.'

He glanced through the door to the office on the other side of the corridor where Ivar Horne was sitting in front of a computer. 'That's the picture of the victim that Harald Ryttingen wants to take with him into the courtroom on Monday,' he said. 'If we scrape off that surface, some of the sympathy for the victim might disappear, but we might also find a motive.'

He sat back and viewed the investigation material. An introductory, crucial question in every murder enquiry was whether the victim had been killed because he or she was a specific person, or whether the victim could have been any other person who happened to be in the wrong place at the wrong time. In the New Year Murder case, it was assumed that Elise Kittelsen was a chance victim. That had shaped all the subsequent enquiries.

'Her brother thought she was hanging out with the wrong crowd,' Christine Thiis recalled, browsing through the ring binder of interviews with family and friends. 'He didn't like her boyfriend, among other things.'

'He has an alibi,' Wisting said. 'He was already at the party Elise was going to.' He got to his feet, moved round the table and stood behind her.

'Here he is,' she said. 'Julian Broch.'

They read the interview together. Julian Broch dismissed the idea that he and Elise were a couple, but explained that they were good friends and had known each other for just over a year. He was nearly six years older than Elise and worked in a shipping office. He gave an account of his own movements and the plans he and Elise had for New Year's Eve. The party they should have attended together was at the home of one of his friends, and the partygoers were mainly old friends of his.

'These were the people her brother didn't like,' Christine Thiis explained. 'Several of them were involved in drugs.'

'Do we have her log of phone calls somewhere?'

Christine Thiis stood up and leaned over one of the boxes on the table. 'I saw a report that had to do with the search for her phone,' she said, and took out the document she was referring to.

Wisting had read the report earlier. It was included in the case papers to which he had obtained electronic access from his own office. The murderer had taken Elise Kittelsen's mobile phone but had got rid of it, probably when he realised that it was traceable. The report concluded that the phone was no longer connected to the telephone network.

The report contained an overview of the people Elise Kittelsen had been in contact with via her phone on the actual day of the murder. There were text messages and brief calls to and from her girlfriends, and a longer conversation with her cousin in Lyngdal as well as some data traffic for use of the Internet. Immediately after seven o'clock, she had sent a text message to Julian Broch and received a reply. The messages had been discussed when her boyfriend had given a statement to the police. He had shown the text messages in which she had written *Leaving home now. See you soon*, and he had replied *Fine. Looking forward to seeing you*. Both messages were peppered with little smiley faces.

'Maybe we should speak to him?' Christine Thiis suggested.

'Tomorrow. Now I think we'll finish for today.'

He lifted a ring binder he had not yet looked at, to give himself something to work on in his hotel room.

Christine Thiis tidied the papers on the table a little before packing up her laptop and following him into the corridor. Ivar Horne swivelled his chair towards them and stretched his arms above his head, cracking his shoulder joints.

'Are you any the wiser now?' he asked, with a smile.

Wisting did not reply, but stood looking at the picture that filled the computer screen in front of Horne. A man in a suit was on his way into a car. His hair was cut short and he looked very fit. There was something familiar about him. 'Who's that?'

Ivar Horne followed his gaze to the screen.

'That?' he answered. 'That's Mister Nice Guy in person.'

'Phillip Goldheim?'

'Yep.'

Wisting had seen the photo in the criminal records, taken when Phillip Goldheim had been arrested more than fifteen years ago. At that time he had been heavier and had his hair in a ponytail. 'Do you have any more photos of him?'

'Hundreds,' Horne replied, opening a folder of pictures.

Wisting leaned closer to the screen and studied the images. They had been taken in a variety of situations and from various angles.

'Can you enlarge that?' Wisting requested, pointing at a picture of Goldheim with his back turned, talking to two younger men.

Horne did as he was asked. 'Do you know them?'

Wisting did not answer that. 'How long have you been tailing him?' he asked instead.

'We've been monitoring him for three weeks, but during the present phase we're only following him from time to time.'

'By monitoring, do you mean monitoring his communications?'

'Tapping and tracing his phone, yes,' Horne said.

'Do you have an electronic trace on him for Wednesday last week?'

Ivar Horne turned towards another computer screen and grabbed the mouse. 'May I ask what it's to do with?' he said, searching through the files.

'I've seen that back before,' Wisting explained, pointing at the surveillance photograph. 'In a field at home in Larvik.'

Ivar Horne turned and gazed quizzically at him. Wisting told him about the potato cellar in the field behind the barn where Jens Hummel's taxi had been located, and the twelve kilos of amphetamines that had been discovered there. 'Someone was there to check whether we had found the consignment after Aron Heisel was arrested. It could have been Phillip Goldheim who ran away from us.'

Horne managed to find the right data file. 'You could be right,' he said, scrolling down the Excel document on the screen. The columns showed dates and times, who he had called or sent a text message to, who had contacted him and where he had been when the phone was used. They could see how he had travelled out of Kristiansand just after twelve o'clock, followed the E18 road northwards, passed Grimstad at half past twelve, Gjerstad an hour later and reached Larvik at 15.37.

'Who did he speak to when he was in Larvik?' Wisting asked.

'His girlfriend,' Horne answered. 'She phones or sends a message about twenty times a day. Handy for us as we usually want to know where he is.'

'What did he do afterwards?' Christine Thiis asked.

'Not easy to say. It looks as if he switched off his mobile phone. It wasn't in use again until he returned to Kristiansand at eight o'clock that night. We didn't have the box on then, or we could have followed him really precisely.'

'The box?'

Wisting let Ivar Horne explain. The box was a term undercover detectives used for electronic surveillance of a vehicle. It stemmed from the time when the tracking unit was a large and heavy box that had to be attached to the car with strong magnets. The equipment was costly and had limited battery capacity, and it was a challenge to place it without it being discovered. Nowadays the equipment used was the size of a thumbnail, required little power and had pinpoint accuracy when giving location information.

Horne brought up a map program to demonstrate. A red dot stood still on an address in Andøya, less than a mile from the centre.

'He's at home.'

'What sort of car does he drive?' Wisting asked.

'A Range Rover.'

'Then they weren't using his car. They disappeared in some kind of Japanese car.'

Christine Thiis addressed herself to Wisting. 'We have some footprints from the floor in the potato cellar, don't we?'

Wisting nodded.

'Is that investigation material we can have access to?' Horne asked.

'Of course. We have a man in custody who refuses to talk to us. You might want to run his name through your system: Aron Heisel.'

Horne keyed the name into the search field in the locked project database. 'He's here.'

It was an intelligence note from October the previous year. The subject was *Phillip Goldheim – contact in Spain.*

Wisting leaned forward in front of the screen. The actual note was not more than a few lines: *Source says that Phillip Goldheim has returned to Norway after a weekend trip to Marbella. He has had a meeting with a Norwegian who has been living there for a number of years – Aron Heisel. The purpose of the meeting is unknown. Heisel was previously convicted of smuggling spirits.*

The information was classified as having a high degree of reliability, indicating that the informant was tried and tested and was trusted, because accurate information had been provided before.

'Where did the information come from?' Wisting asked. 'Whoever told you might know more about our case.'

Ivar Horne clicked on the tab for more information on the source. What came up was a standard text about the source being contactable via the person who had entered the information.

'It's Robert Hansson,' Horne said. 'He worked here in the department. Then it might be the main source we had, the one who broke off contact. It was Robert who was the handler.'

'Where is Robert Hansson now?'

'In Haiti,' Horne replied. 'Some UN project for the police there.'

'Can you get hold of him?'

'I can send him an email.'

At that moment, a signal arrived on the computer screen with the surveillance map. The red dot marking Phillip Goldheim's car was blinking. At the same time, the police radio on the table crackled into life.

'*Object is moving.*'

'*Received,*' was the answer given.

Ivar Horne snatched up the radio and got to his feet. 'We're intending to hang on to him tonight. Do you want to tag along?'

61

Wisting joined Ivar Horne in the anonymous surveillance vehicle while Christine Thiis returned to the hotel. He wanted to see Phillip Goldheim for himself and to check if he could recognise him from the chase through the field at Huken. The undercover detectives reported that Goldheim was heading into the city, but had stopped at a petrol station.

Horne fiddled with an iPad while he drove and a map appeared on the screen. He scanned it quickly and handed it to Wisting. 'The goods you impounded in the potato cellar match with our information. Goldheim has suffered a substantial loss and needs to make a few moves to cover that. Whoever he's going to meet tonight could prove very interesting.'

Wisting agreed. Electronic surveillance was effective and economical, but the undercover detectives were still dependent on a presence out in the field.

'Any contact?' Horne enquired through the police radio.

'*Negative,*' was the answer. '*He's eating a burger.*'

'It's not going to take place there,' Wisting said. 'Not in front of CCTV cameras at the petrol station.'

'You're right. We can pick him up here if he drives towards the city.'

He turned off, drove under a motorway bridge and stopped at a layby beside the main road.

Wisting checked the screen. The red dot was still at rest beside route 456 at a place called Auglandsbukta. A green dot marked their own location, and three blue dots showed the other units.

'How do you envisage the connection between your case and our man?' Horne asked as he reversed the car behind a boat on a trailer.

'The common denominator is Frank Mandt, everything revolves around him. The murder weapon in both cases was locked in his safe when he died, and the taxi belonging to our murder victim was found on a smallholding on which he had a long lease. Aron Heisel lived on that same smallholding, and Heisel is linked to the consignment of amphetamines in the potato cellar. Goldheim visited Heisel in Spain last October, and he sent flowers to Mandt's funeral.'

Horne switched off the ignition and wound down the window. A soft breeze swept the salty tang of the sea across the land. Above them the traffic thundered past on the motorway. 'Mandt and Goldheim,' he said, as if tasting the combination. 'Were they working together or competing against each other?'

'They could have done both. In the trade they operate in, people enter into cooperation and coalition if it's beneficial financially.'

'*Movement now,*' one of the detectives reported. '*Going on towards the city.*'

Wisting glanced at the screen on his lap. The red dot was flashing and moving, with a blue dot a few hundred metres behind. Ivar Horne grabbed the microphone: 'Kilo 4-2, are you in front?'

'*Picking him up at the roundabout at Vågbygd Centre,*' the unit responded.

'Keep your distance,' Horne warned. 'We have him on the map.'

Wisting watched as the red dot moved north on the main road, turning off after less than a kilometre.

'*It's going towards Slettheia,*' the detective in the nearest car reported. '*Do we have somebody who can meet him?*'

Horne directed a car as the red dot continued into a housing estate. 'Løvsangerveien,' Wisting read. 'Does he have any contacts there?'

'He's probably testing to see if there's anyone following.' Horne took back the iPad. 'Keep your distance,' he warned again over the radio. 'He's driving back and forth through the residential streets.'

'*Kilo 4-2 has lost him!*'

Ivar Horne reported positions as the red dot moved along the streets. Eventually it ended up at the far end of a cul-de-sac and came to a halt. 'Stopped at the far end of Rødvingeveien,' he said.

'*What do you want us to do?*' one of the detectives asked.

'Kilo 4-1, drive along Gransangerveien and see if you can observe the object from above.'

'*Received.*'

A blue dot slid on to the map from the west and followed the road parallel to the cul-de-sac where Phillip Goldheim had parked. Just before the car was in position, the red dot flashed again.

'He's moving,' Horne said, and went on to issue instructions to the other units.

Goldheim drove past the *Hennig-Olsen* ice cream factory, the nickel works, underneath the motorway where he circumnavigated a roundabout several times before driving back, and on to the main road leading to the city.

'He wouldn't be behaving like this if he wasn't on his way to an important meeting,' Horne said. 'He wants to be absolutely sure that nobody's following him.'

'Now he's heading for us,' Wisting said, pointing at the screen. The red dot had increased speed and was moving on to the motorway.

Horne started the car. After only a few hundred metres Goldheim left the motorway and crossed underneath. 'Here he comes,' Horne said, as a white Range Rover swept past, so rapidly that Wisting did not manage to catch sight of the driver.

'We'll follow him,' Horne said, giving the other units instructions about how to position themselves.

They let the car reach so far ahead of them that they became dependent on the GPS unit. The journey went down Vestre Strandgata, turning left along Dronningens gate. The red dot continued past the location where Elise Kittelsen had been shot and killed. When it stopped at an intersection, probably waiting for a green light, they drew closer and when the dot began to blink again they were only four car lengths behind.

Goldheim continued straight ahead, using the Lundsbrua Bridge to cross the River Otra, and then turned right.

'I was here earlier today,' Wisting said, recognising the grocery shop where he and Christine Thiis had eaten their hotdogs. 'We were here talking to one of the witnesses in the New Year Murder case. He lives in one of the penthouse flats down beside the river.'

'Høivold Quay,' Horne said, pulling further back. 'Expensive neighbourhood.'

They drove through a residential area with old timber houses where the branches of ancient fruit trees hung over white picket fences. The red dot turned towards the modern apartment block on the riverbank. Ivar Horne snatched the police radio. 'Driving down to Høivold Quay. We're dropping him.'

They drove past the turn-off Goldheim had taken and swung the car on to the pavement. The red dot on the map stopped at the water's edge. 'There's a pair of binoculars in the glove compartment,' Horne said. 'Jump out and see if you can watch him while I turn the car.'

Wisting took the binoculars and stood behind a tree to survey the road below.

Phillip Goldheim was already out of his car and walking along the quayside. Tall buildings blocked Wisting's view and he had to change position to follow him. When he raised the binoculars again, Goldheim was gone. Wisting moved the lens to and fro. Expensive boats were lined up in rows, a man was out walking a shaggy dog, a flock of gulls were fighting noisily over the refuse strewn round a rubbish bin. Goldheim could not have managed to enter one of the buildings, but he could have got into another vehicle.

Wisting lowered the binoculars. An open motorboat slipped away from the quayside. He put the binoculars to his eyes again as Goldheim sat down in the stern. A younger man was standing at the tiller.

Ivar Horne strode up behind him. 'Can you see him?'

Wisting handed him the binoculars. 'In that boat there,' he said, pointing.

Horne stood open-mouthed as he studied what he saw through the lens. Then he spoke again on the police radio: 'Object on board a day cruiser, on its way along the Otra. Do we have a telephoto lens that can capture it?'

'*Kilo 4-1.*'

They watched the boat as it disappeared out of the mouth of the river. The sun had set behind the hills east of the city, and a warm, velvety-soft dusk enveloped them.

'Did you recognise the man at the tiller?' Wisting asked.

Horne lowered the binoculars and shook his head. 'No, but it's a bit too late at night to set out on a jaunt.'

'What are they up to?'

'They want to discuss something,' Horne said, looking out at the shimmering sea, 'where no one can hear them.'

The police radio crackled. '*Got some photographs,*' Kilo 4-1 reported. '*Reg. no. looks like KAR247. We're checking the small boat register.*'

Horne smiled and waved Wisting back to the car with him. Once they had settled inside, the radio crackled again: '*Registered to a Gerhard Broch of Prestvikveien.*'

Horne shrugged to indicate that the name meant nothing to him.

'The man at the tiller must have been in his twenties,' Wisting said.

Horne lifted the police radio: 'Age?'

The answer came quickly: '*Fifty-one.*'

'Check family members.'

A woman on an electric bicycle passed as they waited for an answer.

'*One son,*' the voice on the radio said. '*Julian Broch.*'

Wisting felt a muscle pulsate on his temple. 'Bloody hell,' he muttered through tight lips.

'Do you know who it is?' Ivar Horne asked.

'The New Year Murder,' Wisting replied. 'Julian Broch was Elise Kittelsen's boyfriend.'

252

62

It was past midnight when Wisting let himself into his hotel room. Spacious, it had a carpet on the floor and a small balcony overlooking the street. He kicked off his shoes and sat on the bed with too many thoughts whirling in his head to sleep. He had the uneasy feeling that they were closing in on something and would not be able to rest until he had marshalled all his impressions. He lay down and closed his eyes.

This case was different from any other he had encountered. To come close to a resolution, he would first have to break a case that was already regarded as solved. Wisting felt convinced that Harald Ryttingen and his team had gone in the wrong direction. Concentrating on making the case against Dan Roger Brodin, they stood on the threshold of a miscarriage of justice. Wisting's objections were serious, but not serious enough to halt the court case. The climbdown would be too great for that. The court would convene on Monday morning and, if he were unable to point to another perpetrator, an innocent man would stand in the dock.

He opened his eyes and stared at the ceiling. A fly took off from the air vent, buzzed lazily around the room and landed on the curtain. They had come across a great deal of new information in the course of the day, but the cogs did not properly engage. Who was the perpetrator if Brodin was innocent?

All his experience told him that the motive for a murder was often found close to the victim. There was usually a relationship with the killer, but in the New Year Murder case there had been no need to investigate Elise Kittelsen's circle, since the perpetrator had been arrested only fourteen minutes later.

If you were to start looking, then Julian Broch would be

the person of maximum interest. His alibi had not been verified. No one had checked whether he had been at the party the entire time. It had been their intention to visit him the following morning, but now that he had turned up in surveillance they would need to wait to avoid disturbing the current operation.

As the fly flew from the curtain and buzzed away, Wisting struggled to recall whether he had read anything that could be interpreted as a conflict in Elise Kittelsen's life. There was something. He stood up and took out his copy of the documents.

One of Elise's girlfriends had mentioned that Julian Broch was jealous. Wisting spent almost ten minutes hunting for the right paragraph. Guro Fjellborg had known Elise Kittelsen since nursery. They had gone through primary and secondary school together and now both intended to become teachers.

Elise met Julian Broch at Hovden during the winter holiday, he read. *They became an item, but it was a bit of an on-off relationship. Julian was jealous, and Elise had to put a pin code on her mobile phone so that Julian couldn't read her messages.*

Why was it important that her boyfriend did not read her messages? Did he have reason to be jealous? Was there something on the phone that it was important for her to keep hidden? He glanced up from the papers. And why did the killer take her phone?

The questions began to multiply, as he jotted down the name of her childhood friend. There was another possibility. Did Jens Hummel have something to do with the murder?

He crossed to the desk and took a bag of peanuts from a dish. Somewhere in the building a child was crying bitter and broken-hearted sobs. He poured some nuts into his hand and tossed them into his mouth. The child seemed inconsolable. The sobbing rose and fell, ending in a long wail, before starting again. Left alone in a hotel room while the parents were down in the bar? Wakened and scared?

He chewed another fistful of peanuts and counted the days until Line was due to give birth. Seventeen. Ingrid had gone eleven days over her due date when she produced Line and her brother. He had sat in the corridor and gone in when it was all over. He wondered whether Line had in mind that he should stay with her through the entire labour, or whether he could wait outside this time too.

He was in no doubt that Line would be a good mother, but it would be demanding, being alone with the responsibility.

One thing many murderers had in common was that something had gone wrong in their upbringing, lack of intimacy, love, warmth and commitment had done something to them. They carried painful stories they had never dared to share, or that others had not seen or plucked up the courage to see. Stories of disappointment and damage and broken relationships. Prisons were full of young men whose childhood needs had been badly met or not met at all. Men who had grown up without fathers, as Dan Roger Brodin had done, and as his own grandchild was going to do.

He gazed at the door, wondering whether he should listen for the source of the screams, when it dawned on him that *he* would have to adopt some kind of paternal role and give his grandchild the necessary security.

Someone knocked on a wall and somehow silenced the crying.

He sat at the desk, pushed aside the folder of hotel information and put down the ring binder he had brought with him. Neither he nor Christine Thiis had leafed through this one. It contained background material and information from the investigators' special reports, and documents that had no direct relevance to the enquiry. There were staff lists, reimbursement requests, time sheets and copies of press releases. Of all the documents he had regarded these as being of least interest and now only perused them through a sense of duty.

Around the middle of the folder he came across an email attachment that had been sent to the police from Elise Kittelson's phone company, about the tracing of her stolen mobile phone. The printout was an overview of who she had been in contact with on the date of her murder. It supported the police

255

report and, strictly speaking, ought to have been included as a separate case document.

Wisting recognised that Julian Broch's number had received an '*on my way*' text, the only such message. It would have been easy for him to envisage which route she would take. Apart from her family, he was the only one who knew where she would be when the shots rang out at 19.21.

He took out the city map and calculated the distance from the crime scene to the flat where the party was being held. Four blocks would have taken only five minutes to walk. Even though it was early evening, he doubted whether anyone would have noticed if Julian Broch was gone for a few minutes. The problem was that no one had been asked, and now few would remember. In the investigation material, there was not even a comprehensive overview of who had been present at the party.

This was a hole in the investigation, but not large enough to crawl through.

He was about to continue but instead lingered on the print-out from the telecommunications company. The list seemed longer than the one he had seen in the police report.

He opened the folder of official enquiry documents once more. The papers were becoming dog-eared now, but he found the paper he was looking for. The chronological overview of who Elise Kittelsen had been in contact with throughout that day contained seventeen rows. The investigator had reworked the list so that in addition to the time and phone number, it included the names the various telephone numbers were registered to. Guro Fjellborg, the friend who had suggested that Julian Broch was jealous, was one.

Wisting counted the contacts on the phone company list and arrived at a total of nineteen. Then he re-counted the reworked list again: seventeen. His first thought was that the investigator had limited the list so that it applied from a particular time, for instance after twelve noon, but both lists began with the first call at 10.32 to Runa Kittelsen, a cousin of the same age in Lyngdal.

Number by number, Wisting went through the two lists. At

14.42 a mobile number cropped up that had been left out of the police report. An incoming call from a number beginning with forty-five, a number series used by *NetCom* pay-as-you-go cards.

The conversation had lasted for nearly five minutes. Further down the page, the same number appeared again in an outgoing call lasting eight and a half minutes. That was not registered in the police report either.

Wisting took out his own mobile phone. There were two unread messages from Christine Thiis. Two hours ago she had asked if he was asleep. A quarter of an hour later she had sent another message suggesting they meet for breakfast at nine o'clock. He had not heard the messages come in. It was really too late to answer, but he sent her a message confirming breakfast at nine before opening the app for interrogating phone numbers and keyed this one in. He had not expected to find an entry, but the search returned one result: *Jan Larsen, Post Box 502, 4605 Kristiansand.*

It was a perfectly ordinary first name and a perfectly ordinary surname, but he felt certain that he had not seen it anywhere in the case documents.

The report from which the number had been omitted had been written by a police officer, Robert Hansson, whose name was listed as the contact for the source who had given the Phillip Goldheim information. Could there be a connection? Was Jan Larsen the police informant and had the investigator removed his name and phone number from the list?

Wisting needed a date of birth to search the registers to find out who Jan Larsen really was. Even though it was a pre-paid phone subscription, the phone company could have recorded his personal ID. This was something for Nils Hammer to look into. Without bothering that it was the middle of the night, he put the question in a text message and passed on the assignment.

Wisting opened the camera function on his phone and took a photograph of the telephone printout, securing a copy for himself before handing back the papers. The report was a fabrication. Pretending to copy all the information received from the phone company, it withheld one of the numbers. It was a gross dereliction of duty that could have consequences not only for the policeman who had written the report, but also for the forthcoming court case. This fresh information could allow Dan Roger Brodin and his defence lawyer to win their case.

He crossed to the window. On the opposite side of the street, a man was perched on a ladder, pasting a poster on a billboard. A road sweeper with rotating brushes passed, trailing a pair of damp lines on the asphalt. The city was preparing for a new day.

63

The sound of the fly buzzing around the room woke Wisting. It landed on the vacant pillow beside him but took off again at once. Eager, as if short of time. The clock on the TV set showed 08:43. It had taken time for him to fall asleep, but he had evidently slept like a log.

He stepped into the shower and let the water run for a minute or two while he considered. In every case there was someone with something to hide, but in this particular case it was the police who were holding back information.

Christine Thiis was sitting behind a stack of newspapers when he came down to breakfast. He fetched himself a cup of coffee before taking a seat.

'Aren't you going to eat?' she asked.

'Afterwards.' He told her how they had followed Phillip Goldheim on his way to a meeting with Julian Broch.

'Elise Kittelsen's boyfriend?'

'Yes, but we'll have to hold off speaking to him,' Wisting said. 'Does the name Guro Fjellborg mean anything to you?'

He could see that it did, but that she could not decide how.

'One of Elise Kittelsen's girlfriends,' he said. 'There's a brief interview with her among the case papers. She talks a little about the relationship between Elise and Julian Broch, and says that Julian was jealous. Elise had to lock her phone with a pin code to prevent him from reading her messages.'

She looked at him doubtfully. 'A jealous boyfriend?'

'The question is whether he had reason to be jealous. Whether Elise Kittelsen had secrets that have not been revealed in the course of the investigation.'

'We'll need to talk to this friend.'

259

'There's something else as well,' he said, telling her about the discrepancy between the police report and the phone company printout.

'Do you mean they've manipulated evidence?'

He waited until an elderly man had passed their table. 'Strictly speaking, we're not talking about evidence, but they have suppressed vital information.'

'Who is this Jan Larsen?'

'I've put Hammer on to that.' Wisting crossed over to the breakfast buffet, helping himself to bacon and egg and two slices of wholemeal bread. 'I'll call that friend after breakfast.'

'We'll have to press on with this, one way or another. I don't believe Ryttingen is willing to listen. He's no longer concerned with what's right or wrong, just with the outcome of the case.'

'There must be someone we can talk to. Someone higher up the system. The Public Prosecutor or the Police Chief?'

'We don't have anything specific to go on. To make progress we must dig deeper.'

'The court case starts tomorrow,' she reminded him, pushing the Sunday edition of *VG* across. The picture of Elise Kittelsen had returned to the front page, as Line had predicted. Wisting skimmed through to photos of the murder victim and the crime scene. Harald Ryttingen, leader of the investigation, commented on the imminent court case by saying that the police hoped the accused would re-think and give a full explanation in court. Elise Kittelsen's family needed answers.

Wisting shook his head. This was an indirect way of telling the public that the question of guilt had already been decided, reinforcing a wave of opinion that would wash up against the court of law.

'They write about the revolver as well,' Christine Thiis said. Ryttingen had dismissed the idea that the discovery of the murder weapon and the connection to another killing had any relevance for the evidence in this case.

We have expected that the gun would turn up sooner or later by some means or another, he said. *It means little to our enquiry. We know who fired it.*

260

'He's treading dangerously close to conducting the trial in advance,' Wisting said.

Olav Müller had given a brief reply to the journalist's enquiry about his client continuing to claim innocence. Already on the defensive, it seemed he did not believe his client. He was obviously too inexperienced, not only with the media, but also in pleading a murder case. Mere knowledge of law did not help, you also required a command of rhetoric. A case such as this was just as much about convincing as about proving, about how you portrayed and presented the evidence. The person who won was not necessarily the person who told the truth, but the person who succeeded in putting forward the best argument.

Wisting helped himself at the buffet again before returning to his room. Christine Thiis accompanied him in order to take a look for herself at the document with the two missing phone conversations.

'There is a possible explanation,' he said. 'Jan Larsen could be a police informant, so his name has been removed from the case to protect him.'

'That seems illogical. Why should contact between Elise Kittelsen and a police informant be harmful to him?'

Wisting shrugged. If Jan Larsen's name appeared in the investigation document, the lead would probably be followed. It was not a problem for the source as long as he did not have anything to do with the case. However, Wisting was searching for an alternative perpetrator to Dan Roger Brodin, and if it was Jan Larsen someone in the police had shielded him to protect both him and the ongoing surveillance operation. That was a thought almost too terrifying to contemplate.

'It is against the rules of the game, in that case,' Christine Thiis continued. 'No matter what, it's an internal secret that's not acceptable.'

Wisting agreed. He leafed through his notes to find Guro Fjellborg's personal details. She and Elise Kittelsen were the same age, but in the six months that had passed since the murder she had reached the age of twenty-two.

261

He called her number and sat on the bed. It rang for a long time and Wisting was afraid it might be too early in the day. As he was about to disconnect, she answered, cheerful and in high spirits.

He introduced himself and told her what it was about. 'Is it convenient to speak now?'

'Oh yes,' the young woman at the other end assured him, though the sparkle had disappeared from her voice. 'I was just about to check in.'

'Are you travelling?'

'On my way home. I'm in London.'

Wisting switched on the loudspeaker function so that Christine Thiis could hear what was said. 'Have you time for a few questions?'

'What's it about?'

'It's about Elise Kittelsen. I just want to follow up on a few minor details.'

'Yes?'

'You said in your police statement that Julian Broch, her boyfriend, could be jealous. Is that right?'

'Yes, he didn't like her being with other guys.'

'Was she?'

'Not in that way. He became sort of annoyed if she sat too long talking to another guy.'

'You said that Elise had to put a pin code on her phone so that he couldn't read her messages.'

'Yes, she discovered that messages she hadn't read had been opened and realised that he had been snooping.'

'Was there something she didn't want him to see?'

'I don't really think so, but it's not the sort of thing you do, reading other people's phones in secret.'

'She shared everything with you? I understood that you were good friends.'

Guro Fjellborg hesitated. 'Not everything. Sometimes she went out of the room when the phone rang. Or she could be sitting in the middle of a conversation and send messages without saying who she was chatting to.'

262

'Who was she in contact with?'

'I don't know.'

Wisting moved the phone to his other ear. 'Do you know somebody called Jan Larsen?'

'Jan Larsen? No. Who's that?'

'Just a name that's cropped up.'

In the background, he heard a flight departure being called. 'I'll not detain you any longer. Have a good trip.'

He concluded the conversation and got to his feet. 'Let's get going,' he said, gathering up his case documents.

64

They checked out of the hotel, stowed their luggage in the car and drove back to police headquarters. A tourist coach changed gear and whirled up hot dusty air as they lingered outside the entrance, waiting for Ivar Horne to come and collect them. He seemed tired and exhausted when he appeared in the doorway. 'Late night?' Wisting asked.

'Not very. We managed to attach a fully charged box to Goldheim's car while we waited. They came back to the quay again after dark. We followed Broch. He went home before going into the city.'

'And Goldheim?'

'Went straight home.' Ivar Horne held the lift door for them. 'I'm afraid there's not much more for you to do here.'

'We've a few ring binders to browse through,' Wisting said wryly.

'Not any more. When I arrived an hour ago, the conference room had been cleared. Two men on the night shift removed all the documents.'

'Why's that?'

'Orders from Ryttingen. You requested access to all the investigation material, and you've had that. Now he needs the papers himself. The trial starts tomorrow.'

'There was never a time limit,' Wisting said.

Horne threw his arms out in despair as the lift arrived. 'Sorry.'

'Where are the documents now?' Christine Thiis asked.

'Locked inside Ryttingen's office.' Horne led the way along the corridor to the room they had used the previous day. Apart from a ballpoint pen and a blank notepad, the table was bare.

He took cups out of the cupboard above the kitchen worktop and filled them with coffee from the pot.

Wisting opened his document case and removed the folder he had brought with him. 'You can see to it that he gets this one as well.'

Horne nodded and handed each of them a cup.

'Have you made contact with Robert Hansson in Haiti?' Wisting asked.

'I've sent him an email, but haven't had a reply yet.'

'Is there anyone else here at HQ who knows the identity of his informant?'

Horne smiled over his coffee cup. 'Ryttingen.'

Wisting sighed.

'He's a good boss,' Horne said, still smiling. 'I realise that the two of you have had your professional differences, but he's effective and gets things done. He doesn't beat around the bush, but says exactly what he means. That gives good results. We have a high clear-up rate and low processing time which creates confidence among our citizens and that's thanks to him.'

The phone in Wisting's pocket rang. It was Nils Hammer. Wisting took it over to the window to answer.

'You wanted to know all about Jan Larsen?' Hammer began.

'Have you discovered anything?'

'The post box address you sent me is for the local *NAV* job centre.'

'Does he work there?'

'I doubt that, but he probably feels at home there.'

Wisting glanced out the window without fixing his gaze on anything in particular. 'Have you found out his ID number?'

'Yes, but I took a simpler route. I looked up the phone number in our records. He's mentioned in despatches.'

'For what?'

'Violence and narcotics. He's currently serving an eleven-year sentence for possession of heroin.'

'Eleven years?'

'It's on the screen in front of me,' Hammer said. 'He's got nine years left.'

Wisting looked at Christine Thiis and Ivar Horne. 'He's been in jail for two years?'

Hammer verified and read out the details of his prison term. Wisting turned to face the window again. 'Where is he now?'

'Skien Prison.'

Wisting thanked him for the information and let the news sink in. Outside, the sky was dull and hazy. Small birds flew overhead, appearing as indistinct, flickering fine lines. It was the same with phones as with weapons, he thought. They passed quickly through the hands of criminals. Any name at all could be concealed behind the phone number.

He waited for a while in front of the window before turning to speak to Christine Thiis. 'What do you say, then?' He forced a smile. 'Shall we head for home?'

'I have something for you before you go,' Horne said, not giving her the opportunity to answer. He crossed the corridor to his office and returned with two long plastic parcels. 'We boarded Broch's boat last night. The boys found the impressions of the soles of two different shoes on the deck.'

He handed them to Wisting, who held them up to the light.

'I've already checked,' Horne told him. 'Neither of them match the prints in your potato cellar. If it was Goldheim who ran away from you in that field, he was wearing different shoes.'

65

The house was pleasant to wake up in. Line opened her eyes slowly and let them slide closed before opening them once more. The sun shone through the window in places the roller blind did not cover, and long strips of light were cut off at the edge of the bed. There were reflections on the ceiling. She lay listening to nothing more than a few gulls shrieking in the distance.

When she bought the place she had been afraid that the two deaths would fill the space with negative energy. That it would be difficult to live there. In fact, she felt that she had made it her own, and it was a joy to wake in your own house.

She swung her feet outside the bed and sat up, gathering her strength before standing and wrapping herself in a dressing gown. Padding into the kitchen she put the kettle on for tea. Since she had fallen pregnant, she had begun to drink fruit tea instead of coffee in the mornings, following one of many pieces of advice. Caffeine could result in a reduction in a child's birth weight.

She opened the fridge and peered inside. Eating was no longer simply a matter of feeling full. It was more to do with having sufficient nutrition and energy. She took out a pack of liver paté for iron and a yogurt to cover her calcium requirements. While the tea was infusing, she buttered a slice of crispbread.

She took out her iPad and sat at the kitchen table. *Verdens Gang* had written about the New Year Murder case, but the main article did not contain anything new. That the murder weapon had been found and was linked to another case did not appear to worry the investigators.

She drank her tea, wondering whether her father had

discovered anything more, and whether she ought to have told him about the rest of the safe contents, the notebooks, accounts, photographs, newspaper cuttings and cassettes. She had not seen anything to explain where the revolver had come from, and doubted whether Wisting would find anything else. Most of the notes and papers were old.

The phone rang. She and Sofie chatted every day now. Normally she would have felt it excessive to have a friend who phoned every day, several times a day, but now she enjoyed it. She had nobody else, no work colleagues with whom to share thoughts and opinions.

'Can you come over?' Sofie asked, with no introduction.

Line had not heard her sound so agitated. 'What is it?'

'I think somebody . . .' Sofie began, but interrupted herself. 'You need to see this for yourself. Can you come round?'

Line glanced at the half-eaten crispbread with liver paté. 'Give me an hour, then.'

'Come as fast as you can,' Sofie pleaded, ending the conversation as abruptly as it had begun.

Line ate the rest of the crispbread as she cleared away the plate and returned the yogurt to the fridge. She took a quick shower, did not bother with make-up and was standing outside the massive timber villa in the centre of town before half an hour had passed. 'What is it?' she asked again.

'In here.'

They went into the kitchen. Sofie stood with her back to the worktop and pointed at the kitchen table where a number of papers and a box of light bulbs were spread out. 'The lamp.'

The large lamp suspended from the ceiling seemed slightly out of place above the small kitchen table that Sofie had brought in her van full of furniture. It had probably seemed more appropriate when her grandfather had been living there. 'Look inside.'

Line went over to the lamp, took hold of the metal shade and tilted it to one side. She realised immediately what had made Sofie so flustered. A little microphone was hanging beside the light bulb. 'A bugging device,' Sofie said.

Line peered more closely at the black microphone. It was about the same size as a fingernail and seemed old. Though it must once been advanced and modern, by now it seemed rather clumsy. 'I think it's been here for a long time.'

Sofie crossed her arms without uttering a word.

The microphone hung from a black cable that disappeared behind the lamp holder. Above the lamp, the connection must be camouflaged in the electric cable, and ran across the ceiling to the wall. From there, it disappeared behind one of the tall cupboards. Line pulled a kitchen chair over to the worktop and climbed up.

'Be careful!' Sofie warned.

The chair wobbled. Line held her arms out to the side and waited until she was steady before opening the cupboard door. It was almost empty. Sofie had put only a few baking bowls and plastic jugs on the bottom shelf. Standing on tiptoe and using the cupboard door for support, she peered into the top shelf. A black cable continued into the wall. 'It comes out on the other side,' she said, clambering down again.

Sofie was already in the hallway. 'The cloak cupboard,' she said, pointing.

On the wall adjacent to the kitchen was a broad, built-in cupboard. Line opened the doors. One part was shelved, while the other had space for jackets and coats. Sofie had not used it yet, and with the exception of a pair of Wellington boots the cupboard was bare. In the innermost recess of one shelf Line once again located the black cable, only a centimetre-long stub with a connector.

'I think it must have been your grandfather who installed it,' she said. 'He's probably had a tape recorder in the cupboard here.'

'Why would he do that?'

'I don't know, but it looks as if he's made secret recordings of conversations he's had at his kitchen table.'

'The cassettes,' Sofie said, ' . . . the little cassettes lying in the safe.'

Line had come to the same conclusion. 'I can take it away,

if you want,' she said, going over to the lamp again. 'It's just a matter of cutting the cable.'

Maja began to yell from the living room. They went through and Sofie lifted her out of her playpen. 'It might as well stay there in the meantime,' she said. 'I'll soon be renovating the kitchen anyway.'

They sat on the settee, Sofie with Maja on her lap. 'Have you said any more to your father?' she asked. 'About the revolver?'

'He's in Kristiansand this weekend, looking for a connection between the two murders.'

'Has he found anything?'

Line shrugged. 'I haven't spoken to him.'

She leaned forward and tickled Maja on the tummy. Maja was convulsed with laughter.

'Are you ready to look after her on Tuesday?' Sofie asked.

'You'll just have to show me a bit more about how to feed her and so on.'

'She's going to eat soon. We can do it then.'

Line agreed happily and decided to get hold of a Dictaphone machine so that she could play the cassettes while Sofie was at the meeting with the lawyer in Oslo.

'The meeting's at nine o'clock, so I need to leave by seven at the latest, if that's not too early for you,' Sofie said.

'It's fine.'

'It'll probably last no more than a couple of hours, so I should be home again by two o'clock.'

'That's perfectly okay,' Line said, coaxing another burst of laughter from Maja.

Sofie plumped her daughter down on Line's knee. 'What do you think of living on your own?' she asked unexpectedly.

Line thought about it. She enjoyed it, but there were many idle moments when there was no one to share her thoughts with. 'It's fine,' she replied. 'What about you?'

'I thought I'd had enough of men for a while, but the house seems so big.'

'Have you met anyone?'

Sofie shook her head. 'No, but I realise I can't live on my own forever. That I need somebody.'

Line nodded. She recognised this but, as for herself, she was prepared to be on her own for a long time.

Maja grew restless on her knee and her large bump was constantly in the way.

Sofie looked at the clock. 'I think she's starting to feel hungry,' she said, getting to her feet. 'Shall we make her something?'

Line carried Maja to the kitchen and settled her into the high chair at the table.

'She eats porridge for lunch and in the evening,' Sofie said, opening a cupboard door to take out a packet. 'All you have to do is mix it with lukewarm water.'

Line studied the list of ingredients. 'Is there any difference in the nutritional content?'

'I buy the one without palm oil,' Sofie said. 'It tastes best too.'

Line followed the instructions on the packet, put the plate in front of Maja and sat down at the table herself. Maja opened her mouth eagerly, but just as Line was about to give her the first spoonful, she slapped her hand on the plate so that the porridge splashed over the table. She was delighted and smacked it again. Line pulled the dish back out of her reach.

'Easy mistake for a beginner to make,' Sofie said, and came over with a cloth. She wiped Maja's fingers and then the table. Later she carried Maja up to the first floor for a nap. They took the baby alarm and sat in the garden. A heavy, laden bumblebee buzzed around the grass.

'Sorry for phoning you,' Sofie said. 'I was just so put out when I spotted that microphone. It felt so creepy.'

'It's okay.'

'Do you have a large family?' Sofie asked.

Shaking her head, Line drank from the glass that Sofie had put on the table. 'Hardly anyone. There's only Dad and me, Grandad and my brother.'

'Your father would be there for you, if you ever needed him.'

'He'll be with me at the birth.'

271

'Will he?'

'He'll not want to come in with me,' Line said, 'but I'll feel safe knowing he's out there in the corridor.'

They sat chatting until Maja woke again. Line changed her nappy before heading for the car and driving home. Her father's car was in the driveway and she stopped outside his house.

He was at the kitchen table, surrounded by papers. 'Home already?' she asked, with a smile.

He gave her a hug. 'Yes, but I'll have to go back down again on Tuesday.'

'Why's that?'

'I've been summoned as a witness in the court case.'

'Because of the revolver?'

He nodded.

Line took a seat and caught a glimpse of his notes. There was a timeline and a numbered list. 'Have you discovered anything new?'

'Just more questions.'

'What sort of questions?'

Her father considered. 'Maybe you can provide some answers?'

'Maybe.'

'Do you have your phone on you?'

She took it out.

'Do you have a pin code on it?'

'Yes.'

'Why's that?'

'In case it's stolen.'

'But do you have anything on your phone that you don't want other people to see?'

'Yes.'

'What sort of thing?'

Line mulled it over. Throughout her pregnancy she had taken photos of herself, naked in front of the mirror. She'd wouldn't want anyone else to see and, actually, she didn't even want to tell anyone about them.

'Why do you want to know?'

272

'The phone belonging to the woman who was killed in Kristiansand was never found. I spoke to a friend of hers when I was down there. She told me that sometimes Elise went somewhere else when the phone rang, and she was afraid of her boyfriend accessing what was on it.'

Line did not entirely understand where her father was going with this. What he was describing sounded completely normal to her. 'Does it need to have anything to do with the case?'

He did not reply, and she saw from his demeanour that there was something else. Something that might create headlines and that he did not want to tell her yet. 'Don't give it any more thought,' he said.

Line's curiosity had been piqued. 'Did she have another lover, or what?'

'I don't know. That's something the investigators never looked into.'

She looked at her father's notes again, saw some dates and names, and it dawned on her what he was getting at. 'You're no longer investigating the Hummel case. You're investigating the New Year Murder.'

'There's a connection somewhere.'

She studied him. The tiny muscles around his eyes had contracted as he began to toy with a ballpoint pen.

'Don't you believe he did it?' she asked. 'Do you believe it was another man who murdered Elise Kittelsen? The same one that killed Jens Hummel?'

'I don't know what to believe,' he replied.

66

Wisting grabbed the ballpoint pen lying on the table. His eyes strayed to the clock on the kitchen wall. Eighteen hours to go until Dan Roger Brodin would stand in the dock. The points that suggested he was innocent were listed in front of him. He would make an effort to stop the trial.

He picked up his mobile phone and tapped in Harald Ryttingen's number. Ryttengen sounded morose when he answered, but took the initiative. 'Are you satisfied? Did you get what you wanted?'

'Not all of it,' Wisting said, without mentioning how Ryttingen had deprived them of the opportunity. 'But it was useful. That's why I'm calling.'

'Well?'

Wisting jumped in with both feet. 'I must request that you postpone the trial. I'm not sure that Dan Roger Brodin is the right man.'

He heard a snort at the other end. 'I've just come from a meeting with the Public Prosecutor. I put forward the opinions you've already come out with. Do you know what he did?'

Wisting did not reply.

'He laughed at you, and I want to do the same now. I don't know what's wrong with you, whether you lack the ability to read the case documents. We've seldom had a more solid case. We've got three eye witnesses!'

'Witnesses can make mistakes.'

'We have technical evidence and a notorious habitual criminal in the dock. There has to be an end to this now.'

'I met Dan Roger Brodin in prison . . .'

'I know, and now we're informed that you've been called as a witness.'

'He told me something interesting...'

'And tomorrow he'll have an opportunity to do so in front of a judge,' Ryttingen interrupted. 'This conversation is done. I'll see you in court. Try not to make an arse of it.'

67

The summer holidays were over. On Monday morning there were more cars on the road and people he had not seen for some time had returned to the police station. At nine o'clock Wisting assembled the nearest investigators: Torunn Borg, Nils Hammer and Espen Mortensen. They were seated when he closed the door and switched on the red light outside.

'Our main question has been how the murder weapon from Kristiansand could have been used in Jens Hummel's killing,' he said. 'I believe I've found the answer. I think that whoever killed Jens Hummel, hid his taxi in the barn at Huken and concealed the corpse in the dung heap on Brunla Farm, is the same person who killed Elise Kittelsen.'

He scanned the faces of his colleagues, and saw nothing but doubt and scepticism. Nils Hammer held up his hand. 'Wait a minute now. The case in Kristiansand is regarded as closed. What you're saying would mean that the accused is innocent. He was already in jail when Jens Hummel disappeared.'

Wisting agreed.

'There were three witnesses to the murder,' Torunn Borg said.

'I think there were four,' Wisting said. 'We know that Jens Hummel was in Kristiansand on New Year's Eve. I think that he saw what happened.'

'In that case, he could have been the one who phoned the tip-off to Kristiansand and told them they had arrested the wrong man,' Hammer said.

'But it doesn't match what the other three witnesses saw,' Torunn Borg objected. 'They recognised the perpetrator.'

'There were other aspects,' Espen Mortensen said. 'He had gunshot residue on his hands.'

Wisting told them about the eyewitnesses and about the fireworks.

'Have you put this to the police down there?' Torunn Borg asked.

'To deaf ears. It's too late for them to turn back. It's not just that they have the wrong man, but also that the right man has killed again. If they admit the wrongful arrest, they're also forced to admit that it cost Jens Hummel his life. I think they fear that scenario.'

'It's easier to stop a prosecution than to overturn a conviction,' Hammer said.

'He hasn't been convicted yet. I'm to give testimony at his trial tomorrow. Hopefully, we'll have something more specific before then.'

He crossed out the items on the agenda he had been through but hesitated over the final point. 'There's one more thing. It could be that the investigators in Kristiansand have withheld information.'

He showed the pictures he had taken with his mobile phone and explained about the phone number removed from the log of Elise Kittelsen's phone calls. 'Jan Larsen has been inside for nearly two years. Nils, could you possibly discover where his phone is now, and who is on the list of contacts?'

Hammer had personal associates in the telecommunications industry who were willing to compromise their duty of confidentiality if something was important and urgent. 'I can try.'

They were nearing the end of the meeting.

'Just one thing,' Torunn Borg said to Wisting. 'Do you have a theory about who the murderer could be?'

'It's too early to pick anyone out but Phillip Goldheim has become increasingly more interesting.' He explained to the others about the points of intersection between Goldheim and their own enquiry. 'The police down there are following his movements closely,' he said, and declared the meeting closed.

277

From his office he phoned Ivar Horne in Kristiansand. 'Any news from your detective in Haiti?'

'It's not so simple,' Horne replied. 'Robert Hansson is apparently on vacation and has gone to Florida where he has hired a motorbike to travel to the west coast. I've said it's important and asked him to phone you, but I don't know if he's received my message.'

Wisting thanked him. 'Any news on Mister Nice Guy?'

'No, we're still tailing him. He's active, but extremely careful.'

'Let me know if he moves in my direction.'

'You'll be the first to find out,' Horne promised.

Hammer appeared at the door as Wisting put the phone down. 'The number is not in use,' he said.

'What do you mean?'

'Jan Larsen. His phone hasn't been used for the past six months. The history doesn't go any further back.'

Wisting gave a deep sigh.

'If you want to find out who has used the phone, you'll have to talk to him,' Hammer said.

'To Jan Larsen?'

'He's behind bars in Skien, and isn't going anywhere.'

Wisting nodded in silence. If the next few hours did not yield anything, he would visit Jan Larsen in prison this afternoon.

68

Years had passed since Line had been inside the editorial offices of the local newspaper. She had worked there for two years before her temporary post at *Verdens Gang*. It had been a busy place, but now it was quiet and most of the desks were empty. Several looked as if they had been cleared for good. In the newspaper the advertisements were fewer and the contents thinner, the way all local newspapers were going.

Kristoffer Nybråthen was sitting at the far end of the open plan office, with slightly less hair than when she last saw him. He popped his head up from behind a computer screen and brightened when he saw her. He gave her a hug and remarked on her bump. 'That's some news the editor hasn't picked up. Do you have time to sit down?'

'It was you I came to see,' she said.

Nybråthen put his hand on his forehead to retrieve the hair that had fallen to one side, smoothing it back over his bald crown. The familiar movement brought to Line's mind the old saying that Nybråthen covered everything apart from his own napper.

'We could do with a hot news tip,' he said. The story on screen was about youngsters who spent much of the summer holidays in day-care.

'It's not really to do with anything like that,' Line said. 'At least not yet.'

Nybråthen took off his smudged glasses and looked at her. 'How can I help?'

'When I worked here, you used a little tape recorder.'

'I haven't used it for years,' he said, pulling out a desk drawer. 'But I think I have it here somewhere.'

'I've come across some cassettes, but have had difficulty finding a player to suit.'

'You can borrow mine.'

'Until Tuesday?'

He picked it up and handed it to her. 'No problem.'

Line removed the cassette inside, the same type as were stored in the safe in Sofie's home and handed it to him, thanking him profusely.

Before she could leave she had to tell him that she had moved back to her hometown and that the child's father lived in the USA. If Nybråthen had not been given something to write, at least he now had something to gossip about.

69

Skien Prison was a concrete colossus in an area of moorland south of the city. The atmosphere inside the walls, where Jan Larsen was an inmate, was hot and clammy. No one questioned Wisting's visit and Larsen may not even have been told that a policeman was on his way.

Shown into a cramped visiting room, Wisting sat and waited until a door slammed in the corridor and a man in tracksuit trousers came shuffling in, escorted by an officer.

Wisting stood up. 'Jan Larsen?'

The other man nodded and shook hands. Wisting gave his name and sat down. The prison officer backed into the corridor and locked the door behind him. 'What's it about?' Larsen asked, perching on the edge of his chair.

'Your name has cropped up in a case.'

The man facing him sighed despondently: 'I'm serving an eleven-year sentence. Isn't that enough to be going on with?'

'It's not about you. I think someone has used your phone while you've been in here.'

'My phone?'

Wisting read out the number. 'Isn't that yours? A *NetCom* pay-as-you-go card.'

'Could be. I've had a few that I don't remember.'

'You gave a post box address at the *NAV* job centre when you registered your subscription.'

'Sounds like me.'

Wisting returned to his central question. 'Do you know who has used your phone while you've been inside?'

'There must be a mistake. I haven't seen that phone since I was arrested. The police took it.'

281

'What do you mean?'

'It's even mentioned in the verdict. I'd used it to deal with. As far as I know, it's still in the police evidence room in Kristiansand.'

'Are you sure?'

Larsen got to his feet and walked across to the intercom on the wall. A prison officer answered. 'I need some papers from my cell,' he said. 'Can someone come with me?'

'Wait,' the officer said.

Immediately afterwards, they heard footsteps in the corridor and keys rattling before the door opened. Larsen turned to face Wisting. 'It won't take long,' he said, following the officer out.

Five minutes later he was back with the verdict from Agder Appeal Court. He flicked through it to one of the details on the last page.

Wisting read: *Jan Larsen is found guilty in accordance with §34a of the penal code and ordered to suffer confiscation of 70,000 kroner in favour of the public purse and in accordance with §35, second sub-section, to suffer confiscation of an Alfa Romeo private car and a Nokia mobile phone in favour of the public purse.*

It had become increasingly common. Crime should not pay. In addition to confiscation of the proceeds, the police requested confiscation of possessions that had been used in the commission of crimes.

'Who had responsibility for this case?' Wisting asked.

'Ryttingen,' Jan Larsen said. 'Harald Ryttingen.'

Wisting sat, lost in thought.

'If anyone has used my phone, it must have been the police,' Larsen said, reading Wisting's thoughts.

70

The afternoon sun, low in the sky, shone in Wisting's eyes as he left the prison precincts. He flipped down the sun visor, took out his phone and rang Christine Thiis. The way this case had developed, she had become a close confidante. Her background as a defence lawyer provided an interesting sideways look to his own task, because she spotted the legal complications faster than he did.

'Are you at home?' he asked, after telling her what he had learned. 'I'd like to talk through the case before I go to court tomorrow.'

'I get the children back then. Why not call in now?'

She had set the table in the living room when he arrived. A summer salad with chicken and focaccia. In front of the table, the TV was on with the volume down. 'I wanted to see if there's anything about the court case on the news,' she said.

They ate while waiting for the broadcast to begin.

The court case was one of the main items. She turned up the sound. A news reporter with bleached hair and an overly tight shirt stood in front of the Justice Building and summarised the first day of the trial:

'*A twenty-five-year-old man is charged with the murder of Elise Kittelsen who was shot and killed on the open street here in Kristiansand on New Year's Eve.*'

The reportage switched to archive photographs while the reporter mentioned the central points in the case. They showed Dan Roger Brodin as he arrived in the courtroom, his face concealed. In the background, Wisting recognised Harald Ryttingen in a suit and narrow tie.

'*When the judge asked the question, the 25-year-old denied*'

having anything to do with the murder,' the reporter continued, *'while the Public Prosecutor gave an insight into the huge
amount of evidence that will be presented in the days ahead.
The court proceedings will continue for the rest of the week.
Tomorrow we will hear from several witnesses before the technical evidence is submitted on Wednesday.'*

She switched off the TV. 'What have you considered saying
tomorrow?'

'I have to tell the truth. Hopefully, it'll be enough for the
judge to order a fresh enquiry and suspend court proceedings.'

'That'll create problems.'

He was fully aware of the impending difficulties. His own
Chief of Police had even warned him against meddling in the
New Year Murder case. 'I don't know all of the truth either,
but I can't keep silent about what I do know.'

They ate as they discussed the case, trying to look at it from
different angles and searching for indications that they might
be on the wrong track. Their aim was not to arrive at any conclusion but to explore the facts.

'Most probably the prosecutor won't have any questions for
you,' she said, speaking from experience. 'They'll tell the court
that what you have to say is of no interest and will turn down
the opportunity to question you.'

'That's what they have done all along. Ignored what doesn't
fit their own picture.'

She accompanied him to the door. 'I probably won't see you
in the morning,' she said, lingering, as if hesitating somehow.
Then she leaned forward and gave him a hug. 'Good luck,
anyway.'

He thanked her and stood still for a moment before turning
on his heel and heading for his car. When he was inside, he
decided to drive out to the riding centre at Brunla where Jens
Hummel's body had been found.

The heat had baked the area in front of the stables dry and
hard. He parked the car in the same place as before, stepped
out and slammed the car door. Several crows rose in the dull
evening sky. Grasshoppers sang in the dry grass all around.

284

The remains of the police crime scene tape were still hanging from the barn ramp. He ripped them off. Inside the stable he heard a horse stamping restlessly.

They did not know where Jens Hummel had been killed, only that he had been shot, stowed in the boot of his own taxi and dumped here before the vehicle was hidden in Frank Mandt's barn. He stepped closer to the heap of sawdust and dung. It had begun to fill again and big flies were buzzing around. His phone rang: a long, foreign number. He answered and introduced himself in Norwegian.

'Robert Hansson here. I understand that you wanted to get in touch with me. I'm on holiday in the States, but Ivar Horne says it's important.'

'I'll keep it brief,' Wisting said. He had prepared what he was going to say when Robert Hansson called. 'It has to do with a drugs enquiry. I have Aron Heisel in custody in connection with twelve kilos of amphetamines.'

'I don't recognise that name.'

'It turns up in a note from an informant that you wrote last October. About Phillip Goldheim visiting Heisel in Spain. Can you remember? It was in connection with an operation you called Mister Nice Guy.'

A black and white cat came creeping along the barn wall.

'That might be right,' Hansson replied after a pause. 'I had a lot on Goldheim at that time, but we never managed to catch him.'

'This could be a new opportunity,' Wisting said. 'He may have a central role in our case.'

'That would certainly be interesting.'

'What I'm wondering is whether your source could know anything more about the contact between Goldheim and the part of his activity that borders on Vestfold and Larvik.'

Again there was silence at the other end of the phone. A young girl pushing a wheelbarrow emerged on to the barn ramp. Wisting followed her with his eyes as he waited for Hansson to say something. The wheelbarrow was full of sawdust and dung that she tipped over the side and on to the heap below.

'There's no more information to be had there,' Hansson said.

'Have you no contact with him?'

Hansson hesitated again, exhaling noisily, almost as if a valve had opened after being shut for a long time. 'The informant is no longer alive,' he said.

71

The child was inconsolable. She screamed until she was red in the face and for a moment or two Line thought she might faint. In the end she distracted her with yogurt and, when she finally settled her in the playpen, Line slipped out of the living room.

It did not look as though Sofie had been in the safe since Line had gone through the contents. Ring binders, pictures, notebooks and the envelope of cassettes were in the same places, the cassettes marked by date. Some of the dates had been crossed out and replaced with new ones, and many had been made far back in time. The most recent were almost two years old. She brought them up to the living room, took out the Dictaphone and sat on the settee.

As Maja crawled around the playpen, Line inserted the cassette with the most recent recording and pressed play. Nothing happened. She tried again, but the tape did not rotate. She removed the cassette, turned it round and inserted it again, but that made no difference. She lifted off the battery cover. They seemed old and, when she examined them more closely, she saw that the date on them had passed well over a year earlier.

'Maybe Mummy's got some batteries?' she said to Maja as she struggled up from the settee.

'Ma-ma-ma?' Maja replied, watching Line as she left for the kitchen.

She opened drawers and cupboards, but could not find any, looked in all possible places but had to conclude that there were no spare batteries in the house. She lifted Maja out of the playpen. 'We'll go for a walk to the shop,' she said. Maja gurgled and babbled, making noises that sounded like contentment.

The shop was only a few hundred metres along the street. She placed Maja in her pushchair and pushed her along, the first time she had done this since she had been a youngster earning pocket money. She liked the sensation, and enjoyed the friendly glances.

Faced with a shelf of batteries she could not remember which kind she needed and ended up buying two packs. In addition, she bought a bottle of mineral water and an ice cream cone for Maja. The last of these was a mistake. The ice cream melted in her hands, ran down her arms and stained her clothes.

When they got back, she took Maja into the bathroom, washed her and put on fresh clothes. It felt as if half the day had gone when she finally sat with the Dictaphone again.

It turned out that the smallest batteries suited. The cogs gripped and drove the tape round, but all that came out of the miniature loudspeaker was a hissing noise. When she spooled the tape back her efforts were rewarded. A conversation, two men speaking, and it sounded as if it had been going for some time.

'Those are tough conditions,' one man said.

'It's the same as last time,' the other man replied. *'And we're completely dependent on his people to get rid of the goods.'*

'We just need to make sure we don't let him find out how little we're actually paying.'

They were obviously discussing a business transaction, clearly illegal. They sounded comparatively youthful. She had not heard Sofie's grandfather's voice, but from the date on the recording he would have been seventy-seven when the conversation took place. Neither of them sounded as old as that.

She continued to listen. They were talking about how much they would earn on the setup:

'Then we'll be left with half a million,' one said.

'That's nice,' the other responded. *'Very nice.'*

They laughed and chatted about a car one of them wanted to purchase. Line pictured them sitting on either side of the kitchen table.

Then something happened. A door opened and a third voice sounded. *'Have you come to an agreement?'*

This voice was gruffer and more sophisticated. Frank Mandt, Line thought.

'*We're in,*' one of the two men said. '*We'll do as . . .*'

The conversation was cut off and the loudspeaker filled with crackling. A radio voice sounded as if someone had wiped out the rest with another recording.

What had happened was unmistakable. Frank Mandt had held a business meeting at the kitchen table and offered to let the two men talk undisturbed. He had left the room, but had ensured that he heard what they were talking about all the same. In that way, he knew where he stood. He insured himself against being tricked, and knew what he could demand next.

Mandt must have monitored his associates for years through his access to police documents and it did not surprise her in the least that he also listened to the ones with whom he did business. However, the recordings could also give him away, so why had he not deleted them? Was it a form of insurance or was he merely careless?

She took out the cassette and chose another at random. The recording began with a scream of pain. Shrill and piercing. Line covered the speaker with her hand to avoid upsetting Maja. When the scream subsided, she removed it again.

'*We just want you to tell us how it went,*' a man said calmly.

'*But I don't know,*' another man protested desperately.

There was another scream.

'*Okay! Okay!*' he groaned. '*It was me and Lasse.*'

Line reduced the volume and continued listening as he stammered out how he and another had stolen part of a consignment of amphetamines. The recording stopped abruptly.

Frank Mandt's voice was not on the tape. Others carried out his dirty work for him, but apparently he wanted to hear with his own ears how he had been betrayed. Line glanced at the kitchen where the ill-treatment had taken place, removed the cassette and picked up another.

72

Wisting was back in the city on the south coast. The sun was just as high in the sky and it was just as hot as it had been two days earlier. Like last time, he drove past the crime scene in Dronningens gate. He was early and took time to stop, get out of the car and look at where the shots had been fired. What he had discovered in the course of the night turned everything upside down. The cogwheels had taken hold. Everything fell into place.

A delivery van drove past, stirring up dust and a crumpled sheet of paper that sank slowly back to the asphalt before another vehicle pushed it farther on. He rehearsed his testimony in his mind, aware that he would be regarded as disloyal by many colleagues and that it would impact severely on individuals and cause damage.

His phone rang. It was Ivar Horne. Wisting sat in the car again before answering. 'I thought you would want to know that Phillip Goldheim left home before nine o'clock this morning and drove north on route E18.'

Wisting started the car. 'Then we probably passed each other. Do you know where he's going?'

'No. We didn't have the manpower to follow. I arranged with the surveillance team in Oslo that they would pick him up once he'd reached there, but it looks as if he's turned off before that.' The end of the sentence disappeared into the ether as the mobile phone transferred the connection to hands-free. 'Which is why I'm calling. He's just turned off for Larvik.'

73

Line took out a cassette that had obviously been used several times. Three earlier dates had been crossed out. The one that remained was 13.10.2005.

This time there were a number of voices, but once again none seemed to be that of Frank Mandt. The discussion was about cars and the need for other registration plates, about which road was safest, where they could change vehicles, and where the police were most likely to be posted.

The men were talking about a robbery, discussing how the four robbers would make their escape. Line sat up straight, grabbed her bag and took out a notepad and ballpoint pen.

'*Konnerud is good,*' someone said. '*Then we can split up. One can drive back and go towards Mjøndalen. The others can drive down to Vestfold.*'

Names were mentioned. Line jotted them down: Aron, Robin and someone simply called PG. She stopped the recording and spooled the tape back to the beginning, but thought she heard a noise. It came from the front of the house. She sat listening, heard nothing more, went out to the kitchen and peered out. Nobody there. She filled a glass with water and returned to the living room.

Maja stood holding on to the bars of her playpen, watching Line as she sat down again and picked up the Dictaphone. There it was again. This time it seemed the noise came from inside the house, as if a floorboard had creaked in the hallway. Maja looked at the door with big eyes and open mouth.

Line felt her blood run cold. It was probably only a noise from the old timbers, but the thought that there might be someone on the other side of the door was chilling.

Footsteps.

Maja looked at her and back at the door. Line grabbed the Dictaphone and the envelope full of cassettes and hid them behind a cushion on the settee, took hold of the armrest and hauled herself up. Before she could get to her feet the door opened. A man with a black balaclava over his head and a pistol in his hand entered the room.

74

The massive doors of the Justice Building slid closed behind him. His footsteps echoed off the walls. A monitor high on the wall indicated that the case against Dan Roger Brodin was being heard in Courtroom 5.

Wisting took his bearings. The large hall with entrances into the various courtrooms was remarkably silent and deserted. There was nothing to suggest that one of the most talked-about court cases of the year was going on behind closed doors.

Courtroom 5 was at the far end of the building. He walked through the hall as a judge in his robes descended the stairs from the first floor.

His mobile phone signalled a text message from Espen Mortensen, who had been given the surveillance assignment: *Have picked up the car. It is parked in front of Stavern Church. Observing. Horne has been informed.*

Wisting frowned. Stavern? What was he intending there? Did he have further contacts in the circle around Frank Mandt?

An abstract painting hung on the wall facing him, resembling a tiny black boat on a huge blue ocean. An engraved sign credited the Vest-Agder branch of the Norwegian Bar Association with the gift.

He examined it more closely. The picture had vast empty spaces and shapeless figures that invited different interpretations. It struck him that this was an advantage in art, but a problem in law. The greater the ambiguity, the more difficult it was to arrive at the right decision.

The door to Courtroom 5 opened and the chief prosecution

witness, Einar Gjessing, emerged. He gave Wisting a brief nod before strolling out of the Justice Building.

Wisting was next. He paced to and fro across the floor as he waited for his name to be called.

75

The man pointed the gun at her. Line gulped down nothing but air, causing a pain in her chest that rapidly shifted to her stomach.

'Just stand still,' he said.

Line was unable to utter a word. The threat was directed not only at her, but also at the child she was carrying. The fear of that life ending before it had begun was overwhelming and paralysed her completely. A feeling of compression grew in her abdomen. She put her hand under her stomach, felt a strange, clammy sensation spread to the small of her back, and hoped it was only because of the sudden fear.

'Relax,' the man said, taking a step forward. 'I just want to collect something.'

Line, struggling to breathe calmly, was totally still in the middle of the room with her right hand carefully holding her belly, trying to feel whether it was actually her womb contracting. As the thought occurred, violent pain coursed through her body.

Not now, she thought.

The pain eased. It was certainly not a normal labour contraction, she thought, trying to set her mind at rest. It could have been the accidental tightening of a muscle, a fear reaction, or Braxton Hicks. She took a deep breath and crossed to the playpen. Maja was holding the bars tightly and staring at the man in black. Tears were not far off.

'Leave the child,' he ordered, waving her away with the pistol. His consonants were soft, she registered, and took some time to stare back at the dark eyes behind the balaclava. He must be from the south coast.

'What do you want?' she asked.

'Your grandfather's papers. The ones he kept in the safe.'

He thinks I'm Sofie, Line thought. 'In the basement,' was all she said.

'You first,' he commanded.

Maja began to cry with an uncertain, hesitant whimpering. Line walked towards the door, her footsteps dwindling, as if each stride caused shockwaves through her body, inducing fresh contractions in her womb. The stairs creaked under her weight. Maja's screams grew quieter as they descended into the basement.

The man at her back pressed the pistol against her spine. 'At the far end,' Line said, moving carefully ahead. He pushed her all the way into the room and ordered her over to the wall.

The door of the safe was open. 'Is that all?' he asked as he crouched down.

Line considered whether she should tell him about the cassettes upstairs in the living room, but that would be the same as telling him she had listened to them. He had mentioned papers, and she took a chance that he actually was unfamiliar with the contents of the safe. 'Yes,' she assured him.

The man pulled out a ring binder and leafed through it. Only now did she notice that he was wearing light rubber gloves. He nodded with satisfaction, replaced the folder and scanned the room. 'Are you expecting visitors?'

'What do you mean?'

'Is anybody coming here today?'

She did not know where that question was leading. 'A friend . . .' she answered, thinking of Sofie.

'When will that be?'

'In a few hours.'

'Okay,' he said, standing up again. 'Come with me.' He led her into the corridor, into what had been an exercise room. 'Over there,' he said, pointing at the wall bars.

She did as he ordered.

'Put your hands out!'

She held out her hands in front of her as he pulled some

296

plastic cable ties from his pocket and grabbed one of her arms.

Line saw what was coming. 'No!' she protested, trying to wriggle free.

The man put the weight of his body against her and pressed her to the wall, forcing one arm between two of the bars and out again under the one below.

'No!' she screamed again. 'Please!'

He brutally bound her hands together with the cable ties and tethered her tightly to the wall. The hard plastic chafed her wrists. She bit back a scream of pain and concentrated on breathing calmly. If it really had been a labour contraction, more would follow if she did not pull herself together.

'Your friend will be here soon,' he said, making for the door. 'You'll be free in a couple of hours.' He stopped in the doorway. 'And you'd better keep your mouth shut about this, both of you. You don't want anything to happen to that squealing brat of yours.'

He used the pistol to point at the ceiling where the playpen and Maja were situated on the floor above. 'Understand?'

Line nodded as he left the room, closing the door without a backward glance. Through Maja's weeping, she listened as he emptied the safe in the adjacent room. She struggled to concentrate on her breathing. By focusing on every single intake of breath, even and quiet, she tried to push everything else out of her mind. She closed her eyes.

In the distance she heard footsteps on the stairs and the front door slam.

76

As the minutes passed Line's hopes increased that the contraction might have not have been the start of labour, but no sooner had the thought relaxed her than she felt the pains again. Exactly the same, spreading to the small of her back and doubling in intensity.

Maja was screaming continuously on the floor above. Line tried to do the same, filling her lungs and shouting loudly for help, knowing the sound could hardly penetrate the thick walls. Frank Mandt had tortured people in his own kitchen without their screams attracting attention.

She struggled with the plastic ties that bound her to the wall bars, and tried to twist her hands free, but they were as hard as handcuffs. She would have to stay here until Sofie came home. How long? Two hours? Three?

Her mobile phone rang from inside her handbag beside the settee and Maja's sobbing abated, but as soon as it stopped she began to howl again. Line tried to tell herself that it was not dangerous. Maja was inside the playpen where nothing could harm her. She was scared and frightened, and would soon be hungry, but in the end would exhaust herself and fall asleep.

Three contractions came rolling, rhythmic and regular, with only six or seven minutes in between. Equally long, equally severe. She sank to her knees, slightly lower each time, as if they robbed her of her strength, sinking until she was sitting with her head on her chest.

Many of the pregnancy training classes and much of the preparation for childbirth had consisted of relaxation exercises. She practised calm and that eased her anxiety. Soon her breathing was regular and she noticed that her heart had slowed. If she could get this situation more under control the birth could take a more natural progress. A first-time birth normally lasted more than twelve hours.

The cable ties rubbed at the skin around her wrists. She stood upright to lessen the searing pain, but her stomach contracted and became hard again. She breathed through her mouth in short, fast bursts, without filling her lungs properly and, when the contraction ebbed, changed to deeper breaths. At the same time she noticed the pressure in her belly diminish. She moved her hand between her legs. Amniotic fluid was pouring out of her and ran down the inside of her thighs.

Her labour was in progress: the contractions from now on would be harder and more frequent.

From the moment she knew that she was pregnant, she had read books and articles about labour to try and remove some of the fear, but she had not succeeded too well. She had thought that the birth was going to be a unique memory, to be remembered always. This was not how she wanted to remember it, but whatever was going to happen, would happen regardless. She was going to have her baby on the floor here, bound fast to the wall as she was.

A fresh contraction started, more severe than the others. She used her breathing method to get through it, trying to count how long it lasted, but lost her thread. The following contractions came closer together, were deeper and washed over her in heavier waves. As the regular contractions came rolling, the pains in her back increased and it felt as if she had lost all feeling in her hands.

She did not notice at first that the crying had stopped on the floor above. Maja must have fallen asleep. How long had she been standing here now? An hour? How long would it be till Sofie returned? At that moment the front door opened. If it wasn't Sofie, it might be the man with the pistol come back for whatever was left. She took a chance. 'Help!' she shouted and filled her lungs again, 'Help!'

Footsteps on the stairs. 'Line?' Sofie called out.

'Down here!'

299

The door opened. Sofie took a step inside, but came to a sudden halt and stood staring.

A fresh contraction took hold of Line. This time she let the pain come out in a yell. 'Untie me!' she pleaded, gritting her teeth.

Sofie came forward, put her arms around her and held her upright. 'Have you had many?'

Line responded with a nod.

'How long between?'

'Four or five minutes. And they're getting harder and harder. We don't have much time.'

77

Wisting hovered outside the courtroom, waiting. One of the parties inside wanted to discuss practical details before they continued, such as the timetable for the next day or a change of sequence in the witnesses. Another message from Mortensen arrived on his phone. Goldheim was back in his car with two bulging carrier bags.

He heard hurried footsteps behind him. Harald Ryttingen came trotting through the spacious hall to slip inside the courtroom. Immediately afterwards, the court official arrived and called out Wisting's name.

The room was full of spectators and press representatives. Ryttingen had taken a seat, seemingly relaxed and self-assured. The counsel for the victim sat on the other side of them with Elise Kittelsen's parents. On the opposite side, the trainee defence lawyer, Olav Müller, sat with the accused, Dan Roger Brodin.

The judge was in an elevated position, looking dignified, behind a raised table with his back to the wall. Associate judges sat to either side. One was an overweight man who seemed sleepy and uninterested, the other a younger woman with her hair gathered in a bun at the back of her neck.

On his way to the witness box, Wisting's mobile phone began to ring, provoking laughter among the spectators. He took it out and dismissed the call, noticing that it came from Line. He activated the silent function and placed it with his notepad on the little shelf inside the witness box. He gazed respectfully at the judge who seemed slightly annoyed, as if impatient and in a rush to be finished.

'Your full name?' he was asked. Wisting gave his name, date of birth, address and position.

In front of him, the phone began to vibrate. The sound was caught by the microphone and relayed into the room. A text message shone on the display. *On my way to the hospital. Think labour has started.*

His heart shot into his mouth. He had promised to be there for her, he was supposed to drive her to the hospital. He ran his tongue over his dry palate, his mind a whirl of concern and confusion. She was '*on her way*' meant she had someone to drive her, probably Sofie. Or she was driving herself, which would be just like her. He could still make it.

He was about to lift his mobile phone to answer, at least to write that he had received her message, but was stopped in his tracks by the judge. 'Have you more important things to attend to than giving your statement to the court?'

A number of people in the courtroom chortled, including Ryttingen. Wisting looked up at the judicial bench. 'Sorry.'

'Then we'll try again. Are you related to or connected in any way with the accused in this case?'

Wisting cleared his throat. 'No.'

'Nor the deceased and her family?'

'No.'

The judge continued with the formalities, saying that Wisting had to tell the truth and nothing but the truth, without concealing anything. 'I affirm,' Wisting said, glancing across at Ryttingen.

'Then you can take a seat, if you wish,' the judge said.

Wisting sat down. It was hot in the courtroom and he regretted not removing his jacket.

Olav Müller embarked on his questioning. After a short introduction he rounded off by letting Wisting explain that he led the investigation into the murder of Jens Hummel. 'Tell us about the murder weapon,' he asked from his position at the bar.

'It was a 7.5 millimetre *Nagant* revolver,' Wisting said, 'part of the estate left by Frank Mandt, who was resident in Stavern and died on 10 January this year.' He added that Mandt had been a prominent figure in a criminal network.

'How did the police get their hands on the gun?'

302

'It was handed in for disposal on 24 July, after it had been found inside a safe that had been locked since Mandt's death.'

'What did you do with it?'

'Following the usual routine, it was send on to *Kripos* who conducted ballistic tests on it.'

'What did they show?'

'To put it succinctly, that the gun had been used to kill both Elise Kittelsen and Jens Hummel.'

The Public Prosecutor cleared his throat, stood up and addressed himself to the judge. 'As a matter of procedure, your Honour, we do not dispute that we are talking about the same murder weapon. So we have no need to spend time on this. The court has no interest in details that, strictly speaking, have no relevance to this case.'

The judge nodded.

'I think that the weapon links these two cases,' Wisting said. 'The risk of being a murder victim in Norway is not great. From a statistical point of view, you are most exposed in your local community, and there is usually a relationship between the victim and the perpetrator. Fewer than one murder in twenty takes place on the open street. It is therefore difficult to imagine that we are dealing with two cases in which unknown perpetrators have used the same murder weapon to kill two random victims. Besides, both murders happened within a short time frame.'

He cast a glance at Ryttingen and saw that he was anxious to give counter arguments and plausible explanations of how the gun could have been used twice. Procedure would force him to wait.

Müller went on: 'In connection with your own investigation, you have also scrutinised the documents in the case against my client. What is your conclusion?'

Wisting leaned closer to the microphone. 'That we're faced with the same perpetrator,' he said.

His statement stirred both the body of the room and the judicial bench. The drowsy associate judge sat up straight and pulled his chair closer.

303

Müller left his words hanging in the air and waited until the mumbling had subsided before he asked, with mock astonishment, whether Wisting was aware that his client had been in custody when Jens Hummel had been shot.

'Yes,' Wisting said.

'Does that mean that you believe Dan Roger Brodin to be innocent?'

Wisting looked across at Elise Kittelsen's parents. Her mother was looking down at the table, but her father met his eyes. He knew that his answer would hurt them, but there was no other way. 'That is correct.' He looked up at the judge again. 'I don't think it was Dan Roger Brodin who shot and killed Elise Kittelsen.'

A gasp from Elise Kittelsen's mother was drowned by muttering in the courtroom. The Public Prosecutor got to his feet and directed himself to the judge.

'We have heard three eyewitnesses here earlier today, who have all pointed out the accused and given very similar statements. Unless the witness has something more to offer than supposition and statistics, this is mere speculation that I can't see any need for the court to waste time on.'

The judge nodded, but appeared more interested in what Wisting now had to say. 'Is this more than supposition?'

'I have spoken to the eyewitnesses,' Wisting said, explaining how the description given by two of the witnesses had been based on a description provided by the third and relayed over the police radio. 'In reality we are dealing with only one witness description. When I spoke to them, both witnesses admitted they had not really recognised Brodin as the perpetrator, but took it for granted that it was him, since the police already had him in handcuffs in a patrol car.'

He flicked through his notepad and referred to what Terje Moseid had said: *'It's only in the movies that police arrest the wrong person.'*

The Public Prosecutor rose from his seat again. 'All three witnesses gave statements in front of this court earlier today. I request that their explanations are given credence, rather than Wisting's interpretation.'

The judge nodded but made no comment.

Müller continued. 'What about the technical evidence? Have you examined that more closely?'

'The central piece of evidence is gunshot residue on the accused's right hand. I don't know how he has explained that in court, but when I spoke to him in prison three days ago, he came out with fresh information about his own movements on the evening of the murder. About why he ran away from the police.'

Müller smiled. 'The court has heard that he fled because he was under the influence of drugs and had therefore broken the conditions of his provisional release.'

'He had another reason to run off,' Wisting said. 'And a reason not to want to tell the police about it.'

The defence lawyer gave him a brief nod as a sign that he should continue.

'Between Christmas and New Year, he committed a theft to order of fireworks,' Wisting said. 'A whole container with contents worth more than 100,000 kroner. He held back some to sell, but some he played about with himself. When he came across the police on the evening of 31 December, he had just blown up a rubbish container outside a *Kiwi* supermarket in the city centre. He ran so that he would not be caught and charged with vandalism and theft. When he was apprehended, his hands were covered in gunpowder from the fireworks.'

The Public Prosecutor protested. 'Should we not have heard this from the accused himself?'

'It's not the accused who is sitting in the witness box now,' the judge pointed out. 'But we could perhaps confer with him?'

Dan Roger Brodin lifted his eyes from the table.

'Is this correct?' the judge asked.

Brodin blinked. 'What he says is true. All that about the fireworks. That's how it was.'

Wisting's mobile phone vibrated again as the judge asked Brodin some supplementary questions. He had already moved it away from the microphone. This time it was a pre-arranged message from Nils Hammer. *Okay,* was all it said.

305

The message led his thoughts back to Line, but he forced them away. He had not yet presented the most telling part of his testimony.

Harald Ryttingen spoke for the first time. 'This is all fabricated,' he objected. 'An attempt to make the facts fit. Why have we not heard all this about the fireworks before now?'

'I visited this *Kiwi* shop last weekend,' Wisting said, without waiting for the judge's permission. 'It turned out that they reported the vandalism to the police the following day, and that the incident was filmed.' He produced the folded photo printouts from his notepad. 'The case was dropped after a short time, but I have copies of the images here. They're of poor quality and not suitable for the purpose of identifying the perpetrator, but they do document that there was indeed a fireworks explosion in the rubbish bin outside the *Kiwi* shop that very evening.'

Ryttingen whispered something to the Public Prosecutor, who stood up to protest. 'This has not been cited as documentary evidence.'

'Nevertheless, I am going to admit it,' the judge answered. He held out his hand to indicate that the court official should give him the pictures.

'I have copies for the others,' Wisting said, handing them over.

Ryttingen slumped in his seat, red in the face. The gunshot residue was one of the central planks of the indictment. He would know that when one plank failed, the rest of the framework would soon collapse. 'This is out of order,' he muttered.

The judge looked over at him. 'Is there something you want entered in the court record?'

Ryttingen shook his head, but it seemed as if there was a sudden flash in his eyes. 'No, your Honour,' he answered, rising to his feet. 'But if it is true that Wisting believes the wrong man is in the dock, then perhaps he can tell us whether he has suspicions of anyone else?'

The judge agreed. 'Do you have a suspect?' he asked.

Harald Ryttingen resumed his seat, folded his arms and leaned back.

'Yes,' Wisting said, moving his hand towards his mobile phone. 'I've just received a message that my men have apprehended and charged a man for Jens Hummel's murder. We also believe that he killed Elise Kittelsen.'

The muttering among the spectators rose like a wave behind him. The judge gripped his gavel and asked for silence in court. 'Who?'

'We have charged the witness who was called before me,' Wisting said. 'The chief prosecution witness, Einar Gjessing.'

The reply prompted another outburst in the court. The judge allowed both spectators and prosecution time to digest the information before he again requested silence. The buzz of voices subsided but even from the witness box Wisting could hear the fingers of the journalists as they raced over their keyboards.

'You must explain this in more detail,' the judge said.

Wisting sat up straight. 'As I explained earlier, I have examined both the case documents and the supplementary investigation material, and have found an unexplored avenue.'

The judge sat with pen poised, making notes. 'An unexplored avenue?'

'It's an expression we use in the police,' Wisting said. 'It has to do with an opening in the case that has been overlooked by the investigators or, as in this case, a direction in the case that the management in the enquiry have not wanted to see. A lead that they more or less consciously have chosen not to follow. Having Dan Roger Brodin pointed out as the perpetrator almost before the investigation had got properly started made them blind to other possibilities. At the same time it was extremely convenient for them. With the arrest as their starting point, they constructed a narrative that did not match the reality, and that meant they need not investigate how far the police themselves were responsible for the murder of Elise Kittelsen.'

Ryttingen whispered something in the Police Prosecutor's ear. He nodded and asked the judge for a recess.

'I want to finish hearing this witness,' the judge said. 'I want to know how the police could have something to do with this murder.'

The courtroom was filled with an attentive stillness.

'Elise Kittelsen was a police informant,' Wisting said. 'She was centrally placed in an organised narcotics network that the police had tried to expose for a number of years. They were on the brink of a breakthrough when she was killed. She knew when and where the next consignment of narcotics would arrive. That knowledge was valuable to the police, but mortally dangerous for Elise. Quite simply, she knew too much, and someone knew that she was passing on information.'

The Public Prosecutor made another effort. 'This information has no place in an open court!'

Olav Müller did not allow the judge time to answer. 'This is absolutely essential information that the police have been sitting on all this time, but which they have withheld from me and my client.'

The judge glanced at Wisting before turning to the prosecution. 'Is this correct?'

Ryttingen's face was ashen as if he had suddenly grown several years older. 'This is not relevant to the case,' he replied, admitting nothing.

The judge addressed Wisting again. 'How have you come by this knowledge? And what relevance does it have for the case?'

Wisting filled the glass in front of him with water. 'The man we have arrested, Einar Gjessing, is one of the participants in this criminal network. So is Elise Kittelsen's boyfriend, Julian Broch. It was first and foremost through him that she obtained information for the police.'

He took a drink and cleared his parched throat, noticing that Elise's mother had taken hold of her husband's hand.

'When the police began their investigation into this scene, they started the way we usually do. On the fringes, working inwards. You start at the bottom with an addict, and persuade him to tell you who sold him the drugs. Via the seller you find the supplier, and in that way you climb higher into the hierarchy. Right on the periphery of this case they came across Elise Kittelsen. Undercover detectives apprehended her one morning as she was making her way to college from her boyfriend's. She had a couple of grams of hash in her possession that she had promised to a friend, and a few more in her locker at college. An insignificant charge, but her entire future lay in ruins. A drugs conviction would destroy her professional ambitions as a teacher, and bring shame to her and her parents. The detectives gave her a chance. They could forget the whole business in exchange for information. She chose to betray her associates, to betray her boyfriend and friends to save herself.'

Ryttingen had not given up trying to force Wisting into silence. 'The witness has no first-hand knowledge of this. He was not present, and this is at best pure guesswork.'

The judge turned to him with the same irritated manner he had shown when Wisting entered the witness box. 'Do you deny that Elise Kittelsen was operating as a police informant?'

Ryttingen shook his head. 'No, but this . . .'

'Continue!' the judge demanded, with a nod in Wisting's direction.

'The informant's handler is now serving abroad, but I spoke to him by phone late last night. He explained that they used Elise in an attempt to approach the main man, whom the police have given the nickname Mister Nice Guy. In the process of the operation, Elise began to feel nervous. She was afraid that her boyfriend had seen through her. Her handler used an anonymous phone, that is to say a random phone with a subscription, borrowed from the police evidence room, but Elise still did not feel safe. The last time her contact spoke to her was only a few hours before she was killed. She was at that point scared of what might happen.'

'This can't be right,' Olav Müller said, riffling through his papers. 'We have Elise Kittelsen's call data and there were no such calls on the day of the murder.'

'They were deleted on the orders of the investigation's management team to avoid creating any unnecessary interference in this case,' Wisting said. 'So that no one would open the door leading to that unexplored avenue.'

'Which member of management?' Müller asked.

'Harald Ryttingen.'

A camera clicked behind Wisting. One of the photographers had broken the embargo on photographs when Ryttingen collapsed in his chair. Several others followed.

The Public Prosecutor pushed his chair slightly away, as if wanting to distance himself.

'We must have a more complete picture of what you believe happened on New Year's Eve,' the judge said.

'It is partly hypothetical,' Wisting warned. 'But Elise Kittelsen had become a threat to the central players in the narcotics market. They had to get rid of her. Julian Broch could not do anything, even though, strictly speaking, he was the leak. Suspicion would fall on her boyfriend if anything happened to her. He had to make sure that he had an alibi, so the assignment was given to Einar Gjessing, who was already in debt to Mister Nice Guy. Documentation exists to show that Gjessing had lost money on a joint business venture after he was declared bankrupt.'

The mobile phone on the shelf in front of him vibrated again. It was Line. *Where are you?*

Wisting mustered all his determination before he continued. 'The killing of Elise Kittelsen also provoked the killing of Jens Hummel,' he said. 'Hummel operated as a courier in this network. He conveyed large consignments of narcotics between the regions of Østland and Sørland in his taxi, from Frank Mandt to Mister Nice Guy. It's our hypothesis that on New Year's Eve he delivered a consignment to his usual contact, Einar Gjessing, but on this particular evening something else happened. Gjessing got Jens Hummel to drive him so that he could intercept Elise Kittelsen on her way to the New Year party. It was also his intention to flee the crime scene in the taxi that would be waiting round the corner. The man the other two witnesses saw running from the scene of the shooting was therefore not Dan Roger Brodin but Einar Gjessing.'

He flashed a look at the defence team. Brodin appeared confused, as if he did not understand what was going on in the courtroom.

'When Gjessing returned to the taxi, he was forced into a sudden, audacious change of plan. His assignment was not only to shut Elise Kittelsen's mouth, but also to find out how much she knew. He needed her mobile phone and had to go back. He handed the murder weapon to Hummel and returned, claiming that he had pursued the killer, but had to give up the chase. In the chaos, as they tried to revive Elise Kittelsen, he found her mobile phone and, when the police turned up, and he was asked to describe the perpetrator, he described a random person whom he recalled having seen earlier that evening: Dan Roger Brodin.'

Wisting noticed that he was beginning to feel impatient. He wanted to finish and was no longer expressing himself with his usual accuracy and precision.

'Jens Hummel, in many ways, was an innocent person drawn into this business,' he said. 'He could have kept quiet and let Elise Kittelsen's killer go free, but the idea of an innocent person being convicted of her murder was too much for him. He tried to tell the police that they had arrested the wrong man, but the tip-off was not followed and, as far as Einar Gjessing and the others were concerned, he became another security risk. What actually led to Hummel's murder is something we don't yet know, but we do know that Gjessing was one of the last people to enter his taxi. A number of partial fingerprints were found on the roof of the car. Fingerprints that wind and weather hadn't completely erased. They were too fragmentary to be used in an automatic search of the fingerprint records, but manual comparison has established that they belong to Einar Gjessing.'

He was nearing the end of his testimony, and this part had more loose threads and unanswered questions.

'Maybe Jens Hummel and Einar Gjessing met up on the pretence of Gjessing wanting Hummel to return the gun,' Wisting continued, flinging out his arms in an expression of uncertainty, demonstrating that the suggestions he now made were merely theories in an unfolding police investigation. 'Perhaps Hummel demanded money in exchange for his silence? All we know is that he did not get the opportunity to tell anyone what he knew about Elise Kittelsen's murder. He was shot and killed, and the murder weapon ended in Frank Mandt's safe.'

Wisting was aware that there were still many questions and that they were facing an enormous challenge in the forthcoming investigation. However, his job in the courtroom was done. He had presented an alternative explanation.

'Has defence counsel any further questions for this witness?' the judge asked.

Olav Müller seemed disconcerted. 'Not now,' he replied. 'But I reserve the right to recall this witness if it proves necessary.'

The judge nodded and turned to the opposing side. 'Prosecutor?'

The Public Prosecutor shook his head.

'Well,' the judge said. 'You can have your recess now. Court is adjourned until tomorrow at ten o'clock. By that time the prosecuting authorities should have decided whether they want to continue.'

He struck his gavel on the block, rose and went out through the side door, the two associate judges following in his wake. As soon as the door closed behind them, all hell broke loose. The journalists pressed forward and divided into two flanks, one group flocking round the prosecution while the other surrounded Wisting.

Wisting grabbed his mobile phone, squeezed forward and headed as fast as possible to the exit without answering anyone. Before he left the courtroom, he threw a backward glance to see Ryttingen also trying to make his escape, but being physically detained. The journalists were all over him and refused to give up. Wisting could not do anything other than feel for him. He had seen it all before, and it was always unpleasant when one of their own crossed that thin blue line and perpetrated an injustice.

78

His phone rang before he reached the car, unknown numbers probably belonging to news editors. He dismissed the calls and keyed in Line's number before sitting behind the wheel.

It rang for a long time with no response. He texted that he had been occupied in court, but was now on his way. As he manoeuvred out of the car park it dawned on him that he had no idea which hospital she was in. She had talked about the hospitals in both Tønsberg and Skien, and he thought she had decided on Skien. In any case, it was the nearer of the two, though it was at least two and a half hours away.

He moved into the left lane when he entered the motorway and considered switching on his blue flashing lights. There was little traffic, so he decided against it. Instead he switched on the police radio and let it scan the channels to pick up any surveillance farther ahead.

When he drove over the bridge at Varoddbrua, just outside the city limits, he called Ivar Horne.

'What a bloody circus!' Horne said. 'Everything's been turned upside down here now. For fuck's sake, you've shot down one of our most important surveillance operations in open court.'

'Sorry. There was no other way of doing it.'

'The whole truth and nothing but the truth? You could at least have told me.'

'Any news on Goldheim?'

'He's on his way home, but he's also received a message. He has his people in the courtroom, of course. His phone's been melting.'

'What have they been saying?'

'He's keeping a cool head. Says nothing to reveal the extent of his involvement, but claims he's taken care of the problems.'

Wisting's thoughts were racing. Goldheim had been in Stavern. Had he been there to take care of the problems?

'Where is he now?' he asked, watching the traffic travelling in the opposite direction.

'He's passed the turn-off for Kragerø. We'll pick him up before he's back in the city.'

Wisting pictured the tiny red dot on the tracking unit. If he had reached Kragerø, he would meet him in approximately forty-five minutes. 'Will you keep me posted?' he asked.

'I'll try but no promises,' Horne said.

Wisting tried Line again. When she did not answer, he called Hammer. 'Did it go okay?'

'We took him by surprise,' Hammer said. 'He's on his way to the remand centre. Torunn and I are searching his flat now. Are you coming here?'

'No. You'll have to assume responsibility. I'm on my way to the hospital.'

'What's up?'

Wisting felt his lips broaden into a smile. 'I'm about to be a grandfather.'

79

Line was lying on her own in the labour suite. Sofie had driven her with Maja whimpering in the child seat. They had not bothered to drive home to Line's house to collect a change of clothes or her toiletries and Line had gradually recounted what had happened. When they reached the hospital, Sofie did not want to go home, partly because she wanted to offer Line support, but also because she did not want to return to the house where someone had just broken in.

Line was whisked into an examination room where they monitored the baby's heartbeat. A midwife had recorded the length and severity of her contractions and measured the cervical dilation as four centimetres. After that, Line had provided a urine sample before being handed a hospital gown and told to change.

Scared and alone, she did not know what the staff had done with her bag and belongings. The irritation she felt because her father had failed to answer was turning into anger, and behind that lay a terror she had never felt the like of before.

Another midwife came in and asked how she was. Line could not articulate anything other than that she was fine. Both she and the baby were in safe hands but, surrounded by strangers, she felt insecure.

'Try to relax,' the midwife said. 'It's going to be all right.'

An alarm sounded in the corridor and Line was alone again. Until now she had felt stronger after each contraction, always with fresh reserves of strength, but now the convulsions grew longer and more difficult, and the pain increased each time. She gripped the edge of the quilt and clenched her fists. Hope that it would all soon be over wrestled with longing for her father to arrive before she gave birth.

80

The road narrowed to a single lane. Wisting was the fifth vehicle behind a heavy goods lorry driving strictly at the speed limit. Lifting one hand from the steering wheel he moved it towards the switch that activated the blue lights. At that moment an Emergency Squad patrol car relayed a message on the police radio. It was calling the central switchboard with the faint sound of a police siren in the background.

One of the operators answered immediately.

'I'm following a white Range Rover that has evaded the checkpoint,' the Emergency Squad officer reported. *'It is travelling south on route E18. Passing through the Sørlandsporten tunnel. Do you have any units that can assist?'*

'Wait.'

Several units responded on their own initiative, as normal when a car chase was announced on the radio. Wisting was the one in the best position. In about ten minutes he would meet Phillip Goldheim and the patrol on his tail. More than enough time to stop a lorry and arrange for a roadblock.

The switchboard operator issued orders. Wisting sat with his hand on the blue light switch, knowing he could not let himself be delayed.

The driver of the police car pursuing Goldheim reported their positions. Other units were being deployed. The distance between Wisting and their quarry rapidly decreased. His phone rang. It was Horne.

'Car chasing Goldheim,' was his short message.

'I've picked that up. I'm going to meet them shortly.'

'We tried to arrange a routine checkpoint to check what

316

he had collected in Stavern. When we waved him in, he just accelerated past.'

'Do you know anything more about what he was doing there?'

'Just that he returned to the car with two jam-packed carrier bags.'

Wisting spotted flashing blue lights ahead. 'Here they come,' he said.

The vehicles in front of him swerved to one side. The white Range Rover pushed forward. As the vehicle in pursuit approached, he could also hear sirens. The Range Rover was now on the yellow mid-line. Wisting dropped his speed and moved out as air pressure from oncoming vehicles buffeted his car. He managed to see that Goldheim was alone and driving with a look of determination.

'I need to hang up,' Horne said.

The traffic resumed its normal flow, and Wisting followed. Announcements on the police radio came hard and fast with a number of units reporting in. It sounded as if a spike mat was being set up a few kilometres away.

Wisting listened intently as he continued northwards. The Emergency Squad leading the chase gave regular reports on Goldheim's speed and the exit roads they passed. In the middle of a sentence he suddenly swore loudly.

'He's driven off the road!' he told them, repeating the message. 'We need an ambulance,' he added, giving the position.

Wisting curled his hands round the wheel with no alternative but to remain a silent spectator to the unfolding drama.

The radio traffic changed into a rescue operation. From what Wisting understood, the car was resting on its roof beyond the verge and Phillip Goldheim was trapped inside. By the time Wisting passed the regional border between Aust-Agder and Telemark, the fire brigade had pulled him out of the wreckage. His condition was said to be critical but stable. The radio signal broke up.

81

Four times Wisting tried to call Line's mobile, though he knew she would have called him if she could. He found a vacant parking space in front of the hospital, wasting time at the ticket machine. Not knowing how long he was going to be, he pushed all the coins he had into the slot. On his way back to the car with the ticket, his phone rang. It was Christine Thiis. 'That was a bit of a performance, if we're to believe the online court reports.'

'That's how it turned out,' Wisting said, placing the parking ticket on the dashboard.

'The Police Chief wants to speak to you. He's on his way here now.'

'He'll have to wait,' Wisting said, explaining where he was. 'I don't know how long I'll be.' He wrapped the conversation, stretched his hand into the car, opened the glove compartment and left his phone.

It was the right hospital, but he had arrived too late. When he asked for Line at the labour suite, he was told that the birth was over and that he was grandfather to a little girl. They showed him to the room where Line was resting. When he pushed open the door, she was lying asleep with the baby at her breast. He tiptoed inside, but the door sliding closed woke her. The baby lay on her chest with her tiny hands clenched just below her chin.

'How are you?' he asked.

Line smiled as she looked down at the new-born baby. 'Fantastic.'

He leaned over and their foreheads met as he kissed her cheek. 'I'm so sorry I got here too late.'

'Sofie drove me here. Did you see her down in the cafeteria?'

Wisting shook his head. 'I came straight here.'

His grand-daughter, who looked strong and sturdy, was wrapped in a woollen blanket. Line shifted to a more comfortable position, and the baby tried to lift her head. Trembling with the effort, she managed to move it slightly.

A midwife entered the room. 'Everything okay here?'

Line replied in the affirmative and Wisting introduced himself as the grandfather.

'Would you like to hold her?' the midwife asked.

Wisting looked across at Line. 'I don't know,' he said. 'Maybe later.'

The midwife would not take no for an answer. She lifted the little bundle from the bed and laid it in his arms. He felt the soft down on her small head against his cheek and a warm, convivial silence descended on him. It was a long time since he had held a baby, but it felt completely natural.

The midwife went out and left them alone. Wisting ran his finger carefully over the wrinkled baby face. The skin was almost sticky, but dry and taut at the same time. Suddenly the eyelids opened and two big blue eyes blinked and stared at him with surprising trust.

'Her name's to be Ingrid,' Line said, 'after Mum.'

Wisting nodded his head as the tears ran down his cheeks. Line had once been a little baby just like this. He thought of all the years that had gone by. Everything that had happened while he had not been there for her. How fast she had grown, and now this, something her mother would not experience.

'How did the court case go?' Line asked.

Wisting returned the baby tenderly.

'Fine,' he said. 'It took time, but I managed to say what I wanted. Was lucky with the judge, who allowed it.'

The baby struggled a little, and Line helped her to settle. Only then did Wisting notice that she had a bandage round her lower right arm.

'What happened?' he asked, taking hold of her hand.

She did not answer, but struggled to hide the other arm

319

underneath the quilt. Wisting took it out and saw that she had deep red marks and lacerations round her wrist.

'I don't know if I have the energy right now,' she said, pressing the back of her head into the pillow.

'How did you get these cuts?'

Line closed her eyes, holding back slightly before describing what had happened while she was looking after Maja.

82

Wisting was back in the car before his ticket expired. He fumbled for his mobile phone in the glove compartment, his mind in furious turmoil. His phone contained a lengthy list of unanswered calls. Ignoring them, he looked up Ivar Horne's number. 'How's it going with Goldheim?'

'He'll survive,' Horne said. 'Serious injuries, but not bad enough to prevent him being locked in a prison cell. Though he'll have to wear a different pair of shoes. The soles of the shoes he was wearing match the footprints in the potato cellar involved in your narcotics case.'

Wisting only just took in what he was saying. 'The bags he collected from Stavern contained Frank Mandt's personal archives.'

'How did you know . . .'

'Have you found them?' Wisting interrupted.

'Most of them. The car turned over several times. There were papers all over the place. We're attending to this.'

'I want them here. I'll come and collect them tomorrow.'

'That's not up to me to decide, but one way or another we'll have to coordinate the upcoming investigation. If nothing else, your murder case impinges on our narcotics enquiry.'

Wisting started the car and reported what he had learned from Line.

'The gun and balaclava were found in the car,' Horne said. 'You'll probably find his footprints in the Mandt house as well.'

'I want it all here. Phillip Goldheim too.'

'I'm not sure that'll be so easy.'

'I don't give a damn about Ryttingen.'

'I've already worked that out,' Horne said. 'But Julian Broch was arrested an hour ago. He came ashore from his father's motorboat with twenty kilos of amphetamines from Denmark on board. He's already started talking about Goldheim. We must try to engineer some cooperation here but, after what he's done today, it's not certain that either you or your police district are best placed to deal with the case against him.'

Wisting was forced to agree.

'One thing's certain,' Horne said, 'there's no more Mister Nice Guy.'

83

Wisting assembled the investigators in the conference room. The events of the day had been numerous and there was a pressing need for a run-through. 'What's Gjessing saying?' he asked Hammer, now returned from Kristiansand.

'Wee only talked about the Hummel case,' Hammer said. 'He's given a short, introductory explanation and denies everything.'

'What about the fingerprints on the taxi?' Mortensen asked.

'He hasn't been confronted with that, but has said of his own accord that before the murder he tried to hail a taxi from outside the city. He went inside, but had to get out again. He claims he already told this to the police.'

Wisting nodded. It tallied with what Einar Gjessing had said when they visited him in his penthouse apartment.

'What else do we have on him?' Torunn Borg asked. 'Have we established a connection between him and Frank Mandt?'

'Not yet,' Wisting replied. 'But there might be something in Mandt's personal archives.'

'There may be a chain reaction,' Hammer said. 'If he goes down for the New Year Murder, then he'll go down in our case too.'

The conference room door opened. It was Police Chief Ivan Sundt, with Christine Thiis behind him. He scanned the small gathering and stopped when he came to Wisting. 'I expected you to report to me as soon as you returned.'

'Apologies,' Wisting said. 'We urgently needed to run through recent events.'

'So do I,' the Chief of Police said sternly.

'Can we do it in ten minutes?' Wisting asked.

'We'll do it now,' the Police Chief said, taking a seat.

The other investigators rose from the table. Christine Thiis moved aside to let them out of the room.

'You can stay,' the Police Chief ordered, waving her in. She sat beside Wisting.

The Police Chief got right to the point. 'What proof do you have?'

Wisting went through the case step by step. In the course of giving his account, he realised that what he had was more than enough to sow doubt on Dan Roger Brodin's guilt. The case against him had ripped asunder like a sail in a severe gale. However, the road from that to a charge against Einar Gjessing was still long and hard.

The Police Chief agreed. 'It's not enough. It may be that you have lengthy experience as an investigator, but I've sat an equally long time as a judge. What you have isn't even enough to hold him on remand. You've acted too hastily.' He rose to his feet and turned to Christine Thiis. 'You both defied my instructions about keeping out of the New Year Murder case, and haven't achieved anything other than a major scandal.'

Wisting was not interested in entering into any discussion. The Police Chief made for the door, but stopped and looked at him. 'If this is all you've got, you'll have to let him go before the trial resumes in Kristiansand tomorrow morning.'

84

Just before eight o'clock that evening, Wisting was back visiting Line at the hospital. After his meeting with the Chief of Police, the hours at the police station had passed fruitlessly, hours that he had not been able to fill with much other than longing to hold little Ingrid again.

He had been to Line's house and gathered up some clothes and toiletries, most of which had already been packed. Sofie and Maja had moved in while the crime scene technicians secured and collected traces left by Phillip Goldheim at their home.

Line had just finished feeding Ingrid when he arrived. Putting down her overnight bag, it sprang to Wisting's mind that he should have brought something with him. Flowers, chocolate or a little teddy bear. He apologised and promised to bring gifts for them both the following day.

Line laughed and handed the baby to him. He sat with her in his arms, nudging her hand gingerly with his thick index finger. Her tiny fingers instinctively grabbed and, with a surprisingly strong grip, held tight.

'How's the case going?' Line asked.

Wisting told her, quietly and calmly, as he studied the expressions on the baby's face.

'Do you have to let him go?'

Wisting smiled, aware that, strangely enough, the thought did not upset him. 'Better that ten guilty persons escape than that one innocent suffer,' he reminded her, thinking of Dan Roger Brodin in prison on the top floor of police headquarters in Kristiansand.

'Have you looked at what was in the safe?'

'Not yet.'

'He didn't take everything, you know,' she said, and went on to tell him about the cassettes tucked underneath a cushion on the settee. 'Frank Mandt had a hidden microphone in the kitchen and recorded conversations round the table. There was a recording of them planning a robbery on an armoured security van. Maybe you can do a voice analysis or something to find out who's speaking on it.'

'Good idea,' Wisting said, without any special enthusiasm.

They sat chatting about everyday matters, such as when Line could come home and how she should decorate her bedroom. He told her that he had phoned Thomas, her brother, and that he would pay a visit the following day. 'Have you told John?' he asked, looking up from the baby's face.

They rarely mentioned the baby's father, but Wisting knew they had been in touch during the pregnancy.

'Not yet. I'll send him a photo tomorrow.'

They went on talking about other things before returning to the murder case. 'Do you think he died of natural causes?' she asked.

'Who?' Wisting moved the baby to his other arm.

'Frank Mandt. Do you think he fell, or could he have been pushed?'

Wisting reflected on the report from when Frank Mandt had been found dead at the foot of the basement stairs. 'There was nothing to suggest anything else,' he said.

'But what was he actually doing in the basement? There wasn't much there apart from the old exercise room and the safe, and he wasn't wearing a tracksuit or gym clothes.'

'Perhaps he was going to the safe?' Wisting suggested.

'Maybe. I just thought it was such a remarkable coincidence. That he should fall downstairs at almost the same time as all the rest of this stuff he seems to have been slap bang in the middle of.'

Wisting handed little Ingrid back to Line. The movement made the child blink her eyes and make cooing noises. Something in what she had said had sparked a thought that turned over in his mind. He leaned across the bed, gave his daughter a hug and promised to return the next day.

85

Beside the driveway leading to the old detached house, the street lamp was surrounded by a faint orb of murky light. Wisting stood outside his car listening to the sound of grasshoppers in the trees, bushes and grass whispering their monotonous tune.

Klaus Wahl was the person who had found Frank Mandt at the foot of his basement stairs at the beginning of January. It had been a run-of-the-mill tragedy. Mandt was seventy-nine years old, had diabetes, and was dizzy and unsteady on his feet. Wahl had given the police a concise statement, but not all the relevant questions had been asked.

Wisting rang the doorbell. It took a while for the old man to answer. He was wearing the same clothes as last time, a pair of blue shorts and a checked shirt.

'Oh, it's you,' he mumbled, and stepped to one side as if Wisting was expected.

They sat at the kitchen table. 'We've arrested a man for the murder of Jens Hummel,' Wisting explained.

Klaus Wahl nodded. He had heard it on the broadcast news.

'Does the name Einar Gjessing mean anything to you?' Wisting asked.

'I know who he is,' Wahl replied.

'I think he may have been one of the last people to visit Mandt at home. I think he may have brought him the murder weapon.'

'I wasn't at Frank's house very often,' Wahl said, busying himself with a pack of tobacco. 'We usually met in cafés and suchlike.'

Wisting sat for a while observing the man facing him. 'You may have been the person who knew Mandt best. What do

327

you think actually happened? He had a lot of people under his thumb, and more than a few who had plenty to gain from his death. Do you think he fell, or was he pushed?'

Klaus Wahl swept flakes of tobacco from the waxed table-cloth into his hand and poured them back into the packet. 'He fell,' he answered firmly. 'It was an accident.'

'You seem very sure,' Wisting said.

Klaus Wahl stood up, went over to the kitchen worktop and opened a drawer. Sitting down again, he placed a black notebook and a small cassette player on the table. 'He fell. If not, the person who pushed him would have taken this.'

Wisting drew the notebook towards him and opened it at a random page. There were names, dates, sums of money and other key words.

'This lay beside him at the foot of the stairs,' Wahl said. 'He must have been on his way down to the safe with it. I took it with me. Thought it was something the police shouldn't get their hands on. Now I think differently.'

'How's that?'

Wahl put the cigarette in his mouth and cocked his head slightly as he lit it. 'There's somebody called Einar who speaks on that, in there,' he said, pointing at the little cassette player. 'And someone they call PG. They're talking about Jens Hummel, among other things.' Wahl inhaled and let the smoke trickle out through his nostrils. 'That was how Mandt consolidated his position in the network. He had something on all of them, and got people to talk about one another behind their backs.'

Wisting lifted the cassette player and pressed the play button. The recording started in the middle of a conversation: *'Listen to Einar for a minute, then,'* someone said.

'Jens has become a problem.' It did not require voice analysis to recognise Einar Gjessing's husky south coast accent.

'There must be ways of solving that, eh?' a third person suggested.

'Frank Mandt,' Wahl said, using his cigarette to point at the miniature loudspeaker.

'There's only one permanent method,' the voice belonging

328

to Gjessing asserted. '*We run far too much of a risk by letting him off the hook.*'

'You *run a risk*,' Mandt corrected him. '*This wouldn't be a problem if they hadn't picked up an innocent bloke.*'

'*Who's innocent?*' asked the voice that Wisting had not identified, but whom he assumed was Phillip Goldheim. '*He may not have been the one who did it, but he's not innocent. Nobody's innocent.*'

'*The problem is that if he starts to spill the beans, then we can't be sure what will come out of that mouth of his,*' Gjessing went on. '*It could be dangerous for all of us.*'

'*He's my man,*' Mandt objected. '*He's invaluable to me.*'

'*You'll get compensation, of course, and we'll find a replacement. But Einar, after all, is willing to get rid of a risky character for us. It'll be . . .*'

The voice was cut off and changed to a hissing sound, as if someone had deleted the rest of the conversation. It was not difficult to understand what they were discussing, but it was not incontrovertible evidence either. The conversation could be interpreted in different ways and the content could be twisted.

Wisting let the tape run. The silence on the recording changed. He heard voices that were far away, but grew louder as they moved towards the room where the microphone was located.

'*Have you come here now?*' Frank Mandt said, clearly irritated.

'*I just wanted to tell you that the problem's been solved,*' Einar Gjessing said, his words followed by the sound of something metallic being placed on a table surface.

'*Fuck!*' Mandt protested. '*Have you brought that here?*'

'*It's yours, after all.*'

'*That's the hottest gun on earth right now!*'

'*Well, I've eliminated the problem, so you can make sure you lose this.*'

A scraping sound followed as something was shoved across the table where the two men were sitting.

'*I don't want to know any more about this,*' Mandt warned.

329

'There's something you should know,' Gjessing said. 'I had to leave his taxi in the barn.'

'In my barn?'

'You don't use it anyway. I'll move it later, but the more time that passes before anyone finds it, the better it'll be.'

'What about the body?'

'It's not there. Take it easy.'

'Is anybody going to find it?'

'Not anytime soon.'

'What do you mean by that?'

'Maybe in the spring, when the dung's spread on the fields,' Gjessing explained without going into further details.

Frank Mandt's voice seemed morose: 'All the same, you shouldn't have come here. Not now.'

Chair legs scraped on the floor.

'I thought you'd want to know.'

'I want to know as little as possible about it.'

The voices grew more distant.

'Give PG a message that from now on he'll have to get somebody to come and collect.'

The tone of annoyance continued until the voices dwindled. Then there was another pause before the recording stopped. Smoke from Klaus Wahl's cigarette rose from his hand, drifted past his face, and left it enveloped in grey billows. 'I thought you would want to hear that,' he said.

86

The custody sergeant pushed a cup of coffee over to Wisting. Only then did he appreciate how tired he was, struggling to shake off the exhaustion and gather his thoughts. Facing the bank of TV screens in the duty room he found the picture of Einar Gjessing, pacing to and fro on the cell floor, dressed in the same clothes he had worn in the courtroom earlier that day. It felt like a very long time ago.

'The defence lawyer was here a couple of hours ago,' the sergeant said. 'He was told there wouldn't be another interview until tomorrow.'

'I just want a few words,' Wisting said.

'I don't think he's very interested in talking.'

The man in Cell 3 sat on the bed. Wisting lingered for a while longer, drinking his coffee, before putting down the empty cup and making his way along the corridor.

Einar Gjessing looked up as Wisting carried in a chair, doing his best to conceal his own uncertainty. He could feel the resentment from the man on the bed, his disquiet and anxiety.

'I've got nothing to say,' Gjessing said.

'I've already heard you talking.' Wisting sat on the chair.

He took the little cassette player from his document case and played the recording from the point where Gjessing was talking about the taxi left in the barn. The voices sounded tinny as they bounced off the cell walls. There was an immediate physical transformation in the man facing him. His face turned ashen, and he collapsed like a burst balloon.

Wisting stopped the player. 'Did you know Frank Mandt made recordings of all the conversations that took place inside his house?'

331

Gjessing sat in silence.

Wisting opened his document case and took out a plastic bag filled with cassettes. 'I haven't listened to all of them yet, but I assume that much of it deals with the same things as he wrote in his notebooks, even though I haven't read them either.'

Gjessing opened his mouth, but closed it again.

'As far as you're concerned, it doesn't mean a lot,' Wisting said. 'You'll probably not be able to receive a harsher punishment than you'll get for two murders, but you can spare others.'

'What do you mean?'

'I don't need to listen to these tapes or read his notebooks. What I need is a confession from you.' He stood up. 'You'll have everything to gain from that. A confession will be the only mitigating circumstance to get you a reduced sentence. I start work at seven o'clock tomorrow morning. The offer stands until then.'

Einar Gjessing continued to sit on the edge of the bed when the cell door slid shut. Wisting trudged slowly back to the duty room where he picked up a yellow Post-it note and scribbled down Nils Hammer's phone number.

'If he wants to talk to anybody, then he can call this number,' he said. 'Anytime.'

87

The confession was on Wisting's desk at 07.00. The written statement had commenced at 03.15 and was signed by both Nils Hammer and Einar Gjessing at 05.50. Eight pages of the most salient details.

He read through it, feeling some of his tension dissipate. There were no surprises, a few blank areas were filled out, but none of the details were out of kilter with how they had envisaged the sequence of events.

Wisting took it to Christine Thiis. He could see how the past few days had drained her. She stood between a rock and a hard place, between conscientious investigators and pragmatic managers. It had given her dark circles beneath her eyes that made her look older.

'It's over now,' he said, placing the confession in front of her. He remained on his feet as she read it, and saw that it seemed to lift her spirits too. 'You can break the news to the Police Chief and the Public Prosecutor.'

She nodded, now with a softer expression on her face, and he realised that the task he had given her was one she relished.

'Where are you going?' she asked.

He glanced at the clock. 'I'm going to Kristiansand again. There are a few practical things that have to be cleared with the investigators down there. Besides, the court case resumes at ten o'clock. I'd like to be there.'

88

Courtroom 5 was full to capacity when Wisting arrived at the Justice Building a few minutes before ten. Several spectators and journalists were huddled in a semi-circle round the door-way, but the official who turned them away spotted Wisting and beckoned him over. He sneaked past the others and took up position just inside the door.

Olav Müller, the trainee defence counsel, was now accompanied by his boss, Gisle Kvammen. On the opposite side sat the Public Prosecutor on his own, with the counsel for the victim a few metres away. Neither Ryttingen nor Elise Kittelsen's parents were present.

The door behind the judge's table opened at ten precisely. All the people in the room stood and the judge in his robes emerged followed by the two associate judges. They sat down, the judge asked everyone present to follow suit and declared the court in session.

'As planned, today we shall continue to hear the witnesses. Do any of the parties have anything to say before we continue?'

The Public Prosecutor rose slowly. 'Your Honour. In light of new developments that have emerged during the court proceedings, the prosecution authorities wish to desist from further presentation of evidence and propose that the accused be acquitted.'

The judge let his eyes linger on him. 'What basis do you wish to cite for the acquittal?'

The Public Prosecutor cleared his throat before answering briefly. 'Not guilty.'

A wave of astonished whispering swept through the court-room.

'Are there other factors apart from what emerged yesterday that form the basis for this conclusion?'

'We received supplementary information in the early hours of this morning.'

The judge waited in silence for him to elaborate.

'Another person has confessed to the murder of Elise Kittelsen,' he said finally.

Fresh mutterings rose from the rows of spectators and spread through the courtroom, echoing off the walls, but fell silent when the judge raised his gavel. 'Is this a statement in which you have full confidence?'

The Public Prosecutor answered only with a nod of the head, but the judge did not let him off with that. 'Is it?'

'Yes,' he confirmed.

'Thank you.'

The judge took his time making some notes before directing his gaze at the female counsel for the victim. 'Have the relatives any comments on what has come to light?'

The counsel for the victim stood up. 'Numerous, your Honour. But nothing that has direct relevance to the recommendation for acquittal.' She scowled at the Public Prosecutor.

She resumed her seat and the judge addressed himself to the trainee defence lawyer, Olav Müller. 'What about defence counsel?'

It was Kvammen who spoke up. 'We request that the accused be acquitted,' he said.

Dan Roger Brodin seemed perplexed.

'Has the accused anything he wishes to add?' the judge asked.

The room fell silent. Brodin leaned forward to the microphone: 'I didn't do it.'

'Nobody any longer thinks so,' the judge said, as his eyes shifted back to the Public Prosecutor. 'Judgment in this case will be given at three o'clock this afternoon,' he informed them, adjourning the court with a bang of his gavel.

Wisting leaned against the wall. In practice, this meant that Dan Roger Brodin would be a free man before the day was over.

335

89

Wisting sat in the chair by the window with his five-day-old grandchild on his lap. He had sat in this same place and in this same way with Line almost thirty years earlier, and it was wonderful to let his mind fill with good memories and thoughts about the future.

It was raining outside, just as it had been that first summer with Line. It had begun at five in the morning and continued all day, a chilly rain that fell obliquely from an iron-grey sky.

He glanced down at Ingrid's head with its downy black hair. Her eyes were closed, her cheeks round and fresh, the mouth tiny, pink and soft. Ingrid. The little face moved almost imperceptibly each time she drew breath.

Line came in from the hallway with a large parcel tied with pink ribbon in her hands. Behind her came Sofie with Maja on her arm. Wisting smiled in welcome. Sofie stroked the baby's cheek before sitting down.

Line opened the present. It was a pink sleep suit and other baby clothes. Before she had time to settle she had to answer the doorbell again, returning with Nils Hammer, Torunn Borg, Espen Mortensen and Christine Thiis. Hammer had brought a bouquet of balloons and an enormous teddy bear that he laid on a chair, while Christine Thiis had wrapped a play mat with music activated when you pressed different figures.

Coffee and cake appeared on the table.

Ingrid looked as if she was thinking of starting to cry, but instead lay with what seemed to be a smile playing round her mouth.

'Can I hold her?' Hammer asked.

'I want to take a photo,' Line said, picking up her camera.

She crouched in front of her father while Hammer stood behind her making strange noises to attract Ingrid's attention.

'Take one with my phone too,' Wisting asked, coaxing his mobile carefully out of his trouser pocket. It rang just as he was about to hand it over. Ingrid began to cry and Line lifted her out of his arms, passing her across to Hammer.

Wisting took his phone to the kitchen and answered in the doorway.

'This is Olav Müller, the defence lawyer,' he heard through the laughter in the living room.

'Thanks for your help with the case,' Wisting said.

'Am I disturbing you?'

'It's fine. What's it about?'

In the living room Hammer made farting noises, making everyone laugh but Ingrid.

'It's to do with Dan Roger.'

'What about him?'

'He's dead.'

Wisting withdrew all the way into the kitchen. 'What did you say?'

'He died of an overdose last night. I thought you'd want to know.'

Wisting had to sit down. The news came so suddenly he felt dizzy. It was difficult to be surprised that Dan Roger Brodin's life would end this way, but he had not imagined that it would happen so soon. It was a possibility to which his eyes had been closed.

Questions whirled in his brain, but all that he managed to do was thank Müller for the information. He pulled himself together, and let the thought sink in that if Brodin had still been in prison, he would also still be alive.

A burst of laughter erupted in the living room, dispelling the bleak thought. 'Grandfather!' Hammer shouted. 'Nappy change!'

Wisting left the phone on the kitchen table. 'Coming!' he answered, grinning broadly, and went out to join the others.

337